THE
SEN-TOKU
RAID

JOHN MANNOCK

A SIGNET BOOK

SIGNET
Published by New American Library, a division of
Penguin Group (USA) Inc., 375 Hudson Street,
New York, New York 10014, USA
Penguin Group (Canada), 10 Alcorn Avenue, Toronto,
Ontario M4V 3B2, Canada (a division of Pearson Penguin Canada Inc.)
Penguin Books Ltd., 80 Strand, London WC2R 0RL, England
Penguin Ireland, 25 St. Stephen's Green, Dublin 2,
Ireland (a division of Penguin Books Ltd.)
Penguin Group (Australia), 250 Camberwell Road, Camberwell, Victoria 3124,
Australia (a division of Pearson Australia Group Pty. Ltd.)
Penguin Books India Pvt. Ltd., 11 Community Centre, Panchsheel Park,
New Delhi - 110 017, India
Penguin Group (NZ), cnr Airborne and Rosedale Roads, Albany,
Auckland 1310, New Zealand (a division of Pearson New Zealand Ltd.)
Penguin Books (South Africa) (Pty.) Ltd., 24 Sturdee Avenue,
Rosebank, Johannesburg 2196, South Africa

Penguin Books Ltd., Registered Offices:
80 Strand, London WC2R 0RL, England

First published by Signet, an imprint of New American Library,
a division of Penguin Group (USA) Inc.

First Printing, March 2005
10 9 8 7 6 5 4 3 2 1

PUBLISHER'S NOTE
This is a work of fiction. Names, characters, places, and incidents either are
the product of the author's imagination or are used fictitiously, and any resemblance to actual persons, living or dead, business establishments, events, or
locales is entirely coincidental.

The Sen-Toku Raid is dedicated to my father, A. J. McKinna, of Alida, Saskatchewan—professional baseball player, World War Two combat flier, renowned neuro-ophthalmologist and surgeon, Professor Emeritus of Medicine, Fellow of the Wilmer Institute at Johns Hopkins—who passed on suddenly in January 2003 as the novel was being completed. In addition to his many professional accomplishments, he was a beloved husband, father, brother, teacher, and friend.

I know you're not gone, Dad—just gone on ahead. Leading the way for the rest of us, as usual.

—J. M.

Author's Note

This book contains an abundance of technical terms relating to World War II. I am solely responsible for any inaccuracies, intentional or otherwise, and for these—as usual—I claim Sanctuary in the Cathedral of Fiction.

Acknowledgments

Many thanks to my literary agent and friend,
Jimmy Vines,

and

my editor at NAL, Doug Grad.

Also

special thanks to my father-in-law,
Master Sergeant Richard E. Durrance, USMC (ret.),
for editorial advice on military content.

And of course

all my love and gratitude to my wife, Teresa,
for whom all my books are written.

The Philippines

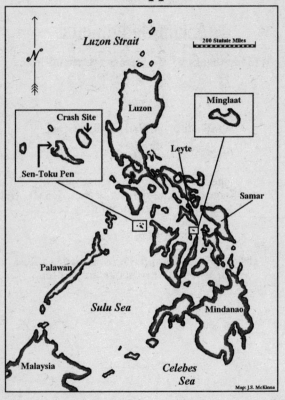

N

Luzon Strait

200 Statute Miles

Crash Site

Luzon

Minglaat

Sen-Toku Pen

Leyte

Samar

Palawan

Sulu Sea

Mindanao

Malaysia

Celebes Sea

Map: J.S. McKinna

Part One

Prologue

April 1942

From its perch on the hillside, the small cedar bungalow with the blue-glazed tile roof had a perfect view of the bay. The modest plot of land on which it sat was bordered by a simple but elegant privacy fence of cedar planks, and within the yard was a garden. The fence was routinely sanded to keep it bright, and the garden—meticulously laid out in interlocking patches of cut stone, clean gravel, sand, loam, and carefully chosen plants—showed a similarly caring touch.

The central feature of the garden was a stone-lined pond ten feet in diameter, which sat near the house, directly beneath the large picture windows that faced the bay. Around the pond and in carefully constructed mounds of earth and stone throughout the garden, bonsai trees, some as tall as a yard or more, stood in shallow clay pots of green and brown and blue and red. Many were in training, bound with soft metal wire to encourage limb growth in one direction or another. All were beautifully trimmed and supported; each was displayed to best advantage in the garden as a whole.

On either side of the pond, framing the perfect view of the bay from the bungalow's picture windows, were two mature cherry trees, in full spring bloom. Normally, their pink-and-white flowers would have created a supremely peaceful contrast with the clear blue sky, but this fine spring morning they bore a different kind of blossom.

They were on fire.

Everything was on fire. The water in the pond was boiling dry; the half-dozen ornamental koi it contained were floating belly up, their once-beautiful orange-and-white bodies now gray and bloated. The numerous bonsai trees inhabiting the garden were crowned by auras of flame, each surrendering its sylvan contours and becoming an immaculate, perfectly balanced torch. The fence was blackened and glowing like a bulwark of vertical embers, crumbling, sheets of fire writhing along its entire length.

The blue-glazed tiles on the roof of the house cracked as the exterior was enveloped in roaring flame. Within the structure, polished cedar floors, silk-covered mattresses, and rice paper privacy walls ignited as the internal temperature climbed. When the pressure within the house increased to a critical point with the rapid expansion of superheated air, the picture windows overlooking the bay blew out with a shattering explosion.

Fresh air rushed through the gaping wound in the rear wall, stocking the house with an unlimited supply of oxygen. A second, larger explosion lifted the roof off its trusses and demolished the load-bearing walls around the bungalow's three small sleeping chambers. The middle-aged woman and the three young men they contained had already succumbed to the concussion of the first blast and the intense heat from the subsequent firestorm, but the collapse of the roof and the walls ensured that little would remain of their bodies. Exhausted firemen combing through cinders days later would find only blackened teeth and a few bits of charred bone.

Other houses in the hillside neighborhood were in the process of being similarly consumed as the great firestorm swept up the slope, engulfing everything in its path. At the base of the hill, the chemical factory continued to burn furiously and emit sporadic explosions as, one by one, its storage tanks of petroleum and hydrogen and turpentine and sulfur caught fire and detonated. Fragments from the explosions reached far out into the bay, falling in long smoky trails like the aftermath of a fireworks display. Billowing columns of sickly green-yellow-black smoke rose into the otherwise pristine blue sky.

Between and beyond the ugly, poisonous columns that were rising at random locations all along the industrial waterfront, a scattered handful of warplanes, seeming to fly barely higher than the smokestacks of the factories they had just bombed, fled southwestward toward the snowcapped peak of Mount Fuji. As air-raid sirens continued to scream their belated warning throughout the great city, the marauding B-25s shrank to mere specks in the distance until, at last, they disappeared in the dirty haze that enshrouded the destruction left by their passing.

Chapter One

October 1944

The naked warrior lay in the gentle surge where the sea met the beach; he was barely covered by ten inches of blood-warm salt water. In the night sky overhead, black rags of cloud scudded across the three-quarter moon, briefly obscuring it. More still even than death in his forced repose—for a corpse would have rolled and bobbed in the soft swell at the water's edge—the warrior prayed against probability that in the next several seconds the clouds would mass together and block out the pale moon completely.

The pinpoint yellow glow of the approaching lantern had grown very large, swinging between the two Japanese sentries as they walked up the beach. The guttering light illuminated the puttees and baggy trousers covering the sentries' legs, as well as the long, sheathed bayonets riding against their thighs, and the wooden stocks of the bolt-action rifles slung over their shoulders.

They were very close now. Still coming.

The naked warrior pressed his body into the sand, his left hand digging in like a claw. His right flexed around

the grip of the Ka-Bar Marine Corps knife with the
blacked-down blade, feeling its reassuring weight. Holding his breath, he hunched his head low, the water lap-
ping at his cheekbones, and squinted so that the glare
from the approaching lantern would not catch the whites
of his eyes.

His heartbeat pounded in his ears, blending with the
soft crunch of coral sand beneath Imperial Japanese
Army issue boots. The patrolling sentries were less than
fifteen feet away now, muttering idly to each other—
as bored men tasked with routine jobs will often do—
in Japanese.

They sidestepped a small mound of sand, which brought
them even closer to the water's edge, and stopped. The
warrior tensed his body.

When they saw him, he would launch himself forward
in a direct attack. There was no other option. The water
was less than eighteen inches deep for at least two hundred yards to seaward—not enough to protect a swimming, porpoising man from rifle fire—and the moon
remained infuriatingly bright. Running, too, was out of
the question: a six-foot-tall silhouette fleeing on foot
through white-sand shallows lit by cold lunar light would
make too good a target.

His mouth and nose were still submerged. His chest
ached dully. How long had it been since his last breath?
No matter. The enemy soldiers would spot him in the
next few seconds and there would be time to breathe as
he lunged.

All the time in the world.

The two Japanese continued to banter in their rapid-
fire native tongue. Even spoken in hushed tones, it
sounded loud to his American ears. Foreign and aggres-
sive. The soldiers were glancing around now, at the low
dunes, the moon, the stars, the sea. . . .

The waterline . . .

Abruptly, the lantern came up between the two sentries, illuminating their distinctive faces—broad, flat features, high cheekbones, slanted eyes. Both men wore

standard-issue forage caps; one wore round-framed glasses. They were not particularly tall, but fit and sturdily built.

They did not look like men who would be slow to react, even when taken off guard.

Here, closer than ever before, was the flesh-and-blood personification of the enemy.

As the naked warrior gritted his teeth and bunched his muscles, the sentry wearing the eyeglasses looked directly at him. Into his face.

And did nothing.

Yellow light flickering over his own face, the Japanese slid up the glass wind cover of the lamp he brandished, cocked his head, and studiously lit a cigarette off the small, wobbling flame. Then he held the cover open as his companion did likewise.

Again, as he drew on his cigarette, he looked directly into the face of the man lying at the water's edge.

And once again, he did nothing.

The lamp came down to a carrying position once more, and the two sentries began to move off down the beach, continuing their languid patrol as they smoked. Eyeglasses let out a sharp guffaw in response to a comment from his companion as the naked warrior— finally—allowed himself the luxury of twisting his half-submerged head to one side and sucking in air through the corner of his mouth. His quivering muscles relaxed infinitesimally as realization of what had just happened dawned on him.

Night blindness.

The sentries' night vision had been destroyed by the light from their own lantern. The effect had been enhanced at the most crucial moment by the act of bringing the flame up close to their faces to light cigarettes.

No wonder Eyeglasses had looked him dead in the eye and still not seen him.

And thank God the two Japanese had stepped around the low mound of sand in their path before halting for a smoke break . . . instead of on it.

The naked warrior raised his head clear of the water,

watching as the sentries ambled around a large coral outcropping at the far end of the beach. Although they were now out of sight, he was able to track them by the faint corona of lantern light moving along the top edge of the dune line.

He pushed himself up out of the water on his hands and knees, bowed his head, and gave his body permission to shake like a leaf for several seconds.

Son of a *bitch.*

Too close.

Cautiously, he got his feet under him and stood up. Looking. Listening.

He was an incredible figure, poised there in the moonlight. One hundred and eighty pounds of lean muscle on a six-foot-one-half-inch frame. Fair hair cropped to a quarter inch all over his head. Short khaki swim trunks, canvas sneakers, and kneepads. Slathered from head to toe with silvery gray aluminum grease. Torso, arms, and legs banded at intervals of six inches with horizontal stripes of waterproof black paint. Heavy canvas GI utility belt from which dangled two small slate boards, two grease pencils, and the long sheath for the Ka-Bar. Canvas gloves stuffed into the top of the belt. Face mask and swim fins hooked by their straps over his left elbow. Dog tags doubled around his neck.

The hard, twenty-six-year-old body was for swimming miles through unknown coastal waters, regardless of weather conditions, at any time of day or night—often under direct enemy fire. The sneakers, kneepads, and gloves were to protect against abrasions when crawling over and around coral reefs. The aluminum grease was partial insulation against the chill of deeper water, as well as camouflage when reconnoitering beaches close in: such grease was a near-perfect color match for the sand found on most islands in the southwestern Pacific.

The black-painted body stripes were for measuring inshore water depths quickly and easily, the slate boards and grease pencils for recording that and other pertinent information: the locations of obstacles, mines, and shore defenses. The simple face mask and fins turned a strong surface swimmer into a truly amphibious human, one capable of seeing, maneuvering, and working underwater. The dog tags were doubled so as not to slip off the neck during intense in-water exertion.

The silver-slathered, black-striped figure bent forward and cupped his left hand around his mouth. Along the dune line far off to the right, the glow of the sentries' lantern was still visible, though continuing to move away. Behind the open beach, a few sparse palm trees fluttered their black fronds against an even blacker sky as the night breeze picked up momentarily.

"Joe!" the naked warrior hissed in a stage whisper. *"Joe!* They're gone!"

The low mound of sand that the two Japanese soldiers had stepped around just before pausing to light up heaved and slowly expanded. An arm revealed itself, followed by a head, shoulders, and the dim whites of a pair of eyes. The arm straightened, the index finger attached to it pointing back into the palm trees and scrub to the left.

"Get down!" the sand mound rasped in reply. "Nambu nest!"

Instantly, the erect man dropped back down onto his belly with a soft splash. The mound heaved once more, and then a second warrior—identical to the first but for his dark hair and the thin layer of sand that clung to every square inch of his grease-coated body—came wriggling like an eel across the beach on his elbows.

He continued on into the water, the sand sheeting off his glistening wet shoulders, until he was temple to temple with the first man.

"God *damn*, Charlton!" he whispered hoarsely. "Why'd you stand up like that? I didn't get a chance to tell you what I saw back there in those trees!"

"You're right, Joe. Sorry. Nambu?"

"Yeah. Heavy machine gun. Four-man squad. Nested up over the dunes, just inside the brush line. About a hundred and twenty yards to the south."

"Another one. You mark it down?"

"Uh-huh." The dark-haired man dashed water on his

face to clear sand from around his eyes. "Dug in so good they're damn near invisible. You can't see the nest at all from the beach. Gotta be right on top of it."

"How'd *you* see it?"

White teeth flashed against a deep tan. "Didn't. I smelled it. Cigarette smoke. Worked my way upwind along the flank until I could make out the exact location and armament. Then I skedaddled out of there like a rat. Thought I was home free until those two Japs came around the far end of the beach and I had to dig in."

The first man swallowed and licked his lips. "Like I told myself, too damn close."

"Yeah."

The fair-haired swimmer glanced at his wristwatch and began to worm his way backward along the bottom. "Come on. We've got thirty minutes to get through the outer reef to the rendezvous point. I could use a cigarette myself—how about you?"

The white-toothed smile flashed briefly again. "Not me, Lieutenant. I think cigarettes are bad for you, no matter what Johnny Weissmuller says in the newspaper ads." A glance back at the darkened dune line and the palm trees beyond. "Get a man killed."

It took Lieutenant (jg) Charlton Randall and Gunner's Mate Joe Garth nearly twenty-five minutes to crawl, wade, and swim the quarter mile across the black expanse of the inner lagoon, traverse the semisubmerged barrier reef, and stroke out into the cold, choppy offshore waters where they and the other four members of their small Underwater Demolition Team squad were to be picked up by the same roving LCI—infantry landing craft—that, earlier, had dropped them off along the reef line in three two-man teams. An October typhoon had passed over the central Philippines only days before, and the ocean was still restless. The two frogmen swam for another long, lonely half hour in the dark predawn swells, alternately gazing back at the enemy-held island of Leyte and searching to seaward where the American invasion fleet lay . . . and all the while they tried not to imagine what might be rising through the black depths toward their pale, kicking legs.

"Where the hell is that incompetent son of a bitch?" Randall panted. He drew a quick breath as a cresting three-foot swell slapped the side of his face. "We're goddamn shark bait out here."

Garth, floating quietly on his back, spat a little stream of water skyward. "Easy, L.T. That LCI'll be along in a few more minutes."

Randall thrashed around, craning his neck. "If we get eaten by sharks, I'm going to have that hick coxswain's ass." He coughed out a mouthful of Philippine Sea. "Aghh. What's his name again?"

"The swabbie LCI driver? Kelso."

"Kelso—that's right. Incompetent son of a bitch." Randall glared into the darkness. "Still nothing."

Garth, continuing to scull gently on his back, cleared his throat. "Lieutenant. Take it easy. Sharks like thrashing movements. Makes 'em curious, remember?"

"Yeah, yeah," Randall replied, calming down. "Sorry."

"And don't worry. No sharks are going to eat us tonight."

"Oh, really? Why is that?"

Garth turned his head and looked at his UDT squad leader across three feet of hissing black brine. "Because we have info the general ordered us to get," he said. His white-toothed grin gleamed in the ambient moonlight. "And nothing that walks on the earth, flies through the air, or swims in the sea interferes with an order from General Douglas MacArthur. Ain't that so?"

By the time the rumble of an approaching diesel reached their ears and the LCI's boxy black shape appeared out of the night, rolling awkwardly atop the moderate swell, they were both numb with cold. Barely able to scramble up the netting that hung over the landing craft's side, they were seized by crewmen—who were anxious to get out of range of any attentive Japanese shore batteries—hauled unceremoniously over the gunwale, and dumped onto the deck plates like a brace of boated tuna.

"Let's get the hell outta here, Kelso," one of the gray-life-jacketed, steel-helmeted sailors called out, his voice hoarse with strain.

"Keep your drawers on, Greer," the coxswain replied cheerfully. He was a dark silhouette standing at the helm in the vessel's stern. A Zippo clinked and flared as he lit a cigarette. "How many is that?"

"Six, dammit. Six frogmen. That's the whole squad. Now can we please haul ass before them Nips get wise and drop a seventy-five-millimeter welcome present into the goddamned boat?" Greer was almost pleading.

The coxswain chuckled and blew a plume of smoke. "Well, I guess, son—since you're about to have a bladder accident."

Greer's four-letter retort was lost in the roar of the gunning diesel as Kelso shoved the throttle lever forward. The landing craft wobbled around onto a south-easterly heading, away from land, as a cloud of acrid exhaust swept across the decks.

The six UDT men crept together in the bottom of the vessel, huddling beneath rough U.S. Navy blankets. Everyone's teeth were chattering audibly, none more so than Randall's.

"Th-that incompetent son of a b-b-bitch," he reiterated, glaring astern at the helmsman's station. "K-K-Kelso. He should have p-picked us all up n-n-nearly an hour ago."

Garth leaned in close to the lieutenant. "Maybe a head c-count, L.T.," he murmured. "Just to keep things by the numbers."

Randall nodded irritably, shivering. "Right." He raised his voice. "Okay. I can s-see everyone's here, but humor m-me and sing out anyway. Bartlett?"

One of the crouching, blanket-wrapped men stuck up a finger. "Here."

"Drexel?"

"H-h-here."

"McNab?"

"Here, Lieutenant."

"Fitzgerald?"

No answer. Randall waited for a few seconds, then reached out and batted the curled-up figure to his opposite left.

"Dammit, Fitz, I'm l-looking right at you. What the hell."

The blanket stirred and a pair of bleary eyes appeared. "S-sorry, L.T. I—I think my lips is f-f-*ffffroze* together."

A ripple of laughter passed through the squad. Even Randall couldn't stifle a chuckle. Count on Fitz to lighten the moment, no matter what.

The seaman named Greer stooped down next to Randall. In one hand he held six small metal mugs by their wire handles, and in the other a liquor bottle. Pulling the cork with his teeth, he poured a generous slug into one of the mugs.

"Have a taste, Lieutenant," he said, offering it to Randall. "Regulations say you UDT guys get a shot to warm you up after a mission. Unlike us poor regular navy swabbies."

Randall took the mug with both hands. "Thanks."

"Don't mention it." Greer proceeded to fortify the remaining five mugs and pass them around. "Just hardly seems fair, that's all. I mean, all of us could use a drink now and again, you know?"

"See, wh-what it is," Fitzgerald cut in, "MacArthur and Nimitz f-figure if they let you swabbies get into the sauce, you'll run amok and end up kicking the shit out of every marine and GI you see. C-could end up incapacitating the bulk of the invasion force." The wisecracking UDT man was barely shivering now, the blanket off his head and exposing a jovial Irish face under a mop of damp, curly hair that would have appeared carrot red had it been daylight.

There was another round of laughter.

"That must be it," Greer said, getting up. "Okay, enjoy the brandy. Kelso says one shot each, then bring him back the bottle."

"Why don't you sneak a taste?" McNab, a swarthy Floridian, grinned over the rim of his mug. "We ain't tellin'."

The seaman sighed and shook his head. "Thanks, but one thing I've learned since bein' assigned to this tub: it may be MacArthur's army, and Nimitz's navy—but this is *damn* sure Mr. Kelso's LCI."

He turned and made his way toward the stern, walking with the wide-apart stance of the seasoned sailor. Randall watched him pass the bottle up to Kelso at the helm.

The lieutenant sipped from the mug, feeling the brandy burn its way down his esophagus. Amazing how even relatively warm waters such as those of the Philippine Sea and Leyte Gulf could drain a man's body heat after only a few hours' immersion. Temperature conductivity of a fluid, or something like that.

The brandy helped in another way. It subdued the vague, twisting knot of fear that Charlton Randall carried around in his belly every waking moment.

It wasn't that he was a coward. He was pretty sure he wasn't one of those. And it wasn't the disorienting chaos of war, although that was certainly a contributing factor. It was something else, something he'd been plagued with since childhood—a gnawing, unspecific dread that no matter what he did or how hard he tried, he would never quite measure up to . . . expectations.

"You feeling okay, L.T.?"

Garth's casual, low-toned inquiry nudged Randall out of his preoccupations and back to reality. Nodding, he sipped again at his brandy. Not for the first time, he acknowledged to himself that he was glad to have the gunner's mate in his squad.

Sometimes he wished he could be more like Joe. Everyone fortunate enough to make it to adulthood, he realized, carried a certain amount of emotional baggage. But if Joe Garth toted any, it wasn't visible. The dark-haired, half-Apache Texan had an inner calm that even the heat of battle could not disrupt. Randall had seen it time and time again, in hard-fought actions on islands like Saipan, Guam, and Peleliu, when the entrenched

Japanese had poured hellfire on the naked swimmers reconnoitering, mining, and blowing up submerged beach obstacles prior to full-scale amphibious landings by U.S. Marines.

Garth would swim unperturbed through hailstorms of machine gun and sniper fire, calmly installing Hagensen packs—waterproof bundles of high explosive named for their inventor, UDT Lieutenant Carl Hagensen—and stretching detonator cord between obstacles. So would Randall—though he was anything but unperturbed. As if a permanent case of butterflies wasn't bad enough, he always had the uncomfortable feeling that Garth, with whom he was permanently paired, was keeping a guardian-like eye on him as well as doing his own job . . . even though *he* was the lieutenant in charge of the squad.

Fortunately, the other guys didn't seem to notice, and his squad had an excellent war record thus far. To top it off, despite all the action they'd seen, they hadn't taken a single casualty.

So by any objective standard, Lieutenant Junior Grade Charlton Randall III of Long Island, New York, was doing a bang-up job of running his UDT squad and performing under fire. He just wished that, like Joe Garth, he could be a little more . . . *relaxed* about it.

He suddenly became aware that Bartlett and Drexel were looking at him. He wondered in a flash if somehow they'd been able to see into his fretful mind. To cover up, he drained the last of his brandy and set the empty mug down hard on the deck plates.

"What are you two looking at?" he growled, making his voice sound tougher than his insides felt.

Bartlett and Drexel, who were always paired up as were McNab and Fitzgerald, shrugged simultaneously. "Just waiting for you to start the mission summary, L.T.," Bartlett said. "But I guess you got something else on your mind tonight." The stocky ex-steelworker from Cleveland glanced at Drexel, the stocky ex-steelworker from Toledo.

They looked like brothers, Randall thought, a pair of

acrobat brothers from some traveling European circus. "We're all pretty cold and tired," he said. "And it's too damn noisy to talk on this bucket. We'll talk back aboard ship."

The two shrugged again, together, as if their muscles were all connected to the same nerve. "Sure, L.T.," Drexel said. He raised his brandy mug to his lips.

The clackety-clack sound of the breech being opened on a heavy machine gun startled everyone, causing them to glance up. On the gunwale above, silhouetted against the stars in an armored swivel mount, one of the LCI's helmeted, life-jacketed sailors—a rangy Nebraskan named Hazelwood—was feeding a fresh belt of ammunition into his fifty-caliber weapon. He felt the six pairs of eyes on him and looked down.

"Got salt spray on my ammo," he shouted over the diesel noise. "I hate salt water on my ammo. Gums up my baby." He patted the top of the machine gun.

"Can you see our ships yet?" Randall called.

The silhouetted gunner turned, looking forward. "Roger that. Blacked out, but less than four miles away, I'd say."

"Thanks," Randall told him. He hunkered down again and pulled the blanket up around his shoulders. "Almost home, gentlemen."

"Fantastic," Fitzgerald said. "I can't wait to get this stinking grease off. I think it's migrating to my balls."

Laughter.

"I get a Purple Heart for suffering greased balls in the field, Lieutenant?"

More laughter.

The troop transport ship USS *Mayhew* was actually a converted destroyer escort—which meant that she was relatively narrow-beamed and rolled like a pig in a crossing sea. With the rhythms of the ocean still confused in the wake of the recent typhoon, every one of the twelve hundred marines crammed aboard her was sick as a dog. Two days earlier, when the typhoon's center had passed

over the invasion fleet, it had been much worse. Even
the captain had blown chow off the port wing of the
bridge, much to his annoyance. Waste of a perfectly
good fried-SPAM sandwich.

Comparable degrees of seasickness existed aboard all
of the seven-hundred-plus warships and transports that
made up General MacArthur's Philippine invasion
force—particularly among the nearly two hundred thousand land troops waiting to disembark and assault the
heavily defended beaches of Leyte Island. The vast majority of soldiers had never been to sea before shipping
out to the South Pacific, much less through a typhoon.
Those that survived the war would never forget the experience. Riding out a Pacific cyclone on an over-
crowded transport vessel was like being under heavy
bombardment from Nature herself.

Kelso's landing craft motored around the stern and
along the lee side of the *Mayhew,* pitching and rolling
even in the reduced swell. From the armored tub of his
forty-millimeter gun mount, Gunner's Mate Samuel
Hatch gazed down with detached interest at the LCI as
it bumped into the hull plates amidships, where a board-
ing net had been hung. Six silver-looking guys in swim
trunks—make that silver with black stripes—swarmed
out of the landing craft and up the net in a tight group,
clambering over the starboard rail a few seconds later.

It took Hatch a moment to clue in. Oh, right. UDTs.
Gone for one of their midnight swims. Crazy bastards.
Wouldn't get me in that friggin' ocean at night for all
the gold in Fort Knox.

He hunkered down under his flak helmet and continued to fiddle with the worn flint of his cigarette lighter.

The UDT men headed down into the bowels of the
ship, picking their way carefully over the bodies of
groaning marines who were camped out shoulder to
shoulder on every available inch of deck space. The air
was stagnant, heavy with body odor and the acidic smell
of vomit. But Randall, Garth, and the others hardly noticed. Seven months of shipboard living, as key partici-

pants in MacArthur's island-hopping campaign up through the southwestern Pacific, had inured them to their own seasickness and that of others.

They reached the sanctuary reserved for them in the *Mayhew*'s stern—a cramped, six-bunk wardroom containing the unheard-of luxury of a private shower stall—and proceeded to strip down. Scrubbing off as much aluminum grease and black paint as could be removed by soap and brush, they dressed and collapsed onto their bunks, exhaustion beginning to take hold.

But within five minutes there was a knock at the door. A young navy lieutenant, the same grade as Randall, stuck his head into the lamplit wardroom.

"You guys alive?" he inquired. He was no-nonsense, but pleasant.

"Hi, Frank," Randall said.

Lieutenant Francis Riley Kaine, known throughout the fleet as "MacArthur's Frogman"—a nickname indicative of both his combat experience and his unique position as the general's personal UDT adviser—smiled sympathetically. "Debriefing in the officers' mess, ten minutes," he announced. "And try to look sharp, gentlemen. You have a special visitor."

After hurriedly making a few notes on the night's reconnaissance information, Randall led his bleary-eyed squad down a passageway lined with the prone bodies of snoring marines and into the officers' mess. Joe Garth's nose wrinkled as he followed his lieutenant over the room's threshold. The place smelled of the last meal served there: chopped steak and onions. Heavy on the onions.

Frank Kaine, tall and slender in clean navy khakis, was leaning back on one of the mess tables with his arms crossed. A large color map of the eastern coast of Leyte Island had been affixed to the bulkhead behind him, and a couple of clip-on lamps rigged to the fire control plumbing overhead. The illumination of the map provided the only lighting in the otherwise dim mess hall. In the center of one of the other tables, a bottle of steak

sauce shifted in a condiment rack every time the
Mayhew rolled to starboard.

"Have a seat, fellas," Kaine said, unfolding an arm
and gesturing at the tables in front of him. "We need to
get started. I know you're tired, but time's an issue
here." Totally professional, but with that easy familiarity
unique to American officers, Randall thought.

Garth repositioned the clunking steak sauce bottle in
its rack as he sat down. One less irritation.

Kaine recrossed his arms and regarded Randall. "Do
you have a handle on the data you and your squad just
collected?" he asked. "Or do you need a few more minutes to discuss it . . . pull it all together in your mind?"

Randall held up a notepad in one hand and tapped a
pile of slate boards covered in grease pencil markings
with the other. "I've pretty much got it."

Kaine nodded, stepped away from the table, and
walked around to the wall map. With a red pencil, he
drew two large brackets around an indented area of
coastline that lay several miles to the southwest of a long
stretch of beach marked "Primary Landing Location."
Then he turned and extended the pencil toward Randall.
"There's the area you just reconned," he said. "Operational code name 'Beach Black.' It's all yours, Charlton.
Summary time."

Clearing his throat, Randall collected the slate boards
and got to his feet. Kaine handed him the pencil and
moved off toward a side door. "Back in a minute," he
murmured. "Get ready."

Randall shot him a puzzled look as he set his slate
boards and notepad down on the table nearest the map.
Ready? Ready for what? He'd done dozens of combat
recon summaries.

He glanced up at the map as Kaine stepped through
the door. Somewhere on the upper decks, a heavy object
fell or was dropped. The muted, metallic echo reverberated through the ship.

"Hey, L.T.," Fitzgerald commented. "We the only audience? You gonna tell us everything we just told you
all over again?"

"Not hardly, son." The voice came from the side door, deep and commanding, stentorian without being particularly loud. The UDT squad members all turned their heads in time to see Frank Kaine step aside and come to attention as a tall, long-legged figure in uniform khakis and a peaked cap entered the mess hall. A corncob pipe jutted from the lower half of a rawboned Scots face that looked as if it had been chiseled from a block of granite.

"Officer on deck!" Kaine barked, saluting.

Randall nearly dropped his pencil.

MacArthur.

There was a banging of knees and ankles on bench seats and table legs as the squad scrambled to its feet and saluted. The General of the Army returned the courtesy with a casual precision that bespoke his authority, then plucked the corncob pipe from his mouth. He didn't even come close to cracking a smile.

"Stand easy," he said, waving his pipe stem in a benevolent gesture. "Be seated."

As the squad sat down again, MacArthur remained standing, his flinty eyes roving over the map of Leyte while Kaine unfolded a collapsible chair and set it on the deck behind him. Once, the general's cold gaze flickered onto Randall's face—giving him a momentary heart palpitation—before returning to the map.

After a pregnant twenty seconds, MacArthur made a rumbling noise in his throat, seated himself, and crossed his arms and legs. He puffed on his pipe, producing a small cloud of smoke, then withdrew it and pointed the stem at Randall.

"Carry on, Lieutenant," he said.

"Yes, sir," Randall replied.

Turning to the map, referring to the notepad he held in his left hand, he rapidly drew in all the details his squad had collected during their reconnaissance, using standard symbols for various types of obstacles and gun emplacements. It took him several minutes. MacArthur sat in silence, coolly smoking his corncob.

"In-water reconnaissance and assessment of Beach Black," Randall said. "Between the northernmost and southernmost boundaries"—he indicated the two brackets Kaine had drawn—"water is three feet deep over soft sand bottom just inside the outer reef, shallowing rapidly to less than eighteen inches along a depth contour that runs consistently more than two hundred yards from the beach proper. The reef itself is partially exposed at low tide, jagged and irregular, with no greater controlling depth than two and a half feet at high tide.

"The entire central section of the inshore lagoon, inside the barrier reef, is devoid of man-made obstacles. There are no mines, rock cribs, or tree trunk stakes. On the other hand"—Randall paused and looked directly at MacArthur—"Gunner's Mate Garth and I were able to count at least four heavy-machine-gun nests placed just behind the dune line in this area, along with several mortars and one small antitank artillery piece of unknown caliber. To confirm the exact locations of these positions, Gunner's Mate Garth reconnoitered behind the dunes for a short distance—"

"He left the water?" Kaine interrupted.

Randall licked his lips. "That's correct. In his estimation, taking into account the intermittent moonlight and the cover he had to work with on that beach, the need for accurate reconnaissance of enemy defensive positions justified the risk of going ashore. Knowing that Gunner's Mate Garth has unusual stalking skills, I concurred."

Actually, he'd nearly hissed himself hoarse trying to order Joe back when the Texan had first slithered out of the water and across the darkened beach. But it hardly seemed appropriate to mention that now.

Kaine's handsome face hardened, but he said nothing more. At the table opposite him, Garth smiled down at the deck in silence. Technically, UDTs were not supposed to leave the cover of the water, a point that would almost certainly be debated by Kaine and Randall at a later date.

"Continue, Lieutenant Randall," MacArthur instructed.

The general's stony expression had not softened one iota, but there was a hint of amusement in his rasp of a voice.

"Yes, sir," Randall responded. "As I was saying, the central beach and dunes are heavily defended by strategically placed machine gun nests and mortar positions. The shallow lagoon contains no obstacles of any kind, all the way out to the reef."

MacArthur nodded, drawing on his pipe. "Why do you think that is, Lieutenant?"

Randall consulted the map briefly before answering. "It's a killing ground, sir. The Japs haven't put any obstacles in that lagoon because they don't have to. It's too shallow for landing craft and too soft-bottomed for tanks. Any infantry trying to wade across the whole quarter mile from reef to beach would be cut to pieces."

The general nodded again, the crevices in his face shifting like geologic fault lines, forming a slight smile. "I'd say so. But the extreme north and south ends of Beach Black—they're different, isn't that so?"

"Yes, sir," Randall went on. "The team of McNab and Fitzgerald was able to confirm that there is a navigable channel through the reef at the beach's southern end. It is forty yards wide by twenty feet deep. This channel extends all the way to shore, where it merges with the delta of a small river flowing down from the hills."

"A natural outflow channel," Kaine mused, "carved by the river over time."

"All the rainwater falling on those hills has to go somewhere," MacArthur said. "It looks like we've got a landing-craft highway right to that delta."

"McNab and Fitzgerald also report," Randall continued, "the presence of stake-mounted mines just inside the reef, several rock cribs farther in, and a strange spherical obstacle on the bottom of the channel about one hundred yards from the delta itself. In addition, the shoreline and hillsides bordering the mouth of the river are infested with defensive positions, including machine gun nests and light-artillery bunkers. My men were unable to get close enough to identify specific locations and armaments."

"Understandable," MacArthur grunted. "And the northern end of the beach?"

"The team of Bartlett and Drexel surveyed that area. They report an area of broken coral in the reef with a controlling depth of five feet, approximately seventy yards wide. They marked it with two small red cork buoys before proceeding inshore."

Kaine turned to MacArthur. "That'll be from the preliminary bombardments, sir. Some of the battlewagons dropped their shells short. Occasionally that results in an unexpected benefit—like a navigable gap blasted in an inconvenient barrier reef."

"Indeed," the general said. "Carry on, Lieutenant Randall."

"Yes sir. While there is no definable channel inshore of the breach in the reef, the lagoon in this area is deeper, with a controlling depth of four feet over sand bottom. This shallows abruptly to less than a foot along a consistent depth contour some seventy-five yards from the beach proper.

"The deeper waters of the lagoon contain numerous stake mines, more than five dozen tripod obstacles constructed of tree trunks, and several large rock cribs. The beaches, again, appear to be heavily defended by machine gun nests and bunkers."

Randall drew a slow breath, then let it out. "That's all, sir."

Silence dominated the room. Randall placed his notepad gently on the table next to the stack of slate boards, studying his own handwriting, and waited.

"Cheery, ain't it?" Fitzgerald cracked.

MacArthur turned his head and looked at him. The redheaded UDT man seemed to wilt like a poisoned dandelion. No one else, including Kaine, budged an inch.

Then the general grinned, his glacial expression instantly rearranging itself into the very picture of good humor. Getting to his feet, he rose to his full height, waved everyone else to stay seated, and turned to face Fitzgerald.

"By God," he said, "I like a man with the brass nuts to joke in the face of death—or in my presence. Very nearly the same thing, you know, to most people." He gazed down at Fitzgerald. "It's 'Fitz,' Lieutenant Kaine tells me."

"Yes, sir," Fitzgerald said in the voice of the doomed.

"Well, Fitz, you're right. It *is* cheery." MacArthur stalked over to the wall map. "Cheery because the channel at the southern end of Beach Black offers us a high-speed route through the reef and into that river mouth. Cheery because, that being the most obvious point for an amphibious penetration, the Japanese have concentrated a considerable number of defensive assets *around* that river mouth. That makes me happy. Do you know why that makes me happy, Fitz?"

Kaine rubbed a finger over his upper lip to hide a smile. The notoriously autocratic MacArthur almost never bantered with the common soldiers who fought under his leadership, much less explained the reasoning behind his tactics. A function of his ironclad opinions about the hierarchy of command. But the general liked his frogmen.

"Uh—no, sir," Fitzgerald said weakly, still unsure whether or not his mouth had gotten him into serious trouble.

"Because," MacArthur said, "knowing they're there makes it possible for me to concentrate part of the final preinvasion bombardment right on the hills bordering that river mouth, with a reasonable expectation of achieving maximum damage to the enemy. They'll be less able to interfere with your underwater demolition work and engage the LCIs and troops that follow after enduring four hours of targeted shellfire from the fleet's heavy batteries."

The knot in Randall's stomach tightened slightly. Something wasn't clear. Across the room, Joe Garth shifted in his chair, his dark eyes very attentive, fixed on the general.

"I beg your pardon, sir," Randall said, "but may I ask when you plan to start the final bombardment? I mean, since immediately following it, we'll be swimming in again to blow the obstacles, sir."

MacArthur surveyed the map. "In about ten minutes. As soon as I'm done here."

The knot in Randall's stomach turned over. "And we *will* be going in immediately afterward to blow the obstacles?" he persisted.

MacArthur looked at him, all traces of good humor evaporating from his expression. "Yes. The route has to be cleared before the landing craft can assault the river mouth."

Randall felt the blood drain from his face. "But sir," he said, "that means we'll be swimming around in front of those enemy guns in broad daylight!"

"Correct."

"Sir—"

"Let me explain something to you, Lieutenant," MacArthur cut in, wheeling around, "and to the rest of your squad. I have nearly two hundred thousand men sitting out here on more than seven hundred ships—all of them bored, scared, seasick, and becoming less inclined to fight with each passing hour. Somewhere north of Leyte Gulf, perhaps in the Philippine Sea proper, the Imperial Japanese Navy is lurking. We are well within striking range of enemy aircraft operating from bases on Leyte and Luzon. This invasion force is eminently vulnerable to attack.

"Ground troops are useless—helpless—while they are penned up aboard ship. They are simply targets, priceless human assets at risk of being wasted for want of being used. A soldier killed while taking an objective, on the other hand, has not been wasted. His life has not been lost in vain." The general paused, eyeing each UDT man in turn. "I intend to waste as few of my men as possible. I owe them that."

"Yes, sir," the squad murmured in ragged unison.

"We are invading Leyte on the twentieth of October," MacArthur declared. "That, gentlemen, is today. If you are concerned about approaching the enemy shore in broad daylight, I remind you that you will be followed closely by thousands of other fighting men—also in broad daylight—who must land, engage the Japanese, and push them back into the hills. Eventually, they will push them off this island.

"A significant number of these men are going to die. Those that do so today at the southern end of Beach Black will enable their brothers-in-arms to perform the absolutely critical task of penetrating inland along the coastal plain, turning north, and providing flank support for the primary invasion force as it comes ashore at the town of Dulag. Proceeding with this flanking maneuver is a last-minute decision, which is why you will have to remove the obstacles from that channel this morning, as soon as the bombardment lifts, just ahead of the first wave of landing craft."

Once again, MacArthur's gaze fell on each man in turn: Randall, Garth, Bartlett, Drexel, McNab, and Fitzgerald. "They cannot land," he said, "unless you clear the way."

He turned to face the map and gravely went about relighting his corncob pipe. Kaine leaned back against the edge of a table in silence, his arms crossed, and observed the effect of the general's words on the UDT squad. A short speech, rendered with typically MacArthurian melodrama—and, as usual, compelling. Delivered on the brink of battle, with the power of Douglas MacArthur's personality behind it, melodrama became inspiration, bluntness clarity. Kaine's eyes flickered over the tall, aging figure. Whatever one thought of the man, he knew how to lead.

"A few LCI gunboats will make a feint at the gap blown in the northern end of the reef," MacArthur mused, puffing on his pipe. "But the assault on Beach Black will focus on the channel to the south." He glanced at his watch. "You men will open the door. Understood?"

"Yes, sir," the squad chorused.

The general headed for the mess hall entrance. "Carry

on, Lieutenant Kaine," he said, "and when you've finished up here, join me on the bridge. We will transfer back to the *Nashville* once the bombardment commences." The *Nashville* was the U.S. Navy heavy cruiser currently serving as MacArthur's command post.

The men got to their feet again, but before they could come fully to attention MacArthur was through the door and gone, leaving a trail of cherry-bourbon tobacco smoke hanging in the reddish glow of the passageway battle lanterns.

Somewhere deep within the hull of the ship, there was another dull, resonating boom.

After a while, realizing that the general was not coming back, the men began to relax. Kaine remained silent, giving them time. Ten minutes of close contact with Douglas MacArthur often necessitated a certain amount of decompression.

"Whew," Fitzgerald said at last. "Who was that masked man?"

Everyone smiled. Even Kaine.

"Frank," Randall said. "Tell me there's some way we can put off having to wire up the obstacles in that channel at least until sundown, when we've got a fifty-fifty chance of blowing everything and getting out of there alive."

Kaine shifted his gaze to the far corner of the room. "You're exaggerating a bit, Charlton. I wouldn't say your chances are worse than fifty-fifty even in daylight."

"Exaggerating? I'm exaggerating? We're going to get our asses shot off if we swim within three hundred yards of that river mouth without the cover of darkness. The Japs have defensive positions up on those steep hillsides. They're going to be able to see us even when we're underwater, and they'll be firing down on us from a high angle. It'll be like shooting fish in a barrel."

Kaine patted the air in a "take it easy" gesture. "Look. You'll be greased up in camo silver, hard to distinguish against the bottom, especially in that murky water. For the next four hours, the hills around that river mouth are going to be hit with so many battlewagon broadsides and naval air strikes, there probably isn't going to be a Jap left to poke his head out."

Fitzgerald couldn't resist. "Sure, Lieutenant," he muttered sarcastically. "Just like at Peleliu. All that ordnance really softened those bastards up."

"They went to ground in those coral caves," Kaine shot back. "It was the First Marine Division that took the beating, not us. Offshore covering fire neutralized every asset that tried to target UDTs—except for the odd sniper, which you know as well as I do we can't eliminate completely. We worked in broad daylight there, didn't we?"

"The circumstances were different," Randall persisted. "We weren't in as close, and the Japs didn't have that high angle of fire. I'm telling you, we'll be swimming into a slaughter."

Kaine looked at the floor, then up at his fellow lieutenant. His expression was hard, resigned. "The General can't afford to wait," he said. "Give me your reconnaissance data. I'll take it over to Team Three and brief them."

"What?" Randall blinked, off-balance. "What for?"

"So they'll have some idea where they're going when they swim in to blow that channel clear."

"Wait a minute—"

"I'll tell MacArthur you all came down with food poisoning. No arguing with that. It happens."

The color drained from Randall's face. He stood stock-still as Garth moved up beside him. The Texan's gimlet eyes were steady on Kaine's. "We're not doing that," Garth said quietly. The other members of the squad closed in behind Randall. "Are we, L.T." It was a statement, not a question.

"Hell, no," Randall affirmed. His voice was hoarse. "That wasn't called for, Frank. I was just—"

Kaine straightened and took a step toward the mess hall door. "So you're telling me you'd rather *not* have UDT Three pick a squad to do your job for you." His hard expression didn't quite conceal the pain his own tactics caused him.

"Hell, no," Randall repeated, ashen. Behind him, all the squad members nodded silently.

"Fine," Kaine said. "Prepare to move inshore with a full supply of explosives at oh nine hundred hours. The first wave will be coming down that channel as soon as you detonate the main shot."

He started toward the door again, then paused. Turning to face Randall, he extended his right hand. "Good luck, Charlton," he said.

Randall shook with him. "Thanks."

Kaine looked at the other men and touched his fingers to the corner of his right eyebrow before turning to leave.

"Good luck to all of you," he said.

Chapter Two

It was difficult to concentrate as the bombardment intensified. Even in the depths of the long, tunnellike cave, well protected by several hundred feet of limestone, the concussion from the shells and bombs the Americans were laying on the hills around the river mouth rattled a man's bones, popped his ears, and made the breath catch in his throat. Overhead, the meager string of electric lights flickered as rock dust sifted down from the cave roof.

Imperial Japanese Navy lieutenant Kentaro Higuchi furrowed his brow and focused on the task at hand. As leadoff man for his *Shinyo* squadron, he would be first out of the cave and into the water when the signal was given. It was essential that his boat be in top working order. He bent farther over the reconditioned six-cylinder Chevrolet automobile engine, preparing to adjust the throttle linkages.

"Wrench," he said, reaching back without looking. "Number two."

When there was no response, he shifted in annoyance

on top of the engine and twisted his head around. "Wanabi! Hand me the number two wrench."

Through the rock walls came another muted, air-shaking series of concussions that brought a fresh cascade of dust seething down on top of the short, pudgy-cheeked soldier crouching at Higuchi's feet. The little man was shaking visibly, hugging his knees, his eyes darting this way and that.

Exasperated, Higuchi raised himself up on one elbow. *"Private Second Class Wanabi! I am speaking to you!"*

The man came partially to life. *"H-hai,* Honorable Lieutenant!" His eyes still darted feverishly over the rock ceiling above his head.

"Compose yourself, Wanabi," Higuchi ordered, trying and failing to keep the disgust out of his voice. Some of these low-grade army privates who'd been assigned to his squadron as helpers were hopelessly sorry specimens—uneducated conscripts from rural areas, mostly. A seaman with technical training or a private of the *Rikusentai*—Imperial Japanese Marines—would have been much more dependable. But of course skilled sailors and elite marines could not be wasted on menial labor.

"The wrench, Wanabi," Higuchi said again. The little private stopped shaking long enough to pass it to him.

As Higuchi bent over the engine linkages once more, another rumbling series of detonations pulsed through the dusty, fume-laden air. The overhead bulbs fizzed out, then came back weakly with perhaps one-fifth their former brightness. It was not enough light to work by. Higuchi cursed under his breath, waiting.

"Honorable Lieutenant," Wanabi began.

Whamwhamwhamwhamwhamwham . . .

The rock dust drifted down. As Higuchi spat limestone powder off his lips, the overhead lights flickered back to full strength. He pulled the throttle linkages into alignment and set the wrench over the locking nut.

Wanabi was shaking again. "Honorable Lieutenant," he stammered. "Do you—do you think the cave will collapse in on us?"

"Anything is possible, Wanabi," Higuchi said, working.

A sound that was a cross between a whimper and a groan escaped the private's lips. "Hon-Honorable Lieutenant, sir?"

"Yes?"

"Do you think that we—that many of us—on land, I mean—will be killed today?"

Higuchi let out a deep sigh, put down the wrench, and propped himself up on one elbow once again so he could look back at Wanabi. His expression was firm, but not unkind. Unlike many of his fellow officers in the Japanese military, he preferred to reinforce orders and the discipline of enlisted men with verbal abuse and physical blows only when absolutely necessary.

"Dying is not the worst thing that can happen to a soldier," he said.

Wanabi did not appear comforted or inspired by this simple truth, and hugged his knees even tighter, goggling at Higuchi in pitiable fashion.

Higuchi's expression hardened. The man needed to be reminded of his duty, his obligations.

"Private Second Class Wanabi," he stated, "you will now recite for me the First Precept of the Imperial Rescript to Soldiers and Sailors. Until I tell you to stop."

As another string of violent explosions echoed through the rock walls, Wanabi, breathing hard, began to mutter: *". . . be resolved that while duty is heavier than a mountain, death is lighter than a feather. . . ."*

As Coxswain Kelso's LCI bucked over the early-morning swells toward the coast of Leyte Island, Fitzgerald, crouched low out of the wind and spray with the other five members of the UDT squad, dug an elbow into his partner's ribs. McNab stopped working on his gum and frowned at him.

"You're disturbin' my preswim tranquillity, here, Fitz." McNab had the exaggerated calm of someone actively controlling a tremendous amount of inner tension. All of them did. And despite their relaxed expressions, every member of the squad, with the exception of Joe Garth, had a tell—a nervously tapping foot, a twitching finger, a gnawed-upon lower lip. McNab's was chewing gum; in the anxious minutes just prior to a combat deployment, he positively punished the Juicy Fruit.

"Lookee here," Fitzgerald whispered with a grin. He pulled out the waist of his swim trunks. Tucked in next to his hip was a roll of bright red cloth. "When we get the last obstacle wired, I'm gonna set it up on that first sandbar in the river mouth."

McNab began working on his gum again. "This ain't the place for that. It's gonna be hot in there. A stupid sign ain't worth getting killed over." When he was really nervous his Florida cracker speech patterns became more pronounced.

Fitzgerald winked at him. "Piece of cake. Those slanty-eyed bastards can't hit shit, anyway." He thumped his silver-greased, black-striped chest and let out a snort of laughter. "The Fitz is too slippery for 'em."

Randall turned around abruptly. "Fitz, I hear you cutting up back there. Listen to me—no stunts, no heroics. We go in; each pair wires up its assigned obstacles; we back out together, blow the shot, and then get the hell out of the way before the first wave of LCIs runs us over. Clear?"

"As a bell, L.T.," Fitzgerald said cheerfully.

Randall eyed him for another second or two, then turned back toward the bow. His stomach felt as though it contained a cast-iron bowling ball. He swallowed, then swallowed again. It was his tell. But he didn't have even a drop of spit. His mouth and throat were as dry as sandpaper. He glanced to his right, wondering if Garth had noticed his nervousness. But Joe was looking straight ahead, his expression as placid as that of a meditating monk.

Bartlett and Drexel were arguing baseball, as usual. Women's baseball—all able-bodied men had been drafted. They spoke in hushed tones and short sentences.

Randall stood up and peered over the gunwale of the landing craft. Less than half a mile ahead, the barely submerged outer reef was a brown smear in the murky blue water, frosted with the white crests of breaking waves. Beyond it was the pale green of the lagoon, the deeper aquamarine of the channel, and the dark green of the hills above the river mouth. The hills and countryside were pocked with shell craters and seemed to simmer with smoke, tendrils of which coiled upward to hang in a low, dirty pall over the entire length of Beach Black.

Maybe they're all dead, Randall thought. But he knew better.

He dropped back down into the bottom of the LCI as the shriek of the first enemy mortar shells filled his ears.

In the armored tub of the USS *Mayhew*'s starboard forty-millimeter antiaircraft gun, Gunner's Mate Samuel Hatch pulled one of his prize possessions from beneath his bulky gray life jacket. It was a set of binoculars, the high-grade kind issued only to submarine captains. He'd won them from a fat bozo of a quartermaster in a poker game back on Guam. Nice. You could see clear to China with these babies. Not that the damn place was that far away.

He tipped back his steel helmet slightly, brought the binoculars to his eyes, and focused them, searching the Leyte coastline. Dark blue water, still unsettled and murky from the recent typhoon . . . the reef line . . . a few whitecaps . . . smoke hovering like rain clouds over dingy green hills . . .

An erupting spume of white water caught his eye, then another. Seconds later, he heard the dull *thud . . . thud* of back-to-back explosions at a distance. He sharpened the glasses' focus, squinting.

There. There was Kelso's LCI, still humping along parallel to the outer reef after being bracketed by mortar shells. Jesus, he was a sitting duck that close in.

As Hatch watched, three more geysers of white water burst upward around the zigzagging landing craft.

He lowered the binoculars and rubbed his eyes. Whew. No goddamned way he was ever getting himself into a situation like that. You had to be smart to survive a war. That was why he'd angled his way aboard the *Mayhew*—into a plate steel gun tub on a fast, heavily armed DE. He was relatively safe here. If the Japs wanted him, they'd have to come and get him. He wasn't going to motor—or *swim,* for chrissakes—right up to their doorstep and say hi.

Too damn dangerous. No, Gunner's Mate Samuel Hatch was keeping his head low and his eyes open, hunkered behind four inches of good American steel, for the duration. Getting killed in the name of liberty wasn't necessary, not when there were so many heroes out there willing to do it.

They went over the side in pairs—Randall and Garth, Fitzgerald and McNab, Bartlett and Drexel—just to seaward of the opening in the reef that marked the channel. To prevent the LCI from becoming a stationary target, they bailed out on the fly, each team dragging a wooden pallet buoyed by blocks of cork. The pallets carried an assortment of Hagensen packs, spools of detonator cord, fuses, and a unique example of UDT field inventiveness: ten-foot lengths of common fire hose, stuffed with C-2 plastic explosive, the cut ends tied off so that they floated.

The LCI bucked away over the light chop, leaving a trail of sizzling white foam and diesel fumes. Randall kicked furiously, swimming with a powerful one-handed sidestroke, towing the pallet toward the gap in the reef. On the opposite side of the makeshift raft, Garth was doing the same. Randall looked up, saw Kelso wave from the stern of the LCI, then turn back to his steering console and spin the wheel hard to port.

Instead of veering off toward the fleet and out of range of the Japanese mortars and light artillery, the LCI came charging back in the direction of the swimmers, running parallel to the reef. A wave slapped Randall's face, momentarily blinding him, and when he shook it off the LCI was twenty feet to the south, roaring past the little knot of UDT men. The life-jacketed, helmeted sailor who was finicky about salt water on his ammunition belts was braced behind his fifty-caliber machine gun, firing long bursts over their heads toward shore. Farther up on the bow, Greer was doing the same with a lighter thirty-caliber, looking wild-eyed.

"Nice of 'em to lay down covering fire," Fitzgerald yelled, not quite breathless from the effort of towing, "but I wish he'd get the hell away from us. He makes a pretty good range marker, big as he is."

As if in direct response, the ragged shriek of mortar shells filled the air. Every man in the UDT squad gritted his teeth, wondering. In the water, even a miss could kill you.

Two more geysers erupted near the LCI, one thirty feet astern, the other directly alongside the craft's starboard bow. Garth caught a glimpse of Greer reeling back from his machine gun in a cascade of spray, one hand clutching his face, the other clawing the air, as the LCI was knocked over seventy degrees on its beam ends.

Then the dual shock waves from the exploding mortar shells hit him, a brutal one-two punch. It was like being slammed with a sledgehammer in every part of his body simultaneously—bones, joints, organs, muscles. The density of seawater turned what on land would have been an inconsequential puff of air from a near miss into a fast-moving pressure wave of potentially lethal force.

Garth gasped for air, the wind knocked out of him. His muscles spasmed, temporarily losing their coordination. Somehow, he got an elbow on the edge of the pallet.

He glanced around. Everyone else had been similarly affected. There was McNab, ten feet away, his cheeks puffing like a bellows as he tried to breathe, keep his head above water, and pull the floundering Fitzgerald onto the corner of their raft, all at the same time. Moving up on his flank were Bartlett and Drexel, their dark faces twisted with pain, doggedly propelling their pallet forward.

"Charlton!" Garth shouted hoarsely. A hand appeared above the pile of Hagensen packs and slapped down on the soaked canvas, and Randall came clawing around the front of the raft. His stare was bloodred. Having been swamped by a wave and submerged at precisely the wrong moment, the shock waves from the exploding mortar shells had ruptured all the tiny surface capillaries in the whites of his eyes.

"Too . . . too close," he gasped, blinking hard.

"Can you see all right?" Garth asked, starting to swim again.

"I—I think so . . . Yeah." Randall rubbed his eyes. "Just feels strange." He resumed his towing sidestroke. "Why? Does it look like there's something wrong with me?"

Garth managed a grin. "Not a thing."

"Huh," Randall said. He fixed his crimson stare over Garth's shoulder, northward along the reef line. "They're cueing on Kelso's LCI. He's drawing their fire." The battered landing craft was still zigzagging close to the breakers, a good quarter mile away, one machine gun spitting a horizontal stream of orange tracers toward the beach.

"That's not all he's doing," Garth panted, eyeing the chop at the channel entrance. "Look back to the southeast."

Randall threw a glance over his shoulder as he stroked. The USS *Mayhew,* along with a small destroyer, had moved up to within half a mile of the outer reef and turned broadside. The deck guns of both vessels were fully depressed and firing, selectively engaging targets at the south end of Beach Black and around the river mouth. Fresh blossoms of fire and black smoke began to appear on the steep hillsides at the inshore end of the channel.

"Kelso's spotting for 'em, drawing fire and calling in the coordinates of the hidden guns once they open up and give away their positions." Garth paused for breath. "That's a good man, right there!"

Randall spat a mouthful of seawater, laboring to keep the raft moving through the gap in the reef. "Maybe he's not such a son of a bitch after all," he wheezed.

He looked over at Bartlett and Drexel, then at McNab

and Fitzgerald—Fitz was kicking hard again, his wet red hair glinting like copper in the dull sunlight—as a salvo of rockets from the *Mayhew*'s amidships batteries screamed overhead toward Leyte.

"Keep going!" Randall shouted, because even though everyone was doing exactly that, he was squad leader and it seemed like the right thing to say. "The tide's with us! Start with the first mine posts we come to!"

The same explosion that had killed Greer up on the thirty-caliber had sent a shell splinter into Coxswain Duane Kelso's left side, between the second and third ribs. Still, he'd kept his LCI, sprung hull plates and all, weaving back and forth along the outer edge of the reef, drawing the attention of the Japanese gunners, taking the heat off the men in the water. As long as the pumps kept up with the leaks, they could continue their decoy act.

Hazelwood was still pouring lead at the beach with his big fifty-caliber Browning, cool and intense, concentrating on anything that looked like a nest or bunker. Murphy, the other crewman, hadn't yet given up working on Greer in the bottom of the boat, pumping his chest and checking for a pulse that wasn't there. Kelso knew it wasn't. He'd seen the back of Greer's head come off in a red mist. Done. A shame . . . he hadn't been a bad guy, just a little excitable.

His own wound didn't seem too serious, as long as he kept his left arm clenched tightly to his side to stanch the bleeding. Didn't hurt much, no more than a punch to the ribs. He could taste a little blood in the back of his throat, but as long as he could steer, spot enemy gun positions, and radio the coordinates in with one hand, he couldn't see any immediate problem. He was feeling a bit tired, though.

Halfway up one of the hills behind the beach, he caught the bright wink of a muzzle flash, bigger than any of the others he'd seen so far. That one distant flash alarmed him. Artillery piece, large bore.

All of a sudden, for no reason, his mind's eye conjured

up a perfect image of his favorite fishing lake back in Arkansas, just north of Hot Springs. It was beautiful. The lake was as still as a mirror beneath a warm Dixie sun, the bass fat and happy in the shadows beneath the lily pads, waiting for him to drop the perfect cast in front of their greedy noses.

Paradise.

When the well-aimed shell from the Japanese 115-millimeter cannon hit the LCI dead amidships and exploded, Coxswain Duane Kelso, already dying from the three-inch metal splinter that had lacerated his left lower lung and embedded itself in his liver, was smiling.

"Jesus Christ!" Bartlett exclaimed, staring across the reef at the ugly blot of black smoke where, seconds before, the LCI had been. "Poor bastards took a direct hit!" Nothing remained of the vessel but a scattered slick of burning fuel. The other members of the squad paused, looking, then turned back to the task at hand.

They were halfway down the channel, being pushed shoreward by a modest tidal current. Randall had just put his mask on and begun to search the marly white bottom fifteen feet below when he saw the shadowy shapes of the first obstacles: heavy tree trunks driven vertically into the seabed and extending up to within eighteen inches of the surface, topped with disk-shaped contact mines. He could make out at least two dozen of them, spanning the channel about six feet apart.

He raised his head and yelled to Bartlett and Drexel, "Start here! Joe and I'll take the opposite side! Work toward the center, then on down toward the river mouth!"

Bartlett nodded, pulled his mask down over his face, and dove to secure his raft's painter to the nearest tree trunk, followed a second later by Drexel with the first Hagensen pack. As their fins kicked below the surface, a burst of fire from a Nambu heavy machine gun stitched a three-foot-high curtain of spray across the water between the two teams.

"*God,*" Randall gasped, fighting to put some distance

between them. They were too bunched up. He could feel
Garth kicking like fury on the other side of their pallet.
He choked, spat water, and caught a glimpse of McNab
and Fitzgerald about twenty yards farther up the channel, driving hard toward land. By prior arrangement,
since they'd reconned this section of Beach Black earlier
and knew firsthand where everything lay, they would
wire the rock cribs closer in, as well as the large, dome-
shaped obstacle just in front of the river delta's first
sandbar.

Once again, the distinctive sound of the Nambu cut
through the air, and another line of bullet strikes walked
across the water and over the top of the pallet. The
Hagensen packs jumped as the rounds hit them. Randall
felt his heart lurch in his chest: the odds were seventy-
thirty *for* that a heavy-caliber machine gun bullet would
set off a pack of C-2 plastic explosive on impact. A
tracer round—forget it. One hundred percent.

They were across. He looked down. Below him, where
the edge of the channel began to shallow, Garth was
tying off the raft's painter to one of the stake mines.

Randall clawed a Hagensen pack off the raft, sucked
in a deep breath, and dove. The last thing he heard
before the water closed over his head was the angry
chatter of the Nambu resuming fire.

Gunner's Mate Samuel Hatch considered himself good
at his job, which was to hit things—usually flying
things—with his forty-millimeter antiaircraft gun. He
liked moving targets, possessed a natural eye for deflec-
tion shooting, and had knocked down, by his count, at
least nine Japanese planes. Well, he and the other two
men in his gun crew—a pointer and a trainer—had
knocked them down. But he was gun captain, so that
made them his kills. Three more he really wasn't sure
of, but figured there was no harm in claiming credit for
anyway. That was an even dozen little red Rising Suns
he'd been able to paint on the rim of his gun tub.

Today was a bit different. All the planes in the sky
were American—dark blue Hellcats, Wildcats, and big

gull-winged Corsairs, for the most part, along with Avenger dive-bombers and a few battered-looking Dauntlesses. No targets overhead. This morning all the shooting was horizontal, toward the beach.

There weren't many instructions from gunfire control coming through Hatch's headset, other than general reminders to concentrate fire on the cluster of four or five steep hills to the northwest. Even with his superb submarine binoculars, he couldn't pick out any specific targets—all he could see was a smoking wasteland of shattered rock, torn foliage, and splintered tree trunks. He couldn't see the LCI anymore, either. Kelso had finally come to his senses and checked out of the hot zone, obviously.

He sighed. What the hell. It was easy work, lobbing ordnance at a distant coastline with very little return fire to worry about. He called out instructions to his gun crew, keeping them on their toes, and methodically began to saturate the second hill in the cluster with forty-millimeter cannon shells, starting at the base and moving back and forth up to the crest.

Corporal Adeki Fujikawa was the only man left alive in his Nambu squad. He and his three companions had been weathering the bombardment reasonably well until a five-inch shell had struck only a few yards to their right. The explosion had collapsed the heavy palm logs that formed the roof, front barricade, and firing slit of their machine gun nest. Now Ito and Ariga were dead of shrapnel wounds, and Shimizu, the teenage music student from Kyoto who loved jazz, was lying pinned beneath the butt end of a fallen timber, his chest crushed. It had taken him less than thirty seconds, kicking like a flattened insect, to gasp out his last breath and die. Even though Fujikawa had thrown his shoulder against the log and heaved with all his might, he had been unable to budge it.

Bleeding from both ears, the corporal hauled his heavy machine gun out of the shredded leaves and churned earth into which it had fallen and steadied it on what remained of his bunker's forward barricade. There was no firing slit now, and no roof. The sun beat down on the back of his neck, and he turned to look up at it as his well-trained fingers fed another clip of ammunition into the Nambu's breech. It was a silver yellow disk today, gleaming rather than shining through a thin gray haze of cloud and cordite smoke. Its warmth felt good on his face.

He realized all at once that he was happy. It was a fine day. A fine day for a soldier's soul to fly away to Yasukuni, the shrine of heroes. His three companions were already there, in their new incarnation as *kami*—demigods of the Shinto religion—waiting for him to join them.

He did not think they would have to wait very long.

On the horizon, the American fleet had massed, the bulk of it concentrated to the north. Already the black dots of landing craft were scurrying between the ships like ants. Two destroyer-type vessels had moved up to within a mile or so of the outer reef and were continuing to bombard the hills upon which his machine gun nest and others were positioned, overlooking the river mouth.

He brushed the sweat and dirt from his eyes and looked down along the barrel of his weapon at the water. From his vantage point on the hillside he had an excellent view of the channel the river had cut through the lagoon and out to the reef. In the center of the channel, a few hundred yards away, he could clearly see two men swimming on either side of what looked like a small, square raft.

They were such an easy target that he wondered why no one else had opened up on them already. He blinked and lifted his head to glance around outside the bunker. Surely he wasn't the only one left alive? The thought made him feel lonely and he crouched back down behind his machine gun.

The two men were still coming, swimming hard against the outflow of the river. Fujikawa shifted the Nambu to the right and settled its sights on the raft. A couple of short bursts would suffice. No sense in wasting ammunition. He'd need all he had soon enough.

The men had stopped swimming, were diving under the raft. Corporal Fujikawa relaxed his trigger finger and raised his head again. Then he swung the barrel of his weapon to the left and slightly up. Something else had caught his eye.

There appeared to be two more swimmers and another raft a good 150 yards farther down the channel. A more challenging shot. The two directly below him he could take at any time. He would try for the more distant pair first.

He settled his cheek against the stock of the Nambu as another salvo of rockets impacted the hillside. With his ruptured ears he could not hear the explosions, only feel them in his breastbone as the ground beneath him shook.

Drexel's lungs were bursting as he jammed the twenty-pound Hagensen pack up against the base of the last mine post, pulled the short retaining leash around the waterlogged wood, and clipped it back onto the pack to hold it in place. Making sure that the charge's three-foot pigtail of detonator cord was fully extended, he kicked for the surface.

He popped up about five feet away from Bartlett, who was resting on the corner of the raft trying to catch his breath. Drexel stroked forward, got a hand on the pallet, and shoved his mask up on his forehead.

"You set a charge . . . on that . . . other one?" he gasped, sucking air.

Bartlett nodded. "Yeah."

"Okay. Let's run the det cord." Drexel seized a spool of what looked like brightly colored clothesline. "You feed. I'll swim and tie this time."

"No argument here." Bartlett held up his left forearm. The flesh on one side of it was shredded and bloody. "Something hit me as I was reaching for that last pack. Don't even know what it was."

"Jesus. Hurt?"

"What the hell d'you think?"

Drexel gave him a chummy grimace and tossed over the spool. "Hold this. I'll be back in a flash, Dash." He repositioned his mask on his face and dove again, pulling the detonator cord with him.

He swam about six feet under the surface, deep enough that even heavy-caliber bullets could not reach him. Reaching the first stake mine, he stress-relieved the detonator cord by taking a couple of wraps around the tree trunk, located the pigtail of the Hagensen pack, and tied the two ends together with a square knot.

Something brushed his shoulder, then his back. He flinched slightly and looked up. Little black nuggets, each one streaming a trail of tiny bubbles, were tumbling down on him like falling leaves. Machine gun bullets.

Maybe I won't breathe right now, he thought, and kicked for the next post, pulling the bight of the cord with him.

His chest burning with air hunger, he reached the second pack and tied its pigtail to the primary cord with a snug timber hitch. Then he had to breathe. He pulled upward, willing the Japanese gunners to look in some other direction for just a few seconds. . . .

His head broke the surface and he sucked in air. Then, in one continuous motion, he arched his back and ducked under again, heading down. Gathering the bight of the detonator cord with a sweep of his arm, he kicked for mine post number three.

A movement caught his eye and he watched for several seconds, distracted, as a four-foot-long blacktip shark cruised past about ten feet in front of him, just off the bottom, heading up the channel. Its lazy, unhurried swimming motion seemed to underscore its total indifference to the chaotic affairs of Man. Drexel forgot about the animal immediately as the shock wave from an exploding mortar shell—at least a couple hundred yards distant—gave him a moderate body punch.

Swim and tie, you bastard, he told himself. Swim and tie . . .

*   *   *

Corporal Fujikawa had already decided that the swimmers in the channel must be demolitioneers sent to blow up underwater obstacles in advance of the invasion. That would mean the rafts they towed were in all likelihood loaded with explosives. Brave men, he thought fleetingly, to undertake such hazardous work. Most American soldiers, he had been told, demonstrated a distinct aversion to dying for their cause, which was proof of their inherent lack of character. This lack of character was why they would ultimately lose the war in the Pacific.

However, the swimmers in the channel were certainly the exception to the rule. Though it was hard to see them through the smoke, the constant shell strikes, and the sunlight glinting off the murky water, they appeared to have nearly completed the mining of the channel obstacles.

Fujikawa had tried twice to rake the two farthest rafts with machine gun fire, in hopes of detonating the explosive packs they carried. They had not blown, although he was reasonably sure he'd hit them, and he thought he knew why. He had been in the military long enough to know that modern explosives were far more stable than earlier nitroglycerin-based compounds. To set them off required not just heat or impact, but heat and impact in combination—such as that provided by a blasting cap.

Or a tracer bullet. The trouble was, Colonel Toriushi, the commanding officer of his battalion, had expressly forbidden the use of tracer bullets by his machine gun crews on the grounds that while they helped a gunner key his fire onto a target, they also made it easier for an enemy to visually track that fire back to its point of origin. Which could be fatal for a concealed Nambu nest.

But the Honorable Colonel was not here, and this, in Corporal Fujikawa's opinion, was an extenuating circumstance. Fortunately, he was the kind of soldier who prided himself on being prepared for any eventuality, and as such had reserved several ammunition clips from which the tracers—one round out of every four—had not been removed. He dug one out of the canvas satchel

at his feet and locked it down into the machine gun's
breech.

A sudden volley of light-caliber cannon shells hammered into the ground and logs at the front of the bunker, throwing dirt and wood splinters over Fujikawa as
he flinched back from his weapon and covered up. A
random burst from one of the destroyers outside the
reef. They had the range but not the luck. He was still
alive. He removed his hands from his face and looked
directly into the sightless eyes of Shimizu.

Revulsion welled up in him, and ashamed of his reaction, he scrambled back behind the Nambu. Later, at
Yasukuni Shrine, he would apologize to his honored
dead comrade for his moment of weakness.

He settled behind the machine gun again and aimed
carefully at the raft that was farthest away. It was now
in the center of the channel. Beyond it, outside the reef,
like dark roaches swarming across the sea's surface,
landing craft were beginning to head inshore in droves.
They were coming.

Corporal Fujikawa steeled himself. He would make
every burst—every single bullet—count.

Drexel was highly annoyed. Bartlett had dropped the
sonofabitching spool of detonator cord—why else would
the slack leading back to the raft be slanting down instead of up? He finned rapidly along the hard white
bottom of the channel, following the blue-and-red line.
They didn't have time for this shit.

There it was, just like he'd thought. Lying on the broken coral marl fifteen feet down. He seized it and got
ready to push off the bottom. All the Hagensen packs
they'd placed were now tied into the common detonator
cord. They'd meet up with Randall and Garth and Fitz
and McNab, who'd have two more common cords, tie
them all together, and then haul ass for the outer reef,
trailing one last cord through which they'd blow the entire multicharge shot from a safe distance.

Drexel pushed off the bottom, carrying the spool, and
stroked upward once. He craned his neck to look at the

surface, and that was when he saw Bartlett drifting down. His teammate was spread-eagled, facing the bottom. His mask was gone and he wore an expression of shocked surprise. Something soft and grayish was flopping over his forehead from a crack in the top of his skull, and clouds of red-brown blood were billowing from at least half a dozen baseball-sized holes in his chest and abdomen.

"Eeaaghh!" Drexel blurted, recoiling in horror—and involuntarily inhaled seawater. He dropped the spool and pulled for the surface.

He banged his shoulder on the edge of the raft, coughing up brine, and at that moment the first tracer round from the second burst Corporal Adeki Fujikawa had begun to fire from his heavy machine gun hit one of the three remaining Hagensen packs dead center.

With a blast that flattened the water for a hundred yards in every direction, the raft, Bartlett's corpse, and Drexel abruptly disintegrated.

Corporal Fujikawa felt a surge of elation course through him. *Yes!* The tracers had done it. Only two short bursts and the explosive-laden raft had gone up like a giant firecracker.

Now for the remaining two teams. One pair of swimmers was still near the sandbar at the river mouth; the other was quite a bit farther out, in the shallow water at the very edge of the channel. As before, he would target the more distant team first.

He shifted position behind the Nambu and tilted his head back to stretch his aching neck. As he did so, a volley of cannon shells from the USS *Mayhew*'s starboard forty-millimeter antiaircraft gun—directed by Gunner's Mate Samuel Hatch, who'd tracked the sudden burst of Japanese tracer bullets back to their point of origin with his fine submariner's binoculars—smashed into the jumbled logs at the front of the machine gun nest. There was a momentary flurry of wood splinters, flying dirt, and leaf confetti, accompanied by a cacophony of explosive impacts.

When the volley was spent, Imperial Japanese Army corporal Adeki Fujikawa lay on his back beside the crushed body of his comrade Shimizu. A single forty-millimeter shell had caught him under the chin, decapitating him instantly.

The only reason Randall and Garth had not been killed by the explosion of Drexel and Bartlett's raft was that the detonating Hagensen packs had been on top of the water, not under it. Most of the blast force had gone upward into the air, taking the path of least resistance. But even the reduced shock wave had been almost bone-cracking.

"They . . . they're gone," Randall groaned, clutching the raft and staring at the frothy white spot on the water where Bartlett and Drexel had been. "We should . . . search for them. . . ."

Garth reached across the remaining two Hagensen packs and clapped a hand on his squad leader's forearm. "Charlton, listen. If we get punched by any more shock waves, we're gonna be too crippled to swim. Bartlett and Drexel are dead. We've got to recover their det cord, tie it into our own so their work doesn't go to waste." He pushed away from the raft, grimacing with effort. "Drexel was running the common line. If he got all the charges tied in, the only thing I have to do is find the end of it. Wait here. Watch for Fitz and McNab."

"Joe—"

Before Randall could argue or suggest that he go instead, Garth inverted himself in a surface dive and disappeared. The lieutenant swore aloud, his own words lost to his ears as yet another salvo of battlewagon shells passed overhead with a long, whistling screech. With considerable effort, he pushed his upper body clear of the water on his aching arms and looked toward the river mouth.

He could see no sign of Fitzgerald and McNab at first glance, and before he could blink and look again, a skiff of spray kicked up two feet to his right. Then another a foot to his left. He dropped back down into the water immediately. *Sniper.*

Well, he could stay busy until Joe got back. The extra Hagensen packs would be less of a threat if they were secured at the bottom of one of the mine posts, out of the line of fire. A rifle bullet wouldn't set them off, but there was no telling when another tracer like the one that had punched Bartlett and Drexel's ticket might fly his way.

He swallowed hard, grabbed the carrying straps of the last two explosive packs, and dove once more for the bottom of the channel.

Best damn binocs a man could ever hope for, Gunner's Mate Hatch told himself for the hundredth time that morning. He'd been watching a tall, spindly-trunked palm tree topped by a great leafy crown of fronds that stood by itself on the left-hand shore of the river mouth. Ah—there it was again: a little puff of smoke and, in the foreground, a reaction—a sudden flinch—from the UDT man hiding behind the one raft in the channel he could still see.

"Come up two points," Hatch told his gun crew. "Come left three points." The twin barrels of the forty-millimeter swung imperceptibly. "Hold that."

He fired. The gun tub shook as brass shell casings tumbled out of the breeches and clanged to the deck, the recoiling twin cannon barrels punching out and back like fists.

The top of the palm tree shredded like salad, turning into a whirlwind of chopped green foliage, flying coconuts, and white smoke. Hatch kept firing for a full five seconds, just to be sure.

When at last he stopped and carefully examined the palm through his binoculars again, the limp body of a Japanese soldier was hanging from the ruined treetop by a six-foot rope leash. Dangling below him by its strap was a scoped sniper's rifle.

Gunner's Mate Samuel Hatch grinned and lowered the glasses.

Damn, he was good.

*   *   *

Fitzgerald was hoping everyone else in the squad had been as lucky as McNab and he. They'd been kicking, ducking, and towing their way along the edge of the channel, working right in under the noses of the Jap gunners, taking a lot of heat despite the heavy suppressing fire being laid down by the ships outside the reef—when all of a sudden they'd run into perfect cover. One of the rock cribs—a ten-foot-square, six-to-eight-foot-high corral of thick palm logs, filled with limestone boulders—had been built up out of the channel and onto the shallow lagoon flat. Low tide had exposed the top eighteen inches of it, providing a relatively safe place to secure the raft and from which to operate.

Fitzgerald was almost smiling as he stroked along six feet beneath the surface, heading for the river's delta. He and McNab, the best breath holders in the squad, had been able to swim repeatedly out from behind the convenient rock crib underwater, plant Hagensen packs on the other cribs, and make it back across the channel, all on the same lungful of air. *Beautiful.* If they didn't have to stick their heads up, there was no way a Jap sniper or machine gunner was going to get a clean shot at them. A mortar shell was another story, but there didn't seem to be that many dropping anymore.

The outflow from the river was tough to swim against, making him kick hard and burn oxygen. He arched for the surface in a classic UDT porpoising move— breaching like a small whale to grab a breath and ducking back down to a safe depth before the enemy gunners could get a bead on him.

The last thing McNab and he had done was haul two ten-foot-long snakes of explosive-stuffed fire hose up the channel to the strange, domelike concrete obstacle located about fifty yards from the river delta's first sandbar. It looked like nothing they'd ever seen before: one-half of a fifteen-foot-diameter egg sitting on the bottom. They'd wrapped the charges around the top of it in a deadly halo, secured them with short lengths of twine, then popped up to the surface for a few quick breaths.

"Run the det cord back to the cribs and tie it in," Fitzgerald had panted. "Then take it on back to the L.T. and the other guys. I'll catch up with you in a couple of minutes."

Without waiting for McNab's comment, he'd ducked under again and headed for the river delta. There was one personal mission he had to take care of.

The thing people like Lieutenant Randall and even his buddy McNab didn't understand about him, Fitzgerald thought as he swam along, was that he was a competitor right down to his bone marrow. Any sport—baseball, football, swimming, boxing . . . hell, even horseshoes— he had to be the best at or die trying. And what was war but the ultimate competition, for the ultimate stakes? Win at this game and you were really the toughest boy on the block. Especially if everyone knew it.

The spearhead marines that came down the channel in their LCIs—they were going to be thinking they were the first Americans to set foot in the Philippines since MacArthur had taken a fast PT boat out of Corregidor back in '42. But they'd be thinking wrong. One look at the sandbar in the river mouth would tell them who was *really* the first man to hit the shores of Leyte Island.

Fitzgerald porpoised again, caught a breath, stroked hard, and felt the hard sand of the bottom against the palms of his outstretched hands. The water was less than six feet deep and shallowing fast. He was only yards from the exposed sandbar.

This was going to have to be quick. All the Japs couldn't be dead, regardless of how much pounding they'd taken from the battlewagons and airedales.

Fitzgerald dug into his swim trunks and pulled out the thick roll of red cloth, still holding his breath. He was crouching now, in less than three feet of water, legs curled under him and feet planted firmly on the bottom.

Go.

Launching himself forward and up, he burst from the water and dashed for dry sand, high-stepping it, holding his unfurled red banner in front of him with both hands.

The high-tide line. Where was it?

There.

As his feet left the last two inches of water, he dove forward onto his belly, reaching.

A flurry of rifle shots kicked up sand all around him, the reports distant, muted.

They all missed.

Jap punks.

Fitzgerald stabbed down hard with both fists—then pushed backward, rolled off one shoulder to his feet, and sprinted back into the water. More rifle shots kicked up spurts of sand at his heels. Fitzgerald couldn't resist. Just before diving beneath the channel's murky green surface, he whirled and threw the finger at the smoking, leaf-torn hillsides.

The three-by-one-foot banner of red cloth remained upright, supported at each end by an eighteen-inch length of straightened coat hanger wire. A belated slug from the rifle of a frustrated and quite possibly insulted Japanese marksman punched through it, but did not knock it over.

There was lettering on the seaward side of the banner, carefully rendered in waterproof white tape.

Welcome Marines! it read. *The Fitz Was Here.*

Chapter Three

"McNab!" Randall shouted, waving an arm. "This way!"

Thirty yards away, the tanned Floridian paused to reorient himself before ducking under the surface and continuing to swim to seaward. Pushing their now empty pallet, Randall and Garth moved out into the middle of the channel to meet him.

McNab came up spluttering and slapped a hand onto the raft. Then he lifted the spool he was carrying into view, detonator cord trailing off into the water behind him.

"Where's . . . where's Bartlett and Drexel?" he panted.

Randall shook his head. "Dead."

McNab looked from Randall to Garth, his breathing harsh. "For sure?"

"No mistake," Garth said. "Machine gun tracer caught their raft and it blew. Took them with it."

McNab hung there at the side of the pallet for a long moment, blinking salt water out of his eyes. "Fuck," he said.

Randall looked back up the channel. "Where the hell's Fitz?" he asked.

"Should be right behind me."

"Well, he's not."

McNab twisted around, gazing at the river mouth, and shook his head in frustration. "We got all the cribs wired . . . and that dome thing just off the delta." He tapped the spool sitting on the pallet. "Everything's ready to blow. This here's the end of the common line."

"Let me have it," Garth said, bringing up his own spool. "I'll connect it to ours."

"What about Bartlett and Drexel's?" McNab asked, passing it over.

"It's already tied in. They got the job done."

The Floridian nodded and spat seawater. "Good," he said softly. "Good for them ol' boys."

"Dammit," Randall exclaimed, searching the waters behind them. "Where's Fitz?" He turned to McNab. "Where'd you see him last?"

"Well . . . he was . . . sorta swimming in toward that first sandbar."

"What? You mean in past the dome?"

"Er—yeah, L.T." McNab looked evasive. "Toward the sandbar."

"What the hell for?"

McNab let out a long sigh. "He had a sign. He wanted to set it up on the sandbar for the marines to see."

Randall sagged down in the water and looked over at Garth, who'd just finished tying the det cords together. "Jesus Christ," he said in disbelief. "A stunt. He went in there just to pull one of his goddamned stunts. Jesus Christ."

"Well, he oughtta be along any minute now, L.T.," McNab said. "We did get all the charges set first. You know Fitz—everything's a game to him. He just wanted to put a little . . . icing on the cake, I guess."

"He's making the rest of us wait for him in a fire zone," Randall shot back. "We—"

He was interrupted by a burst of machine gun fire

that threw up a fast-moving wall of spray five feet to their right.

"That's it!" Randall yelled, wild-eyed. *"We're going! Swim for the reef, now!"* He grabbed Garth by the shoulder as they pushed away from the pallet. "Joe! When you get to the end of that det cord, stick a four-minute fuse on it and *pull* it! We can't wait any longer!"

"What about Fitz?" McNab shouted, stroking around the raft.

"If he's not already dead, he'll be right behind us!" Randall told him. "We've got to blow these obstacles or the LCIs won't be able to get through to shore! Those marines will be caught out in deep water, like at Tarawa!"

"You want Fitz's blood on your hands?" McNab hollered.

"You want a massacre on yours?" Randall yelled back.

The exchange was ended by another burst of machine gun fire. The two UDT men dove for their lives, following Joe Garth, who was already underwater and kicking hard for the gap in the outer reef, paying out the last of the detonator cord as he went.

The *Fukuryu* had lain in wait in their submerged, flooded concrete bunker for nearly twenty hours. There were six of them, each man wearing a loose-fitting rubber wet suit, a clumsy brass diving helmet, and a bulky rebreather with oxygen tanks strapped across his chest and back. They had been sustained, there in the claustrophobic darkness, by containers of liquid food and their own unshakable belief that the highest honor a soldier could attain was to die willingly in service to the emperor and Japan—which were one and the same. And of all the *Fukuryu* to come, they would always be remembered as the first to have gone into battle—the first of the Crouching Dragons.

Their presence on the bottom of the channel was an experiment—a field test of the *Fukuryu* concept. Much

depended upon the performance this day of Imperial
Japanese Navy lieutenant Sekio Doi and his five men, a
fact of which Doi was acutely aware. The commanders
who had selected him to lead the first *Fukuryu* attack
against an invading force would be observing the operational effectiveness of his small unit closely. He must not
permit his concentration to waver.

Close to hand was each man's primary weapon: an
eight-foot-long wooden pole with a twenty-two-pound
impact-fired explosive charge mounted on one end. A
small flotation tank incorporated into this unwieldy
"lunge mine" gave it neutral buoyancy, making it somewhat easier to handle underwater. When the time came,
the *Fukuryu* would rise from the bottom of the sea and
jam their explosive lances against the hulls of incoming
landing craft, sacrificing their lives in order to destroy
the invaders. Doi himself would lead the first three; the
other two would not emerge from the bunker until they
heard at least two lunge mines detonate—this to ensure
that the entire squad would not be killed by a random
shell strike.

Lieutenant Doi squinted through the condensation on
his leaky faceplate at the luminous dial of the small underwater clock he had been given. It was morning, 0930,
and the long on-again, off-again bombardment seemed
to have ceased. The dome-shaped concrete bunker had
done its job—the *Fukuryu* were unharmed, untouched
by the massive pressure waves generated by exploding
aerial bombs and battleship shells. Very soon now, according to intelligence predictions, American landing
craft would be approaching via the channel to invade
this sector of Leyte. Doi was firmly resolved that they
would get a surprise.

Working by feel in the utter darkness, he knelt and
unbarred the small steel door that sealed the underwater
bunker's only entrance. The three-foot-square plate
swung outward when he pushed on it, letting in a flood
of pale green light. Grasping his lunge mine, Doi crawled
out through the opening and onto the seafloor.

He stood up, and unexpectedly the sense of relief he

felt at being surrounded by sunlight one more time, even under fifteen feet of seawater, almost moved him to tears. Turning to face the bunker, he stretched his arms over his head as far as the awkward rebreather gear and helmet would allow, and looked up toward the surface.

That was when he noticed the thick hose that had been draped around the top of the dome and secured with lengths of twine to various small protrusions in the concrete. It had not been there twenty hours earlier when he and the other *Fukuryu* had entered the bunker.

Doi stepped up beside the next man crawling out of the tiny entrance and bounded off the seafloor onto the dome's upper curve. He put a hand on the hose, squeezed it—and then with a throb of horror noticed the thin leads of red-and-blue cord running out of the hose ends and into a single common line, which stretched off down the channel into the milky green distance.

Explosives! While he and his comrades had huddled within, the bunker had been mined! Scrambling forward, pulling his sheath knife, Doi seized the single cord into which all the leads were tied and slashed it through. Then he whirled, searching the surrounding water—just in time for his chest tank to deflect the stab of Fitzgerald's Ka-Bar as the red-haired UDT man drove down on top of him, kicking furiously.

Doi shouted in surprise inside his helmet and grappled with his assailant. The American—for who else could he be?—was at least half again his size, naked but for swimming shorts and a thick layer of gray grease that made him virtually impossible to hang on to. Doi gasped in pain as the big man's knife stabbed through his wet suit and into the trapezius muscle above his collarbone. The power behind the thrust was incredible; the man was as strong as a bull.

But Lieutenant Doi knew something of hand-to-hand fighting. Warding off another stab with his left forearm, he twisted sideways, turned his right hand palm up, and rammed the tips of his rigid fingers into the American's larynx. He saw the man's eyes bug behind his mask face-

plate, a gust of bubbles erupt from his contorted lips.
Doi closed his left fist and punched into the American's
right armpit, hitting the nerve plexus that controlled the
arm on that side. Then he floundered backward to a
sitting position, groping blindly on top of the dome for
his own dropped knife.

The American broke away, heading for the surface
nine feet above. Doi found his knife, struggled to his
feet, and saw three of the other *Fukuryu* clambering up
the side of the bunker, looking like sea trolls in their
cumbersome helmets and breathing gear. He was about
to wave them off—give the signal to take up their lances
and deploy across the width of the channel in readiness
to engage incoming landing craft, as rehearsed—when,
incredibly, the big American with the reddish hair came
back, swooping down with his knife arm extended.

He slashed at Doi as he went by, but did not attempt
to close with him. Instead, he kicked deeper, arcing over
the dome toward the bottom of the channel. Less maneuverable in his clumsy gear, Doi struggled to follow,
his booted feet scrabbling against the curved concrete.
The other three *Fukuryu* did likewise.

The American grabbed the cut cord lying on the sandy
marl, inverted himself, and sprang back the way he had
come, pushing off hard with his legs. In a flash Doi understood: he was going to try to reconnect the detonator
cord to the explosives. Brandishing his own knife, the
lieutenant lunged forward.

Not if he could help it.

In the long, dark tunnel housing the twenty boats of
Lieutenant Kentaro Higuchi's *Shinyo* squadron, chaos
reigned. The overhead electric lights had gone out completely, to be replaced by torches, kerosene lanterns, and
poor-quality flashlights. A cave-in had occurred at the
rear of the tunnel, crushing the last half-dozen boats as
they sat on their rail trolleys and trapping several dozen
soldiers and sailors under tons of rock. The screams of
those who were not quite dead and the frenzied shouts

of would-be rescuers joined with the throaty roar of revving engines, filling the cave with a hellish din.

Higuchi was standing in the cockpit of his boat, nearly asphyxiated from dust and engine fumes, looking down helplessly at the disoriented men running back and forth along the railway track that supported the entire line of attack boats on their launching trolleys. Were they all going to die in this miserable hole without ever getting an opportunity to strike at the enemy? It was too bitter a possibility to contemplate.

He turned and glanced past his *Shinyo*'s bow at the huge wood-and-steel double doors that sealed the entrance to the cave. They were still closed. Camouflaged from the outside, the standing order had been not to open them until given express instructions to do so by the sectional commander in chief, Colonel Toriushi—so as not to risk forfeiting the element of surprise. But surely the order should have come by now? Perhaps the Honorable Colonel—

"Open the doors!" a voice screamed, the sound piercing, ragged. *"Colonel Toriushi's command post was destroyed by American planes half an hour ago! Open the doors! Launch the boats! Launch the boats!"*

Lieutenant Higuchi's pulse tripled and he squinted back into the flickering haze of the inner cave. Waddling out of the darkness came squat, rotund Major Ozawa, waving the samurai sword he always carried, his normally immaculate tunic torn half off his shoulder. He was a myopic little bully of a man with oiled hair and a toothbrush mustache. The pomposity he usually displayed had now been replaced by a barely controlled panic. He stopped, stared up at Higuchi through thick eyeglasses, and shook his sword at him.

"Launch!" he shrieked. *"Launch, coward! Traitor! What are you waiting for?"*

Higuchi looked down at him for a moment, then shrugged and pointed over the bow of his boat. "The doors," he said calmly. There was little point in contending with this hysterical buffoon. However, said buffoon was a ranking officer and might be able to harness enough manpower to get the manually operated doors pulled open. It required a minimum of six men per door—the same number it took to push a boat-laden trolley down the tracks, out of the cave, and into the water.

Ozawa looked bewildered for a few seconds, then turned and waddled forward, screeching at the men milling around in front of Higuchi's *Shinyo*. He began to lay into them with the flat of his sword, attempting to flog them into two separate working parties. Many evaded him and fled back into the depths of the cave, but a dozen or so crowded up around the massive bombproof doors and began to undog them.

Good, Ozawa, Higuchi thought. You are not entirely useless after all.

He immediately felt a vague sense of shame at thinking in such derogatory terms about a superior officer— even one who happened to be a posturing humbug—and made a silent apology to the major. Without respect for duty, loyalty, and the chain of command, nothing in a military context was possible.

A vertical crack widened between the two great doors, the outside camouflage layer of cut branches and foliage dropped away, and daylight flooded into the cave.

The moment had come.

Higuchi seized the steering wheel of his boat with one hand as the doors swung open to their fullest extent. With the other he pounded on the wooden cockpit coaming.

"Private Second Class Wanabi!" he shouted, fixing his eye on the cleft in the rock where his helper had been cowering for the past ten minutes. "Come here!"

Shaking so much that he could hardly stay erect, Wanabi emerged from his hole and scurried over to the trolley supporting Higuchi's *Shinyo*.

"*H-h-hai,* Honorable Lieutenant, sir?" he managed to say.

Try a touch of psychology, Higuchi thought—*an ap-*

peal to what little pride the man has. What could it hurt?
Life was short and death was certain.

"Wanabi," he declared, "it is time to launch the boats, starting with mine. Someone must take charge. You are hereby promoted from private second class to superior private." Higuchi had little doubt that the quaking infantryman would be unaware that as a navy lieutenant he had no right whatsoever to arbitrarily increase the rank of an army private.

"I . . . ?" Wanabi said, wincing as a shell exploded against the side of the hill, sending rock fragments tumbling to the sand outside the opened cave doors.

"You. And now, Superior Private Wanabi, you will select five men and push my boat out to the river, at once." Higuchi tried to transfer confidence to Wanabi through his eyes. "Then you will launch the rest of the boats. Do you understand me, Superior Private?"

Considering the urgency of the current situation, the change came over Wanabi slowly. But come it did, like the light of dawn creeping down a long hill. He straightened, his shoulders went back, and he got his heels together with a dusty click, saluting.

"*Hai,* Honorable Lieutenant, sir!" he said, his voice steadier. "Thank you!"

"Get on with it, Superior Private," Higuchi told him.
"*Hai!*"

The lieutenant turned and looked out through the doors again. They were wide open now, the gray white sand, green foliage, and aquamarine river blaring daylight colors into the dimness of the cave. Off to the left, Major Ozawa was pursuing a trio of soldiers at full waddle, shrieking for them to man the trolleys and swiping at them with his sword. Additional shouting arose from below the gunwales of Higuchi's craft, on either side.

With a sudden jerk, his *Shinyo* boat began to move forward, gaining speed, rolling toward the open doors on the narrow-gauge railway tracks that led across the sand to the river. He felt a surge of adrenaline. The sequence of events for which he had trained so long and hard had begun. He braced himself behind the wheel and touched the throttle, testing it. The well-tuned Chevrolet engine roared in response, as he had known it would.

As *Shinyo* Number One trundled out into the sunlight on its rail trolley, the half-dozen men pushing it shouting encouragement to each other, Lieutenant Kentaro Higuchi sat down in his helmsman's seat, throttled the engine back to a fast idle, and took in everything. There was the salt-and-cordite smell to the air, the fluttering green fronds of the few undamaged palm trees, the swirling blue outflow of the river. The healthy purr of his boat's power plant, and the warmth of the sun on his face and the backs of his hands.

Everything was in its place; everything was in order. He had only to carry through, as Honor and Duty demanded. How fortunate he was not to have been crushed in the rear of the cave like so many of his comrades.

His would be a beautiful death, after all.

Fitzgerald reversed his fist and smashed the steel ball at the butt end of his knife into the faceplate of the Japanese lunging at him. The heavy glass shattered, there was an explosion of air, and the enemy diver reeled back, clawing at his helmet. That was number three. There was one more, coming up over the dome holding what looked like a spear with a five-gallon kerosene can for a tip. Weird.

Working quickly, Fitzgerald knotted the main detonator cord back into the combined leads, dropped them, and pushed off for the surface. The diver brandishing the spear stabbed at him with the drum end as he went by, but he was too far away. Hungry for air, Fitzgerald made it up in three hard pulls.

He hyperventilated for five seconds, then inverted himself and headed back down. Whoever these Japs in the brass helmets were, he had their number. They might be able to breathe underwater, but their gear was heavy and awkward. He could outmaneuver them at will, like a sea otter dodging around a crab. Three of them lay on the channel floor beside the dome—two with smashed faceplates, drowned inside the heavy gear they could not shed in time, the third dying by inches with a Ka-Bar stab to the throat. Life was tough, Fitzgerald thought, riding an adrenaline rush so intense it was almost painful, when you were a Japoon bastard and got into a rumble with The Fitz.

He had to take them all out: anyone left alive when he hightailed it for the outer reef would simply cut the detonator cord again. He finned down on the fourth diver, flanking him, his knife at the ready. The helmeted Japanese tried to turn, follow him with his bulky pole spear, but Fitzgerald was too fast. Plunging down behind him, Fitz ripped his knife blade through the tangle of hoses connecting the diver's back and chest tanks with his helmet.

There was a great whoosh of air, and the man's upper body was instantly enshrouded in bubbles. Fitzgerald finished the job by burying his Ka-Bar to the hilt, twice, between the diver's shoulder blades, just above his back tank. The Japanese tumbled off the dome, contorting in agony, and drifted down toward the bottom. Fitzgerald pushed off for the surface again to breathe.

For some reason, the other diver or divers in the dome—he had seen a booted foot just inside the tiny door that he and McNab hadn't noticed earlier—were not coming out. Fine. He could shut it and jam it with a piece of steel concrete-reinforcing rod he'd seen lying on the bottom. That would be one or more fewer he'd have to kill. They could stay in there and go up with the dome when Randall blew the shot.

Fitzgerald filled his aching lungs again and dove back down to the base of the dome. It seemed as if the divers remaining inside were somehow unaware of the deadly hand-to-hand fighting that had just taken place mere feet away from them. Why they were still in there he couldn't imagine—but fuck 'em. That's where they were staying.

He seized the four-foot-long piece of one-inch rebar lying in the sand, dragged it over to the dome entrance, and kicked the door shut. Before the men inside could react, he threaded the steel rod through two lifting pad-eyes set in the concrete on either side of the door—he spanned it and barred it closed.

Done.

It was time to go. Catch a breath at the surface and begin the long, porpoising swim to the outer reef—hopefully before Randall ran out of time and had to set off the charges. He was already late.

Fitzgerald tensed his legs to push off the bottom, and that was when Lieutenant Doi, coming up from behind, reached around and sank his sheath knife deep into Fitzgerald's belly.

Higuchi's *Shinyo* boat rolled down the last twenty feet of railway under its own momentum and hit the water with a smacking splash. The trolley dropped off the submerged end of the track and tumbled to the riverbed. Higuchi rammed the *Shinyo*'s throttle forward. The boat roared off in a tight turn, heading for the lagoon some two hundred yards downriver.

Elated, Wanabi and his five-man pushing detail broke into cheers and ran back toward the cave. Already, the next boat in line was about to plunge into the water; five more were queued up across the narrow strip of sandy shore behind it. Wanabi was amazed to discover that he felt no fear, only a kind of light-headed exhilaration. It was wonderful—*wonderful*—to be moving in the open air again, like a living human being.

In the cockpit of his *Shinyo,* Higuchi crouched low behind the wheel and adjusted his goggles. Despite them, the windblast was making his eyes tear. Like Wanabi, he was experiencing an emotional transformation—but in his case exhilaration was accompanied by an incredible sense of calm, of professional and personal relief that he was finally engaged in the performance of his sacred duty.

Duty that was heavier than a mountain, but would soon be swept away by death.

Death as light as a feather.

*   *   *

What the hell was that?

Gunner's Mate Samuel Hatch nestled his submariner's binoculars against the underside of his brows and touched up the focus. Coming out of the river mouth at high speed were two—no, dammit, at least four or five— small speedboats, possibly more. The lead boat, already into the channel, was weaving in what looked like a predetermined pattern. Probably avoiding known underwater obstacles and mines.

There were no guns on the boats, nor any torpedoes or rockets. Hatch couldn't figure out what the little Nipponese sons of bitches were up to now, but he always listened to his gut, and his gut told him that he didn't want those speeding powerboats anywhere near him. He opened his mouth to order the forty-millimeter trained on the middle of the channel when the flat, disembodied voice of the *Mayhew*'s gunfire control officer crackled in his earphones.

"All gunnery stations, *do not fire*—repeat—*do not fire* on small craft outbound at high speed through lagoon channel. Maintain fire on selected shoreline and inland targets only. American demolition personnel may still be inside the outer reef. Repeat: all gunnery stations are forbidden to fire upon outbound high-speed craft until ordered to do so."

Oh, fuck. Hatch didn't like that at all. What was the point in having a big gun if you couldn't shoot it at the enemy? An enemy that was coming your way, no less. He glanced up at the bridge in irritation. What species of asshole was in charge up there, anyway?

He stared through his binoculars again at the tiny, onrushing boats. There were at least ten of them now, weaving back and forth one behind the other, creamy white wakes intertwining on the channel's blue green surface. Heading for the gap in the outer reef.

He didn't like it. No sir. Not one goddamned bit.

Fitzgerald had made it all the way to the surface with Doi on his back. The dying Japanese diver had held on like a limpet, one arm locked around the American's throat, the other stabbing repeatedly with his sheath knife. He'd managed to drive it twice more into Fitzgerald's abdomen before the frantically struggling frogman had been able to seize Doi's wrist and twist his fingers off the knife haft.

They'd sunk to the bottom three times, fighting all the way down, and three times Fitzgerald had clawed his way back to the surface—Doi doing his best to stab or strangle him—before his wind gave out. But despite the UDT man's size advantage and tremendous strength, he'd been unable to dislodge his enemy. Faced with drowning, he'd instinctively headed for shallower water—back toward the sandbar at the river mouth.

Now Fitzgerald, to his astonishment and for the first time in his life, could feel his great strength and athletic ability deserting him. Adrenaline continued to override the pain of the deep stab wounds in his stomach, but he could feel himself growing feeble, his muscles failing to respond. His vision was becoming tunnellike, darkening on the periphery, closing down like a camera shutter. His head was swimming, his focus slipping away.

It scared him. No way was he ready to die. That wasn't in The Fitz's Grand Plan for Success and Long Life. He forced himself into another frenzied effort, stroking for shore with his one free arm, squeezing his enemy's wrist with the other, kicking madly with his powerful legs. . . .

Lieutenant Doi choked, swallowing his own blood, barely getting enough air to inflate his lungs halfway. In addition to splitting his voice box, Fitzgerald's knife had nicked his carotid artery. Doi was losing consciousness, and he knew when he did, it would be for good.

He could feel his left arm weakening, starting to slip from around the American's throat. His mind began to drift . . . to begin the long, unknown journey away from earthly concerns. He was intensely sad for a moment—sad because rather than achieving a glorious and meaningful death by destroying an entire boatload of enemy soldiers, he was about to become just another unexceptional casualty of war at the hands of a single American.

He hoped the other *Fukuryu* would do better than he. It was important to do one's best for the emperor and homeland, after all.

He noticed that he was wreathed in a cloud of Japanese and American blood. Odd, he thought, his vision fading—the two were unarguably very different, but when mixed together, they still made the same red.

That he had died in battle like so many of his brothers-in-arms was a great comfort to him as he slipped gently to the seafloor. He, too, would dwell forever in the shrine of fallen warriors.

In the distance, not too far ahead, he was certain he could see the gates of Yasukuni.

"That's it!" Garth called, pausing in midchannel to tread water. He held up the end of the detonator cord in one hand and the depleted spool in the other. "No more slack."

Randall turned and looked out to sea. They were about seventy-five yards short of the outer reef. On either side of the channel gap, yellow brown coral heads had been exposed by the low tide, some protruding above the surface as much as two feet. Beyond the reef, in a distant line, a dark armada of bouncing, rolling landing craft was rushing forward, growing larger by the second.

"Christ," he muttered, spinning in the water to stare back at the now distant river mouth. "How'd we end up short? We've got to blow it. . . ."

McNab swam up beside him. "L.T., we've gotta wait for Fitz. He's coming, I tell ya. I know he is."

Randall chewed his lip, treading water in the light chop. He caught Garth's eye. The dark-skinned Texan had extracted a four-minute igniter fuse from his belt.

"Charlton," he said, "listen. We can climb up on the reef. Avoid the underwater shock wave. I can tie the fuse short—maybe a minute and a half, two minutes. We sprint for the coral, climb out, and *bang*—the shot blows. Then we dive back in on the seaward side and swim toward the fleet. Flag down a ride on one of the LCIs."

"What about Fitz?" McNab persisted.

Garth looked at him. "Fitz isn't here," he said. "His choice. If he'd stayed with you, he would be."

McNab searched the waters behind Garth in desperation. "Where the fuck *is* he?"

Randall made a decision. "Joe, stay here. Tie the fuse short and stand by to pull it." He looked at McNab. "Come on. You and I will swim to the reef, climb up on it, and see if we can spot Fitz." A shadow of pain flitted across his face. "It's his last chance."

The two frogmen kicked themselves horizontal and took off for the exposed coral heads, swimming on the surface. Garth doubled the fuse over, halving its length, and mated it and the detonator cord to a small blasting cap.

McNab was the first to reach the reef. He clambered out of the wave wash onto a large head of brain coral and stood up, balancing precariously. Randall followed, finding stable footing on a thick chunk of staghorn. They looked more like creatures of the sea than of the land— a pair of haggard, silver-and-black-striped mermen.

The first thing they saw was the flotilla of high-speed motorboats racing down the channel in their direction.

The second thing they saw, on the tip of the sandbar at the river mouth, was Fitzgerald.

Lieutenant Higuchi steered the *Shinyo* into yet another planing turn, throwing sheets of white spray across the blue-green surface of the channel. His many weeks of attack training were now paying off. He was able to navigate through the irregularly placed mines and underwater obstacles without thinking about it, almost by reflex. He doubted that the invading American landing craft, which he could see lined up across the horizon several miles ahead, would find the correct passage so easily.

He threw a quick glance over his shoulder. Flying along in his wake were at least a dozen more boats of his *Shinyo* squadron. Higuchi laughed aloud for joy. It was obvious that the majority of his fellow pilots had escaped a futile death in the cave. Now the *Shinyo*—the Ocean Shakers—were on their way to glory. How accurately they had been named! The ocean, crawling with Americans, was truly about to shake.

Higuchi peered over the low windscreen of his boat and concentrated. The guiding principle of the *Tokkotai* suicide warrior was to not be in too big a hurry to die, but to choose a death that would achieve a maximum result. He ran his eyes over the long dark line of landing craft and dismissed them from his mind. He could engage only one, and the individual vessels were too small. As leader of the squadron, he would set a proper example and choose a worthy target.

Lying half a mile in front of the landing craft, her guns still firing intermittently, was the USS *Mayhew*.

Higuchi set his jaw and pressed the throttle lever as far down as it would go.

Son of a *bitch*.

This was all wrong.

This wasn't supposed to happen to *him*.

Fitzgerald groaned, tasting blood, as spasms of crippling pain continued to lance through his abdomen. He tried to inch his way farther up the sandbar, lying on his right hip, propped up by his right elbow. His left hand was occupied keeping his guts from spilling out through the deep gashes inflicted by Lieutenant Doi's knife.

He looked at the sign he'd planted earlier, only a few feet away. The three-foot-long red banner had a few bullet holes in it, but was still standing. He had to grin at the irony of it. Still standing. That was more than he could say for himself.

He watched with detached interest as yet another Japanese speedboat roared past the sandbar, heading out to sea. The helmsman crouching behind the wheel turned his goggled head to stare at Fitzgerald briefly as he went by. He did not attempt to alter course or raise the alarm; rather, he merely looked surprised to see a naked, bleeding, silver-and-black-striped American lying on the end of the sand spit.

Grimacing, Fitzgerald pushed himself up to a sitting position, toed off his fins, and painfully crossed his legs. He pressed his other hand to his abdomen. Blood leaked out between his fingers in a warm flood.

God *damn* it.

What a lousy break.

He blinked, trembling, and squinted hard to focus on the pack of outbound speedboats bouncing and banking down the channel. He blinked again. It looked as if the lead boat had almost reached the gap in the reef.

Then he saw them, on top of the exposed coral at the left side of the channel. Two tiny silver figures, waving frantically. One of them paused, then held its arms out from its sides and pumped them up and down as if doing an overhead press with a barbell.

Sure, Fitzgerald thought. What the hell.

He removed his hands from his stomach. Blood gushed over his groin and into the sand. Slowly, he raised his arms above his head and duplicated the overhead press motion. Three times. Then he paused. Then he did it again.

Then he brought his hands back down, replaced them over his torn abdomen, and lowered his chin onto his chest.

"Shoot it!" Randall yelled at Garth. *"Fitz just signaled us to shoot it!"*

Garth pulled the brass igniter attached to the fuse, let it go, and swam for the reef with everything he had.

"Come on!" McNab shouted, eyeing the approaching speedboats. *"Come on!"*

Randall stepped down off the chunk of staghorn, nearly falling, and took a wobbly stride toward the edge of the reef. He extended his hand as Garth reached the coral and began to climb out of the water. "Hurry up, Joe!"

At that moment, twenty-six seconds after Garth had pulled the igniter, the fuse malfunctioned, flaring and burning down the rest of its one-minute length in the span of a heartbeat. Its hot, traveling coal hit the blasting cap connected to the end of the detonator cord. With a muted underwater *SNAP,* the cap fired.

The detonator cord—nothing more than a greatly elongated form of the same high explosive contained in the Hagensen packs—discharged instantaneously along its entire length. All the hundreds of yards of interconnected cord strung by the UDT squad vaporized in the blink of an eye.

Every one of the dozens of twenty- and thirty-pound Hagensen packs planted on mine posts, rock cribs, and tripod obstacles exploded simultaneously. The very reef seemed to shake under Randall's, McNab's, and Garth's feet as the aquamarine waters of the channel erupted skyward in multiple gigantic fountains of white spray and foam.

More than half the speeding *Shinyo* boats were caught in the explosions. Some disintegrated completely, their fragments blown upward. Others remained whole, tumbling end over end through the air before smashing down on the water again like flung toys. A few, their hulls fractured by the massive crisscrossing shock waves, simply slowed, settled, and sank.

The two lead boats, Higuchi's and the one immediately behind, narrowly escaped destruction, skittering wildly across the surface of the channel as the multiple concussions battered them. Still, the two *Shinyo* pilots were able to maintain control and continue to head for the gap in the reef, which was now very close. Far behind them, bursting through the fog of water vapor and smoke, three more boats emerged, their helmsmen maneuvering desperately to avoid the sudden abundance of floating wreckage cluttering the channel.

"Yeeeee-haaaaaaw!" McNab whooped, pumping his fists like a boxer. *"How 'bout that, Tojo?"*

Garth was helping Randall to his feet. The lieutenant, who had been knocked flat by the explosions, was bleeding from a nasty barnacle gash on his right thigh. Wincing in pain, he refocused on the onrushing speedboats as Higuchi's lead *Shinyo* began to line up on the center of the navigable gap.

Randall stared. The first boat was clearly going to head straight on through to open water. But the second was starting to alter course . . . to veer out of the wake of the one ahead.

Toward them.

"Hey!" Randall yelled, leaning on Garth's shoulder. *"Watch out! Watch out for that second goddamn boat. . . ."*

Beautiful. It was a beautiful thing.

Fitzgerald grinned around clenched teeth, nodding his head slowly, as he sat there cross-legged on the end of the sandbar. His hands were slippery red halfway to the elbows with his own blood. Beneath him, the wet sand was dark and sticky.

Beautiful. It looked like every single thing they'd wired had blown—especially that fucking dome about fifty yards down the channel. *Boom.* So much for the Jap divers.

He was surprised to still be alive. Earlier, when he'd dashed up on the sandbar to plant his banner, he'd attracted a hail of bullets. But now—so far—nothing.

He had no way of knowing that sustained offshore fire from the USS *Mayhew* and various other warships, concentrated on the hillsides above the river mouth, had finally killed every last Japanese sniper and machine gunner with a clear view of the sandbar.

Fitzgerald spat blood off his lip. Well, if the Nips were too stupid to shoot while he was sitting right out in plain sight, that was their problem. He wasn't going anywhere.

He shifted slightly on the sand, grunting, and gazed out to seaward. He couldn't see through the huge columns of mist thrown up by the explosions, but he knew that right now Randall, Garth, McNab, Bartlett, and Drexel were swimming out beyond the reef into deep water, their demo mission accomplished, looking for a pickup from a patrolling LCI or torpedo boat. He felt really good about that.

And pretty soon a whole lot of extremely serious U.S.

Marines were going to be coming up the channel to land at this river mouth. That was a comforting thought, too.

As a matter of fact, he was feeling quite a bit better in general. True, there was a lot of his blood soaking into the sand, and his gut was pretty torn up—but his mind was clear, the pain of his wounds had subsided for some reason, and his body had stopped its uncontrollable trembling. Something like a warm calm seemed to have descended over him. Contentment, maybe, Fitzgerald mused.

Yeah. Contentment.

He had just decided to let himself relax and enjoy the feeling when Private Second Class Wanabi, who'd grabbed his army issue bolt-action rifle and run along the riverbank to watch the *Shinyo* squadron race off to glory, took careful aim from behind a charred palm tree—the top of which was adorned with the hanging body of a dead Japanese sniper—and shot him between the shoulder blades.

"All gunnery stations," the disembodied voice in Hatch's earphones said, "commence firing upon small craft approaching at high speed off starboard forward quarter. Repeat: commence firing upon small craft approaching at high speed off starboard forward quarter."

About fucking time.

"Track 'em, track 'em!" Hatch barked to his gun crew. He stared nervously over the edge of the armored tub as the twin barrels swung around, and watched the lead boat, which had just made it through the reef. It bounced and jinked off the open-water swells, throwing sheets of spray with every impact. It was heading directly toward the *Mayhew*. A freezing, tingling sensation began at the base of Samuel Hatch's neck and spread rapidly up over his scalp. His chest tightened, making it difficult to breathe.

He began to fire—*pom pom pom pom pom*—but the forty-millimeter was not sufficiently depressed. The cannon shells were overshooting badly, kicking up geysers of spray several hundred yards behind the approaching speedboat.

"Lower! *Lower!*" he yelled at his trainer and pointer, the pitch of his voice rising with his fear. *"Get me on the bastard!"*

The pilot of the *Shinyo* boat following Higuchi's was an eighteen-year-old named Tatsu Mizuro. His father was a hard-line career military officer and devoted follower of the ultranationalist Kodo-ha, the Imperial Way, dedicated to the preservation of samurai and Bushido values. Mizuro's father had indoctrinated his only son from an early age—with rewards, punishment, and endless repetition—in the concept of *yamato-damashii*, fighting spirit based on Japanese superiority and racial purity. As a result of this and other teachings, Mizuro, unusually hotheaded even for a teenage male, had developed a deep personal hatred for Americans, though he had never actually met or even seen one. They were all soulless imperialists—morally bankrupt and racially inferior.

So when he spotted three six-foot-tall, grease-coated frogmen standing on the exposed reef just off his *Shinyo*'s port bow, that long-cultivated hatred combined with an excess of adrenaline to overwhelm his better judgment. With a yank of the wheel he turned his boat directly toward them and stood up.

In the waistband of his combat jumpsuit was a silver-plated, jade-handled .32-caliber revolver—the finest work of a Kobe master gunsmith and a gift from his father upon his posting to Higuchi's *Shinyo* squadron. "Go, now, into battle!" Colonel Mizuro had told him, standing at attention in his dress uniform and sword—taking care *not* to use the Japanese form of speech that implied "go . . . and then return."

Tatsu Mizuro pulled the pistol from his waistband as he stood behind the wheel, his long black hair and white *hachimaki* head scarf streaming out behind him, and took aim at one of the Americans. He would bank off at the last minute, thereby missing the reef and preserving his boat for a strike at the larger vessels offshore, but with any luck would be able to kill one or two of the frogmen. That they were *here*, so brazenly close to the Japanese shore defenses, filled him with a white-hot rage.

His father had drilled him in small-arms shooting from the age of six. So even though the boat was vibrating badly and traveling at a high rate of speed, when he fired, emptying the revolver's five-shot cylinder in as many seconds, he was still able to achieve a respectable grouping.

The first three shots hit McNab in the center of the chest, knocking him off the brain coral head. The other two went wide. Randall and Garth were scrambling over the reef, cutting themselves to ribbons on the razor-sharp coral, trying to get clear of the onrushing speedboat. They dove into the open water on the far side as Mizuro turned the wheel hard and banked the *Shinyo* around to starboard.

He'd misjudged the edge of the reef. With a screeching crash the boat drove aground, ripping off most of its hull below the waterline, and went airborne. It turned over slowly, presenting its damaged keel to the sky, and smacked back down on the water in an explosion of spray. Tatsu Mizuro's neck and spine snapped instantly.

Gasoline from the *Shinyo*'s ruptured fuel tank ignited as it spread across the water, but the boat itself did not explode or burn. Remaining upside down, it merely foundered, flames licking at its splintered hull, until, in less than thirty seconds, it disappeared completely beneath the rolling swells of Leyte Gulf.

Black and blue, cut and bleeding, joints swollen from concussion edema, and near exhaustion, Randall and Garth locked arms across a yard-square piece of floating *Shinyo* decking, laid their heads down on the sodden wood, and lapsed into a state that was not quite sleep, not quite consciousness, but somewhere in between . . . where the sight, sound, smell, taste, feel, and fury of war faded into a dim gray void of stillness and silence.

* * *

Gunner's Mate Samuel Hatch was beside himself with fear and frustration. The lead speedboat—there were a total of four of them out beyond the reef now—was proving nearly impossible to hit. Every gun on the starboard side of the *Mayhew* that could depress below the horizontal was firing at it, but still the goddamned Nip came on, zigzagging in unpredictable high-speed turns like a broken-field runner.

Pom pom pom pom pom . . .

"*Track him, track him!*" Hatch yelled at his gun crew. The fucking shells were landing *everywhere* but right on top of the speedboat.

Pom pom pom pom pom . . .

All right, all right . . . he and Miller up on the forward twenty-millimeter had the Nip bracketed now. All they had to do was converge their fire—

The speedboat dodged abruptly to the left as the twenty– and forty-millimeter cannon shells crisscrossed ten feet in front of its bow, missing it.

"*Fuck!*" Hatch screamed at the sea.

Pom pom pom pom pom . . .

Lieutenant Kentaro Higuchi was in a state of grace. His attack was unfolding like a haiku poem—that very essence of elegant simplicity. This was how he had always known it would be. The difficult made easy. Overwhelming abundance defeated by deftly applied economy.

When he turned three times port to starboard, the American gunners always clustered their massive firepower as if expecting him to turn in similar fashion a fourth time. But of course he wouldn't. A haiku contained three lines of five, seven, and five syllables, respectively. This was the pattern of zigzagging turns he had decided to follow: three, five, seven, five. The Americans could not catch the rhythm of it—the repetition inside the irregularity—and it kept their fire walking away from him at every crucial turn.

He knew there were more *Shinyo* behind him, seeking

targets of their own, but he did not dare turn around and look. His example had to be definitive, inspirational; his attack execution, flawless. It was his Duty.

Reaching beneath the cockpit dash, he pulled the lever that disengaged the safety lock of the electrical firing mechanism in the *Shinyo*'s bow.

The big Chevrolet engine roared beneath him, the cannon shells burst around him, but all he heard was the wind in his ears.

Pom pom pom pom pom . . .
"Get on him!" Hatch screamed. *"Get on him!"*
POM POM POM POM POM . . .

"Miho," Kentaro Higuchi breathed, uttering his mother's name.

His *Shinyo* suicide boat struck the USS *Mayhew* just below the starboard forty-millimeter antiaircraft gun mount. Upon contacting the American vessel's hull plates, the stem of the *Shinyo* crushed back, as designed, completing a battery-powered electrical firing circuit.

The one-thousand-pound explosive charge contained in the bow of the boat detonated, ripping off the *Mayhew*'s entire starboard forward quarter from the main deck to ten feet below the waterline. The blast killed every officer, seaman, and gunner on that side who was stationed forward of the amidships launch davits.

Chapter Four

United States Marine Corps captain Aaron Smoltz had managed to survive no less than nine separate amphibious invasion operations in the nearly two years since his initial deployment to the South Pacific—some of them involving close combat of almost unbelievable savagery. He'd seen friends and enemies alike burned alive, decapitated, dismembered, riddled with holes, and blown into unidentifiable fragments. He'd watched men and boys from half a dozen nations die slowly of horrible wounds—screaming, whimpering, or making no sound at all.

His physical aspect had been shaped by the things he'd seen. His short black hair was now salted with gray, his cheeks were sunken, and his complexion was sallow. His eyes were hard and distant, scored by deep crow's-feet and underlined by dark, baggy circles. His posture was that of a man in late middle age: stoop-shouldered and weary. He was not quite twenty-two years old.

He had a rule—Rule Number One—about riding in landing craft: never stick your head above the gunwale or expose yourself in any way until the ramp drops down and there is nothing else to do but go. He'd seen enough men get their chips cashed in by random slugs and shrapnel to have a healthy respect for statistical probabilities—even considered himself a student of the math. As a result of this interest, he'd developed what he liked to call the Smoltz Principle. It was the basis for Rule Number One and went thusly: if the head remains low while in a hot fire zone, there is a much greater likelihood of it not being suddenly detached from the body.

So it was with considerable unwillingness that he edged up beside the coxswain of the LCI transporting him and his men up the channel to the small river delta at the southern end of Beach Black. He was feeling quite put out. The Leyte invasion was the Sixth Army's assignment; for once the marines were getting a break. Except for *his* unit, which had been tapped to do a last-minute penetration and sweep on the southwest flank of the main beachhead. Just lucky, he supposed. Remember the Smoltz Principle, Aaron, his brain kept repeating. Remember the Smoltz Principle.

"Hey, Captain, I'm serious," the coxswain said, glancing down at him across his bulky gray life jacket. "Why don't you just stick your head up real quick and take a look at what's over here to starboard?"

"It's against my principles," Smoltz replied, still hunched below the level of the gunwale.

The coxswain looked annoyed. "There ain't a shot being fired up here, sir. No kiddin'. We must've pasted them Nips but good." He squinted ahead at the charred, barren hills. "No movement, no fire."

"Yet," Smoltz commented, "I'd advise you to stay low. Japs can appear out of cracks a rat couldn't get through."

"Yes, sir. I 'preciate that. But you really oughtta take a look over thisaway. . . ."

Captain Smoltz sighed and clapped his helmet down on his head more firmly. He was going to regret this; he just knew it.

He raised his head and peered out to starboard through the narrow slit between his helmet visor and the top of the LCI's gunwale.

On the end of a nearby sandbar, a man was sitting cross-legged—hands in his lap, slumped forward slightly, his head bowed. He appeared to be wearing only khaki shorts and a coating of silvery gray paint, interspersed with horizontal black stripes. Just behind him, fluttering in the breeze, was a bright red strip of cloth. It was pinned to the sand at either end by small uprights, like a banner, but seemed to have worked loose in the wind and sagged over.

"Gawd," the coxswain said. "We ain't even took the beach and already the fuckin' tourists are here." He cupped a hand around his mouth. "Buddy! Hey, buddy! What the hell are you doin'? Halloween ain't for ten days yet!"

The figure on the sandbar was well within earshot, but didn't move or respond.

"Save your breath," Smoltz said, gazing through a small pair of field glasses. "That man's dead."

"Yeah? Sonofabitch."

"Very dead. Massive wound in the lower stomach— lots of blood . . . and shot right through the upper back, too." Smoltz adjusted the glasses. "Yep. There it is: exit wound in the center of the chest. Nice big hole where his heart used to be."

"I knew a girl like that once," the coxswain said, looking away from the sandbar. "Hole where her heart shoulda been."

Captain Aaron Smoltz didn't feel like smiling at the coxswain's bland humor. All the way up the western rim of the Pacific, on island after bloody island, he'd seen the naked warriors in action. Always in first. Always alone. Like the man on the sandbar. Clearing the way for him.

"UDT," he said quietly. "Poor bastard."

He recited a short Torah verse for the dead under his breath.

Picking up on Smoltz's chilly reaction to his wisecrack,

the coxswain tried to make amends. "Jeez, yeah, sir, that's too bad. Damn shame." The captain looked up at him for a moment, his old-young face utterly devoid of empathy, then went back to his binoculars. "Er—who ya think he is, sir?" the coxswain soldiered on.

"Looks like . . . some kind of . . . *sign* behind him," Smoltz muttered, half to himself. "That red cloth. It has white lettering on it."

"That a fact, sir? What's it say?"

Smoltz studied the sandbar for another full minute before lowering the binoculars.

"I don't know," he said, shaking his head. "It's fallen over too far. I can't read it."

Later that same day, farther north on the main beach-head near Dulag, another incoming landing craft accidentally grounded itself more than fifty yards from shore. The coxswain gulped and felt the color drain from his face as the tall figure in the bow, wearing peaked cap and sunglasses, turned to frown back at him. His insides dissolving, the LCI driver gave the nod to his deck crewman. The bow ramp unlatched and dropped forward, hitting the water with a loud splash.

MacArthur's patrician features wrinkled in annoyance as he regarded the 150 feet of muddy brine between the end of the ramp and the beach. He had not intended to execute what he and everyone else in the civilized world knew would be a pivotal moment in history with his pants soaked from cuff to midthigh. That the personal vanity of the Pacific's most powerful general was being tweaked by the slight course miscalculation of a lowly LCI coxswain and a dropping tide did not amuse him in the slightest. Nor did he appreciate the situation's inherent irony. Douglas MacArthur did not like irony unless he was on the beneficent side of it.

But he was not a man who failed to capitalize on attention when it was focused upon him. The photographers and newsreel cameramen were there on the beach, waiting. Behind them, waves of American infantrymen of the U.S. Sixth Army pushed inland through the towns of Dulag and Tacloban, accompanied by armored vehicles of every description. Out to sea, from the horizon to the very edge of Leyte's barrier reef, one of the greatest military armadas ever assembled lay in support of one of the greatest amphibious invasions ever undertaken. In the afternoon sky, swarms of U.S. warplanes continued to strafe and bomb ahead of the advance.

The moment he so craved, MacArthur knew—that glorious, fleeting, axial point in history—was now.

So he threw one last autocratic scowl at the quaking coxswain, shot the buttoned cuffs of his khaki military field shirt, and turned briefly to Sergio Osmeña, president of the Philippines, who was standing beside him.

"Let's go," he declared, and marched down the ramp into the muddy water. His staff generals, aides, and Osmeña did likewise, a step or two behind.

Cameras clicked as MacArthur and his entourage strode through the knee-deep shallows and emerged onto the beach proper, their progress observed from every landing craft and staging area within eyeshot. At a nearby command post set up by officers of the Twenty-fourth Infantry Division, a microphone connected to a mobile-radio-communications truck was waiting. The soldiers in the makeshift CP came to attention. Nodding, MacArthur grasped the microphone, cleared his throat, and began to speak, his voice rich with emotion.

"This is the voice of Freedom, General Douglas MacArthur speaking," he said, the background rumble of artillery fire providing dramatic context for his words. "People of the Philippines, I have returned. By the grace of Almighty God our forces stand again upon Philippine soil—soil consecrated in the blood of our two peoples. We have come dedicated and committed to the task of destroying every vestige of enemy control over your daily lives, and of restoring on a foundation of indestructible strength the liberties of your people. . . ."

The general paused as the crack of a sniper's rifle, not far off, initiated a flurry of return fire from the infantrymen around the command post. A dozen army Rangers fanned out toward a grove of trees about six hundred yards to the southwest, each man moving with the peculiar, skittering run of the trained soldier. MacArthur cleared his throat once again and continued: "By my side is your president, Sergio Osmeña. . . ."

About twenty yards from the CP, two combat photographers—one military and one civilian—were sitting behind a stack of field-kitchen crates. It was a safe place, with Japanese snipers still working the beachhead, to reload camera film and listen to the crackly feed of MacArthur's radio speech through a hastily wired horn speaker.

The civilian, a jaded type with fifteen years of beating the streets for a major New York newspaper behind him, stuck a Lucky Strike between his lips and gave a sardonic snort as he flicked his Zippo. "Ol' Mac's purpling the prose again," he muttered. "Chewing the scenery. Guy should have been an actor."

The military photographer, a kid of nineteen, looked distressed, as if his companion had just pissed on the altar. "I don't know, Vince," he said. "He's a great man, talking about something real important. You shouldn't say stuff like that."

Vince rested his wrist on his drawn-up knee, the cigarette cleated between his dangling fingers, and exhaled a long cloud of smoke. "Look, kid, don't get me wrong. You're right. That's a great man over there, and a great general. He's exactly the guy we need, doing exactly what he's doing, at this point in time. But let me tell you something about MacArthur. He's as vain as an English duke. *And*"—he raised his Lucky as the younger photographer began to interrupt—"to quote a columnist buddy of mine, he has an insatiable thirst for military glory, more characteristic of a general of the eighteenth century than the twentieth. Unquote."

"Holy cow," the kid said, lowering his voice. "He wrote that in the newspapers?"

Vince smiled around his cigarette. "Hell, no. He's too smart to get himself run out of Manhattan on a rail, or charged with subversion or even treason. But he can express his opinions privately—like to me in the Knickerbocker Bar over a couple of bourbons."

The young photographer began to wind fresh film into his camera. "Well, I don't believe it," he said. "Sounds like your buddy's just got it in for General MacArthur. Maybe he's jealous."

Vince laughed out loud as another thunderous roll of artillery fire echoed down from the hills. "Sure, kid, sure. He's just jealous." He drew on his cigarette, then plucked it from his mouth and gestured with it. "Tell you what. I'll bet you a sawbuck that MacArthur's going to personally review the photos and newsreel films of him and his staff coming ashore today, before they're released to the public. That ten bucks says there's a better-than-even chance that he's not going to like the way he looks, and he'll restage the whole scene at a later date for us to shoot again."

The military photographer looked at him, wide-eyed. "You mean like with him as star and director?"

Vince chuckled. "Yeah. Something like that."

The kid stuck his hand out. "You're on," he said. "That'll never happen."

Throughout the night, an endless stream of landing craft continued to ferry men and materiel from the offshore supply vessels to the beachheads. By the early morning of October 21, over two hundred thousand troops had landed and pushed westward into the interior of Leyte, liberating the coastal town of Dulag and the island's capital, Tacloban. Initial progress was good, though they'd had to fight for every inch. The Japanese had decided to cut their initial losses from naval bombardment by withdrawing from the beaches and retreating into the hills.

Now, almost twenty-four hours after the spearhead landings, the advance was slowing down. Japanese resistance had stiffened, aided by deteriorating weather conditions that limited the ability of army air force and navy planes to provide close air support. The terrain had become difficult: mountainous and overgrown, traversed only by footpaths, mule trails, and a few washed-out dirt roads.

After landing the previous day, Captain Aaron Smoltz and his marines had pushed up the river valley at the end of Beach Black, encountering minimal resistance for the most part. The exception had been at a large cave—complete with double doors and train tracks—where they'd come under rifle fire from an unknown number of Japanese defenders. Smoltz and his men had rushed the entrance, tossed grenades, burned out the interior with flamethrowers, and sealed the cave mouth with demolition charges.

Before firing the charges, Smoltz had picked up a souvenir: an ivory-handled samurai sword clutched in the claws of a charred corpse that had once been a rather chubby man. He didn't feel particularly bad about it—like he was robbing the dead or anything like that—because the guy was a Jap and had enough of his face left that Smoltz could see he wore a Charlie Chaplin mustache just like Adolph Hitler.

After sealing the cave, Smoltz and his marines had continued their penetration upriver for another three-quarters of a mile, turned north toward the main invasion force, and fought their way steadily across the intervening hills. Just before dark, they'd hooked up with advance troops of the army's Thirty-fourth Infantry Battalion. Final tally: two dead, four wounded, everybody dog-tired. Smoltz decided that the operation had been a relative success and fell asleep in a muddy foxhole, wondering for the umpteenth time what a nice Jewish boy from Flatbush was doing in a place like this.

Far out to sea, three separate Japanese naval-strike groups—two from the south and one from the north—were bearing down on the central Philippines. In opposition were the aircraft carriers, battleships, and destroyers of Admiral Bull Halsey's Third Fleet. Over the next four days, these monumental naval forces would collide with each other in the largest sea engagement in modern times—the Battle of Leyte Gulf.

In the confusion generated by the most ambitious and complex amphibious landing of the Pacific war to date, a confusion exacerbated by the impending conflict between the U.S. and Imperial Japanese Navies, no one spotted the small section of broken decking—or the two exhausted, grease-covered men clinging to it—that spun slowly past the support ships of the invasion fleet and out to sea on the prevailing current.

Chapter Five

"Well, bugger me," Flight Lieutenant Simon Parrish declared, looking down through the side window of his banking aircraft. "Looks like a pair of Robinson Crusoes down there, Pidgey."

"Wot, Guv'nor?"

Parrish winced slightly. In addition to a piercing nasal voice, his replacement radio operator, Warrant Officer Alvin Pidgeon, had a thick and grating cockney accent. They were still getting used to each other. Parrish's previous radioman had been killed eight days earlier in an encounter with a lone Japanese Zero that had pounced on their Royal Australian Air Force Beaufighter from a late afternoon cloud bank.

"Crusoes, Pidgey, bloody Crusoes." Parrish put the heavy twin-engine fighter into a shallow, turning dive. "A couple of blokes draped across a floating chunk of wood. We'll take another look. They might be ours."

"Righty-o, Guv. An' wot if they ain't?"

Parrish didn't hesitate or change his tone of voice: "If they're Japs, we'll strafe their yellow arses, then fly on home and say no more about it. Agreed?"

"I'm wiv you, Guv'nor," Pidgeon replied immediately. "Me bruvver Alfie was killed in Singapore when they overran the place. Sod the little perishers."

Simon Parrish smiled. "You'll do, Pidgey. You'll do."

He leveled the Beaufighter fifty feet off the calm blue surface of Leyte Gulf, reduced airspeed to just shy of a stall, and did a flyby of the flotsam. One of the two men clinging to it raised an arm and waved as the powerful fighter roared past, its twin Hercules radial engines shaking the air.

"What do you think, Pidgey?" Parrish intoned over the intercom.

"I fink," the radio operator said, "that I ain't never seen a Jap wiv blond hair. Nor as big as those two cobbers, neiver."

Parrish nodded unconsciously as he began to bank the aircraft around a third time. "That's what I think, too."

"Yanks, you figure, Guv?"

"Possibly," Parrish said. "Go ahead and radio their position in to our new outpost on Minglaat. They'll send a Hawker seaplane out to pick them up. And Pidgey— do it before I get another look at them, eh?"

"Sure, Guv, sure. But 'ow come?"

Flight Lieutenant Simon Parrish wrinkled his itching nose and sniffed. "Because," he said, "if I find out they're both bloody bird-stealing Americans, I may just leave them to soak where they bloody well are."

Two hours later, UDT men Charlton Randall and Joe Garth were picked up by an RAAF seaplane, given immediate medical aid for superficial wounds, dehydration, and exhaustion, and transported to the newly established motor torpedo boat base on the tiny island of Minglaat, forty miles south of Leyte. They'd been drifting with the ocean currents for nearly six days, bypassed but somehow not seen by ship after ship, plane after plane. During the last forty-eight hours, fading in and out of consciousness, their strength all but gone, they'd lashed themselves together across the piece of broken *Shinyo* decking using their web canvas belts. Only that precaution had kept them from succumbing to fatigue, slipping beneath the waves, and drowning.

While the establishment of the air/sea base and depot on Minglaat was primarily the responsibility of the Australian military, the place was a hotbed of activity for the combined Allied forces taking part in the invasion of the Philippines. Not just Australians but Americans, Brits, and Canadians frequented it—if only to refuel, drop off or take on supplies, or visit the small field hospital that had been set up in the island's old Catholic-mission building.

The mission was located near one end of a short, narrow landing strip, which had been in existence for less than three days and was still under construction. Two Bristol Beaufighters bearing RAAF róundels sat at the opposite end, angling up at the sky as if poised to leap into it at a moment's notice. Parked next to them, looking rather toothless by comparison, was an unarmed Lysander observation plane. Gasoline drums were piled at random up and down the length of the strip, along with a miniature mountain range of stacked crates containing everything from ammunition to medical supplies to toilet paper. Moving in and around the makeshift depot and on down to the beaches was a hurrying, sweating, cursing mass of men—like ants in a stirred-up nest—clad in military fatigues of blue, olive drab, and khaki.

At the mission end of the strip, lying askew about thirty feet off the runway proper in the partially cleared palm scrub, was a U.S. Navy Wildcat, its dark blue fuselage pocked with bullet holes. Its port wheel strut had buckled, dropping it onto its thick, wide wing on that side. The outboard third of the wing was torn off. Farther forward, the Plexiglas cockpit canopy was shattered and the cowling of the fighter's huge radial engine was charred black and streaked with oil. Only the American star insignia on the plane's side looked unscathed.

Randall and Garth had been stretchered from the seaplane to the field hospital, put on intravenous electrolyte drips to speed their rehydration, given mild sedatives, and ordered to get some sleep by a stern Royal Australian Army doctor who looked and sounded like an out-back Neville Chamberlain.

It was an order neither of them had any inclination to disobey. They both promptly drifted off and slept for the next fifteen hours straight.

When Randall awoke—slowly, as if dragging himself back up out of a netherworld that did not want to let him go—the hospital sheets were twisted around his legs and he was covered in a light film of sweat, though he did not feel sick. It was just hot. Hot and humid, even in the interior of the thick-walled mission building.

The intravenous needle had been removed from the inside of his forearm and replaced with a small patch of gauze and adhesive tape. A tall glass of what looked like lemonade was sitting on the upended crate that served as a bedside table. The top inch of the drink was clear and colorless, where ice had been floating and melted. Randall reached over and stuck the tip of his finger into it. It was as tepid as old bathwater.

The cot beside him was empty. He gazed around at the other beds in the field hospital, noting that at least as many patients looked malarial as wounded, and finally located Garth through one of the three open Spanish archways that led out onto the second-story balcony. He was sitting in a rattan chair with a bedsheet draped around his shoulders and was sipping from a glass of iced tea. Another man in a white cotton hospital smock was sitting next to him, his leg in a cast from ankle to hip and propped up on a five-gallon paint can.

Randall rubbed his eyes and swallowed with effort. His mouth tasted foul. He waved a hand at a passing orderly.

"Excuse me," he said, his voice a dry croak. "Do you think I could get some ice for this?" He indicated the glass on the crate.

The orderly barely paused in midstride, but smiled and nodded. In a few minutes he returned with a small metal can and slipped several pieces of crushed ice into the lemonade.

"Thanks," Randall said, and gingerly lowered his legs to the floor. Keeping the top bedsheet around his hips with one hand, he picked up his refreshed lemonade and made his way out through the archway to where Garth was sitting. In addition to Joe and the man in the cast, there were two other patients nearby, sipping tea and luxuriating in the ocean breeze that wafted across the open balcony.

"Feeling better?" Garth asked, as Randall sat down unsteadily next to him.

"I'm not sure yet," Randall replied, settling back in the rattan armchair. "You?"

"I'm good. A little sore in the joints from all those underwater concussions." Garth pointed at his lieutenant's right thigh. "That looks nasty."

Randall looked down and ran his forefinger gingerly along the four-inch gash on top of his upper leg. It had been stitched up with heavy sutures and swabbed with some kind of antiseptic that had turned his skin a lurid yellow-orange. The edges of the wound were puffy and it was leaking a small amount of clear fluid, but it was not infected.

"Doesn't hurt," he said to Garth. "I guess it'll be all right."

"Hey, mate." One of the men sitting to his left—a rake-thin Australian with a jaundiced complexion and protruding collarbones—leaned forward and grinned around his cigarette. "How'd you get that, then? Shrapnel?"

Randall smiled and shook his head. "Uh, no. I fell on a coral reef. Hit a barnacle, maybe."

The Australian chuckled heartily and shot his gaze around at the other men. "Blimey! You're sayin' you fell on a fokkin' *clam,* then?"

"More or less."

The thin man slapped his knee and let out a guffaw that was half laugh, half emphysematous rattle. *"Ha-haaaaa!* The biggest bloody shootin' war in history goin' on all around him, and he gets racked up by a clam!"

He looked back at Randall, exhaling smoke. "Hey, mate, hey, you think your Yank generals will give you a Purple Heart for bein' wounded by seafood?"

Instantly, Randall was reminded of Fitz. The same basic joke had been pretty funny when he'd told it—what? Only six, seven days ago. An eternity. It didn't seem nearly as amusing now. He glanced up at Garth, caught his eye, and knew he'd had exactly the same thought.

Still, what had happened to their UDT squad on Beach Black was hardly the Aussie's fault, so Randall forced another smile. "You never know," he said. "Maybe they will."

Garth chose that moment to redirect the conversation before the Australian—who clearly enjoyed the sound of his own voice more than anyone else did—could continue in the same vein. "Lieutenant," he said, gesturing across his body toward the man in the cast on his opposite side, "say hello to Captain Art Lucas, U.S. Navy flier *extraordinaire*—or so he's been telling me." He grinned, his white teeth flashing against his tan. "He's a nice guy, for a pilot. Captain Lucas, my UDT squad leader, Lieutenant Charlton Randall."

Garth leaned back as Randall and Lucas reached across him and clasped hands. "Nice to meet you," Randall said.

"Likewise," Lucas responded, accommodating his immobilized leg with some effort. He was a tall, rawboned man with the look of a Midwestern farmer about him. Except for his eyes, which were icy gray-blue, fixed in a permanent squint, and rimmed with deep, slashlike wrinkles. Gunfighter's eyes, Randall thought . . . or more precisely, fighter pilot's eyes. Eyes that looked as though they could see what was on the surface of the sun at high noon. Or diving out of it.

"Captain Lucas was just telling me how he came to be here," Garth said. "Apparently he's only been on Minglaat about a day longer than us."

Lucas nodded and raised his tea glass. "Yup. Little less than a day."

"How's the leg?" Randall asked. "Not too bad, I hope?"

"Not worth a damn," Lucas said matter-of-factly. "Broken in four places. They tell me they'll probably have to rebreak it once I get back Stateside so they can fix it properly. I'm really looking forward to that, let me tell you."

"Damn," Randall muttered. "How'd it happen?"

Lucas sipped his tea, then extended the glass and pointed with his middle finger at the crumpled Wildcat on the opposite side of the landing strip. "Hard slide into home plate."

"The captain's had a tough couple of days all round," Garth said. He glanced at Randall. "We weren't the only ones. You won't believe this. Go ahead, Art."

"I was telling Joe," Lucas said, shifting his cast, "that I'm a Wildcat flight leader from the escort carrier *St. Lo*—part of Rear Admiral Sprague's Task Unit 77.4.3 naval group. 'Taffy Three' for short. We've been flying support for the Leyte invasion—strafing enemy airfields on Leyte, Cebu, Samar; doing air-to-ground attacks ahead of the troops; dogfighting Jap planes that get airborne; that kind of thing.

"We were cruising off Samar a couple of days ago. . . . I guess it was the morning of October twenty-fifth. Admiral Halsey'd taken the big guns of the Third Fleet up north through the San Bernardino Strait to catch the Jap carriers that were sneaking around up there trying to get an angle on us. Taffy Three kept supporting the Leyte landing, 'cause we figured Halsey had the strait and the other northern approaches covered.

"Somebody got their signals crossed somewhere, because at about seven o'clock, here comes an entire Jap battle group sailing out from under a rainsquall. Led by the *Yamato*, no less! You know about the *Yamato*, don't you?"

"Largest battleship in the world," Randall said. "A superbattleship."

"Right." Lucas's ruddy complexion began to pale as his recollection sharpened. "She's an awful thing—a monster. Anyway, as we come under fire, Taffy Three turns tail and runs—Sprague needs time to turn the carriers ninety degrees into the wind so he can get all his remaining aircraft launched—except for our screening destroyers and one destroyer escort. The destroyer *Johnston* charges the Jap battle line—I'm talking heavy cruisers, battlewagons, the whole bit—followed by the destroyers *Hoel* and *Heerman,* and the DE *Samuel B. Roberts.* Four Davids against twenty-three Goliaths.

"The *Johnston* went in firing everything she had— torpedoes, light and heavy guns—everything. The Japs just hammered her, but she kept on coming. It was the bravest goddamn thing I've ever seen." Lucas's eyes welled up, and he swallowed hard. "Ernest Evans is her skipper. That's the fightingest American captain since John Paul Jones." He looked over at Joe Garth, taking in his high cheekbones and dark skin. "He's a Cherokee Indian, from Oklahoma. God *damn*—he made you proud to be in the same ocean with him."

"Jesus," Randall said. "That was just a couple of days ago? I thought you said Halsey was chasing the Jap fleet up north of Luzon somewhere. Where'd this other big battle group come from?"

Lucas shrugged, his brows knitting. "I don't know. From that base in Brunei, maybe, across the Sulu Sea. There'd been activity to the south the night before, too, at the top end of Mindanao in the Surigao Strait. More Jap destroyers and cruisers coming out of nowhere. A real mess, if you ask me."

"What happened to you guys in Taffy Three?" Garth asked.

"Right, right," Lucas said. He cleared his throat. "I finally got airborne off the *St. Lo* and went after the big battleships—the *Yamato* and the *Kongo*. I was trying to keep their antiaircraft gunners off our Avenger torpedo bombers as they made their runs. There was so much flak coming up I could hardly see through it, but I could damn sure see the *Johnston* getting pasted. She gave as good as she got, though. So did the other three: the *Hoel,* the *Heerman,* and the *Roberts.*

"Four little ships against all that firepower. No way they could win. But they fought those Jap battlewagons and heavy cruisers tooth and nail. It was kind of—what's that word?—*surreal*. Whenever I got a second or two to really look around, the ocean seemed to be covered by giant chrysanthemums—red, yellow, purple, green. The Japs were using dye markers with their big shells. When a fourteen-incher landed in the water and went off, it blew out a blossom of color a quarter mile in diameter.

"The *Hoel* had her bridge blasted off and went down first, still firing. The DE, the *Roberts*—she was next. They must have hit her in the magazine, because she just came apart in one huge explosion. Then the *Johnston* sank, like the *Hoel*—firing with every gun that would still work. Only the *Heerman* shot off her fish and got away alive."

Lucas's steely eyes were fixed on a point somewhere just beyond infinity. "Four little ships," he said, his voice as stark as an echo.

The men sitting around him on the balcony were silent. On the far side of the crushed-coral runway, a lone white heron came gliding in over the palm trees, gracefully put on the air brakes, and lit upon the propeller hub of Lucas's mangled Wildcat.

"What happened to you, Art?" Garth asked gently.

Lucas blinked and shifted in his chair. "Sorry. I was just . . . picturing it, there. Me? Like I said, I flew support for the Avengers as they made their torpedo runs. See, Taffy Three escort carriers like the *St. Lo* and the *Gambier Bay* carry what are called composite squadrons: eighteen Grumman Wildcat fighters and twelve Grumman Avenger torpedo bombers. We kind of . . . watch out for each other, you know?"

Randall's lips tightened in a grimace. "Watch out for each other," he said. "Yeah. I know." There was a slight tremor in his voice. Garth looked at him carefully for several seconds.

"There were some Jap planes above the battle group, complicating things. I shot my guns dry and had to break off. I was low on gas, too. We'd been ordered not to try to land back on the *St. Lo* during the battle, but to head for Tacloban on Leyte to rearm and refuel. The Sixth Army just took the town and got the airstrip up and running the other day.

"I didn't notice that my plane was half shot to shit until I landed, jumped out to grab a Coke, and looked back at it. More holes in it than a sieve. But it was still flyable, so what the hell. I was back in the air with another load of fuel and ammo in twenty minutes.

"I picked up a couple of wingmen and headed back toward Taffy Three. We wasted a few minutes tangling with a small flight of Zeros, shot down one and scattered the rest, then kept on heading east. I was expecting to get right back into it—probably get killed, if you want to know the truth—but when we found our ships, the entire Jap battle group had already broken off the attack and hightailed it for the open ocean! I couldn't tell you why—they had Sprague and our escort carriers dead to rights. The only thing I can think of is that they must have just lost their nerve."

"Lost their nerve?" Garth muttered, raising an eyebrow. "Doesn't sound like the Japs *I've* been fighting."

The men sitting nearby nodded, as did Lucas. "True enough," he said. "I just can't figure why they'd have cut and run like that."

"I guess they was just bent on snatchin' defeat from the jaws o' victory," the skinny Australian blurted. He let out a long, rattling guffaw.

Lucas ignored him. So did everyone else. "Anyway," the pilot said, "here's the capper: we were trying to reorganize, get a decent air umbrella flying cover over the carriers while we collected information on how badly damaged they were. All at once somebody screams over the radio that there are about sixty Jap planes above us, moving in on Taffy Three from the direction of Luzon and Mabalacat.

"So we climb and engage. Zeros—we call 'em Zekes—Kates, and Judys, mostly. All hell breaks loose, as usual. But about a third of these Jap planes act differently. Instead of trying to set up conventional attack runs on the carriers, they dive straight down on top of them—straight into the antiaircraft fire. They don't strafe bow to stern, they don't release bombs, and they don't bank away at the last minute.

"They crash-dive right into the ships. On purpose."

The listening men were stunned.

"What?" Randall said.

Lucas scratched the stubble on his chin, his hand shaking slightly. "Suicide pilots. Their planes must be loaded with explosives, like flying bombs, 'cause when they hit, they blow up with a lot bigger bang than just a fuel tank going off.

"I saw three of them hit. There were probably more, but I was so busy with the Zeros I couldn't tell. See, not all the planes are suiciders; at least half of them are flying cover. They had us tied up but good while their buddies dove on the carriers.

"The last one I saw was the worst. A Zeke dove straight through the flight deck of the *St. Lo* and blew up. It must have hit the aviation fuel storage tanks because there were several small internal explosions, and then one huge blast that nearly tore her in half. She sank a few minutes later.

"That was my ship. The first wave of Jap planes had pulled away, so I circled a few times. Hundreds of men in the water, oil and fuel burning, other ships damaged and on fire—it was terrible.

"I didn't have very long to think about it, because another wave of suicide planes and escorts showed up and it was back to the party. This time I ended up being chased into a cloud bank for miles by a pair of Zeros. My tail was so shot up I couldn't turn tight anymore." Lucas pointed across the runway at his crashed Wildcat again. "See? Stabilizer's almost gone. I lost the Zeros in the clouds but had to crash-land here."

He looked around at his audience and smiled a haunted smile. "And now here I sit, sipping tea."

No one spoke for the better part of a minute. On the other side of the landing strip, the white heron standing on the propeller hub of Lucas's Wildcat extended its broad wings and flapped into the air with a prehistoric croak. The men on the balcony watched as it soared across the runway toward them and disappeared up over the mission roof.

"Bloody Japs," the thin Australian snarled finally. "The little beggars are fokkin' insane."

"Not insane, Booth," said the older man sitting next to him. "Motivated." It was the first time he'd spoken. He recrossed his legs and carefully adjusted his dark green robe over the large burn dressing on his right shoulder. Garth took a good look at him for the first time. The man was slender and long-limbed, with salt-and-pepper hair and a neatly trimmed mustache. By his accent, he was obviously English, and by his diction, obviously well educated.

Booth glowered around at everyone over the cigarette clamped between his lips. "This 'ere's the Prof," he said grumpily. "Major Barnaby, my boss."

The older man gave a well-mannered nod. "Quentin Barnaby, late of the cushy sanctums of Cambridge University. I wish I could say I was delighted to be sitting here with you gentlemen." He smiled.

Garth, Randall, and Lucas managed a polite chuckle or two, and were glad of it despite the effort. It seemed to lighten the atmosphere.

"Prof is a real, honest-to-God professor," Booth explained, somewhat redundantly. "That's why I call him Prof, see?"

"We see," Garth assured him.

"What's your area of expertise, sir?" Randall asked.

"Quentin, please," Barnaby said. "I'm enjoying the informality of our discussion here." He smiled again. "My specialty lurks somewhere between anthropology, politics, and history. A relatively new discipline generally referred to as sociology, although my interests remain rather . . . expansive. Particularly in light of my temporary appointment to His Majesty's armed forces."

Booth chortled. "He's a bleedin' spook."

Barnaby cut his eyes at him. "Let's be careful, shall

we, Sergeant?" he said, his tone cool. "Accurate definitions are always important, but not always appropriate."

Garth noted the exchange with interest. So much for dispensing with rank. There was pure British steel beneath Barnaby's deceptively soft, academic exterior.

"Sorry, Prof," Booth mumbled, chastened.

The hardness faded from Barnaby's face. "All right, then." He regarded the three Americans again. "I find Sergeant Booth quite invaluable, you know. The Royal Australian Army has seen fit to loan him to me as an aide for the duration of my tenure as field researcher and adviser to CAID in the Pacific Theater of Operations."

"What's CAID?" Lucas asked.

"Combined Allied Intelligence Directorate," Barnaby told him. "You'll understand if I can't be too specific, but it's rather a sort of clearinghouse for information gathered about the Japanese as we prosecute the war. Modern warfare requires that we address psychological factors as never before, in purely scientific terms. In other words, we want to know our enemy. If we know what makes him tick, we will ultimately know how best to defeat him."

"Makes sense," Garth commented. "You can't bait a coyote with a head of lettuce."

Barnaby brightened. "That's quite good," he said. "And quite wonderfully rustic. It illustrates my point exactly. Did you read that somewhere?"

Garth shook his dark head. "Nope. Learned it riding fence in West Texas with my daddy when I was six years old. You want to bring a varmint in, fox him at his own game, you've got to know his habits. Why he does what he does."

"Ah, your father was a rancher," Barnaby said.

Again, Garth shook his head. "Texas Ranger."

"How marvelous!" The Englishman was genuinely intrigued. "And your mother?"

"Chiricahua Apache," Joe Garth said. "Full-blooded."

"Ah, that would explain your distinctive physiognomy," Barnaby continued, gathering steam. "Typically Native American, with the characteristic cheekbone structure and vestigial Mongolian fold of the eyelid—"

He caught himself, looked down, and smiled sheepishly. "You must forgive me," he said. "I'm afraid my enthusiasm for social anthropology occasionally leads me off into interminable digressions. I beg your pardon."

"It's all right," Garth told him.

"My original point," Barnaby said, "is that the Japanese are not insane, but extraordinarily motivated. That you witnessed such extreme combat tactics recently, Captain Lu—pardon me—*Art,* alarms me . . . but it does not surprise me. For many months now, we have received scattered intelligence reports of the deployment of special enemy squadrons with a suicidal mandate. In my opinion, what you saw two days ago was the first full-scale operation by aerial units of the *Shimpu Tokubetsu Kogekitai*—which translates as 'Divine Wind Special Attack Force.' Nisei translators, American soldiers of Japanese descent, at CAID have come up with the shorter, somewhat more derogatory term *kamikaze* when referring to these units. Like *Shimpu,* the word means 'divine wind'—a reference to a great typhoon that blew away an invading Mongol fleet and saved Japan from being overrun in the thirteenth century—but has pejorative overtones of foolishness or recklessness when used colloquially."

"Collo . . . *what*?" Booth interrupted.

"When used commonly, Sergeant," Barnaby rephrased. "And *Tokubetsu*—sometimes referred to as *Tokko-tai* or simply *Toku*—means 'Special Attack,' which is a euphemism for *suicide* attack." He coughed. "We in the intelligence-gathering community have known for some time that the kamikaze existed, but many of my colleagues had hoped that the Japanese high command would not go so far as to actually use them. Not to sound immodest, but I myself have entertained no such illusions.

"I can tell you that the contemporary Japanese soldier is a warrior such as the United States has never before encountered in a conflict of this international scale. He is not merely willing to die if necessary for his country, as most of us on the Allied side are, but to *plan to die on purpose* for his nation and his emperor. The emotional heat of banzai charges—of which you have all no doubt heard—notwithstanding, legions of completely sane, intelligent, sober-minded young Japanese men are currently prepared to lose their lives while executing preplanned strikes against the enemy if in so doing they will further the cause of the empire. They have the capacity to make themselves do this because in Japan, at the moment, certain social prerequisites have been met that enable the common soldier to metamorphose into a suicide soldier.

"The first and most important of these is an absolute belief in the existence of an afterlife. Not just any afterlife, either—but an *attractive* and *rewarding* afterlife. The state-approved religion in Japan is Shintoism, and Shinto doctrine teaches that all Japanese soldiers killed in battle are reincarnated instantly at Yasukuni Shrine, to live forever in glory as minor gods."

Garth nodded slowly. "Makes sense. It's pretty tough to fight a man who believes that even if he gets killed, he doesn't die."

"And that he's going off to a life better than the one he's got here on earth," Randall added.

"Exactly," Barnaby confirmed. "And by the way, this concept of a rewarding afterlife for the fallen warrior is not at all uncommon in the religions of the world. The Vikings believed that if killed in battle they would be admitted to Valhalla, the great hall of the supreme Norse god Odin, where they would feast, drink, fight, fornicate, and otherwise engage in riotous debauchery until the end of time. Not an unappealing fate, if you happened to be a Viking.

"I just stated that the United States has never before encountered, on an international scale, a foe willing to sacrifice his earthly life for a supposed existence in the hereafter. But your country has come up against such an opponent on a *smaller* scale—during the Moro Rebellion right here in the Philippines, at the beginning of this century. The religion was Islam in this case, with its concept of the heroic martyr. The Moros, as you probably know, are devout Filipino Muslims of the southern islands, and were engaged in a nasty protracted conflict with the U.S. Marines after Spain lost the Philippines to America as a consequence of the Spanish-American War."

"See, when the Prof gets goin'," Booth interjected, exhaling smoke, "there's no bloody stoppin' him."

Barnaby smiled tolerantly at the sergeant, then glanced at Garth, Randall, and Lucas. "He's quite right, you know. I hope I'm not boring you."

"Far from it," Randall said. "I've been fighting this war for a long time without really understanding why the Japs do what they do, and it's good to hear something that sounds like straight talk instead of propaganda for a change." Garth and Lucas nodded their agreement.

"I appreciate that," Barnaby said. "Back to the Moros. A warrior would prepare himself with prayer and ritual, then run, sword in hand, directly into a marine encampment, cutting and slashing as he went, taking down as many of the enemy as he could before he himself was killed. His reward for this, according to the Koran—the Islamic Bible, if you will—was and is an eternity in the Muslim paradise, endlessly serviced by droves of 'dark-eyed houris'—the beautiful and willing slave girls that apparently abound in the afterlife."

"Hell, sounds good to me," Lucas said. "*Droves of houris,* you say? God*damn.* I like this religion."

Everyone laughed politely except Booth, who laughed out loud. Barnaby shrugged. "Perhaps you can convert after the war."

"Well, I'd consider it," Lucas replied, " 'cept I don't think it'd go over real big with Henrietta back in Des Moines. Henny—that's my wife."

"Anyway," Barnaby went on, "armed with little more than their religious beliefs, the Moros were extremely effective against you Americans during your initial occupation of the Philippines. The nickname 'leatherneck' comes from the leather-and-steel collar the U.S. Marines began wearing during the height of the Moro Rebellion—too many slashed throats and beheadings to suit them.

"So, you see, the concept of a glorious afterlife for the martyred soldier is not unique to Shintoism. Now, you combine that idea with something like the traditional Bushido ethic of the samurai warrior, which holds that loyalty to one's lord and clan—the emperor and Japan, internationally speaking—outweighs every other consideration, including personal survival, reinforce it all with modern military codes of behavior like the Imperial Rescript to Soldiers and Sailors, and you get tremendous social pressure for the individual combatant to perform his duty—even to the extent of sacrificing his own life.

"Japanese society as a whole accepts these extreme standards of conduct for the nation's military as part of the twentieth-century doctrine of *Kokutai*—the 'National Policy.' Every man, woman, and child in Japan, for the past several decades, has been raised to believe that they are members of an utterly unique race and culture that must defend itself against the imperialism of Western nations in order to preserve that uniqueness. These concerns are not without merit. Look at history: prior to the outbreak of the present conflict, the Dutch controlled the East Indies, the French controlled Indochina, the British—as usual—had their fingers in every pie, including mainland China and of course India, and the United States controlled the Philippines and aggressively promulgated its economic interests throughout the western Pacific.

"Is it any wonder that Japan began to fear being carved up piecemeal by traditionally imperialist nations from the other side of the globe, like the rest of Indo-Asia? Hence the virulent nationalism that has seized the Japanese people as a whole and provided, in concert with the Shinto and Bushido beliefs I've already described, a logical construct by which they can accept the

notion of their sons fighting to the death on the battle-
field rather than surrendering—or killing themselves in
premeditated, suicidal attacks on the enemy."

"You sure you're on our side, Quentin?" Lucas
mused.

"Just playing devil's advocate, I assure you," Barnaby
said. "Again, I must warn you—I was a compulsive lec-
turer at Cambridge. Old habits die hard, I'm afraid, particularly when one finds a receptive audience."

"Don't get me wrong," Lucas said. "I like listening to
you. I just don't see how knowing all this helps us win
the war. So they had some gripes. Don't we all. How
does that justify them sneaking up on us at Pearl Harbor
like they did? Or murdering all those Chinese civilians
at Nanking? You make them sound so civilized. Well,
buddy—they don't act like it."

"From their point of view," Barnaby said, "they're
so civilized that they can't stand the thought of their
civilization being dominated by barbarians like us. Any
means of advancing the interests of the Empire of Japan,
therefore, are justifiable. And I maintain that the contemporary Japanese would rather perish as a race and a
nation than live some kind of diluted existence as just another Asian country absorbed by Western imperialism.

"They are not going to give up, gentlemen. What you
saw two days ago, Art—the kamikaze assault off
Samar—is only the beginning of many such attacks to
come. As we press closer to the Japanese mainland, I
predict these suicide attacks will increase in both frequency and variety. The Japanese are an industrious and
innovative people. They have no end of unpleasant sur-
prises in store for us. This is why I do what I do—collect
information that may help us understand their current
national state of mind, anticipate what they will do next,
and figure out how best to counteract it."

"Good luck," Booth commented acidly.

"As you can tell," Barnaby said, "Sergeant Booth is
not exactly the eternal optimist. You might well imagine
that this could be a sticking point in our professional
relationship, but fortunately I find his earthy simplicity

an effective counterbalance to my own predilection for arcane hypothesizing."

"Pardon?" Garth said.

"He keeps me in touch with reality," Barnaby explained.

"Okay." The Texan grinned good-naturedly.

"You know," Randall said, "when we were trying to get clear of the Leyte beaches at the end of our UDT op the other day, about to shoot our charges, a whole pack of Jap speedboats came roaring out in our direction—heading for the fleet, I guess. Some of them got caught in the explosions we set off, but a few got through. I was pretty out of it, but I thought I saw one of 'em ram a converted destroyer escort—the *Mayhew*—and explode."

Garth nodded. "It did. I saw it, too."

Barnaby leaned forward, his eyes bright with interest. "Indeed? And what did these speedboats look like, may I ask? Were they approximately twenty feet long? Made of wood?"

"That's right," Randall replied, exchanging a confirming nod with Garth.

"A single helmsman? Sitting in the stern behind a small pair of deck-mounted air scoops?"

"Yeah, that's right," Garth said. "I remember that. Two small scoops."

"Ah!" Barnaby sat back in his chair. "A *Shinyo*. A type of EMB—explosive motorboat. CAID has received random reports of their deployment throughout the Philippine Islands. You may have witnessed the first operational use of this weapon, I think."

"The helmsman put his boat right into the *Mayhew*'s side," Garth stated. "Blew her starboard bow clean off."

Barnaby nodded slowly. "Suicide planes, suicide boats. We've even heard rumors of manned torpedoes called *Kaiten*. It's started, gentlemen—Japan's do-or-die defense of her empire and homeland. Mark my words. As ugly as this war has been to date, it's about to get even uglier."

"I thought you said these little yellow bastards were

sane," Booth blurted. "I thought you said they were fok-kin' civilized."

"They are," Barnaby said. "As civilized as we are."

"But look what they're capable of," Lucas exclaimed. "And you claim they're just like us?"

"Yes. And ultimately, that's the most terrifying thing of all."

"What?" the pilot persisted. "That they're just like us? Why?"

Barnaby looked at him. "Because it means that the inverse is true," he said. "We, in spite of all our self-righteousness, are just like *them*."

"Bah!" Booth ground out the stub of his cigarette under his sandal. "I don't bloody well believe it, Prof," he growled. "You ain't never goin' to see us Allies kill thousands of innocent civilians like the Japs did at fok-kin' Nanking and Singapore."

Barnaby sighed and lifted his eyes to the horizon, thinking of the day-and-night bombing raids carried out by American Flying Fortresses and British Lancasters that had all but incinerated the civilian populations of German cities like Hamburg, Essen, and Bremen. Men would remember what they wanted to remember and forget what they wanted to forget. It was mandatory in war to elevate one's own atrocities to the level of justifi-able necessity, while at the same time condemning those of the enemy. And, he reminded himself, wars were not fought primarily by PhD lecturers from Cambridge, who had the luxury of stepping back off the front lines and indulging in analysis and philosophy. They were fought by working-class men like Sergeant Booth, who needed simple answers to hard questions so they could dehu-manize the enemy they had to kill.

Out on Leyte Gulf, to the southwest, an afternoon thunderstorm was building, its towering cumulonimbus cloud starkly white against the vivid blue of the sky. The Englishman gazed into the immense mushroom-shaped formation and smiled faintly.

"I pray you're right," he said to his aide.

Chapter Six

Early the following morning, while Randall was still tossing in his sleep, Major Barnaby, Sergeant Booth, and an RAAF pilot boarded the small Lysander that had been parked at the far end of the airstrip and took off, heading eastward. The British intelligence officer had been able to bid a quick farewell to Joe Garth, who, as per his habit, was up before dawn with a cup of black coffee.

"You never mentioned how you got that burn on your shoulder," Garth said as he shook hands.

Barnaby, fully dressed in khakis, short olive battle jacket, and sidearm, patted the fresh bandage under his shirt. "It's terribly embarrassing, I'm afraid," he said, smiling. "Not heroic in the least—unlike the injuries sustained by yourself, Lieutenant Randall, and Captain Lucas."

Garth smiled back. "Fall asleep in the steam room, Major?"

"Not quite that bad. I bent down to tie my bootlace and inadvertently leaned against the hot exhaust pipe of an amphibious tank. Damned nuisance. My own fault. It hurt worse than being shot in the foot."

Garth raised an eyebrow as he sipped coffee. "You were shot in the foot? How?"

Booth, standing nearby, cackled past his ubiquitous cigarette. "How? Bloody hell, the Prof here puts your Sergeant York to bleedin' shame! He—"

"You are undoubtedly the most talkative intelligence operative in the entire history of human intrigue, Sergeant Booth," Barnaby declared, cutting him off. Again, the soft, academic voice was firm—but not without humor. As Booth grumped in place, shuffling his feet, Barnaby winked at Garth and touched the fingertips of his right hand to his eyebrow. "A tale to be told another time, Joe," he said. "In another place. Good luck to you."

Garth returned the salute. "You too, Quentin."

The dregs of his coffee were cold and gritty on his tongue as Garth watched the Lysander carrying Barnaby and Booth bank gently into the thin mist of a distant rainsquall and disappear. He was sorry to see the personable, astute Briton go, but he had come to know that war was always like that. People appeared, began to make an impression, good or bad—and then abruptly vanished: wounded, killed, transferred, or just swept on by in the great uncontrollable flow of events like spindrift on the ocean surge. Paths crossed momentarily, fates intersected—but the contact was always fleeting. War distilled a person's entire existence down to a few key words or deeds that affected one or more other individuals within a fragment of time . . . and then that fragment, and that person—friend or enemy—was gone.

Joe Garth didn't worry much about fate. Everybody had one, and it was inescapable. End of story.

When he reached the top of the balcony stairs, he saw that Randall was up, hovering around the ward's pair of coffee dispensers. A rare cigarette was clamped between his lips, and he was squinting against the smoke coiling up around his eyes. Garth didn't like the way his friend looked.

" 'Morning, Charlton," Garth said, trying to tiptoe around his friend's troubled aura. "Sleep okay?"

"Mm—I guess. On and off. You?"

"Like a baby." The Texan lifted the top off one of the dispensers, releasing a cloud of aromatic steam. "You leave any for me?"

"The other one's full." Randall drew on his cigarette and gazed out through the Spanish archway toward the airstrip. "That Lysander's gone," he remarked.

"Yeah," Garth said, refilling his mug. "It took Barnaby and Booth off toward Samar about ten minutes ago."

"Huh. I would've liked to say good-bye." Randall moved toward the balcony chairs. "Interesting man."

"Yep."

They drew the chairs up near the balcony's low masonry railing and sat down. As they did, a trio of odd-looking aircraft overflew Minglaat's small natural harbor. They were twin-engine and twin-tailed, like the P-38 Lightning fighter, but noticeably larger. The main fuselage pod between the engine nacelles was bulky and bristling with guns. Unlike all the other planes frequenting the skies over Leyte Gulf, they were painted flat black, and together they resembled a close swarm of huge, predatory dragonflies.

"Now those are some evil-looking planes," Garth said. "Fast, too." He sipped coffee as the patrol droned off toward the northwest. "Never seen 'em before."

"P-61s," Randall said. "Black Widows. They're night fighters, equipped with twenty-mil cannon and radar. The latest thing from Northrop. A Black Widow can find a Jap plane in a cloud bank at midnight and shoot it down without the pilot actually seeing it."

"That right?"

"Uh-huh. And it makes me feel good to know they're up there, because this was on the foot of my bed when I woke up this morning." Randall passed a small sheet of paper over to Garth.

"Communication from Kaine, Frank, Lieutenant, UDT," Garth read aloud. "Aboard the USS *Nashville*

Leyte Invasion Support Fleet. To: Randall, Charlton, lieutenant, UDT, and Garth, Joseph, gunner's mate, UDT. Quote: *Where the hell have you two been and thank God you're all right. C-47 transport rerouted to Minglaat arriving October 27 approximately 1500 hours to evacuate you to rear-area facilities on Peleliu. We'll talk soon. Well done and welcome home.* Unquote. Signed: Frank."

Randall exhaled smoke. "The doctor who's been taking care of us—the one who looks like Neville Chamberlain . . ."

"Sheffield," Garth said.

"Right, Sheffield. He lifted our vital stats from our dog tags and sent a radio inquiry out to fleet the day we arrived. They've got some kind of clearinghouse set up to track missing personnel from the Leyte invasion. Turns out Frank Kaine's been going crazy trying to locate anyone left alive from our squad. When he saw our names he jumped on Sheffield's message and followed up."

Randall swallowed, cracked a weak smile, and drew on his cigarette. His fingers were trembling, and moisture glistened at the corner of his eye.

Garth looked him over for a moment. "Charlton," he said gently.

"Mm . . . yeah?"

"Sheffield told you Kaine's been going crazy trying to find anyone left alive from our squad?"

"Yeah."

Garth cleared his throat. "Sheffield tell you anything else?"

Randall shifted uncomfortably. "Sure. He told me that Kaine was looking for two other surviving combat swimmers named Bartlett and Drexel. So far, you and I are the only ones he's been able to find. So if we're the only two, and he doesn't know about Bartlett and Drexel . . ."

"That means he wasn't able to talk to Fitz or McNab during the past week," Garth filled in. "McNab would have told him about Bartlett and Drexel's raft blowing up, if he survived being shot. And Fitz—he was sitting on that sandbar, remember? Still in one piece, according to what you saw just before you told me to shoot the charges."

"Like I said," Randall muttered, "as far as Frank Kaine's concerned, we're the only two left alive from the original squad. That tells me Fitz and McNab didn't make it, like we were hoping, or Frank wouldn't be looking for 'anyone left alive.' And even if he doesn't know what happened to Bartlett and Drexel, we do. So unless Fitz and McNab turn up floating on a raft in the next few days, like us . . ."

His voice trailed off. Without warning, a look of pure anguish contorted his features. Garth was shocked by the suddenness, the intensity of it. Randall put one hand over his face, his cigarette still burning between his fingers, and bowed his head. His shoulders heaved once, and he let out a single harsh sob.

"Charlton," Garth said, touching him on the arm.

Randall moved his hand down until it covered only his mouth. His eyes were streaming, horrified, staring off at the horizon. "My whole squad," he said in a choked voice. "I lost my whole squad."

"Hey, hey," Garth told him, sitting forward in his chair. "Easy, now."

Randall's eyes wavered around onto his, focused, then welled up and overflowed again. "I lost them all, Joe," he whispered. "I lost them all."

Sheffield eased away from the side of Randall's cot and motioned to Garth, who was standing nearby.

"He'll doze until after lunch now," the doctor said. "The sedative is fairly mild."

Garth studied his friend, who was lying prone on the narrow bed with one elbow crooked over his eyes. His six-foot-plus frame suddenly looked very frail atop the rumpled sheets.

"What's wrong with him?" Garth asked. "Just exhausted, right?"

The doctor lowered his long Anglo-Saxon nose and regarded him over a pair of half lenses. "Partly," he said.

"But your lieutenant seems to be exhibiting preliminary symptoms of a full-blown case of battle fatigue. Delayed onset."

"Battle fatigue?" Garth repeated. "You mean like shell shock?"

"Shell shock is a term that came out of the First World War," Sheffield said. "Something happens to men when they get hammered by artillery for months on end while cowering in trenches. Their nerves are shattered, sometimes permanently. I'm sure you've seen it in veterans of your father's era."

Garth nodded. "Yes, sir. We had a few around town back in Laredo. They shook all day long. Any sudden noise, even a car horn, would drive them batty. They drank to stop shaking, and the drink made them shake even more. Folks around town wouldn't have much to do with 'em. Rummies with weak character, everyone said."

"That's a cruel and uninformed assessment," Sheffield declared. "I've seen too many brave men come down with battle fatigue to believe it has anything to do with weak character. Men simply have a point at which the accumulated strains of combat overwhelm them, some sooner than others. I consider it a legitimate medical condition. Of course, I don't get a lot of sympathy from the powers that be for my opinion. Commanders like General Patton would rather slap soldiers into shape than accept that men can take only so much. Of course, I concede that there'd probably be a stampede off the front lines and into the hospital wards if Eisenhower or MacArthur legitimized battle fatigue by publicly admitting such a thing exists."

"Lieutenant Randall doesn't have battle fatigue," Garth said. "He's just tired. We had a bad time during the Leyte landing, and ended up drifting around in the ocean for a week. He'll be okay. He's a stand-up guy. Always carries his own weight."

Sheffield smiled down at his overloaded clipboard and shook his head. "You see? You don't really understand what I'm saying to you. Whether or not your lieutenant

is a stand-up guy, quote-unquote, has *nothing whatsoever
to do with it.* Every man has a point at which his nervous
constitution starts to collapse inward, like a house of
cards. If Lieutenant Randall has been subject to continuous strain over the past months—as indeed most of us
have—he may have reached such a point.

"Uncontrollable feelings of guilt, paralyzing melan-
cholia, physical tremors—these are all symptoms of battle fatigue. I think your lieutenant is in the early stages
of it. If you like, I can evaluate him, give you a report
to take to the hospital on Peleliu. Maybe you can find
a sympathetic physician there."

"How do you evaluate someone for battle fatigue?"
Garth asked.

"Interview them, basically," Sheffield replied. "Ask
questions, observe how they respond. Note peculiarities,
odd mannerisms."

Garth shook his head. "He'll never do it, sir. Trust
me. Not Randall. You see, UDT men . . . they don't . . .
well . . . let's just say, we don't *get* things like battle
fatigue in UDT, sir. That's just the way it is. And we
have to be on that C-47 in a few hours."

Sheffield shrugged, suddenly looking very tired. "Suit
yourself, Garth. I have plenty of other patients in this
ward to keep me busy." He flipped over the next chart
on his clipboard. "Get your lieutenant up and moving
by two o'clock this afternoon. If he's traveling, it'll be
good for him to get his blood flowing again, and we can
use the bed."

"Yes, sir," Garth said. "Fourteen hundred hours."

He started to salute, but the doctor had already turned
away and begun walking toward the far end of the
infirmary.

Garth lay in his cot for the rest of the morning, reading. Back issues of *Life, Time,* and *The Saturday Evening
Post,* mostly. All war stuff: Rosie the Riveter, Allied
combat successes, Betty Grable's legs, Roosevelt's latest
comments to reporters, et cetera.

What he liked the most were the ads; they reminded

him of home. Pictures of apple pie and familiar skylines.
Baseball, Coca-Cola, and Camels. That new singer who
used to be with Tommy Dorsey's band—Fred Sinatra or
something—grinning up off the page with eyes like
bright blue headlights, surrounded by dancers from
Radio City Music Hall. Some guys had all the luck.

Randall, lying in the next cot, moaned once or twice
in his sleep but otherwise didn't move for four hours.
Garth went to find some lunch just after twelve, and
when he returned, bearing a plate of hot food, Randall
was beginning to toss himself awake. Garth let him wake
up slowly, and read a new copy of *Stars and Stripes* as
he sat on the edge of his cot.

"Aaghh," Randall said, rubbing his eyes. "How
long've I been asleep?"

Garth glanced at his watch. "A few hours. Brought
you some food." He indicated the plate on the bedside
table.

"Mm. Thanks. I think I'm hungry."

"Eat up, L.T.," Garth told him. "You need to grab a
wash and get dressed. That transport plane's supposed
to be here to pick us up in a couple of hours. We want
to be ready."

"Right, right." Randall pushed himself up to a sitting
position. "Whew. Feels like my head's stuffed with cotton." He rubbed his eyes again and blinked. "What'd
that doc give me?"

"A sedative," Garth explained. "Things caught up to
you a bit, that's all. You just needed a little more rest."

"Oh, yeah." Some of the pain returned to Randall's
face . . . then seemed to ebb away. "Rest. Yeah, that's
what I needed, I guess." He picked up the plate.
"Thanks for the grub. Any good?"

Garth grinned. "As good as powdered eggs and beans
can be."

He sipped his coffee and watched as Randall dug in.
There didn't seem to be anything wrong with his appe-
tite. And it took a robust man, to say the least, to keep
that army field-kitchen food down.

No, Sheffield must have been mistaken, Garth decided. Lieutenant Charlton Randall was going to be just fine.

The C-47 came floating in like a big silver sausage and bumped its wheels down on the very end of the airstrip in a puff of coral dust. Garth thought it odd that the transport didn't have some kind of military paint job, but what did he know? It had a big American star emblazoned on the fuselage and it was their ticket off Minglaat. Good enough. If the pilot thought it was safe to go roaring around the Philippine sky glinting in the sunlight like a shiny new dime, that was his business.

The C-47 managed to slow just enough to make a precarious 180-degree taxiing turn at the far end of the airstrip. It jockeyed around in front of the two parked Beaufighters, its twin props shimmering like disks of vibrating glass. Garth and Randall, dressed in borrowed khakis and carrying small canvas tote bags, jogged down the strip toward it.

The side door was open when they reached the aircraft. A crewman wearing a battered flight cap, headphones, and dark sunglasses beckoned impatiently.

The plane was starting to taxi forward again as first Randall, then Garth, threw their bags into the dark opening and hauled themselves inside. The door banged shut, and the roar of the engines began to rise in pitch before they could grope their way to the nearest of the small seats that lined both sides of the fuselage interior.

"Park it there!" yelled the crewman, who was on his way forward. He grabbed Randall by the shoulder and steered him toward a seat. "And there!" he yelled again, maneuvering Garth the same way. "Okay! Buckle up! Make it snappy!" Without another look at the two UDT men, he staggered forward to the cockpit. He was actually the copilot, Garth realized. There probably wasn't much chance he'd be bucking for head steward at TWA after the war.

Garth's teeth rattled in his head as the C-47 jounced down the crude runway, gathering speed. Hot sunlit colors—coral white and palm frond green—flashed past the small round view port directly opposite him. The floor of the plane leveled as the tail rose off the ground, and then, with a final shuddering bounce, the transport was airborne. Garth caught a glimpse of the mission's whitewashed walls as the C-47 cleared the end of the runway.

It banked immediately, dipping the wing opposite Garth and Randall, and the colors in the view port changed rapidly to aquamarine and ocean blue. Small naval craft of every description dotted the waters below, coming and going from Minglaat. The plane continued to bank steeply for a full ten seconds, then rolled back onto an even keel and began to climb through a low cloud.

Garth and Randall exchanged a look. There was no point in even attempting to talk at normal volume; the racket inside the aircraft was deafening. It was also difficult to see. Garth rubbed his eyes, waiting for them to get accustomed to the relative darkness.

It took him the better part of two minutes to realize that he and Randall were not the only passengers aboard. There were at least six or seven other men occupying the cargo compartment, most of them seated farther forward. Two were sprawled on top of the canvas tarp that covered pallets of supplies in the aircraft's tail. Another man sat apart from the others, occupying a seat about halfway down the cargo bay, arms folded and chin on his chest as if dozing.

Randall's vision continued to adjust to the dimness of the plane's interior until at last he was capable of making out some real detail. The first face he was able to see clearly gave him a nasty start. From the other side of the compartment, what appeared to be a parched human skull was staring at him out of heavy-lidded Asian eyes.

Randall blinked and looked again. It wasn't a skull—it was a living man. But *what* a man. Of medium height, whipcord-thin, long in the arm, and somewhat bow-legged, he was naked but for a patterned sash and loin-cloth, grass sandals, and some kind of elaborate headdress made of cloth and bird feathers. A machete-like sword hung at his hip. Brass bands adorned his upper arms, and strings of beads dangled around his neck. His face was Oriental in the extreme, with slanted eyes, a flat-bridged nose, and high, sharp cheekbones, but in a way not typically Japanese or Chinese. Rather, his features had an almost childlike delicacy, and his skin, stretched tight over his prominent facial bones, was quite dark. Complicating the man's appearance was the fact that his face had been finger-painted—decorated with short stripes of black, white, and red pigment.

"If that isn't war paint, I'll eat my mama's moccasins," Garth called into Randall's ear.

Randall nodded and leaned in close. "Looks like a Malay, doesn't he?"

"Yeah. Or something. From down around Java, maybe."

The slitted obsidian eyes moved from Randall to Garth and back again, while the incredible face to which they belonged remained absolutely expressionless.

"How about if we don't stare?" Randall suggested. "I'd hate to see this guy mad."

Garth laughed and leaned back in his seat.

Randall looked toward the rear of the compartment. The two men sprawled on the supply tarp were more typical of the soldiers he'd encountered throughout the Pacific campaign. Many months ago, on early assignment to the Solomon Islands, he'd shared temporary quarters with several members of the Royal Australian Army's Seventh Division—the unit that had turned the Japanese back from Port Moresby in Papua New Guinea, fighting hand-to-hand along the Kokoda Trail in the dense jungles of the Owen Stanley Mountain Range.

The gritty heroism of the Seventh in those desperate battles had saved Australia from certain invasion, and the representative soldiers Randall had met all shared the same look: starvation-lean, careless of their worn appearance, wary—like predators—even at rest, and as tough as ten years' hard labor. They'd told him their nickname for the rain-soaked, disease-infested killing grounds of New Guinea: "Green Hell." With characteristic Australian nonchalance they'd recounted their experiences in jungle fighting the Japanese—but such nonchalance, Randall soon realized, was misleading. Only the very toughest and very luckiest had made it out of the green hell of the Owen Stanley Range alive. And the ordeal had stamped them like a die.

The two men lying on top of the supply tarp had that same look. One of them was about Randall's height, six feet or so, and wore a short khaki battle jacket with the sleeves ripped off, exposing his powerfully muscled arms. Tattoos decorated his left biceps and right forearm. His threadbare khaki trousers were tucked loosely into the tops of his unlaced jungle boots, which were propped up on a crate of bulk medicinal quinine. A broad-brimmed Australian bush hat, similar to an American cowboy's Stetson, was tugged forward over his eyes, and longish locks of auburn hair curled down his tanned neck—Scots-Irish coloring burned biscuit brown. He appeared to be snoring.

His companion was a smaller man, several inches shorter and considerably less muscular. He bore a passing resemblance to Major Barnaby's aide, Booth, though without the sergeant's almost tubercular scrawniness. And his face, while thin, had none of Booth's vulpine quality; rather, his expression seemed to be one of live-and-let-live amiability. He wore a khaki battle shirt with the sleeves rolled up to the elbow, the same scarred jungle boots as his comrade, but instead of standard-issue Australian army khaki trousers, his lower half was clad in U.S. Marine Corps camouflage pants. They were at least a size too large for him, and the lower cuffs were ragged where the legs had been hacked off to the right length, probably with a knife, and left unhemmed. The baggy pants made him look smaller than he actually was.

Both Australians wore heavy gear belts with bullet pouches and holstered side arms, and had Sten submachine guns leaning up against their bodies within easy reach. The weapons, Randall knew, had been so placed out of unconscious reflex. For jungle fighters, old habits died hard—or they did.

Randall looked forward again. The man sitting alone in the middle of the plane stirred and lifted his head. He was American, dressed in U.S. Navy seaman's denim fatigues, and a Negro. Recrossing his arms, he looked around briefly, locked eyes with Randall for a split second, then lowered his chin back onto his chest and continued to doze.

The cluster of passengers near the cockpit bulkhead consisted of a swarthy Filipino in cutoff black pants, sandals, and a camouflage combat shirt; an older Caucasian of perhaps fifty-five, very tall and slender, wearing olive drab clothing and a sweat-stained Australian bush hat; and another Caucasian, perhaps ten years younger, in olive-and-khaki battle gear, with a chiseled face, broad mustache, and the look and carriage of a British career officer. The mustachioed man wore a black beret slanted over his right temple, as did two similarly clad soldiers of lesser rank sitting on either side of him.

Quite an odd assortment, Randall was thinking—just before the C-47 shuddered violently and a line of bullet holes ripped down the length of the fuselage roof from tail to cockpit, filling the cargo compartment with dust, shards, and thin, hot shafts of sunlight.

Chapter Seven

"*Z*eros!" a voice screamed from the forward section of the plane. "*Hang the fuck on back there!*"

Randall caught a glimpse of the copilot, twisted around in his seat and yelling, through the open cockpit door. Then the aircraft rolled into a ninety-degree port bank and all of a sudden Randall was lying on his back, still belted in place, his head spinning and his guts sliding into his throat. The larger of the two Australians who'd been napping on the cargo tarp landed on top of him, flailing. He clutched instinctively at the soldier, stopping his wild cartwheel across the compartment. On the other side of the big man, Garth did the same.

"*Bloody hellllllllll!*" shrieked the smaller Australian, flying past. He tumbled and bounced up the length of the transport and crashed into the trio of black-bereted soldiers just aft of the cockpit bulkhead.

Randall and Garth hung on to their man in desperation as the C-47 rolled past ninety degrees and went partially upside down, its hard port bank becoming a screaming dive. Their ears popped with the sudden change in altitude as they were first lifted out of their seats, lap belts straining, then pressed back against the wall of the fuselage, with the Australian pinned between them. The g forces acting on their bodies tripled as the pilots fought to pull the transport out of its plummeting nosedive.

Just as Garth thought his lungs were going to collapse, the giant invisible hand crushing his chest lifted off and the aircraft heaved level. The big Australian tumbled away from the two UDT men and crashed to the floor of the compartment. He got to his hands and knees, dazed, and in the next second Randall and Garth had him by the upper arms, hauling him into the seat between them.

"Belt in!" Garth shouted into his ear. The big man didn't have to be told twice; in one fast motion he locked the seat belt across his lap and yanked it snug.

Not a moment too soon. Without warning, a succession of ear-shattering explosions shook the aircraft. The cargo compartment was suddenly filled with sparks and choking black smoke. Blinded, Randall and Garth felt pressure increase against their backs once more as the C-47 rolled again to port.

A tremendous blast of air whipped the breath out of their mouths—and then the smoke was gone. They found themselves staring across the compartment at brilliant blue sky and a fast-changing panorama of white-and-gray clouds. The slipstream howled with banshee intensity past the tattered aluminum edges of the huge gap that had suddenly appeared in the opposite side of the aircraft.

The starboard rear quarter of the fuselage had been ripped away from the side door back to the tail assembly, and from the midline overhead to below the cargo compartment floor. Stunned, Randall watched as the Malay-looking tribesman huddled away from the enormous void at his left elbow, the feathers of his headdress fluttering wildly in the windblast.

A second later the blue-and-white skyscape was obscured by a huge, flashing silver form that roared downward past the stricken transport, seeming to avoid collision by mere inches. Garth caught a glimpse of the bright red meatball on the wingtip of the Japanese fighter as it corkscrewed by, and then the C-47 was pitching and yawing in the enemy interceptor's prop wash.

"Stay in your fuckin' seats!" the copilot screamed over the slipstream howl. *"We're gonna try to lose these bastards in the clouds! It's our only chance!"*

Lieutenant Gishiro Akiyama grimaced behind his flying goggles as he pulled his Mitsubishi A6M5 *Reisen* out of its dive past the crippled American transport and up into a steep, looping climb. He could literally feel the blood draining from his upper body and pooling in his legs as the g forces generated by the maneuver flattened him against his seat. The sleek fighter's powerful Nakajima radial engine sang in a throaty, rising howl as it drove up, up into the eye-burning blue sky.

At the apex of the loop, upside down, Akiyama craned his neck back and looked straight up at the deeper blue of the sea directly overhead. Then he was diving again, gathering speed, and the sea was back on the nose of his aircraft. The sun and the sky were behind him; to either side rose towering cumulonimbus thunderheads. Far below, like a tiny silver beetle fleeing through an immense white-sided canyon, the wounded C-47 flew on, trailing black smoke.

He watched as his friend and wingman, Ensign Jemmu Gato, completed his second firing pass and executed a snap roll over the helpless American. Akiyama grunted deep in his throat. He'd seen pieces fly off the transport's tail, but otherwise it appeared to have sustained little additional damage. Jemmu would receive an unmerciful roasting from his comrades upon their return to the squadron airfield on Luzon—he'd see to that—and serve him right. Ammunition was too valuable to waste these days.

Of course, the American cargo plane was so slow that it was easy to overshoot in their high-speed fighters, but that was no excuse. Jemmu—"Little Lover" to his fellow pilots, since at twenty-one he was still a virgin—had taken his first run at the target, and was an experienced enough combat flier to have made the necessary adjustments during his second pass. Probably dreaming of women again.

Akiyama concentrated as the speed of his dive increased. The unarmed transport was a sitting duck; there was no need to rush things. He would pull out well behind the target, reduce airspeed, and give it a good long rake with his twin twenty-millimeter cannon. One engine was smoking already. A leisurely, well-aimed burst would finish the job.

Lieutenant Akiyama smiled to himself. Life was good. The gods of war had offered up beautiful flying weather and a fat, easy kill. Tonight there would be sake to drink, comrades to laugh with, and a comfort woman from the barracks bordello to ease his overtense muscles. And best of all, there would be another morning . . . another opportunity to watch the rising sun climb above the horizon and spread its warm glow across the blue Pacific.

One more day. One more good day.

Gishiro Akiyama continued to smile as he pulled up a thousand yards behind the C-47 and began to close, his mind still partially occupied with thoughts of how good it was to be alive—and so did not notice the P-61 Black Widow boring in on his starboard flank before its twenty-millimeter cannon shells blew the canopy from his cockpit and his head from his shoulders.

"Yeahhh! We got us some help, boys!" The copilot was hollering again, gesturing out the C-47's forward windscreen. He turned and sent a thumbs-up back through the open cockpit door. *"American goddamned fighter!"*

Thank Christ, Randall thought. As he sat helpless in the damaged transport, the familiar knot of fear in his stomach seemed twice its normal size. He glanced past the big Australian beside him and located Joe Garth. As he'd expected, his teammate was looking calmly out through the giant gash in the fuselage, his tanned face impassive. Randall swallowed, tasting envy. It was as if the Texan had no nerves at all.

He shifted his gaze and locked eyes with the Australian. The big man's tough face broke into a grin.

"Dry mouth, mate?" he shouted.

Randall swallowed again and nodded, annoyed that his nervousness was so apparent. The Australian looked amused.

"Don't fret about it," he shouted again. "Me, I'm about to soil me trousers any second now." He turned and gazed up toward the forward section of the cargo compartment. *"Hey, Mick!"* he bellowed. *"You still in one piece, mate?"*

His comrade, who'd been grabbed by the black-bereted soldiers and strapped into a seat, raised his palms, shrugged, and mouthed a grimacing *"What?"*

"Never mind!" the big man yelled, waving a hand. *"Forget it!"*

There was a change outside the aircraft and Randall's eyes swung again to the huge breach in the fuselage. Wisps of gauzy white mist were beginning to stream past the tattered edges of the gap. A gust of rain beat into the rear of the cargo compartment, drenching the fluttering tarpaulins that covered the supplies, and another smell—clean, tangy, metallic—mingled with the odors of engine exhaust and burnt aluminum: ozone. As the gap began to white out completely, Randall realized that the pilot had to be taking them directly into one of the nearby thunderheads, seeking cover.

A second blast of rain whirled into the compartment. The cloud became thicker, then abruptly cleared, revealing a few more seconds of blue sky. Randall took the opportunity to search for signs of other aircraft, but could see nothing. He was aware of a prickling at the back of his neck. There were still fighters out there—some friendly, some not. No way to know how many.

The gap opposite him went into whiteout—and then the C-47 was shaking like a broken jalopy again as cannon shells smashed into the forward fuselage. There was a shattering sound. A human scream, barely audible, came back from the cockpit. Randall stared toward the front of the plane, trying to see what was happening, but the cockpit was filled with dirty smoke that billowed out into the cargo compartment through the bulkhead door.

He caught a glimpse of the black-bereted British officer lurching out of his seat and clawing his way forward as the stricken C-47 began to roll over on its starboard wing—and then the white wall of cloud darkened to charcoal gray and torrents of rain began to batter in through the gaping wound in the plane's side.

Ensign Jemmu Gato's heart was hammering in his throat as his *Reisen* dodged over the bullet-riddled American transport and arced up through the center of the boiling thunderhead. Flying blind, he kept the stick pulled back between his legs until he was completely inverted at the top of his looping climb, then rotated the plane 180 degrees on its long axis, executing a perfect Immelmann roll by feel alone. Two seconds later the fighter shot out of the clouds and into clear blue sky again, several hundred feet higher than the transport and heading in the opposite direction.

Except for the pounding in his throat, Gato felt numb. Gishiro Akiyama had been like an older brother from the days of flight training onward—friend, mentor, and watchdog. They'd flown and fought wing to wing for more than two years and had shot down seventeen Allied aircraft between them—mostly the slower, less maneuverable Grumman F4F Wildcat.

Those had been great days for pilots such as Gishiro and him. Nothing the Americans or British had could match the speed and agility of the sleek aerial hunter they'd nicknamed the Zero. But those days were long gone . . . a sweet, distant memory. Gone like Gishiro, erased in an instant in a ball of fire. Now there were terrifying new enemy aircraft in the skies, warplanes that could outrun, outmaneuver, and outshoot the durable *Reisen* in any head-to-head contest: Hellcats, Corsairs, Lightnings, Spitfires, Beaufighters, Thunderbolts. . . .

Jemmu Gato stared down past his port wing. . . .

And this thing.

It was black, ugly, alien. It had twin tails like the feared P-38 Lightning, but was much, much larger—almost the size of a Nakajima *Donryu* heavy bomber. But it was also *fast* . . . clearly faster than his game little *Reisen*. And it was certainly more heavily armed.

It was coming, climbing toward him across the great cathedral of clouds in a rapid turn . . . *accelerating* upward!

Raw courage was all very well and good, but the smart money was on the guy who had an edge. That was the way U.S. Army Air Forces captain Albert Sennett saw it. And a brand-new, radar-equipped, quadruple-cannon P-61B Black Widow night fighter was a whole lot of edge.

God *damn*, he loved this plane.

Nothing the Japs had could touch it. Nothing was as strong or fast, or packed as much of a punch. He and his crew, gunner Bob Gales and radarman Dave "Smitty" Smith, had taken down twenty Jap planes in a little over seven weeks, alternating day and night patrols. The smoke trail from number twenty-one was still hanging in the air behind them. Number twenty-two was just coming onto the Black Widow's nose about two miles ahead.

Sennett licked his lips, a little tense as usual but feeling fine. It was good to be the guy with the edge. That was why he'd campaigned to get into P-61s, tapped every connection he knew in order to transfer out of Wildcats and into something more up-to-date. Hell, back over Bougainville he'd had to run like a singed jackrabbit during a couple of Wildcat-Zero dogfights . . . would have gotten his ass shot off like the other guys in his flight if he hadn't. Screw that.

Now he had *Dark Lark* to carry him around the Pacific theater. He'd come up with the name himself. Even painted the combination bird-and-pinup-girl nose art himself, and it hadn't turned out half bad for an amateur effort. The *Dark Lark* babe had *real* big tits.

Captain Al Sennett was in the military for life, as a career, and had no intention of getting himself killed in this war or any other. He'd given the subject a lot of thought. The thing was, you had to participate in enough combat that you built up some credit, collected a few laurels—but you couldn't be stupid about it. You couldn't be flying around shooting at high-performance Jap fighters in some antiquated piece of junk. That shit would get you killed. You had to stack the deck in your favor, but still have enough sense to book for home if the fight began to get out of your control. That was it, basically: you had to stay in control of things. Maintain a nice cushion of safety in a very dangerous business.

You had to have an edge.

Dark Lark was his. Engaging a lone Zero with a P-61 Black Widow was like taking on a caterpillar with a steamroller. He almost felt sorry for the Jap. Almost.

The Zero was diving now, trying to keep *Dark Lark* from lining up directly behind it. Al Sennett smiled. The Jap would try to evade him using a split S—a snap roll into a dive followed by a pullout. It was a favorite maneuver of Japanese fighter pilots, and one he was far too experienced to fall for.

Very soon now, he'd splash Nip number twenty-two. Then he'd locate that shot-up C-47 and escort it to the nearest airfield. And then he'd go back to home base and sample some of that rice-and-raisin hooch the squadron bootlegger had recently acquired.

Business as usual.

Jemmu Gato held tight into his descending turn, keeping one eye on the twin-engine black demon behind his left shoulder. There had been a day when the *Reisen* could maintain a tighter turning radius than any American fighter—it was possible to spiral and spiral until a Yankee pursuer either broke away or *you* were on *his* tail. But not now. Big as it was, the black plane turned just as tightly as he did, even as it gained on him.

Gato yanked the stick and threw his fighter into a downward half snap roll, initiating the split-S maneuver. The scream of the Nakajima engine was deafening as the *Reisen* plummeted toward the ocean far below. Gato felt his buttocks lift away from the pilot's seat as he free-fell with the aircraft, held in place only by his harness.

As he neared the bottom of the dive and began the pullout, he was startled to see the American warplane, like a great black phantom, shadowing him directly off his port wingtip. It was both close enough and far enough away to be able to compensate for any escape maneuver he might attempt.

Toying with him.

Gato peeled away to starboard, knowing the American would follow.

"Jesus, Al—you gonna splash this guy or what?"

Dark Lark's gunner sounded agitated. Sennett fingered his throat mike and grinned. "Sure thing, Bob. He gets any lower, he's gonna run out of sky. He'll have to flatten out over the water. We'll punch his ticket there."

"Well, okay." Gales's exasperation seemed to moderate.

"How you doing back there, Smitty?" Sennett called.

"Good, boss," the radarman replied, his voice crackling in Sennett's earphones. "Just along for the ride."

"Stay sharp. We're gonna take this sonofabitch out in a few seconds."

"Roger that."

Al Sennett ran his thumb over the firing button of the twenty-millimeter cannon as the Black Widow's nose tracked around onto the fleeing Zero.

He just loved a sure thing.

Ensign Jemmu Gato was thinking several things simultaneously.

If he stopped twisting, turning, and diving . . . if he

flew level even for a second . . . he would be shot down. And there was no point to that.

Gishiro Akiyama—and many others—were watching him expectantly from Yasukuni. The emperor, the living god, was watching him. The souls of his ancestors were watching him. Reminding him that, above all else, there was Duty and Loyalty.

His comrades in the squadron, knowing that he admitted to being a virgin, called him "Little Lover" and assumed he was afraid of women. He did not feel obliged to explain that he had promised his heart to Toshi, a student girl he had met just before enlisting, and wished not to defile himself with meaningless sex acts before returning at war's end to marry her. His thoughts toward her—and she herself—were that pure.

Toshi, like his father and mother, would expect him to do his best.

He had long been an admirer of the great Japanese fighter ace Hiroyoshi Nishizawa, whose flying skills, leadership, and commitment to emperor and empire were second to none. Nishizawa had once boasted that he would never be defeated in air-to-air combat, and then gone on to prove it by downing over eighty enemy planes. On one memorable occasion, over the Solomon Islands, after having shot down six Wildcats in a single engagement and thinking he would not be able to make it back to base in his damaged fighter, he had sought to claim one more American by using the *tai-atari* tactic. But the skies around him had been empty. Those opponents he had not destroyed already had fled. So Hiroyoshi Nishizawa had simply limped home to fight another day.

Such exemplary conduct was nothing short of inspiring.

Ensign Jemmu Gato swallowed hard. There was no way he was going to be able to shake off the black American fighter, much less shoot it down.

He yanked the stick back, stood the *Reisen* on its tail, and drove it straight up into the sky.

* * *

"Hang tight," Al Sennett radioed his crew. "This little bastard isn't throwing in the towel yet."

He pulled the Black Widow up into a near-vertical climb, following the Zero. The distance between the two aircraft began to close rapidly. Again, Sennett smiled to himself, satisfied. Got to have that *edge*. The Jap couldn't outpower the P-61 in a straight climb. A little closer and he'd end it.

The Zero grew large in his windscreen gunsight, not quite centered. He tweaked the steering controls as he kept the throttles of the P-61's twin supercharged Pratt & Whitney engines fully depressed. The Black Widow continued to gain on the Zero as the two planes clawed their way skyward, one behind the other.

Unconsciously, Al Sennett rubbed his thumb once more over the smooth surface of the twenty-millimeter firing button. The Jap was losing momentum as he maintained his vertical climb. Very soon now he would have to wing over into another dive—probably some variation of the split-S maneuver—or stall. A fast adjustment, and *Dark Lark*'s cannon would catch the Zero before it could build up speed.

Six hundred yards ahead of the Black Widow, Jemmu Gato cut his engine.

The Zero floated up another few feet, hung motionless in the air for a long second . . . then dropped tailward straight down. The weight of its engine, combined with Gato's last-minute aileron adjustment, flopped it over on its back. The nose fell, the engine coughed back to life— and then the plane was diving straight back down the way it had come.

The oncoming American fighter was a huge black mass before Ensign Jemmu Gato's wide, triumphant eyes.

Al Sennett's jaw dropped and he yanked the controls hard to starboard, knowing it was already too late. The Japanese pilot's unconventional maneuver had caught him completely off guard.

A horrible freezing sensation gripped his spine, neck, and skull.

The Zero was going to ram.

"God—no," Sennett whispered.

The two warplanes collided at an altitude of eleven thousand feet and exploded. In the partially intact rear third of the Black Widow's central fuselage pod, Radar Operator Smitty Smith, hideously burned, lived long enough to be aware of his own death when, forty seconds after Ensign Jemmu Gato's *tai-atari* counterattack, the wreckage entrapping him hit the sunlit blue surface of Leyte Gulf.

Chapter Eight

The C-47 was standing on its starboard wingtip, banked ninety degrees in a shuddering shallow dive. Garth, Randall, and the big Australian were dangling from their lap restraints on the port side, looking straight down through the great rip in the fuselage opposite them. They could see nothing outside the aircraft but a swirling vortex of gray black vapor, punctuated by frequent lightning flashes. It had taken Randall the better part of a minute to realize that the ear-splitting concussions shaking the plane were not twenty-millimeter shell strikes but nearby claps of thunder.

The solid wall of dark cloud shredded momentarily, and for a second or two, Garth could make out several tiny islands, green blots in a carpet of aquamarine blue. The coastline of a larger island slid into view—and then the vibrating panorama was obscured by black cloud once again.

Yells came from the front of the transport. Randall cranked his head sideways and stared forward. The smoke from the cockpit had thinned, but the interior of the C-47 was so dim that he could barely make out the seats and passengers immediately behind the bulkhead.

"Where'd those black berets go?" Garth shouted to him.

Randall looked again. Yes—there was the skinny Aussie who'd been catapulted the length of the plane during the initial attack, belted in place on the starboard side and nervously chewing his lower lip. But the three British soldiers who'd been seated near him were gone.

There was a change in the engines' ragged pitch and the transport began to roll back to port, leveling out. Garth sucked in deep gulps of air as he felt himself settle back into his seat, the pressure across his gut easing.

"Everyone brace for crash-landing!" The voice was young and shrill. Garth and Randall glanced forward to see one of the black-bereted soldiers standing in the cockpit doorway, hanging on for dear life. His face was streaked with blood. "The major is going to try to set her down on a strip of beach up ahead!"

The *may-juh*. The young Englishman's accent was even more proper and crisp than Quentin Barnaby's, Randall thought. As if he should have been chasing batted balls on some Etonian cricket pitch rather than going down in a shot-up warplane in the southwestern Pacific.

There was a loud bang, and a pennant of orange flame began a frenzied dance in the slipstream outside the void in the fuselage. The C-47 jerked to starboard and began to roll again. There was a tremendous vibration, as if the blades of a giant fan had suddenly begun hitting the top of the aircraft.

"Bloody right engine's burning up!" was all Randall heard before the fire and the dark cloud opposite him changed to blue sky . . . then to a sunlit mist of whirling raindrops . . . to a blurred chaos of green foliage. . . .

Something walloped the plane with tremendous force, and the aircraft heaved upward. Garth's stomach bottomed out in his groin. Everyone who hadn't already done so bent forward and locked their fingers behind their necks in the crash-ready position.

This is stupid, Randall thought, staring at the scarred metal floor between his knees. *As if hunching into a ball is going to help when this crate hits a mountain.* But he kept his hands behind his head.

A second impact, even more violent than the first, shook the transport. For a moment Garth was sure his spine had snapped. There was a high-pitched thrashing sound, and a flurry of shredded foliage blew in through the gap in the fuselage.

"Hold on!" someone shrieked. *"We—"*

The third impact cracked the plane in two.

The fuselage broke apart just behind the wing roots. Randall watched in helpless fascination as a ragged ring of daylight appeared around the midsection of the cargo compartment . . . widened. . . .

There was a screech of tearing metal, and sunlight flooded into the interior, accompanied by a blast of fresh air. A blinding font of sand and spray followed, and the rear half of the transport was wrenched sideways.

Choking, his senses rattled by vibration, Garth twisted his head enough to look forward and see clouds of spray whirling against blue sky and green sea . . . the emerald water split by long, parallel lines of white foam. . . .

The tail section of the aircraft was skimming backward along the surface of the sea, leaving a wake like a planing motorboat.

"Fokkin' hell . . . ," Garth heard the big Australian beside him exclaim.

The hammering vibrations ebbed rapidly as the tail section lost momentum. With a fresh thrill of alarm Randall realized that he and the others had no time to rejoice at being alive. When the fuselage stopped skimming, it would sink.

"Get unbuckled!" he heard himself yell. The tail section shimmied to a halt and tilted. Water began to surge in over the lower lip of the break. *"Everyone get out!"*

Stupid thing to say.

Randall fumbled for his own lap belt as green water boiled up the slanting floor, and the horizon and blue sky and sunlight slid out of sight above the top edge of the fracture. The aluminum of the fuselage groaned and popped as the sea clutched at it.

Garth got his belt unhooked and glanced up in time to see the black seaman go under, still struggling to free himself from his seat. Garth pushed himself to his feet, lunged toward the drowning sailor—but was engulfed by an onrushing wall of foam as the wreckage rolled to port and the air trapped in the tail belched out through the gap in the side of the fuselage. The surging water slammed him backward, sideways, then hurled him out through the gap as well.

Something raked his shoulder, his lungs stung as they took in salt water . . . and then he was on the surface, spluttering and coughing. He felt suction tugging at his legs, kicked and clawed in the opposite direction, and caught a glimpse of the C-47's vertical tail fin—half shot away—sinking into a churning cauldron of white foam.

"Charlton!" he yelled.

As if in direct response, three wooden crates erupted to the surface around him. He floundered toward the nearest one, got an arm over top of it, and hung there, retching salt water. Fifteen feet away, the tip of the damaged tailplane sank slowly out of sight.

Joe Garth heaved in three great breaths of air and dove, pulling hard for the aircraft. His overstressed body felt depleted of oxygen almost immediately, but he ignored the gnawing air hunger, swallowed, and kept stroking downward. The water was clear, a bright, pale green. Just ahead and ten feet below him was the silver-gray bulk of the fuselage, simmering streams of air bubbles. Garth kicked for the forward section where the final, catastrophic fracture had occurred.

Two human forms rose past him, heading for the surface. One was small and dark, the other larger and lighter in color. The Malay tribesman and the big Australian. Good. He wouldn't be the only survivor.

The fuselage was lying on a white sand bottom at a depth of about twenty feet. Thank Christ it wasn't deeper. He placed a hand carefully on the torn metal at the top edge of the fracture and pulled himself around and down into the wreckage.

Randall was coming out of the dim interior, struggling to make headway with the limp body of the black seaman in tow. There was a feebleness to his movements that told Garth he was only seconds from passing out. Ignoring the ache in his own lungs, the Texan took two strokes forward, pried Randall's fingers from the seaman's shirt collar, and shoved him toward the surface. Then, one arm around the sailor's chest, he kicked off the top of the fuselage himself and stroked upward with all his remaining strength.

His temples were throbbing and his brain was shutting down when he broke the surface. He threw back his head and sucked in a huge gulp of air; sending pins and needles stinging through his chest. He reeled in the water, dizzy with oxygen.

"Let go, Joe! I've got him!"

It was Randall, maneuvering up beside him. Exhausted, Garth released the black sailor and drifted onto his back, wheezing. He felt a hand press between his shoulder blades, keeping him up.

"Easy, mate, easy," the big Australian panted, treading water next to him. "Get your wind, now."

Garth nodded, too spent to answer. Another hand came up under his neck and he turned to see the tribesman—face paint smeared, and feathered headdress matted but miraculously still in place—swimming on his opposite side. The yellow-brown skin on the gaunt face looked as taut and shiny as that of a shrunken head.

Then, unexpectedly, the tribesman grinned, his fierce visage rearranging itself into a display of fine lines and wrinkles. Garth blinked, taken off guard. The man's front teeth were filed to sharp points.

"How's that for fine bloody dental work, eh?" the Australian grunted. He spat a mouthful of seawater. *"Paagh."*

The three of them sculled through the negligible swell toward one of the floating medicine crates. Garth righted himself as they neared it, his breathing back under control.

"I'm okay," he said. "Thanks." He looked at the tribesman. *"Terima kasih."*

The skull face split into a fresh grin. *"Kembali."*

The Australian moved around to the far side of the crate. "Speak a little island Malay, do ya then, mate?"

Garth shrugged. "No. Just enough to say 'Thank you' and stay out of trouble."

"That's more than I know," the Aussie said, spitting again. He glanced at the tribesman. "What'd he say back to you?"

" 'You're welcome,' I think."

"Look," the big man said, "there's your mate over there."

He pointed. Garth turned and caught sight of Randall draped over his own crate about twenty yards away. He was supporting the head of the black sailor, who was floating on his back and breathing with some difficulty.

"Let's kick over to them," Garth said. "Maybe get the two crates lashed together somehow."

"You're on," the Aussie said.

It took them several minutes to swim the twenty yards. By the time they got there, the black seaman was upright in the water, breathing more or less normally, his hands interlocked with Randall's across their crate. He looked reasonably calm, Garth thought, but very much out of his element.

"Everybody all right?" Randall asked.

Garth and the Australian nodded. The tribesman grinned uncomprehendingly.

"What about you, mate?" the Aussie asked the seaman.

The black man nodded slowly. "Still warm. But I'll tell y'all up front, like I just told the lieutenant here: I cain't swim." The Mississippi accent was thick, but not impenetrable. Garth, accustomed to the subtleties of Southern dialect, automatically took note. The man was an urban Negro, not a field hand.

"That's a fokkin' disadvantage at this point," the Australian commented.

The black sailor nodded again. "Sho' nuff."

"Well, just hang on, mate," the big Australian said. "We'll do the swimmin' for ya." He nudged Garth. "You still see the plane down there?"

"What?" The UDT man looked puzzled. "Why?"

The Aussie had put his head underwater. A few seconds later it came up. "I see it," he announced. "Back soon."

Before anyone could speak, he inverted himself and dove.

"Where the hell's he going?" Randall asked.

Garth shrugged. "To the plane, I guess."

"What is he, crazy?"

"I'm starting to think so."

Randall puffed his cheeks and exhaled slowly. Then he took a long look around. They were in the middle of a narrow lagoon that lay between the exposed coral of an offshore barrier reef and the white-sand beaches of a mountainous, jungle-covered island. Other islands of varying sizes were visible in the near and far distance, hazy in the late afternoon humidity. Isolated thunderheads rose sporadically on the horizon like great puffy mushrooms. "You see the front half of the plane anywhere?" he asked Garth.

"No," Garth said. He rotated himself 360 degrees, treading water.

"Any other people?"

"Not a one."

"Shit." Randall gazed helplessly at the narrow strip of beach. "They can't all have gone down with the forward section . . . can they?"

Garth shook his head. "I couldn't tell you. I hope not."

Suddenly Randall was irritated. Four other guys around him and nobody knew anything. One he couldn't communicate with, another couldn't swim, a third was fucking around underwater somewhere, and even Joe seemed to be thinking in slow motion. He was irritated because The Rules said he was supposed to take charge of the situation, and he was irritated because he was scared. And tired. Tired of being scared. Here he was back in the goddamn ocean again, with everything completely and totally FUBAR—Fucked Up Beyond All Recognition. The familiar ball of dread in his stomach felt like a lead pig dragging him toward the bottom.

"Well, why the hell don't you . . ." he blurted, glaring at Garth—and caught himself. His eyes shifted downward. Taking out his frustrations on his friend would make him look like even more of a jerk; even less in control. "Where the hell's that Aussie?" he growled instead.

Garth regarded him steadily for a moment, then took a couple of deep breaths. "I'll see," he said. There was a light splash as he inverted himself in a surface dive and disappeared.

Randall began a slow frog kick in the direction of the beach, perhaps two hundred yards away, pushing the crate and the dangling black seaman. "Help a little if you can," he muttered.

"Yes, sir. Tryin' to kick some," the seaman replied, puffing. "Think I'm gettin' the hang of it."

"Good."

The silent tribesman, the dark feathers of his headdress bedraggled and hanging limp, moved to one end of the crate and began to push as well, using a one-handed dog paddle that was surprisingly effective. Randall gazed at the island: thin strip of white-sand beach, no surf, overhanging palms with long, spindly trunks angling out from the brush line. Steep terrain, heavily covered by jungle, rising almost immediately from the beach to a high point of perhaps seven or eight hundred feet at the island's center. You could almost smell the heat, the steaming vegetal *density* of the atmosphere under those trees. Feel the presence of the swarms of insects waiting to eat you alive.

Randall felt his spirits sink another notch. If there was one thing he hated about the tropics, it was the goddamn bugs.

A sudden splash off to his right startled him. It was the big Australian, gulping air and rolling over onto his back. He seemed to be weighed down by something. A few seconds later Joe Garth reappeared, also supporting some kind of weight. Together, he and the Aussie kicked over to the crate and hung on to the free end.

"*Bloody. . . . hell . . . ,*" the Australian panted, his long reddish-brown hair plastered down his sunburned neck.

"What was that all about?" Randall demanded.

The Aussie grinned, still puffing. He shifted in the water and the short barrel of a Sten submachine gun broke the surface next to him. "Need our weapons, don't we?" he explained. "Got me and Mick's choppers here, plus our ammo." He glanced at Garth and his grin widened. "Well, your mate's got most of the ammo."

Garth nodded and spat a stream of water between his teeth. "I thought our friend here was going to drown trying to carry all that stuff off the bottom. He sure wasn't about to let go of anything."

"That was a damfool thing to do," Randall told the Aussie. "You could have gotten trapped in there."

The big man lifted an eyebrow at him. "You know for sure there ain't any Japs on that island?" he said. "If there are, what do you want to fight 'em with—sticks and stones? Not me, mate."

Randall felt the rush of irritation return. "Don't do anything like that again," he said. "You're no good to the rest of us dead."

The Australian gave him an incredulous look. Then he laughed, blew out a long breath underwater, and rolled over onto his back. With his free hand on the crate, he resumed kicking.

"Where'd that Malay go?" Garth said suddenly.

Randall swiveled his head. The tribesman, who'd been on his opposite side, was gone. "I don't know. He was just here."

"He wasn't hurt, was he?"

"No—not that I could tell." Randall shrugged. "He was helping me move the crate just now. Swimming pretty well."

"I'll take a look." Garth drew a deep breath and ducked beneath the surface.

Randall resumed his steady push toward shore, which

was now less than a 150 yards away. The black seaman floundered ineffectively, trying to add leg thrust. Beside them, the Australian was still on his back, whip-kicking with one hand on the end of the crate. He was humming fragments of a well-known drinking song between breaths.

Randall was too tired and fed up to be more than mildly annoyed. He bent his head and concentrated on moving the crate forward. Just behind the black seaman, a little shoal of juvenile fish, each less than an inch long and as transparent as glass, jumped out of the water in unison. Moving out of what they perceived to be harm's way.

There was a light splash some yards behind Randall. Heavy breathing accompanied by the sounds of swimming, and then Garth and the tribesman reappeared on either side of him. The tribesman was grinning again.

"What's with him?" Randall asked.

Garth shook his head. "He went back for his spear and his woven grass satchel. They were both jammed in the frames behind his seat. He must have stuck them in there as we were going down. I guess once he saw this guy"— he indicated the Australian with his thumb—"go back down for his weapons, he figured why not him, too?"

"Jesus Christ," Randall said. "Come on, let's quit screwing around and get to the beach." He winced slightly as pain flared in his left side. He'd bruised a few ribs, apparently.

They kicked until their feet scraped bottom. A little farther and they were in shoulder-deep water, walking on soft sand toward a beach that looked as if it belonged on a postcard from Tahiti.

"Look over there," Garth said, pointing.

The others followed his finger. Along the beach to their right, perhaps half a mile away, a ridge of rock extended down the steep hillside, across the sand, and out into the lagoon. It was about twenty feet high, the top of it covered in brush and low palms. There was a gap in the vegetation directly above the beach, as if a giant scythe had scraped clean a large section of the ridge's spine.

Several hundred yards closer to them, right at the water's edge, there was a large divot in the clean sand—a rough pool brimming with seawater—and beyond it, a long skid mark that gradually turned out toward the lagoon. A much shorter skid mark split off from the first just past the pool; at the end of it, another fresh gap had been hacked into the brush and the trees. Broken, peeled palm trunks, mangled foliage, and hanging vines cluttered the opening where something had clearly smashed its way off the beach, into the jungle, and partway up the adjoining slope.

"We must have clipped the ridge as we came in," Garth mused. "Bounced, then come down hard on the beach."

"Too hard," Randall said. "That's where the plane broke in half. The tail section skidded off into the lagoon. . . ."

"And the cockpit went the other way, into the bloody trees," the Australian finished.

They were wading waist-deep now, eyeing the beach. There was no way of knowing who or what might be just inside the tree line. As the big Australian reached thigh-deep water, he unslung one of the two Sten guns from his shoulder, removed the side-mounted magazine, and broke open the breech. Shaking the excess water out of it, he blew down the barrel and worked the trigger back and forth several times. Then he slapped the magazine home again and leveled it to the ready position on his hip.

"Will that thing fire after it's been soaking in salt water?" Randall asked.

The Aussie nodded. "Yeh. She'll fire when she's soakin' wet, choked with sand, and half fouled with rust."

"Must be a high-quality item," Randall said.

"Nah," the big man responded, his eyes tracking back and forth along the green wall of jungle. "Piece of shit. Stamped out of cheap metal. But I took these two apart and filed down all the components, includin' the sticky magazines. That's what keeps 'em from jammin' even when they're full of dirt. Loose tolerances."

"Not too accurate, I guess," Garth commented.

The corner of the Australian's mouth curled up in a

half smile. "Put it this way, mate," he said. "At more than fifty paces, the safest place to be around a Sten is right in front of it."

Randall let out a snort of laughter. "Then why don't you carry something else?"

"Because," the Aussie said, "at *less* than fifty paces, it's the sweetest little murder machine you ever laid eyes on. And in the jungle, mate, all the killin' is done close-up." He eyed Randall for a moment. " 'Course, you'd know that, wouldn't you, bein' a combat officer and all." Pause. "What branch o' the service you say you were in?"

"I didn't," Randall told him. "And what makes you think I'm an officer? I'm not wearing any insignia."

The Australian resumed his intent scan of the jungle as they all walked out of the water onto the sand. "You act it," he said.

Randall flushed. "I beg your—"

"Hey!" the black seaman exclaimed. "Look!" He pointed down the beach.

Coming out of the gap in the trees at the end of the short skid mark were several men, none of them—to everyone's relief—Japanese. Garth recognized them as the black-bereted British major who'd taken control of the crippled C-47, the tall civilian in the battered bush hat, and the swarthy Filipino wearing the camouflage shirt and black trousers.

All were carrying weapons: the major a heavy revolver, the tall civilian a Sten, and the Filipino—improbably—an early-model .45-caliber Thompson submachine gun with twin handgrips and a circular drum magazine. The gangster gun, Randall thought. A fleeting image of Edward G. Robinson in *Little Caesar,* fedora-topped and rubber-lipped, flashed through his mind. The Filipino didn't resemble him at all. But he looked very comfortable with the heavy tommy gun cradled loosely in his arms.

The black-bereted major raised an arm and waved.

"There are five of you, then?" he called, striding forward. "And you're all walking on your own two feet. Bloody good show! That accounts for everyone."

Chapter Nine

Garth moved up on Randall's right side as the two groups of men converged, and continued his assessment of the three new survivors. They were a study in contrasts, even with respect to the way they moved.

The major, in the lead, did not walk so much as march—striding forward with knees high and booted feet clomping down on the sand. Every aspect of his appearance and bearing said career British military: ruddy, granite-slab facial features; ginger-colored handlebar mustache tinged with gray; stern brow, and eyes the color of North Sea ice—a wintry pale blue. Broad shoulders thrown back, spine ramrod-straight, and not a spare ounce on his stomach despite the fact that he was firmly in middle age. The heavy revolver he carried at his side looked like a natural extension of his hand.

The tall civilian, on the other hand, moved in a casual, gangly stroll that suggested a country gentleman out for an easy hike. His olive drab pants and shirt, sleeves rolled up to the elbow, hung loosely from his bony, long-limbed frame; the color lent a military effect, but the clothes bore none of the tailoring details that would have indicated an actual uniform. The man's floppy, wide-brimmed hat concealed the upper third of a thin, sunken-cheeked face peppered with grizzly stubble. His nose was long and straight, a vertical strut beneath the brim of his hat. He carried his Sten the way a photographer carries a camera bag—the strap over his right shoulder, the weapon level, right forearm resting atop the breech and barrel.

Garth, his Apache half tuned in to such things, noted the man's grace and economy of movement. Here was someone capable, he had little doubt, of gliding through dense jungle or over rough terrain like a ghost if the need arose.

The third man, the Filipino, moved forward rapidly on the balls of his feet, maintaining a wide stance. He seemed constantly on the verge of breaking into a trot—only to slow again with a slight change in direction. Garth's impression was of a person accustomed to stalking—picking his way forward in an irregular, elusive pattern like a feral cat. In addition, he noticed that the medium-sized man's face revealed little of the Spanish influence common in many northern Filipinos. Rather, he was Asian: he bore a strong resemblance to the Malay tribesman standing just behind Garth, minus the filed teeth and the face paint.

The two groups halted opposite each other. Before anyone could speak, the tall civilian stepped forward, moved past Garth, and placed his left hand on the tribesman's left shoulder. The smaller man shifted his spear to his right hand and did likewise, reaching up. Across their paralleled arms, the civilian and the tribesman exchanged a series of quietly muttered phrases, in a language incomprehensible even to those close enough to hear the words clearly.

The Australian gave the major a British-style salute, palm out. "Sir. My mate, Corporal Mulgrew—he was with you in the front of the plane. Is he all right, sir?"

The major returned the salute. "Whom am I addressing?" he asked gruffly.

"Foster, sir," the Aussie said, shifting his weight casually to his other foot. "Sergeant Web Foster."

The major's handlebar mustache twitched. "If you had sleeves on your battle blouse, Sergeant, your rank wouldn't be a mystery to everyone except you."

The expression on Foster's rugged Scots-Irish face shifted from friendly to neutral. He started to speak, but the major beat him to it.

"Your unit, Sergeant?"

"Royal Australian Army, Seventh Division," Foster said, omitting the "sir."

"Ah. Bloody good. I was with your unit in North Africa for a few months back in 'forty-two. Chasing Rommel all over that beastly desert. Attached as an adviser while the Seventh was fighting under British command. Good bunch of lads."

Foster nodded slowly, his expression unchanged. "Yeh. Where's Mick, then?"

"Corporal Mulgrew is back inside the wreckage of the transport, tending to one of my men who is seriously injured—unlikely to survive," the major said. "And mind your tone, Sergeant. Being Australian doesn't give you license to play fast and loose with military courtesy. Not around me."

The big Aussie's demeanor cooled another ten degrees. Very deliberately, he brought his hand up to his brow in a second salute. "Sir. If you'll excuse me, I'll see to me mate," he growled. Then he let the hand drop and walked past the major without waiting for a reply.

The British officer frowned, but said nothing further. Instead, he turned to Randall. "Who's the ranking officer here?" he asked.

Randall saluted—American-style, with the edge of the hand out—then extended the same hand. "That'd be me, sir. Lieutenant Charlton Randall, United States Navy. This is my partner, Gunner's Mate Joseph Garth. We serve on the same Underwater Demolition Team. By the way, you'll have to excuse our being out of uniform. We were just released from the infirmary on Minglaat, and these are the clothes we were given."

The major touched his own brow, then shook hands. "A perfectly acceptable explanation, Lieutenant. UDT, eh? Damn fine show you lads have been putting on lately. Your reconnaissance and clearance work has truly expedited MacArthur's amphibious landings over the past year." His smile was hard, professional. "Major Harold Horwitch, British army. Formerly of the Queen's Rifles and the Scots Guards, presently attached to the thirty-third Commando—in both advisory and operational capacities."

"Pleased to meet you, sir," Randall said.

"Likewise," Horwitch affirmed. "Well, let's complete the introductions, what?" His last word punctuated the end of the sentence like a pistol shot. "May I present Mr. Finian Hooke, formerly of New Zealand and the territory of Sarawak, and his—ah—personal assistant, Yomat Dap." The major indicated the tall civilian and the wiry tribesman at his side. "And this," he said, turning to nod at the Filipino, "is Salih Matalam, a commander of the Moro resistance on the island of Mindanao."

He harrumphed, clearing his throat, before proceeding. "Mr. Hooke was the owner-operator of a rubber plantation in Sarawak until the Japanese dropped in uninvited and appropriated it for themselves. Oh, and I believe there were some oil resources under preliminary development as well, along the western coastal boundary of the estate, that were lost at the time of the invasion. Isn't that right, Mr. Hooke?"

"Correct," Hooke said. He tipped his head back and gazed for the first time, unsmiling, at Randall, Garth, and the black seaman. His eyes were as sunken as his cheeks, chips of flint lurking in dark-rimmed sockets. "They took everything."

Randall nodded uncertainly; the man's voice conveyed a strange chill. Nothing overtly threatening, just . . . odd. Garth picked up on it as well, but came to a more definitive conclusion: at least part of Finian Hooke's spirit— part of his *soul*—was missing. There was a void behind his deep-set eyes—a great emptiness beyond fear or despair. The man was still moving, still functioning, but he was hollow. Like a tall tree slashed at its base, drained of life-giving sap, yet, for the time being, continuing to stand.

"Everything," Hooke repeated.

Randall cleared his throat. "So this . . . gentleman"—he gestured toward the tribesman—"is with you? I have to admit, we were wondering what he was doing aboard a military transport. Yee-mat . . . *Dop,* is it? I didn't quite catch it the first time."

Hooke shuffled his feet and looked wearily out at the late-afternoon ocean haze. "His name is Yomat Dap. He is a subchief of the Dayak people of northwestern Borneo, whose tribal lands bordered the southern boundaries of my estate in Sarawak, and he is my friend. He travels with me at all times, assists and protects me, and has done so since early 1942. He speaks a little conventional Malay, but primarily his own tribal dialect and no English."

"Sounds like a bodyguard," the black seaman said, entering the verbal exchange for the first time.

Hooke nodded slowly. "Something like that."

The seaman grinned and glanced around at Randall, Garth, and Horwitch in quick succession. "What is he?" he asked Hooke blithely. "Your slave or somethin'?"

He kept the grin in place as the three white men he'd just glanced at looked down in discomfort, which was the effect he'd hoped for. The fourth white man—Hooke—did not. Instead, he shifted his forearm atop his Sten gun and regarded the black seaman without expression.

"And you are?" he inquired.

The seaman's grin faltered slightly. "Steward's Mate Henry DuFourmey, U.S. Navy."

Randall turned and looked hard at the steward's mate, annoyed that DuFourmey's question had made him feel awkward, but as certain he would say nothing about it as he was the black seaman had done it on purpose.

"No, Mr. DuFourmey," Hooke said quietly, "Yomat

Dap is not my slave. A Dayak would not tolerate such an existence for even a minute."

He fell silent, continuing to hold the seaman's eye.

"Shee-it . . . me neither," DuFourmey declared.

"Indeed?" Hooke remarked, looking out to sea again. "Your race tolerated it for how long in the Americas? Three hundred years?" He turned on his heel and sauntered off down the beach, back the way he had come, Yomat Dap following quickly behind.

"What'd he mean by that?" DuFourmey demanded, his voice rising in pitch. "What'd he mean by that?"

There was a trace of a smile on Garth's lips as he watched Hooke amble away. "I think it means, Steward's Mate," he said, "that you should be careful whose buttons you try to push."

"What d'you mean?" DuFourmey rephrased shrilly, becoming even more animated. "What chu talkin' 'bout?"

Randall held up a placatory hand. "Take it easy, DuFourmey."

"He messin' with me? I don't want nobody messin' with me, or—"

"All right, all right, then—that's *enough*!" Horwitch barked. He shook his head in restrained disgust. "A mere rating arguing with a commissioned officer. Of all the bloody cheek." He glared at the black seaman, tapping the long barrel of his revolver against his thigh.

DuFourmey looked sullenly at the sand, adopting the role of the unjustly affronted. From off to one side, Garth looked him up and down. That takes care of acts one and two, he thought. Don't think I feel like watching act three.

"I think I'll go see if I can help at the plane," he said to Randall and Horwitch. He saluted briefly and began to walk off. "Lieutenant. Major. Mr. Matalam."

"We'll all go," Horwitch declared. "Come on, then." He gave DuFourmey one final glare. "We're in the same fix, the lot of us, so let's all try to move in the same direction, eh?"

"Excellent advice, Major," Randall said, following his teammate.

Horwitch and Matalam fell in step with Randall and together they caught up with Garth in a few quick strides. DuFourmey slouched along behind them, stewing.

After leaving the beach, it took them the better part of five minutes to pick their way along the 150-yard tunnel of slashed vegetation that the front half of the C-47 had carved through the jungle. Both wings had broken off immediately after striking the trees; they lay crumpled among the broadleafs on either side of the tunnel like great ruined tin sails, streaked with black oil and riddled with bullet holes. The starboard propeller was gone. The blades of the opposite prop splayed out from their hub at the front of the port engine nacelle, bent and twisted.

The fuselage had slid up the steep incline immediately behind the beach and stopped when the nose crunched into an outcropping of rock some forty feet above sea level. It lay in a bed of torn greenery at an angle of about thirty degrees, canted onto its port side. One of the trees it had knocked over had come to rest on top of it, pinning it to the earth.

Randall and Garth followed Horwitch into the interior of the fuselage; Salih Matalam took up a lookout position, leaning against a mahogany tree with his tommy gun nestled in his arms. Fifty yards back down the slope, Henry DuFourmey was still laboring through the slash, grousing not quite under his breath. The air trapped under the jungle canopy was dense and steamy, ripe with smell of organic rot. The sustained humming of innumerable insects needled the ear.

Web Foster was sitting in the cockpit doorway, his long legs braced against the slope of the cargo compartment floor, as he worked on something forward of the main bulkhead. Two thin rivulets of bright red blood had laced themselves down his right forearm, running from wrist to elbow. As Randall approached, pulling himself up the incline along the port-side fuselage ribs, he noticed that the blood was dripping steadily from the point of the elbow onto Foster's upper thigh. The khaki cloth of the big sergeant's trouser leg bore a dark, sticky stain almost the size of a dinner plate.

Horwitch stepped over Foster, ducked his head, and climbed inside the cockpit. Randall and Garth remained at the doorway, on either side of the big Australian. Foster was grimacing as he worked, the muscles flexing along his jawline. A third rivulet of blood snaked down his powerful forearm, twining with the other two.

"Fokkin' artery tore right in half when he tried to move," Foster grunted. "Can't quite get hold of the Christly thing . . ."

A low moan came from behind the bulkhead. Randall and Garth leaned inside the doorway, taking care not to interfere with Foster. The moan repeated.

In a tangle of metal behind the remains of the copilot's seat lay one of the two black-bereted soldiers who had accompanied Horwitch. Randall recognized him as the boy who had warned the passengers that the major was about to attempt a crash landing—the one who looked and sounded as if he should have been concerned about nothing more momentous than the next batted cricket ball. His beret was gone now, and he lay on his back with his arms splayed out to either side. His face had a sickly pallor and was streaked with blood. He had been impaled by a thin metal girder, apparently when the cockpit had caved in upon colliding with the rock ledge.

Both Randall and Garth winced involuntarily. The metal strut had penetrated sideways at a shallow angle between the boy's shoulder blades and emerged from his left armpit. Eighteen inches of it stuck out toward Foster's head; three feet more extended down from the boy's back into a tangle of torn aluminum and wiring on the cockpit floor. Blood was everywhere. Foster was probing the wound with both hands.

His comrade, the Aussie corporal named Mulgrew, was on the injured soldier's opposite side, hunched into a ball in the crushed cockpit. With one hand, he was holding a blood-soaked field dressing to the terrible wound in the boy's armpit; the other was under the back of his neck, supporting his head. Beads of sweat dotted Mulgrew's furrowed brow, and his short black hair was plastered to his temples.

" 'Urry up, Web," he muttered through clenched teeth.

"Move your hand—move your hand a bit," Foster replied, digging. "All right, that's got it. . . . No—Goddamn it . . . Goddamn it . . ."

Fresh blood coursed down his arm. Horwitch hovered above the two Australians, an odd mix of detachment and concern on his craggy face. "He's still alive? What's happened?"

"The fokkin' bloody main artery," Foster replied, forgetting himself. Horwitch remained silent. "The poor lad began to struggle while we were trying to cut him free and the fokkin' thing pulled itself apart. Started squirting like a garden hose."

"Brachial artery," Mulgrew said, shifting his weight. "The torn end's retracted back inside the body. Web's tryin' to get hold of the bastard now."

"Goddamn it," Foster growled. "Goddamn it. . . ."

Randall looked away from the gruesome proceedings, swallowing—and in doing so noticed for the first time that the rest of the cockpit was a virtual study in carnage. The bullet-riddled bodies of the pilot and the copilot were crumpled together on the port side, and the corpse of the other black-bereted soldier was draped out through the smashed port window, the jagged Plexiglas of which was smeared with blood and tissue. It glistened like raspberry jam in the sparse sunlight that penetrated the jungle canopy.

Randall's eyelids fluttered. All of a sudden, the heat, the humidity, the insects, and the sticky smell of warm gore seemed overwhelming. He swayed back, holding on to the doorjamb, then turned and slid down the slanting floor to the port side of the cargo compartment. His heart was hammering in his throat, choking him, and there was an awful roaring in his ears. Certain he was going to be sick, he pushed off the frames of the fuselage and slid the rest of the way down the compartment to the jungle floor, trying to breathe.

"L.T.!" he heard Garth call out. *"Charlton!"*

His feet sinking to the ankles in soft, churned humus, he staggered away from the back of the plane. He gagged, swallowed hard, gagged again. The jungle was whirling around him, light and shadow and vines and leaves blending into an endless moving mosaic of suffocating green. He stumbled over a root, nearly fell, and steadied himself against a tree trunk, breathing hard.

A slight noise caught his attention, and he looked up to see the Moro guerrilla, Salih Matalam, looking at him from a few feet away. The Muslim Filipino regarded him soberly for several seconds, then hefted his tommy gun in his crossed arms and turned away, continuing his slow, methodical examination of the surrounding jungle.

What's wrong with me? Randall almost cried it aloud. But even as the question formed in his mind, he knew the answer. He wanted to be anywhere—*anywhere*—but here. And he wanted to be anyone but Lieutenant Charlton Randall III, scion of the renowned Long Island Randalls—American aristocrats who could trace their lineage through a formidable pantheon of soldiers, adventurers, and profiteering businessmen all the way back to the Revolutionary War.

As so often happened when he was under stress, a sudden rush of images and details from his illustrious clan's history—like a hyperkinetic mental newsreel—shot through his mind's eye.

The family fortune had been built on human conflict and its accompanying material demands, and the pattern of acquisition had always been the same. The male heir of each succeeding generation won himself a warrior's reputation in his first war, thereby locking in an updated set of political and business connections, and then cashed in during his second—as a respectable, middle-aged industrialist filling plum military contracts. One could always count on a convenient war to come along at least once every decade or so. And if one didn't—well, you could always get a family friend like William Randolph Hearst to manufacture one for you. That had been the case with the Spanish-American War—a media-created ferment if ever there was one—which had made his grandfather Charlton Randall, Civil War hero of the Battle of Shiloh, a tidy sum manufacturing brass cartridge casings for the Krag-Jorgensen rifle. The fact that the rifle had turned out to be an inferior weapon almost immediately replaced by the 1903 bolt-action Springfield had made little difference to the old cavalry colonel. The money had been paid, and the Randall Munitions Company had found itself comfortably in the black.

His father, Charlton Randall Jr., had been wounded in action leading a charge through a mustard gas attack in France during the First World War. He'd been decorated on the spot by General Black Jack Pershing himself, who'd pinned the Distinguished Service Cross on his chest as he lay bleeding in the German trench he and his unit had just overrun. The home-front acclaim had been tumultuous, the making of the man. Now, during the current war, his father was reaping U.S. government lucre as one of the military's primary suppliers of pressed-metal goods—everything from mess kits to fuel tanks.

Randall stared at the ground, trying to slow his breathing. Now it was *his* turn to be the family hero. It was his preordained, nonnegotiable destiny.

It was expected.

And at this moment, he was absolutely certain he wasn't up to it.

Garth watched the boy die. Slowly, the light left his eyes, the lines of pain in his young face relaxed, and he stopped breathing. His body actually seemed to deflate as every vestige of living tension seeped from his muscles.

At the age of seven, Garth had seen a small dog—a puppy—run over by a wagon in the streets of Laredo. It had died in exactly the same way: its bright, confused eyes dulling to stone black, its mangled body sagging into a puddle of inanimate plasm as the vital force left it. It was the worst thing Joe Garth had ever seen, even though he had shot thousands of game animals while hunting alone and with his father, grandfather, and uncles.

And it had remained the worst thing . . . until this war. Until Kwajalein, Biak, Peleliu, Leyte . . .

And *here*.

Wherever here was.

Chapter
Ten

An hour later it had begun to rain, the heavy drops pattering and smacking through the broad leaves of the jungle canopy. As the squall intensified, Garth and Foster had each thrown a final shovelful of musty earth on the shallow grave of the young soldier and joined the others as they scrambled back inside the smashed fuselage of the transport plane. Seating themselves on the buckled flooring, they'd gazed out in silence at the four graves that lay between the twisted roots of a giant teak tree; listening to the hollow din of raindrops on the aluminum skin overhead, they watched the tropical deluge flatten the freshly piled earth into slick, sodden mounds.

Horwitch was filling canteens from the miniature waterfall cascading off the top edge of the torn fuselage; he held them in the stream one at a time. The rest of the men shifted continuously, trying to find positions of relative comfort while swatting at the insects that had taken shelter with them in the plane's dank interior.

"I thought they was bugs in Louisiana," DuFourmey grumbled, crushing a mosquito against his forehead. "The bayous ain't got nothin' on this place."

"Here." Mulgrew leaned forward and tapped his shoulder with a small metal tin the size of a sardine can. "Rub some o' this on you."

DuFourmey took the tin and examined it. "What you got here?"

"Outback bug dope," Mulgrew said, settling back against a crumpled frame. "Homemade." He fished in his shirt pocket and extracted a damp cigarette. "Me mum sends it to me along with a regular supply of fresh silk underwear." He chortled at his own humor and lit the smoke with a battered silver Zippo.

The black seaman popped the lid off the tin and sniffed at the greasy brown substance inside. Immediately, his nose wrinkled. "Gawd. What this made of?"

Mulgrew caught Randall's eye and winked. "Oh, a couple o' things," he said, exhaling smoke. "Kangaroo fat, dingo piss . . . a little sweat from a wild steer's balls . . ."

"Damn."

"Steers don't have balls," Garth pointed out.

"Shh," Mulgrew told him, smiling.

DuFourmey snapped the lid back on the tin and held it out. "No, thanks. I'll just slap."

Mulgrew shrugged and took it back. "Suit yerself, mate."

The rain was stopping. The drumming on the top of the fuselage became less incessant, and the cascade of water at which Horwitch had filled the group's dozen canteens shrank to a trickle. A few random shafts of sunlight began to illuminate the wet mist that drifted through the dark tree trunks and dripping foliage of the surrounding jungle.

"Hey," Foster said suddenly. "Where's Hooke and his pet Dayak?"

Randall looked up at Horwitch. "That's right. What with your trooper dying and us having to bury four men, I forgot all about them."

The British major harrumphed to clear his throat. "Mr. Hooke indicated to me before we encountered you on the beach that he intended to make a reconnaissance of the island's higher ground—work his way up the side of this volcano and spy out the land from a better vantage point. He and Dap should be back shortly."

"Maybe they done fell off a cliff or somethin'," Du-Fourmey offered.

Horwitch gave him a bored glare. "Restrain the impulse to be helpful, if you please, Steward's Mate."

Foster got to his feet, extended his powerful arms over his head, and grasped the upper edge of the torn fuselage. "They probably holed up somewhere once the squall hit," he mused, stretching his muscles. "Musta been pretty exposed up the side o' that mountain."

Horwitch nodded. "In all likelihood."

"The rain's going to wash out the skid marks on the beach," Garth said. "Make the crash site harder to spot from the air. I doubt if anyone's going to be able to make much of that tail section on the bottom of the lagoon, even with the water as clear as it is. And this forward section's lying under the jungle canopy. Both wings are ripped off, and they're pretty well covered, too."

"Jap planes cain't notice us so easy, then, huh?" Du-Fourmey commented, looking anxious. "That's good."

"Neither can American planes," Garth replied. He spat between his boots. "That ain't so good."

"We can make us a signal," DuFourmey persisted. "Fire or somethin'."

"Before we do that," Horwitch said, "we're going to find out if anyone is on this island besides ourselves. And have a look at the islands nearby."

Foster turned and grinned at Mulgrew. "Sounds like we may be doin' a little climbin', mate."

"Fair dinkum, I figure, Web," the corporal replied around his cigarette.

"High ground provides us the best lookout," Horwitch declared, "and now here's Mr. Hooke back, finally."

The lanky New Zealander came down the slope without a sound, working his way through the dripping foliage, his floppy-brimmed hat and olive-colored clothing completely soaked. Yomat Dap followed on his left flank, gently parting the glistening greenery in his path with the tip of his bladed spear.

Hooke stepped carefully over a fallen log just behind the fuselage and sat back on it, facing the little knot of men. His Sten gun remained level at his side, his right forearm draped atop it. Without speaking and without hurrying, he removed a waterproof tobacco pouch from inside his wet shirt, opened it, and extracted a short-stemmed pipe with a small, carved bowl. Putting the stem between his teeth, he filled the bowl, tamped it, and lit up with a waxed match. The smoke wafted through the moisture-laden air, drifting in tendrils into the fuselage.

Cherry cognac, Randall thought. *Just like my grandfather smoked.* The sense of nostalgia was almost overwhelming.

Finian Hooke inhaled and exhaled smoke three times before raising his eyes and regarding the men in front of him. His dark gaze came to rest on Horwitch.

"Well, Mr. Hooke?" the major inquired.

"The jungle thins out about a hundred and fifty yards up the slope from here," the lean civilian said. "An old game trail runs in a series of switchbacks up a steep, rocky section to a razor grass plateau at the base of the exposed volcanic cone. It's a long climb, but from there we should be able to see the entire island."

"Decide where we should head next," Randall muttered, thinking out loud.

"Precisely," Hooke said. He exhaled a long cloud.

"Did you actually get to the plateau?" Horwitch asked.

"No, about halfway. We turned back to find shelter when the squall hit, but just before that we could see all the way to the base of the uppermost cone."

The major nodded slowly. "When you got clear of the trees, were you able to get a decent view? And see at least part of the coastline on this side of the island?"

"Yes, adequate." Hooke scratched the grayish stubble on his jaw. "We appear to be in a small archipelago of volcanic islands like this one. Quite beautiful, really." For a split second his haunted eyes took on a warmer, almost pleasant look. "There are at least six other islands to the west, judging by the sun."

"How far?" Horwitch asked.

"Between five and twenty miles, I estimate. Deep water in between."

"Any sign of enemy activity or bases?"

"No, nothing."

"How 'bout any sign of the U.S. Navy?" DuFourmey inquired hopefully.

Hooke sent the black seaman a thin smile. "No."

There was a lull in the discussion. The background noises of the jungle—the scampering of small lizards, the intermittent squawks of birds, the rising whir of reawakening insects—became louder in the absence of human voices, punctuated by the steady dripping of water from the leaf canopy. Randall became aware of a feeling of intense isolation, of the fact that, at present, they were cut off completely from the giant military machine that supported and protected them. Sitting in a void of exotic and indifferent Nature, quite likely in Japanese-controlled territory. Hell, MacArthur had only invaded the Philippines a week ago. Even he couldn't be running the whole place yet.

Garth moved his feet as Foster stepped by to cadge a cigarette from Mulgrew, then broke the silence: "I don't suppose anyone knows exactly where we are?"

Hooke's dark eyes flickered from Garth to Horwitch and back again. "I couldn't say. I wasn't flying. When we took off from Minglaat we were supposed to be heading east toward Peleliu. After a few minutes of playing cat and mouse with those Zeros, though, I doubt very much that we were anything close to being on course."

There was a general nodding of heads. Foster accepted a light from Mulgrew and blew cigarette smoke at the overhead frames of the fuselage interior. "Maybe we got lucky and landed in Hawaii," he said. "Maybe Honolulu's just on the other side of this hill." He grinned at Mulgrew. "Always wanted a two-week furlough in Honolulu."

"I'm game, Web," Mulgrew returned. "You're buyin', right?"

" 'Til me money's gone, mate."

"By the time I got into the cockpit and took over the controls," Horwitch said, "the compass and radio were already smashed by bullets and the pilots were dead. Half the instrument panel was on fire and the charts were the first things to burn up. Owen tried to put out the blaze but couldn't manage it before we crashed."

"Owen?" Randall muttered.

"The lad you just buried," Horwitch clarified. "One of my boys. The one with the shaft through his back."

Randall nodded. "Oh." There was an awkward silence. "He was very young, wasn't he, sir?"

Horwitch looked directly at him. "He was a soldier."

"Yes," Randall said. "Of course he was."

"So, the upshot is," Horwitch continued, "we don't have the faintest bloody idea where we are—except that we're somewhere in the Philippines somewhere south of Luzon. Beyond that, I couldn't tell you."

"If I had to guess, and I do," Hooke said, "I'd say we were southwest of Luzon rather than southeast. These volcanic archipelagoes are more characteristic of the western Philippines than the eastern."

"Japanese-held territory, certainly. The question is, do they have troops on this particular island or the ones nearby?"

Hooke puffed on his pipe. "You know as well as I do, Major, that the Japanese have made a habit out of scattering small, self-sufficient garrisons throughout the island chains from here to the Dutch East Indies. If there isn't an enemy force on this island, there probably is on one close by, tasked with defending the archipelago against amphibious invasion."

"Mm." Horwitch nodded thoughtfully. "What we need to do is pick a location that allows us to remain hidden from Japanese eyes, yet at the same time gives us ample opportunity to signal any Allied planes or ships that chance our way. And the best place from which to do that, as we've already determined, is up there." He pointed up the slope.

"Major," Garth asked, "do you think we ought to start for that plateau now? We're losing the sun. In an hour it'll be gone completely and we'll end up fumbling around on the side of that mountain in the dark."

"Easier to spot the lights and fires of any Japanese bases at night," Horwitch said, "but no. We'll equip ourselves with whatever gear we can salvage from the plane, shelter here for the night, and head up for the plateau tomorrow at first light. Agreed, Mr. Hooke?"

The New Zealander shrugged once and nodded, drawing on his pipe.

"Lieutenant Randall?"

Randall glanced at Garth, then nodded, as well. "Sounds good to me, sir."

"Bully," Horwitch declared. "Gentlemen, let's use what light we have left to check the plane and remaining cargo crates for usable equipment, and set up a bivouac for the night. We'll run sentry shifts, too. One hour, each man, until dawn. That way everyone will get some sleep. Understood?"

There were scattered replies of "yes, sir." A series of grunts and groans followed as the survivors got wearily to their feet and began to climb through the interior of the fuselage, scavenging. DuFourmey bent over a small wooden crate and began to pry at the lid with a small crowbar he'd found.

"*Damn,*" he said, squashing a mosquito that was feasting on his jugular vein. "Hope they got bug nettin' in here."

"Don't get your hopes up, mate," Foster told him, climbing past. He pointed at the stenciled markings on the side of the crate. "See that?"

The markings were upside-down. DuFourmey craned his neck sideways and began to spell out loud: "*H-E-M-O-R-R-H-O-I-D . . . O-I-N-T-M-E-N-T . . .*" He frowned. "Don't know what that is, but I'll bet it ain't bug netting."

"It's for hemorrhoids, mate," Foster called over his shoulder. "Get that open and at least while the mosquitoes are eating you alive you can keep your fokkin' piles cool."

He and Mulgrew roared with laughter and began to break into a small crate labeled PISTOLS—.45 AUTOMATIC. QUANTITY: 24.

Randall took the first watch, then after an hour and ten minutes woke Mulgrew and lay down beside Garth on a makeshift bed of life jackets. The insects were terrible, but could not bite and sting through the tattered canvas tarpaulin he pulled around his body. He covered his head completely, killed the few bugs that had gotten trapped inside the stale-smelling cocoon with him, and then was able to drift off without being devoured piecemeal.

He did not sleep well. Fitzgerald had been visiting him in his dreams with increasing frequency over the past five or six days, the look of accusation on his bloodied, corpselike face more intense each time. Now McNab had shown up, at Fitz's rotting shoulder, and behind him, in the shadows, Bartlett and Drexel were lurking.

Randall wanted to explain, tell them that it wasn't his fault, but the harder he tried to speak, the more his throat closed up—until he clawed his way out of the dream and into consciousness, trembling, bathed in a clammy sweat.

He lay there enshrouded in the musty canvas, breathing hard and staring into the blackness with his eyes wide open. Hard on the heels of the guilt he felt at losing his squad was the deeply ingrained dread of what his father and mother would think of his failure, of his current fragile state of mind. Some war hero. He squeezed his eyes shut and gritted his teeth, trying to push the torturous thoughts away, but it was no good. He felt as though he were coming apart at the seams.

"Hey," Garth said in a low voice. "You okay, L.T.?"

Randall swallowed hard. "Huh?"

"I said, you okay? You're making funny noises in there. Moaning, like."

Randall drew a deep breath and let it out as slowly as he could, hoping it didn't sound too ragged.

"Yeah, Joe," he said. "Yeah. I'm fine."

Chapter Eleven

Horwitch had them moving up the side of the mountain well before sunrise. In addition to two canteens of rainwater and an equal share of the C-47's emergency rations, those without weapons of their own—Randall, Garth, and DuFourmey—carried not one but two of the salvaged .45-caliber automatic pistols, plus ammunition. The two Australian jungle fighters had their sidearms and Sten submachine guns, as did Finian Hooke. Horwitch wore his heavy Bulldog revolver reversed on his hip in its leather holster, and carried a short M1 carbine that had belonged to the transport pilot. Salih Matalam, silent as ever, bore his tommy gun easily across his chest. Yomat Dap glided through the foliage just off Hooke's left shoulder, parting the leaves with his spear, one hand on the hilt of his sword.

"Why I got to carry two of these damn pistols?" Du-Fourmey grumbled, sweating profusely as he worked his way up the rocky grade. "I cain't aim but one of 'em at a time."

"Firepower, Steward's Mate," Horwitch declared, overhearing him. "If we run into the enemy, you point both of those in the appropriate direction and pull the triggers until I tell you to stop. Understood?"

"Yes, sir." DuFourmey stepped with difficulty over a large rock. "One gun be plenty," he reiterated, keeping his voice low.

Garth was right behind him. "Look, Henry," he said. "You have two and one jams—you still have a backup. You have two and they both malfunction—you use parts from one to fix the other. See?"

"Long as the Japs ain't shot me dead by then," Du-Fourmey countered gloomily.

They emerged from the jungle after climbing about four hundred vertical feet and found themselves on a gradually leveling trail that continued to wind its way upward through exposed lava rock and razor grass toward the plateau at the base of the volcanic cone. To the east, the sun was a cold silver ball, partially obscured by streaks of purple cloud, clinging low to the ocean horizon. The dawn thermals began to stir, and a balmy breeze wafted up over the shoulders of the mountain, cooling the panting men as they labored on toward high ground.

They were about two hundred yards from the top when Mulgrew, leading the way through razor grass that was now shoulder-high, stopped abruptly, crouched, and raised a fist. In an instant, Foster and Horwitch were beside him, weapons at the ready. Randall and Garth, held up on the trail behind DuFourmey and Matalam, knelt where they were and watched intently.

"What's goin' on?" DuFourmey said shrilly. "What's happenin'?"

Matalam whirled and glared back at the black seaman. *"Hsst!"* he exclaimed, one finger to his lips. It was the first utterance the three Americans had heard from him. The look on his exotic face made DuFourmey take a step back.

"What the—?" he began.

"Shut up, DuFourmey," Randall hissed.

Up forward, Foster put a hand on Mulgrew's shoulder. "What is it, mate?"

"Something's movin' in the grass just ahead and to the right," Mulgrew whispered. "Good size."

"Man-sized?" Horwitch inquired.

"Could be."

"Bugger." The major turned, looked at Randall, and touched his pistol. The Americans responded by drawing an automatic each. "Can you work up the trail a little farther and get a look, Corporal?"

Mulgrew nodded slowly. "Think so, sir. Point man's me favorite game." He looked sidelong at Foster, rolled his eyes, and moved forward, so low he was almost duckwalking.

"I'll give him close cover from behind," Foster whispered. "He—"

All of a sudden there was a flurry of movement beside Mulgrew, and a khaki-colored form exploded from the thick grass immediately to his right, emitting a loud shriek. The wiry corporal was bowled over before he could bring his weapon to bear and went tumbling into the growth on the opposite side of the trail.

Brrrrrraaaaaap! A burst from Foster's Sten scythed through the razor grass just beyond Mulgrew as the attacker rushed off to the left.

"Wait!" Horwitch roared, flinging out his free hand.

Foster held his fire, breathing hard, and glanced over at the major. Ten feet away, Mulgrew thrashed his legs clear of the entangling grasses and sat up, wild-eyed.

"Bloody fokkin' hell," he gasped, clutching his right forearm.

"You all right, Mick?" Foster hissed. "He knife you or anything?"

Mulgrew shook his head. *"Bloody . . . fokkin' . . . hell,"* he repeated, trying to regain his breath.

"Quiet—*quiet!*" Horwitch exclaimed. Cautiously, he rose off his knees, peering over the top of the razor grass. He stared for a few seconds, then straightened. From the back of his throat came a deep laugh.

Foster looked up at him, blinking, then got to his feet and followed the major's line of sight across the grass to a small outcropping of lava rock some fifty feet away.

On top of the outcropping squatted a light brown creature about the size of a large dog. Its forearms were covered in thick silver fur, as were its legs, belly, and the long, heavy tail that was draped over the rock behind it. It gazed unperturbed across the intervening stretch of grass at the startled men with two expressive, jet-black eyes, which were set on either side of its most improbable feature: a bulbous pink nose the approximate size and shape of a large zucchini. As the nine crash survivors watched, it belched, plucked a handful of leaves from a nearby bush, and began to munch, looking bored.

"W—what in the name o' sweet Jesus is that thing?" DuFourmey said, pointing his automatic at the alien.

"Put the pistol away," Hooke said, keeping his voice low. "That animal is harmless. It's a rather large male proboscis monkey."

"Don't look like no monk I ever seen at the zoo," DuFourmey said.

"Harmless, eh?" Mulgrew rubbed his forearm, which was bleeding from several long, parallel scrapes. "How harmless?"

"Ninety-nine percent harmless," Hooke told him. "Any animal will lash out if cornered or injured."

The corporal scowled and held up his arm. "Ninety-*eight*."

Hooke shrugged. "The monkey was alarmed. He bolted and got his nails into you as he went past."

Mulgrew frowned at the open welts. "Not as alarmed as me, mate," he muttered.

Garth put a hand on top of DuFourmey's still-leveled automatic, sticking his thumb between the hammer and the firing pin, and gently pushed it down. "Easy, Henry," he said.

"Gawd-damned ape," the seaman croaked. "Scared the shit outta me."

Garth watched him uncock the pistol with trembling hands. "Don't feel special," he told DuFourmey. "It scared the shit out of all of us."

"Here, Corporal," Horwitch said, tearing open a small envelope of sulfa powder and handing it to Mulgrew.

"Disinfect those scratches and let's go." He turned to Foster. "Sergeant—you take the lead up to the plateau."

Foster eyed the major, looked casually away for a few seconds, then touched his temple with his middle finger. "Yes, sir."

Horwitch's expression darkened and he opened his mouth to speak, but the big sergeant was already half a dozen yards past him, climbing through the razor grass with his Sten cradled loosely against his hip. Biting his lip, the major waved the party on and followed.

It took only an additional ten minutes to reach the base of the volcanic cone, which towered another two hundred feet above the plateau. The small clearing was littered with rocks, sparse grasses, and a scattering of brilliant orange-and-white orchids that garlanded the boulders at the periphery. Far below, 360 degrees around, lay the rolling topography of the island, carpeted in lush green jungle. From its beaches, the rich blue plane of the sea spread out in a vast panorama to the horizon. To the north, east, and south, the seascape was uninterrupted by land, but to the west a cluster of small islands—some with volcanic cones of their own—curved off into the distant haze.

"As I said, the closest one is less than five miles away," Hooke remarked, producing his tobacco pouch. He pointed. "That one there, with the twin volcanoes."

The men spread out around the clearing, unbuckling canteen belts and shedding pouches of ammunition. Everyone drank, and some stripped off sweat-soaked shirts to take advantage of the cooling breeze. All the while, they gazed around at the dramatic scenery surrounding them.

"Beautiful," Randall said to Garth as they shared a canteen. "But not a settlement or ship in sight."

Garth nodded, swallowing. "A whole lot of empty."

Horwitch was crisscrossing the clearing, examining the vistas in every direction. The others watched him in silence. When he'd covered all four compass directions he stood in the center of the plateau with his arms folded, stroking his mustache, his brow furrowed.

"What we gonna do now, Major?" DuFourmey called.

Horwitch glanced over at him in irritation, but did not reply. Instead, he began to pace slowly.

"Let the man think," Randall said to the steward's mate.

"He don't know," DuFourmey grumbled. "He got us all the way up here, and now he cain't see nothin' and he don't know what to do."

"That's enough, DuFourmey," Randall snapped. "Keep a lid on that talk."

The seaman sucked his teeth and leaned back against the wall of the volcanic cone with his arms crossed as if he were loitering outside the neighborhood pool hall.

"I think I hear water tricklin' out of somewhere," Foster said, catching the last drop from his inverted canteen on his tongue. "Must be a spring just down the other side o' this clearing." He rolled to his feet and began to stride off. "Lemme see if I can find it."

Randall watched the big Australian walk to the north edge of the clearing and disappear down the slope. "Think someone should go with him?" he asked.

Mulgrew lolled back on a large boulder and drank a large swig from his canteen. "Nah, mate," he said. "Web can take care o' himself. Been doin' it for a long time."

Randall nodded and shrugged. He resumed gazing around the plateau at the exotic orchid blossoms that seemed to leap from the green-beige grass and black rock like small, brilliant splashes of oil paint. Amazing how the greatest beauty often showed up in the most godforsaken places—after the devastation of a forest fire, or on the barren, windswept shoulder of a Pacific volcano. As he was appreciating the vibrant colors of the orchids, Major Horwitch passed through his line of vision, still pacing.

"*Hey!*" The voice was Foster's, slightly muted as it carried up over the edge of the plateau. "*HEY!*"

The men bolted to their feet as if stung, grabbing for their weapons. Horwitch spun on his heel, yanked his Bulldog from its holster, and ran toward the spot where Foster had disappeared from view. Mulgrew was right behind him, followed by Randall and Garth.

The big sergeant was charging up the slope at a dead run, his powerful arms pumping. The other four men dropped to their knees, bringing their weapons to bear. Twenty feet to the left, Hooke slid into position behind a huge boulder and steadied his Sten gun on top of it.

"Where are they, Web?" Mulgrew yelled, eyeing his friend over the sights of his own Sten. "How many?"

"No, no!" Foster bellowed. *"Over there! Over there!"* He gestured furiously with one arm.

Everyone looked to the northeast. Coming out from behind the verdant bulge of one of the island's lower hills was the unmistakable shape of an American PT boat, as tiny in the distance as a matchstick, skirting the outer reef where the azure blue of deep water met the emerald green of coral shallows. Twin threads of white water creamed out from its bow, forming the narrow, trailing V that marked its passage.

As Foster regained the top of the rise, all the men began shouting and waving their arms at the same time. It was several seconds before Randall realized the futility of it: at so great a distance they were little more than animated pinpricks. Unless they came up with a more effective signal, and quickly, the PT boat was going to pass them by.

Horwitch had arrived at the same conclusion. Raising his revolver over his head, he fired three evenly spaced shots into the air. Then he fired three more.

"Mr. Matalam! Mr. Hooke!" he shouted, breaking open the Bulldog's cylinder and shaking out the spent casings. "Fire off some short volleys! See if the sound will get their attention!"

The Moro guerrilla stepped to the edge of the plateau, brought his tommy gun up to a forty-five-degree angle, and let loose a three-second burst. The chugging of the heavy submachine gun reverberated off the side of the volcanic cone. A few seconds later, Finian Hooke fired half a clip from his Sten, the lighter-caliber weapon chattering at a higher pitch.

The PT boat did not slow down or alter course. It was

now directly opposite the plateau, continuing its cruising-speed patrol along the side of the island.

"Keep trying!" Horwitch fumed, reaching inside his shirt. "I'll try to get their attention with my signaling mirror!" He glanced back to the east as he produced a small rectangle of highly polished steel. "The sun needs to rise clear of those clouds, blast it!"

He twisted the mirror in his hands, desperately trying to find the optimum angle at which to catch the few dawn rays that were escaping the thunderhead-cluttered horizon.

"Web," Mulgrew said breathlessly, "what about smoke? We can set some of this dry grass on fire, then smudge it down. If that damned Yank looks back and sees our plume, maybe he'll want to have a closer look, eh?"

"Bloody hell, let's give it a try," Foster replied, turning and heading for the nearest tuft.

"Good idea," Garth said. "I'll help."

Working quickly, the three men ripped up a few dozen handfuls of dead grass and weeds and piled them on the bleached roots of a lightning-killed thornbush. Mulgrew was bent over coaxing flame from his old Zippo, Foster beside him, when an odd whistle, like the cry of an exotic bird, cut through the general cacophony of frustrated shouts and intermittent bursts of machine gun fire.

Forty feet above the plateau, Yomat Dap was kneeling on top of a spire of rock that had somehow split off from the side of the volcano and remained standing. Black feathered headdress and topknot fluttering in the light wind, he let out the strange call once more. As the men stared up at him, he pointed to the west with his spear, at the island nearest their own.

Three aircraft were emerging from behind the island's cojoined pair of steep volcanic cones, one after the other. Banking to the south, they closed up neatly and flew in single file toward the motoring PT boat.

"What are they?" DuFourmey shouted. "What side they on?"

Still behind the boulder at which he'd taken up firing position upon hearing Foster's initial yell, Hooke propped an elbow on the black rock and squinted through a pair of opera-glass-sized binoculars he'd produced from a pouch on his hip. After a few seconds, a trace of a smile grazed his thin lips.

"American," he announced. "High-performance seaplanes of some sort. Single-engine. Navy blue paint job, U.S. star insignia on the wingtips and fuselage."

A spontaneous round of cheers burst from the little group of men. Randall felt the lurking ball of fear in his stomach suddenly diminish in size by a factor of ten. He stole a look at Joe Garth. His friend was smiling, calm as a cucumber—as usual.

The line of planes descended to within a hundred feet of the water, flying parallel to the beaches and the reef, and rapidly closed the distance between themselves and the PT boat. As they overflew the boat and drew nearer the volcanic cone and plateau, it became easier to make out their design details with the naked eye. Sleek, powerful fuselages with relatively short wings. In-line engines, like the German Messerschmitt 109. Large twin pontoons beneath, attached by stout single struts. Streamlined cockpit canopies glinting in the early-morning sun.

The aircraft continued to follow the coastline for approximately another mile, gaining altitude as they did so, until they were just below the level of the plateau and almost directly opposite it. The men began to wave and shout again as the leader rose to within what seemed like a stone's throw, engine whining, then abruptly banked hard to port and soared off toward the ocean once more. The two others followed in his wake, and in thirty seconds the entire flight had wheeled around 180 degrees, heading back the way they had come.

"Bloody good turn of speed on those buggers," Horwitch commented. He eyed the aircraft as they descended to sea level and began to follow the reef line back in the direction of the PT boat, now a good two miles distant. "I'm not familiar with the design. It must be another one of those new American wonder machines. Mr. Hooke? What say you, sir?"

The New Zealander scratched his grizzled chin. "As a coast watcher, I've been identifying aircraft at distance for nearly three years now. I make it a point to know all combat fighters, bombers, and transports—old and new—in the Pacific theater. But I have never seen planes like those before."

"Ever see a P-61 Black Widow?" Garth asked.

Hooke shook his head. "Not yet. But I've heard of it."

"Mm." Garth smiled inwardly. Even the rather superior and remote Mr. Finian Hooke hadn't seen every new U.S. warplane in the Philippine skies.

He touched Mulgrew on the shoulder. "Corporal. How about we get the smudge fire going? Just to make sure they see us."

The Australian turned and grinned. "Now, there's a worthy thought, mate," he said, and flicked his Zippo open.

On the bridge of the PT boat, Lieutenant Thomas Mercer, the vessel's twenty-five-year-old captain, shielded his eyes against the glare of the morning sun with a hand over his brow and squinted at the three aircraft approaching from the stern. "I've never seen planes like those before," he said to his executive officer, Lieutenant Junior Grade Marlon Pike.

Pike, a blond college quarterback type from Alabama, pushed his cap back on his head in rakish fashion and blew a quick gum bubble. "Well, boss," he drawled, popping it with his side teeth, "they turn out these new sky buggies so fast, there ain't no way to keep track. Less'n you work for Grumman or Boeing or something."

"I suppose," Mercer conceded. The two officers spoke in moderate yell—the standard method of carrying on a conversation when the PT boat was traveling at anything more than idle speed. The roar of the eighty-foot vessel's three fifteen-hundred-horsepower Packard engines was all but deafening.

"Good to have them boys up there, anyway," Pike

said. He raised an arm and waved at the oncoming lead plane. "Makes a poor swabbie feel safer."

"Say what?" Mercer cupped his fingers around his ear.

"I said it's *good to have them boys up there,*" Pike hollered, continuing to wave as the aircraft approached.

He was still grinning and waving when the very first 12.7-millimeter bullet fired from the lead plane's machine guns smashed through his front teeth.

Up on the plateau, the relieved conversation was suddenly replaced by silence. The men stared in stunned disbelief as the first seaplane strafed its way up to the PT boat's stern, puffs of smoke streaming back from its wing guns, and released the single small bomb it carried beneath its belly. The bomb overshot the bullet-chewed vessel and exploded fifty feet in front of its bow, sending a white blossom of churned water into the air. The PT boat bucked as the shock wave struck its hull. The attacking plane banked hard toward the beach, winging over and regaining altitude. Two seconds later, the sound of the detonation, muted by distance, reached the plateau.

Crump.

Horwitch whirled. "Put that fire out!" he barked. "No smoke!" As Garth and Mulgrew leaped to stamp out the smudge they'd just lit, the major began to move toward the base of the volcanic cone, waving the remaining men in front of him. "Everyone take cover behind the boulders! If the planes come back this way, stay low!" He glared back down at the chaos on the outer reef, his jaw muscles working. "Bloody *bastards!*"

"What they doin'?" DuFourmey asked, scrambling behind a natural rampart of black lava. "They be outta their minds?"

"Not hardly," Garth answered, taking cover nearby. His face was grim. "Crazy people aren't that well organized."

The second seaplane had just finished its strafing run and was pulling up over the smoking PT boat. It did not

release a bomb. Like the leader, it banked hard toward
the beaches, powering for altitude.

The third seaplane bore in toward the PT boat's stern,
machine guns hammering.

"Somebody get on those fifties!" Mercer screamed,
clinging to the ship's wheel on one knee. He groaned
and tried to wipe away the blood running into his eyes,
but it was difficult because the entire right side of his
face was studded with large wood splinters. The fusillade
of machine gun bullets that had killed Pike had also
shredded the PT boat's small open-air bridge, throwing
out a spray of plywood shrapnel.

Mercer blinked hard, clearing his vision enough to see
two long fountain trails of exploding white water racing
up the wake of the PT boat. The terrible high-intensity
whine of the attacking plane's engine, the stuttering tat-
too of its guns, and the shock of being shot up and
bombed by U.S. aircraft nearly drove him to insensibil-
ity. He watched in helpless dread as the pursuing fountain trails reached the stern and were instantly replaced
by parallel flurries of splintering wood and sawdust as
the seaplane's machine gun bullets chopped their way
up the deck.

"Why the fuck are they shooting at us?" The despairing shriek came from the young seaman Hernandez as
he clawed his way into the port fifty-caliber gun turret.
"We're Americans!"

Lieutenant Thomas Mercer did not answer, because
Lieutenant Thomas Mercer was dead, lying in the ruined
bridge beside the bullet-torn body of Lieutenant (jg)
Marlon Pike.

Tears of hurt and rage sprang from Seaman Hernandez's eyes as he racked the firing mechanisms of the twin
fifties and swung the long barrels onto the U.S.-marked
seaplane that was hurtling overhead. He was about to
depress the triggers when the two-hundred-kilogram
bomb the aircraft had just dropped hit the aft deck dead
center and plunged into the engine room.

The bomb exploded, simultaneously blowing out the bottom of the plywood hull and igniting the remaining two thousand gallons of high-octane fuel in the vessel's main tanks.

The PT boat came apart with a blast that flattened the water for a quarter mile around. A fiery cloud of red and black boiled up into the sky, shot through with pieces of tumbling debris. A few seconds later, multiple small splashes began to pepper the periphery of the explosion as the first falling fragments hit the ocean's surface.

The delayed sound of the detonation reached the plateau well after the PT boat had been replaced by a large blot of flaming oil and gasoline.

Randall felt the reverberation off the volcanic cone penetrate his body right down to the soles of his feet. Beside him, Joe Garth's tanned face twitched with the unconscious tightening of his mouth.

A dirty pillar of black smoke rose even with the plateau, then higher into the blue morning sky, where it began to thin and dissipate. As it did so, the three U.S.-marked seaplanes circled the site of their kill, like hungry raptors searching for living movement.

It was an unnecessary exercise. Of the fourteen crewmen aboard the PT boat, not one had survived. Not a single body was even intact enough to float.

The seaplanes circled for several minutes more. Then, one after the other, they banked away and headed in single file back to the west, toward the twin-coned volcanic island that had spawned them. Upon reaching it, they soared around behind its jungle-covered highlands and descended. They were soon out of sight behind the towering central cones.

They did not reappear on the volcanoes' opposite side.

Part Two

Chapter Twelve

In his private quarters, deep within the metal bowels of the giant submarine, Captain Toshiko Yarizuma was praying.

Although for the sake of appearance he paused daily at the large Shinto shrine mounted just aft of the officers' wardroom, he did his true reflective thinking out of sight of the other 213 members of the crew. Sincere though they might be, their prayers were necessarily of less gravity than his, unburdened as they were by the responsibilities of command. And as he enjoyed the solitude of omnipotent rank, he enjoyed—relished—the solitude of private prayer.

The small personal shrine in his quarters was built of cherrywood and incorporated Shintoism's three essential symbols of virtue: a mirror—for wisdom; a short sword—for courage; and a small selection of jewels—for benevolence. Attached to opposite edges of the mirror were framed pictures of Emperor Hirohito—the living god—and Yarizuma's own family: his wife, Nima, and their three young sons.

Kneeling on the end of his small bunk, the captain

straightened, placed his palms upon the tops of his thighs, and gazed at the portrait. His eldest boy, Keiji, would surely have graduated from the Naval Academy at Etajima by now, possibly even been in command of his own submarine, hunting the vast Pacific for American and Allied targets. What a source of pride that would have been, to have one's own son engaged in the Great Struggle alongside his father, fighting in the same elite undersea service!

But it was not to be . . . courtesy of one Lieutenant Colonel James H. Doolittle and the crews of sixteen U.S. Army Air Force B-25 bombers. Slightly more than four months after the Imperial Japanese Navy's successful attack on Pearl Harbor, Doolittle and his flying henchmen had committed the unspeakable atrocity of dropping incendiary bombs on Tokyo itself, setting fire to key parts of the great city. Soon after, the American press had shamelessly published the names of the perpetrators, hailing them as heroes and claiming that the B-25s had struck only specific military targets in the factory and waterfront districts.

What had not been reported was that the resultant firestorm from the destruction of a chemical factory had spread uphill into a nearby affluent neighborhood, consuming houses like so many matchboxes. In one of those houses—the small cedar bungalow with the blue-glazed tile roof and the perfect view of Tokyo Bay—Captain Toshiko Yarizuma's wife and three sons had burned to death.

He had accepted the news stoically, without a flicker of emotion crossing his face. He had graciously declined the personal offer from Vice Admiral Komatsu, then commander in chief of the Sixth Imperial Japanese Fleet, to take a special hardship leave, that he might have time to grieve appropriately. *It is not necessary*, he wrote in his formal reply to the admiral,

> to grieve for my wife and children, imbued as they all were with yamato-damashii. Undoubtedly, they wait for me in the hereafter, to usher me through

*the gates of Yasukuni on the day when my Final
Duty is done. Until that day, my only cause for grief
will be that which removes me, however temporarily, from my responsibilities as a warrior and commander in our Great Struggle. I respectfully decline
your generous offer of leave and request that I, my
crew, and my vessel be assigned further combat duty
as soon as possible. Long live the Emperor!*

What Toshiko Yarizuma had not indicated to the admiral or anyone else was that in the moment when he
had first read the news of his devastating personal loss,
the core of his soul had turned to ash—like the cremated
bodies of his family—and dropped away, leaving nothing
but a black, empty hollow. And so it had remained.

It was rumored that Admiral Komatsu had been so
moved by Yarizuma's statement of courage and fighting
spirit that he had promptly directed the veteran captain
to assume command of the Imperial Navy's newest,
largest, and most top secret submarine, the *I-403*—the
first of the mighty *Sensuikan-Toku* class.

Yarizuma had accepted his new assignment without
hesitation, outwardly humbled that he would be placed
in charge of his nation's most technologically advanced
undersea weapon, but feeling privately that it was no
more than his due. The sacrifice he and his family had
laid upon the altar of emperor and country notwithstanding, his career in the submarine force had long been
stalled by his unwillingness to accept the established tactical doctrines—specifically pertaining to submarine
warfare—of the Imperial Japanese Navy's high command, doctrines that he considered outdated, unimagina-
tive, and ineffective.

As a younger man, he had endured the galling inertia
of a naval establishment in love with old victories, specifically, the spectacular defeat of the Russian navy by
Admiral Heihachiro Togo at Tsushima Strait in 1905,
during the Russo-Japanese War. An engagement of fleet
battleships, Tsushima Strait, like the Battle of Jutland in
the First World War, had been a four-square confronta-

tion between surface warships of massive size, maneuvering like chess pieces on the open sea, hammering
away at each other with their immense guns, each combatant in full view of his opposition. The echoes of this
great maritime victory, combined with the Japanese Admiralty's love affair with the British archetype of the
twentieth-century navy, had given Japanese naval theo-
reticians a severely restricted notion as to the proper
composition and tactical priorities of the post-1918 Imperial Japanese Navy. Oceangoing warfare, their conventional wisdom dictated, should be conducted by great
fleets of capital ships meeting each other head-to-head
in titanic and decisive contests on the open sea.

Submarines, a relatively new technology, were rele-
gated to the limited secondary role of supporting the
main battle fleet. This despite the arguments of keen
young submariners like Yarizuma, who protested that
their undersea vessels should be deployed as far-ranging
hunters, able to wreak havoc on enemy merchant shipping and lines of communication, and who offered as
supporting evidence of their claims the impressive combat achievements of Kaiser Wilhelm's German U-
boats—operating as unrestricted predators in the North
Sea—between 1914 and 1918. Their arguments had
fallen on unsympathetic ears, and Yarizuma—more vola-
tile of personality in those early days—had found himself
in conflict with a navy establishment that had the power
to both shut him up and inhibit his career advancement.

Thus he had found himself assigned to small coastal-
patrol submarines throughout most of the 1920s and the
early 1930s, chafing inwardly even as he learned the hard
way to control his temper and keep his nonconformist
opinions to himself. But time had rewarded him. By the
late 1930s old grudges held against him had faded, and
he had returned to large combat submarines as a command officer of nearly twenty years' experience. Still,
the Japanese Admiralty thought of submarines only in
terms of battle fleet support, but that attitude was slowly
changing. How could it not, with the example that Nazi
Grossadmiral Karl Dönitz's modern U-boats, hunting in

their feared wolf packs, were setting in the Atlantic? Yarizuma had kept silent as his reputation within the submarine service gradually evolved from loose cannon to forward-thinking mainstay, and contented himself with the unshakable belief that he had been a man ahead of his time, who had been persecuted by myopic imbeciles for his advocacy of revolutionary ideas, and who was now in the process of being vindicated.

He shifted his gaze and examined himself in the shrine's mirror. Oiled black hair salted with gray, kept rather long after the samurai fashion, combed back and pulled into a neatly bound bundle at the back of the head. Extremely slanted eyes, black as obsidian, captured between arching brows and very high cheekbones. A rather broad face tapering to a pointed chin. A small mouth set in a grim line. Ever deepening creases of stress and weathering, and a certain looseness around the jowls—despite a Spartan diet and a rigid daily calisthenics regimen—that evidenced the onset of later middle age.

He accepted the subtle ravages of time with little concern. It was the way of things. A man could not hope to live forever. But he could hope to die nobly—particularly if he was a samurai, and a true son of the Rising Sun.

Yarizuma finished his meditation by silently reciting his favorite five of the ten major precepts of Shinto: *I will not transgress the will of the gods; I will not forget my obligations to my ancestors; I will not become angry even though others become angry; I will not be sluggish in my work; I will not be carried away by foreign teachings.*

He had long deleted the other five precepts from his thought processes, particularly the maxim *I will never forget that the world is one large family.* In Toshiko Yarizuma's world, there was but one family: his own, and by extension, the Japanese race. All others were barbarians. Like so many xenophobic extremists before him, he practiced a selective form of religion, putting constructs of intolerance on specific teachings within a certain established theology—teachings that were adaptable to his own personal philosophy—and conveniently discarding the rest. Such monomaniacal interpretations lent a spiritual foundation to his deeply ingrained abhorrence of anything that inhibited the forward progress of expansionist Japan, and to his pathological hatred of foreigners—particularly Europeans and Americans: the colonizers, imperialists, and murderers who had continuously looted the world with impunity since the time of Magellan.

Yarizuma unfolded his legs and stood beside his bunk, still looking at himself in the shrine mirror. Despite the adversity he had endured in his life—or perhaps because of it—he was still strong. And now, at long last, he had the tools, the *weapons,* with which to extend that strength, to unleash it against the enemy. He, Toshiko Yarizuma, was the right man in the right place at the right time.

He balled an exercise-hardened fist and raised it in front of his reflection.

With his last breath, he would fight to expel all presumptuous foreign opportunists from Japan's rightful sphere of influence, which he defined as the western Pacific in its entirety. And if he could manage to kill thousands of Americans in the process, so much the better. His beloved Nima and their sons would be avenged.

The insistent low-frequency vibration of active machinery that always pervaded the giant *Sen-Toku,* whether docked or at sea, underwent a subtle change in pitch. Yarizuma's finely tuned commander's ear caught it immediately, and he nodded at his reflected image in satisfaction. Engineers switching diesels to perform routine daily maintenance, exactly on schedule. Similar maintenance would begin on the attack aircraft within the hour. The submarine was running like clockwork, her crew's performance honed to a fine edge. He, and no other, had made it so.

And so it would continue.

Chapter Thirteen

High up on the plateau at the base of the volcanic cone, the shared mood was one of apprehension and bafflement. Unsure whether or not the group had been spotted by the attacking seaplanes, Horwitch had ordered the men into a large crevice near the spire of rock atop which Yomat Dap had first spied the oncoming aircraft.

"Being in here will give us better cover in the event that any more planes come our way," the British major said, "but I want everyone ready to move, and move fast, at a moment's notice. If we were seen, there could be ground forces searching for us as we speak. We may be in for a running fight through the jungle."

"Run to *where*?" DuFourmey spat sarcastically.

Horwitch ignored him.

"Hold on, hold on a minute," DuFourmey pleaded. " 'Zackly how you so sure them planes wasn't ours? I mean . . . you know . . . what if the Japs done *stole* that PT boat—captured it, like—and was tryin' to get back to their own people? What if the U.S. Navy sent them planes to sink it before it got away?"

"Unlikely," Finian Hooke commented, leaning back against the lava rock on one elbow.

DuFourmey turned on him. "How you know that, Mr. High-and-Mighty? You stuck up here on this damn rock, same as me! You got special sight or somethin', lets you figger the answers better than anyone else?"

"That's enough, DuFourmey!" Randall barked. "Keep it civil. The last thing we need to do is start fighting with each other."

DuFourmey pointed a trembling finger at Hooke. "He ain't no ranking officer, Lieutenant; hell, he ain't military and he ain't even American. Ain't no rule book says I got to be civil to him. And he ain't got no call to look down his long nose at me like he been doin' since we hit the beach, nor talk down to me, neither."

"Lieutenant Randall," Horwitch said quietly, gazing across the plateau at the windswept blue expanse of ocean, "pull your man into line. Or I'll do it."

From his seat on top of a large boulder, Hooke blew smoke and looked down idly at DuFourmey, who was breathing hard and staring daggers at him. "In my opinion," the New Zealander calmly said, "it was the aircraft that were questionable, not the PT boat. First of all, when the boat was initially overflown, it did not change course or increase speed. Not a single crewman moved to man a gun. And when the planes came in from the stern for their first strafing run, the two men on the bridge were waving, as if the last thing they expected was to be attacked."

"Now *how* you know that?" DuFourmey said. "That boat was so far away we couldn't hardly see the men on it, never mind what they was doin'."

Silently, Hooke reached inside his shirt and held up the small pair of high-powered binoculars with which he had observed the action.

Joe Garth cleared his throat. "You don't think it's possible that the boat had been seized? After all, we figure we're a pretty long way from Leyte and Minglaat. You think the PT boys are running patrols this far out already?"

"Point taken," Hooke said. "But if there had been a Japanese prize crew aboard that vessel, they would have made ready to fire their antiaircraft weapons and take evasive action upon sighting a formation of American planes—even if they planned to try to bluff their way through initially."

"Makes sense," Foster remarked. The big sergeant was sitting next to Mulgrew at the open end of the crevice, opposite Horwitch. He shifted his Sten across his knees. "They'd have been ready to make a fight of it, the little yellow sons o' bitches. Eh, Mick?"

"Yeh," the swarthy corporal agreed, lighting a cigarette and passing it to Foster. "All the little yellow sons o' bitches I've run up against have."

"Secondly," Hooke said, "those planes came from the west, and as far as we could tell, returned westward to that next island. By our best reckoning, the American and Allied forces are concentrated to our east. I doubt very much that a friendly seaplane base just happens to be conveniently located right beside us—deep in what has to be Japanese-controlled territory.

"And then, thirdly, there are the planes themselves. None of us recognized them. I am ninety-nine percent sure that no such planes exist in the combined Allied air arsenal. And there is something else. During the attack on the PT boat, the aircraft machine guns—"

"I heard it," Foster said, straightening. "But it was so far off, I couldn't be sure. That sound . . ."

"I heard it, too," Mulgrew chimed in. "Web's right—it was far off, sort of muted and echoey, but it had that same bloody sound we heard over and over again in New Guinea. A kind of *tak tak tak tak tak*—real distinctive, that you only hear—"

"From a Nambu-manufactured machine gun," Horwitch finished. He looked up at Hooke. "You're right, sir. I heard it, too."

"So what are you saying?" Randall cut in. "We've got Japanese Nambu machine guns in an American seaplane?"

"That," Joe Garth said slowly, "or we've got Japanese Nambu machine guns in a Japanese seaplane painted with American colors and markings." He looked up and caught Hooke's eye. The lanky New Zealander cracked a thin smile.

"Japanese aircraft disguised with American markings," Randall repeated.

DuFourmey, disgusted, stared around from one man to the next. "Ain't that against the rules?"

"Yes, indeed," Horwitch growled. His ruddy face was dark with anger.

"Look at it," Hooke said. "The Japanese are losing this war, island by island. Once they're pushed out of the Philippines, it will only be a matter of time before Japan itself is invaded. They're getting more desperate day by day. I heard rumors during the Leyte invasion that certain Japanese pilots had crashed their planes into American vessels on purpose—executing something called a kamikaze attack."

"We can confirm that," Garth said, glancing at Randall. "When we were in the hospital on Minglaat, we spoke to a navy Wildcat pilot who saw it happen off Samar a few days ago. Kamikazes sank his carrier."

"And we personally witnessed a suicide attack on the Leyte invasion fleet by high-speed Japanese motorboats loaded with explosives," Randall added. "The helmsmen drove them right into the sides of our ships. Blew themselves up."

"*Shinyo,*" Hooke remarked. "Yes, I know about them. Suicide weapons and tactics. These are the options the Japanese, in their increasing desperation, are being reduced to, gentlemen. And the closer we get to Japan itself, the more we will see of them." He tapped out his spent pipe on the edge of the boulder. "So I don't think any of us should be surprised to see Japanese planes painted to look like American aircraft. Believe me, there is no extreme to which the Japanese will not resort in order to glorify themselves, their country, and their emperor." Hooke's flinty, dead eyes fell on Randall. "They will not give up, you know. Not until we have killed them all." The knife blade smile again.

It was the matter-of-fact way in which the New

Zealander rendered his final comment that sent a chill through Randall. Vaguely, he wondered what the Japanese had done to Hooke in the past, that the thought of wiping them all out filled the man with such a cold, ghoulish enthusiasm.

Foster grimaced around his cigarette, locked his fingers together, and stretched his powerful arms out in front of him. "Fokkin' slanty-eyed little monkeys," he declared. "Take it from me an' Mick: they don't even act like human beings." He gazed around. "Back in New Guinea, on the Kokoda Trail in 'forty-two, we musta been on the receivin' end of at least a dozen Banzai charges. They'd keep comin' until every man jack of 'em was dead. Sometimes, we had Japs surrender, then set off hand grenades hidden in their pockets once we got up close." He glanced at Mulgrew and gave a bitter laugh. "So we stopped lettin' 'em surrender, eh, mate?"

"Bloody right," the corporal grunted, fiddling with his lighter. "They made better fokkin' targets with their hands in the air, anyway."

Foster shrugged, his face set in grim amusement. "What can you do with people like that? I'm with Mr. Hooke over there; I've had a bellyful of 'em. If we end up killin' 'em all, it won't cost me any fokkin' sleep, and that's a fact."

"It's the slanty eyes," Mulgrew remarked off-the-cuff. "Slanty eyes squeeze on a man's frontal lobes and give him permanent brain bruise." He grinned over at Foster. "Makes him fokkin' batty, mate."

The two Australians shared a brief chortle, and Mulgrew's dark, lively eyes flickered around the little group of men. His jokey expression faded somewhat as his glance fell on Salih Matalam, who was sitting back against a rock opposite Hooke, looking down at Mulgrew through heavily slanted lids, his tommy gun in his lap. His Asian face was impassive, impenetrable.

Mulgrew dropped his eyes momentarily, then smiled and gazed back up at the Moro guerrilla. "You know," he said, a note of casual challenge in his voice, "I don't recall ever hearin' you speak a word, friend, not once.

Not since we got aboard the same plane." He paused
for effect. "Kinda makes a man jumpy, havin' to keep
company out here with someone who looks Japanese
and don't ever talk to the people he's movin' with. Now,
this Dayak here"—he gestured with his cigarette at
Yomat Dap—"we've already been told he don't parley
so good, 'cept in his own language. That's fair enough."
The customary affable set of Mulgrew's face dropped
away, and for a moment he looked very dangerous.
"What's your story, mate? Don't you speak English?"

Matalam lifted his tommy gun from his lap and rested
it in the crook of his elbow. His expression did not
change one iota. "I speak English okay, Corporal Mulgrew. And I understand better than I speak. Also Japanese, Malay, Spanish, French, and Philippine Tagalog.
These five I speak much better than English."

Mulgrew lowered his head, somewhat nonplussed.
"Well, you oughtta speak up a little more often, mate,"
he grumbled.

"Because I understand better than I speak," Matalam
said, "I listen more than talk." He blinked slowly, like
a living idol. "Listen more than talk is good rule,
Corporal."

Mulgrew's head came up. "You ain't crackin' wise
with me, are you, mate?" Matalam continued to regard
him with heavy-lidded eyes. " 'Cause if you start crackin'
wise with ol' Mick, I promise you, he can cure you of it
in a fokkin' hurry." He tapped a finger on the hilt of
the long knife in his jungle boot.

"That'll do, Corporal," Horwitch growled. "Steady on.
There'll be no more bickering in this group as of now."

Mulgrew sat back against the rock, his affable expression returning. "Yes, sir." To Matalam, he said, "You
be a good little coolie, now." A ghost of a dangerous
smile flitted across the Moro's face.

A sudden gust of cool wind whirled into the crevice,
accompanied by a few raindrops. The sun dimmed, and
then rain began to fall in earnest as a small squall drifted
across the plateau. The men sat in silence, listening to

the deluge chatter softly against the lava rock that surrounded them, each temporarily lost in his own thoughts.

The squall passed quickly, and within five minutes the sun was shining again, its rays turning the wet lava into lumps of black diamond. Water droplets, falling from the top edge of the entrance, formed a thin, glittering curtain through which the men could gaze across the plateau, over top of the bordering fringe of razor grass, and out to the blue line of the distant horizon.

Horwitch was studying the ground between his jungle boots, frowning.

"What do we do now, Major?" Randall asked quietly.

The Englishman straightened and squared his shoulders, shifting his hands to the tops of his thighs. "I'll tell you what we're going to do, Lieutenant. Inasmuch as we are a de facto unit of Allied military personnel, sworn to prosecute the current war against the Japanese, we are going to reconfigure our thinking—undergo a metamorphosis *right now* from a group of castaways into a viable combat and reconnaissance force. Then we are going to make our way across the intervening strait to that next island and find out exactly what the Japanese are up to over there. At the very least, we will have something to report once we are rescued. At best, we may be able to disrupt or destroy whatever illegal operation exists on that island."

The silence was total.

The major continued: "I include Mr. Hooke; his companion, Mr. Dap; and Mr. Matalam in my definition of military personnel. Although they are all technically civilians, they are experienced combatants dedicated to defeating our enemy in the western Pacific. I am confident of their willing participation in any actions we undertake." He paused to glance at Matalam, who nodded, and Hooke, who did the same. Dap, squatting on his haunches near Hooke, responded to the major's glance with a grin, showing filed teeth.

"Illegal?" DuFourmey asked.

"Correct," Horwitch said. "Illegal. Japan was a signatory to the Geneva convention of 1929, which—among other things—requires that all combatants wear uniforms clearly displaying their nationality. The same principle applies to the markings on tanks, ships, and aircraft. It is against international law to don the colors of one's enemy and then attack him. Japan is well aware of this, and even though some of her diplomats have made noises about the 1929 Geneva treaty not being ratified at home, thereby—they claim—creating a legal technicality which excludes Japan from having to abide by the rules of the convention, the Japanese government formally announced in 1942 that they would consider the Geneva agreement in full force for the duration of this conflict." Horwitch eyed DuFourmey. "Therefore, Steward's Mate, the action of the falsely marked Japanese seaplanes in attacking and destroying the American PT boat was, in fact, illegal."

Foster sagged back against the rock, drew a deep breath, and began to laugh uproariously, holding his stomach. "Illegal!" he managed to gasp. *"Illegal?* Oh, bloody hell, mate—that's a good one! Illegal!" Horwitch kept silent, watching. Foster nudged Mulgrew. "You hear that, Mick? Fokkin' illegal, the major says." He locked eyes with Horwitch, his blue-collar contempt for the British officer and the social class he embodied undisguised. "You've gone off your bloody knob, mate. The whole fokkin' world's in the process of blowin' itself to pieces, people murdered by the millions—bombed, shot, burned, or dyin' of some bloody pox—and you're talking about legal and illegal. Me an' Mick—the more men we kill, the more medals the soddin' brass gives us. It's got so I don't think no more of killin' than I do of takin' a crap. Less maybe . . . I've had dysentery so many times I worry more about me bowels than I do about blowin' some Jap's head off. If there wasn't a war on, they'd call me and Mick both mad-dog murderers." He glanced at his friend, and there was a wild, desperate glaze to his eyes. "Sometimes I wonder how I'm ever gonna be able to stop, once I get back to me cattle station south o' Darwin. Some beered-up stable hand'll give me some lip, and I'll just blast the bugger." He looked back at Horwitch. "Illegal? Callin' one little air attack illegal in this war is like pinchin' Jack the Ripper for jaywalkin'!"

Foster sagged back against the rock, glaring at the major and breathing hard. Horwitch let a full minute pass before he spoke: "Feel better now, Sergeant?"

The big Australian blinked several times and licked his lips before answering. "I'm all right," he muttered.

"Good," Horwitch said. "Because I am the ranking officer here, and if you ever address me with such disrespect again, I'll have you up on charges before the courts-martial." He leaned forward, looking Foster directly in the eye. "And if you do it while we're under fire, I'll blow your bloody head off on the spot. Understood?"

Beside Foster, Mulgrew shifted, muscles tensing. His fingers dangled near the hilt of his boot knife.

For a long moment, none of the men watching were sure what Foster would do next. Then the big soldier let out a raspy laugh, folded his arms, and leaned back against the lava rock. "Aye, Major," he chuckled. "Understood."

Horwitch sat up, his hard glare diminishing. "Good," he said. On Foster's opposite side, Mulgrew relaxed.

"One of the things a British officer candidate is taught at Sandhurst," Horwitch said, "is a certain appreciation of political and military history. It gives one an understanding of what he is fighting for, his place in the bigger scheme of things. Questions of illegality may seem superfluous, even ludicrous, right now—but mark my words, gentlemen: this war will not last forever. And when it is over, those individuals and governments that have contravened the established rules of war—committed atrocities, used immoral tactics and weaponry—will be brought to account. Civilization will reorganize itself, using the *rule of law,* and move beyond these troubled times. That is what I mean by 'legal' and 'illegal.'"

"Bravo," Hooke said from atop his boulder. "Well said."

"Christ, we may all need a good lawyer," Randall mumbled to Garth.

"In the meantime," Horwitch went on, "we are going to go about our duty, which at present consists of moving down the north side of this mountain, traversing this island to its far western point, and devising some way of getting across the strait to that *next* island." He rose to his feet. "Gentlemen, let's move out."

There was a general sighing and shuffling as the men gathered themselves to follow Horwitch out through the curtain of water droplets at the crevice mouth. Garth caught DuFourmey's eye as the black seaman picked his way across the rocks, muttering under his breath. His expression was that of a man being led to the gallows for a crime he didn't commit.

Garth steadied him with a hand on his shoulder. "You okay, Henry?"

DuFourmey looked up at him and blinked. "Hell," he said. "I'm still workin' on 'illegal.'"

Chapter Fourteen

To Flight Technician Kameo Fujita's eye, the Aichi M6A1 *Seiran* floatplane was one of the most beautiful high-performance dive-bombers ever conceived. It reminded him of the British Supermarine seaplane racer he had seen capture the world speed record in its class in the mid-1930s, charging through the air off the Brighton coast, scant meters above the gray waters of the English Channel. He had been a twenty-year-old student of aeronautical design back then, studying in London at the behest of his employer, Mitsubishi Heavy Industries.

He felt a pang of nostalgia as he removed the retaining screws from the machine gun access plate of the first *Seiran*'s starboard wing. Those had been happy times: carefree days consumed by study, nights spent wandering the streets of one of the world's great cities— absorbing the language, visiting legendary sites and monuments, haunting the clubs of Soho and Piccadilly. A young man growing and learning.

It was not for nothing that Mitsubishi had seen fit to bankroll his ongoing education and maintenance halfway around the world in England. Kameo Fujita, the son of a potter from Japan's poor Kagoshima Prefecture, had demonstrated from an early age an almost diabolical facility with things mechanical—let him get his hands on a piece of troublesome machinery, simple or complex, and in short order it would be dismantled, repaired, and reassembled. Word of the boy's aptitude had spread as he progressed from the local high school workshop to the regional technical college, finally reaching Mitsubishi's personnel development offices.

The forward-thinking corporation had invested in him, plucking him away from his humble home and setting him to work under the wing of a senior engineer in its aviation design department. The engineer had liked him, had taken pains to mentor him in the department's highly competitive environment. Ultimately, however, he had been forced to conclude that Kameo, despite his uncanny mechanical intuition, lacked breadth of vision—a crucial attribute for a top designer. Nevertheless, the engineer was optimistic that this flaw could be remedied by further education. Such had been his written evaluation of Kameo Fujita, submitted to the head of Mitsubishi's aviation division a mere three months after the young man had first set foot inside the main corporate building.

So, off to London, on the company ticket. Eighteen glorious months of travel, casual romance, and high times. And all the advanced aeronautical learning he could cram into his reeling, often hungover brain. More nightlife. More high times.

And then came the recall. Political relations with Great Britain had been deteriorating steadily with the rise of Japan's new militarism, and just as Kameo Fujita was beginning to feel like the party was really getting into gear, the ax had fallen and Mitsubishi Heavy Industries had ordered him to return to Tokyo.

He'd found himself back in the aviation design department under the scrutiny of his old mentor, with the place virtually on a war footing and the country in the grip of a militant nationalism that bordered on collective mania. It was back to work with a vengeance, and this time there was little in the way of understanding from the senior engineer. Abruptly, Kameo Fujita realized that he'd had his coddling, his apprenticeship. Now he was expected to produce.

It had not gone well. On September 5, 1939, four days after the sword of Nazi Germany had fallen across the neck of Poland, courtesy of Hitler's blitzkrieg, a sword of another kind fell across the neck of Kameo Fujita—courtesy of the departmental head of Mitsubishi Heavy Industries' aviation division, who held in his hand a job-performance evaluation confirming the awful truth that while employee Fujita possessed undeniable instinctive mechanical gifts, he lacked the fundamental imagination and mental discipline to become an effective design engineer. At best, he would always be a talented shop mechanic.

But before the stunned and bewildered Fujita, who had become accustomed to a considerable amount of deference befitting his status as boy genius, could digest the harsh reality of his first genuine failure—before he could even clean out his desk—an even harsher reality had manifested itself. The senior engineer who had penned the damning performance evaluation that cost him his privileged future with Mitsubishi had also seen fit to report his termination to the recruitment offices of the Imperial Japanese Navy. Since Kameo Fujita's services were no longer required by an essential war industry, went the engineer's suggestion, and since he was a gifted mechanic with a sizable amount of costly additional training in modern aeronautics, perhaps the IJN could use a fresh recruit who already possessed most of the skills needed to work on its most modern military aircraft? Mitsubishi Heavy Industries, exemplar of Japanese patriotism that it was, considered it unconscionable that so much expensive education should not be put to some practical use as the empire continued to expand its influence in the southwestern Pacific.

For Kameo Fujita, it had been the beginning of a five-year running nightmare. Rushed through a brutal six-week course of basic infantry training—which he had barely survived—he had subsequently been posted to a large naval-aviation airfield in the coastal city of Yoko-suka. While his technical talents ensured that he would be kept busy working on the most up-to-date warplanes in the Japanese arsenal, they did not guarantee him anything in the way of special treatment in his humble capacity as a mere seaman second class.

A better man might have learned humility from the jarring rejection at Mitsubishi; in Kameo Fujita—immature, spoiled, and self-absorbed—it generated only indignation and bitterness. His wounded ego exacerbated his longstanding tendency to fire off sarcastic retorts at anyone who had the temerity to question or even try to examine his work.

The Japanese military in 1940, however, bore little resemblance to the local school workshop or even the marginally more daunting environs of a corporate aviation design office. The first time Kameo Fujita, up to his elbows in a stripped-down aircraft engine, had snapped over his shoulder at the senior warrant officer whose responsibility it was to see that maintenance on the warplanes under his care was performed to the letter, the NCO had broken off three of Fujita's front teeth with the heel of his hand.

There had been other rude awakenings, including a thirty-day stint at hard labor on a punishment detail for malingering with a faked stomach ailment, but eventually Fujita had gotten the message that it was less troublesome—and less painful—to do things the navy way and not his. As war was declared against the English, the Dutch, and finally the Americans, his knack for hands-on tinkering had kept him moving, if not up in rank, at least into more and more interesting aircraft maintenance assignments.

This lateral promotion had eventually resulted in his posting to the first *Seiran* dive-bomber unit, which was being deployed in conjunction with Captain Toshiko Yarizuma's *I-403*—the first of the colossal *Sen-Toku* submarines. To his dismay, Fujita—now close to thirty—had been given double duty: in addition to being a primary *Seiran* mechanic, he was also to be a lead field technician for one prototype variant of a curious new aircraft—a rocket-powered flying bomb poetically named the "Cherry Blossom," or *Ohka*. It was a single-pilot suicide weapon, originally designed to be carried to an enemy locale beneath the belly of a heavy bomber and then released. The *tokko* pilot would then fire up the rocket engine, which had only enough fuel for a few minutes' operation, and dive at incredible velocity onto the target, destroying it. The prototype variant assigned to Fujita's care was larger and more complex than the basic design, with both rocket and jet engines, as well as improved—though still limited—flying range.

The pilot of this single experimental *Ohka* that had been attached to Fujita's small *Seiran* seaplane unit was named Sekio Yagi. He was a classic young warrior turk of the Japanese empire—elitist, ultranationalistic, and consumed by notions of military glory and romantic death. Kameo Fujita—who unlike most Japanese had traveled outside the country and considered himself far too worldly and intelligent to credit the jingoistic ravings of the current crop of twenty-year-olds—had hated him on sight.

Yagi was a full naval lieutenant, however, despite his youth—and as such was Fujita's superior. Soon after his posting to the new *Seiran* unit, Fujita had found himself on a transport ship to an unknown destination in the Philippines—seaplanes and all—with the intolerable Lieutenant Yagi and his modified *Ohka* in attendance. Inevitably, conflict had arisen between the two men, which from Kameo Fujita's point of view had made for a very long trip.

Fujita ground his teeth as he struggled to remove the sticky breech mechanism of the *Seiran*'s wing machine gun. Even now, months after their initial arrival on the isolated island in the western Philippines, Yagi was still the bane of his existence. The man had all the besetting weaknesses of youth: he was vain; he was temperamental; he was overly sure of himself; he was arrogant. Never having had to take orders in the field, he did not know how to give them. He bullied rather than led, threatened rather than inspired. He often reinforced his semiludicrous commands with the lowbrow Japanese officer's discipline of choice: a punch, a slap, or a kick.

In addition, Yagi seemed unaware that Fujita had three other *Seiran* aircraft in his care besides the *Ohka*. If Yagi had his way, Fujita would have done nothing but disassemble, tweak, and reassemble the flying bomb over and over, twenty-four hours a day, seven days a week. There would have been no on-the-spot improvements to the *Seiran,* such as Fujita's installation of forward-firing machine guns in the wings of the dive-bombers, which had previously only had a single rear-firing defensive gun mounted at the back of the cockpit canopy.

Kameo Fujita heard footsteps and looked up from his work. Yagi was approaching. The mechanic ground his teeth again and steeled himself for the coming verbal assault.

For months now, he had been praying for the day when Lieutenant Sekio Yagi wrapped his *hachimaki* around his swollen head, climbed into his *Ohka,* soared off into the wild blue yonder, and blew himself to hell.

Chapter
Fifteen

It had taken most of the day to descend the side of the volcano and bushwhack through the lower hills to the island's far western tip. Horwitch had kept them moving quickly in single file, no talking, one man walking point several dozen yards ahead of the main body. Periodically, the major had changed the point man, alternating between Foster, Mulgrew, Matalam, and himself. Finian Hooke had brought up the rear, hanging back somewhat, while Yomat Dap lurked through the trees like a black-feathered ghost, appearing first on one flank, then the other.

"You hear somethin'?" DuFourmey had kept whispering. "I think maybe I hear Japs." But they had encountered no one.

By the time they'd reached the island's western extremity, they were all dehydrated and muscle-sore. Even with the sun starting to dip below the horizon, it was still brutally hot. Mercifully, after finding no freshwater all day, they'd discovered a small stream running out to sea in the little sand cove that faced the next island. "No fires," Horwitch had ordered. "Treat the water with iodine."

"Looks clean to me," DuFourmey protested, staring at the stream water he'd scooped up in his cupped hands.

Mulgrew squatted on his haunches beside him and began filling canteens. Nearby, Foster searched his pockets for purification tablets. The swarthy corporal gave DuFourmey a Mephistophelian grin. "Hey, mate," he said. "I knew an outback bloke from Queensland once who swore up an' down that he was so used to the bush, he never had to treat his water—just drank it straight down whether it came from a river, a swamp, or a wild-pig wallow. And he ate like ten men, too—steaks, bread, desserts—you name it. Funny thing was, though, he never gained a pound. Skinniest little sod you ever saw."

"Yeah?" DuFourmey replied warily.

"When he got down to about ninety pounds and started havin' dizzy spells, he went to see the local doc. Turns out he was carryin' around a twenty-three-foot tapeworm in his lower intestine."

DuFourmey opened his hands and dropped the water back into the stream with a splash.

"Always treat your water, mate," Mulgrew said. He handed a canteen up to Foster, whose big shoulders were shaking with suppressed laughter.

Farther down the beach, Randall and Garth were standing on either side of Horwitch and gazing with him out across the purple-blue evening waters of the strait, examining the twin volcanic cones of the neighboring island. Nearby, Hooke stood with Dap and Matalam, doing the same.

"Ideas for getting across, gentlemen?" Horwitch said.

Garth spoke up: "Well, Major, I make it every bit of five miles, like Mr. Hooke here said. That's a long way to swim without some kind of buoyant support, especially since we're toting boots, clothing, weapons."

"We don't know about the currents, either," Randall pointed out. "The tides can squeeze a lot of water back and forth between these islands. We could end up being pushed halfway to Borneo."

Horwitch nodded. "My thoughts exactly. So we're

looking at putting together some kind of raft. Something we can paddle."

"Or sail," Randall suggested. "Right now the breeze is blowing directly at that island. It'd be a downhill run and a lot less effort if we were able to ride it across." He turned and looked back at the tree line. "All we really need are a couple of large logs lashed together with a few short crosspieces—like a ladder. It'd float low, and be wet, but with some luck, we wouldn't have to be on it very long. We'd be in position to paddle, too."

Horwitch considered. "I like the idea of some kind of sail," he said. "But we don't have any material . . . *blast*! The cargo tarps from the plane!"

Randall nodded. "They'd work. But you're talking about a day and a half to backtrack over the mountain and pick them up. Maybe we can make something here, Major."

"Palm fronds," Hooke said. "If we make a light grid out of bamboo—maybe six feet wide by ten tall—and then weave palm fronds into it, we'll have a flat surface like a square sail. We can rig it upright on one end of the raft and it will pull us downwind."

"Rigging materials?" Horwitch inquired.

Hooke gestured at the jungle with the muzzle of his Sten gun. "Strangler vines," he said. "Nearly as strong as hemp rope."

"All right, then," Horwitch declared. "We'll split up the labor. Half of us can work on the sail; the others can search for suitable logs for the raft. We—"

"Not necessary, Major," Hooke interrupted. "We can all work on the raft." He turned to Yomat Dap and rattled off something incomprehensible. The Dayak grinned and responded in the same guttural tongue, dropping to his haunches. Working quickly, he sketched out a rectangular framework in the sand with his index finger, muttering as he did so.

"*Ya*," Hooke said, nodding. Without further comment, Yomat Dap stood up, drew his long sword, and stalked off toward a tall thicket of green bamboo.

DuFourmey, approaching from the stream with several canteens, stepped sideways and gave the Dayak a wide berth as he went past. Shaking his head, he began to hand out the water. "Damned if that fella don't give me the heebie-jeebies," he said. "What he got there, anyhow? A machete?"

"That is a parang," Hooke informed him. "All Dayak warriors carry them."

DuFourmey blinked at the New Zealander. "What for? Cuttin' cane?"

Hooke sent him a glinting smile. "Cutting heads."

"Say what?"

"Cutting heads. A parang is a traditional beheading sword. Dayaks are headhunters."

DuFourmey stared at him. "G'wan . . . the hell you say . . ."

"When the Japanese first invaded North Borneo," Hooke told him, "they treated the indigenous people with great brutality—raiding their villages and imposing martial law. They killed a significant number and forced many others into slave labor, using them to construct coastal bases and roads. However, it wasn't long before the Dayaks under their control began to disappear— simply melt away into the jungle. It was impossible to stop them; they just seemed to evaporate overnight.

"So the Japanese began to send killing squads into the backcountry villages, to try to restore their dominance over the Dayaks through fear. Bad idea. The larger squads usually returned to base having seen no one. The smaller squads quite often did not return at all. When search parties in force located the bodies, they were always minus their heads."

Hooke paused as DuFourmey swallowed hard and stared through the gathering dusk at the wiry figure of Yomat Dap, hacking away with his parang at the base of the bamboo thicket. Randall exchanged glances with Garth. "So your friend Mr. Dap," he said. "He . . . er . . ."

"The last time I was in his mountain lodge," Hooke stated, "he had the heads of nine Japanese soldiers hanging from the central roof support pole. Two of them were still wearing their spectacles. Fourteen other heads were stored in baskets around the room. My friend Yomat Dap took them all, single-handed."

"Extreme," was all Randall could think to say.

"My friend, who as I have told you is a subchief within his tribe, does not appreciate uninvited foreigners marching into his home territory and abusing those under his care," Hooke said. A black gleam pulsed momentarily in his dead eyes. "Neither do I."

He shifted his gaze out over the open strait and reached for his tobacco pouch.

Salih Matalam moved up beside Horwitch. "Excuse, Major. I am thinking, a sail will make the raft much easier to see, yes? Perhaps even at night. Maybe paddling is better."

"An excellent point, Mr. Matalam," Horwitch said. "Certainly, we will cross at night. And, weather permitting, *tomorrow* night. As to the visibility of our sail, if you will take note over your right shoulder, just above the ridgeline—"

The Moro smiled immediately without turning to look. "Ah," he said, nodding. "Of course. Tonight, a waning moon. Tomorrow, no moon at all."

Horwitch lifted his eyes to the darkening sky. "Exactly."

It was well after midnight when the raft was finished. Constructed of two logs fifteen inches in diameter and twenty feet long, with ten six-foot tree limbs serving as cross braces, the entire affair was held together by numerous lashings of vines. It lay just off the beach behind the tree line, covered by the palm frond sail Yomat Dap had framed and woven in less than an hour.

From the air, it was completely invisible. The last thing Horwitch did, as the exhausted men bedded down on foliage mats beside the raft, was sweep the beach clean of footprints above the high-tide line with a leafy branch. Then he, too, crawled in beneath the woven sail, pulled his neck bandanna up over his face and eyes against the biting insects, and went to sleep.

Hooke, who had volunteered to keep watch, sat at the end of a short finger of rock that jutted out from the southern end of the cove like a natural jetty. He was almost out of tobacco, and so had loaded his pipe bowl only half full with his remaining Cherry-Bourbon Amsterdam Darkleaf. He drew on the pipe slowly, savoring the rich smoke. Its taste and aroma triggered intense memories of the home he'd had, the life he had lost.

He was an educated man, a worldly man, with an agile, questing intellect and the pragmatic toughness to make it work for him in business, a student of history and human nature, a believer in the lessons of history.

Opportunism was the name of the game in international politics. Always had been, always would be. It had been so clear to him in mid-1940, sitting in his plantation home in Sarawak, listening to ominous radio broadcasts from British Singapore and reading private communiqués sent to him by friends in the consular service and the oil business, that the great chess game of warring nations was about to repeat itself in the western Pacific. To Finian Hooke, the very predictability of events was what had made them so frightening.

Japan had been at full-scale war with China since 1937. It had also signed alliance pacts with Germany and Italy. By 1939, the Nationalist Chinese were hard-pressed but still fighting, supplied primarily by the United States via a rail line from Haiphong Harbor in French Indochina, and the long, twisting Burma Road. In 1940, as France fell to Germany, and Britain fought for her life, the Japanese saw an opportunity.

With the cooperation of Nazi-occupied France's new Vichy government, Japan took over air bases in French Indochina and closed the rail line from Haiphong Harbor. Check.

Japan then threatened Britain with war if the supply line from Burma remained open. Prime Minister Winston Churchill, not wanting to enter a second conflict with Nazi Germany already battering down his country's door, closed the Burma Road. Check.

China was cut off.

Then, at the end of 1940, Japan had declared its intention to put in place what it termed The Greater East Asia Co-Prosperity Sphere. With that, Finian Hooke's blood had really begun to run cold, and he'd made inquiries of his diplomatic friends. Translation: Japan sought complete control over all the territories and raw materials of the western Pacific, as well as uncontested dominance over all the peoples of Asia. Check.

Hooke had been in the process of wrapping up his plantation and oil business affairs and arranging transport to Darwin, Australia, for his wife and daughter when Japan had bombed Pearl Harbor. Check.

Two days later, elite Japanese paratroopers deployed out of Saigon had landed in his backyard. Their primary task had been to initiate attacks against the weak British garrisons in Sarawak and Brunei, paving the way for a larger, seaborne invasion force to overrun Borneo and secure for Japan's military machine the vital oil fields of Miri, Tarakan, and Balikpapan. Check.

Their secondary task had been to suppress the activities of the civilian population through intimidation. Of particular interest were wealthy foreign nationals—primarily British and Dutch—who held positions of influence in the society, and who represented for the Japanese the colonial European powers they were trying to oust. They were to be made examples of.

That was how Finian Hooke had found himself tied spread-eagled to the wheel of an oxcart, the right side of his face smashed in by a rifle butt, watching through a red mist of blood and pain as his Malayan wife, Liu, and eleven-year-old daughter, Kim, were dragged out into the center of the patio terrace of their home and repeatedly raped and beaten by several dozen laughing, hooting Japanese paratroopers. His wife had managed to keep her eyes on his for a few minutes, her beautiful face calm even in its despair. His daughter had only screamed.

At some point in the brutal assault, both of them had died. The soldiers had continued to take turns for a while, bellowing encouragement to each other, then had concluded their entertainment with a gang bayoneting of the women's bodies. By that time Hooke had gone past insanity into catatonic numbness.

The paratroopers had turned their attention back to him. After discussing it for a few minutes, they decided they would teach him the honor of dying by a belly slash, seppuku-style. The lieutenant in charge had drawn his boot knife, knelt down, and plunged it into Finian Hooke's stomach. He'd jerked it sideways as Hooke let out a long, bubbling scream, then yanked the blade free. Rising to his feet, he'd made a grim comment about leaving appropriate examples scattered around the countryside, and then spit on Hooke for good measure. Then he and his paratroopers had left.

Population suppressed. Check.

But Finian Hooke had not died, although he'd wanted to. His hard, fit body had been tough enough to last all night and halfway through the next day—though by the time Yomat Dap and his warriors found him, half the blood in his body had pooled on the ground beneath him.

Hooke stared out across the dark strait at the twin-coned island in the middle distance. His pipe was dead, and he removed the stem from his mouth so he wouldn't risk cracking it between his clenched teeth. He blinked slowly, trying to erase the memory of Liu's face as she'd lain on the terrace being raped and beaten to death.

Example made. Check.

Finian Hooke's fingers tightened around the magazine of his Sten.

Check—but not checkmate.

Not yet.

Chapter
Sixteen

Lieutenant Sekio Yagi had no patience for Seaman Technician Kameo Fujita. He saw in him a kind of pernicious malaise, an unfocused, noncommittal cynicism about Japan's sacred struggle for self-determination that ran completely counter to Yagi's own ardent patriotism. Individuals like Fujita, who went around affecting an air of dissatisfied ennui—as if they were above it all—were, in his opinion, more than an irritant; they were subversives who undermined the collective *yamato-damashii* of the nation. If he'd had his way, they all would have been taken out and shot.

As with most young men, Sekio Yagi's idealism was untempered by experience. He viewed right and wrong as absolutes, without gray areas. No interpretation, evaluation, or compromise necessary.

Japan needed commitment and decisive action from her sons right now—great acts of sacrifice that would ultimately force the Americans to abandon all attempts to dismantle the recently expanded empire. Yagi himself existed in a state of barely contained exhilaration, knowing that he would soon have an opportunity to martyr himself for his emperor. So it galled him no end that the technician on whom he had to rely to keep the vehicle of his martyrdom—his specially modified *Ohka*—in peak operating condition had turned out to be such a dilatory croaker.

But a *talented* croaker, he had to admit. Fujita was a veritable surgeon when his hands were inside a piece of machinery. His skills almost made up for his appalling lack of Bushido virtue.

Almost, Yagi thought angrily—but not quite.

He strode up behind the technician, who was working on the wing of one of the *Seiran,* and stopped, clacking his heels down hard on the steel deck. Fujita stiffened, then slowly turned his head and glanced over his shoulder, giving off blasé insolence like a gas.

Yagi's smooth, boyish face creased in irritation. "So, Fujita, have you found a way to increase the solid-fuel capacity of my *Ohka*'s rocket engine, as I ordered you to do?"

Fujita was gripped by a sudden urge to smash the heavy wrench he was holding into Yagi's mouth—the young officer was so pompous and smug. Summoning what he felt to be a superhuman amount of self-control, he refrained from doing so.

"Not yet," he said.

" 'Not yet'—*Lieutenant!*" Yagi shouted.

"Not yet, Lieutenant."

"Get on your feet and come to attention, Seaman Technician Fujita!" Yagi barked, clasping his hands behind him.

Not again. Kameo Fujita set his wrench on the deck, pushed himself to his feet, and let his arms hang at his sides. This military-school puppy was unendurable.

"Sir," he said wearily, "I most respectfully remind you that I am responsible for the maintenance and tuning not only of your *Ohka*, but also these three *Seiran.* Each of the other pilots has a list of checks and repairs he wants performed before the end of the week. The *Ohka*'s schedule of standard maintenance is completely up-to-date. What you are asking for is a time-consuming customization—"

Yagi's white-gloved hand whipped up and cracked across Fujita's cheek. "Do not presume to tell *me* what I am asking for!" the lieutenant shouted. "*I* will tell *you!* And my orders are not requests! You will follow them to the letter, not debate them with me! Do you understand, Seaman Technician Fujita?"

Fujita looked sideways at him, his cheek stinging. "Sir," he said, "what you ask is impractical. It will be difficult to increase the *Ohka*'s fuel capacity without destabilizing it in flight. There is only so much room—"

Yagi struck him again. *Crack.*

Fujita took a step back, recovered, and held his position of attention. Inside, he was seething with anger; on the outside, nothing showed. He had been hit so often by officers over the past five years that he had come to expect it. He had never come to accept it.

"Sir," he began, "I protest—"

"You are derelict in your duty, Fujita!" Yagi declared. "Your reputation as a malcontent precedes you. It is in your service record—and in your deportment—for all to see. If you were not the *former* Boy Wizard of Mechanics from Kagoshima, you would undoubtedly have been executed by now for your treasonous complacency!"

To argue was pointless. Yagi was puffed up like a fighting rooster. Fujita clamped his teeth together so the next blow would not dislocate his jaw, and fixed his eyes on a point just above the lieutenant's head. "I will look at the *Ohka* again, sir," he muttered, "but as I said, it is impractical—"

"Impractical is not *impossible,* Seaman Technician," Yagi told him. "Especially not for a mechanic of your renowned ability." He smiled suddenly. "Now, then, you will get me the improved range I need, won't you?"

Fujita lowered his eyes to meet the lieutenant's. The fool did not even have the sense to be consistent. He had the changeable emotions of a child—one minute squalling, the next, smiling. And his transparent attempts to use psychology on a man nearly ten years his senior were lame and patronizing.

To make Yagi go away, Fujita knocked his heels together and stiffened slightly. "I will do my best, sir," he said.

Captain Toshiko Yarizuma lay in his bunk and stared into the darkness, listening to the mechanical pulse of his submarine. In the past year and a half he had remained on board almost continuously, whether the boat was at sea or moored in one of the IJN's many hidden sub pens. The *Sen-Toku* had become his whole world. There was no reason to leave.

A notable exception had occurred in April of 1943, when Admiral Isoroku Yamamoto himself, commander of the Japanese Combined Fleet, had made a surprise visit to the little Philippine island with the twin volcanic cones, not long after the arrival of Yarizuma's *I-403*. The great admiral, architect of the Pearl Harbor attack and many other Japanese naval successes, had flown in by seaplane transport, escorted by seven Nakajima single-float fighters. Yarizuma had been stunned to see Yamamoto emerge from the transport, benevolently returning salutes, but had quickly recovered. The admiral was known as something of an eccentric, given to doing the unpredictable, such as showing up in out-of-the-way places unannounced. Despite this, and the fact that they had met only twice before, Yarizuma admired and respected him—as did nearly every other serving member of the IJN.

Together, they had walked alone up the rocky path above the garrison compound—the jungle highlands and the huge cojoined volcanoes towering above them in the evening sky. After having made a routine inspection of the relatively new sub pen and its supporting fortifications, the admiral had seemed in a pensive, philosophical mood.

"You are well, Yarizuma?" he'd asked.

"Very well, sir, thank you," Yarizuma replied.

"Good, good," Yamamoto said. "I am pleased that you have been able to reconcile yourself to the loss of your family—yes, I remember Vice Admiral Komatsu telling me about it soon after the Doolittle raid—and persevere in your duties. Experienced submarine commanders are getting scarcer all the time, I'm afraid."

The Toshiko Yarizuma of 1922 would have responded immediately to such a comment with an impassioned outburst criticizing the tactical doctrines of the entire Japanese naval establishment. The Toshiko Yarizuma of 1943 was an older, subtler man.

"Yes, sir. Submarine duty is exceedingly hazardous these days."

Yamamoto looked at him, one eyebrow raised expectantly. "Yes, it is." A pause. "But you do not care to volunteer your opinion as to why this is so?"

Yarizuma kept his expression placid. "I have not been asked for my opinion, Honorable Admiral."

Yamamoto tipped back his close-cropped gray head and laughed, his intelligent face reorganizing itself into a welter of crow's-feet and laugh lines. "No longer the young fire-eater, eh, Yarizuma?" he said. "That is as it should be. Age and experience make cautious men of us all." He scratched his chin with the back of his hand. "Come, now, I want your input on this."

Yarizuma took a deep breath. "The submarine fleet is being used incorrectly, sir. Attack subs are deployed as cargo transports delivering food and ammunition to ground troops in New Guinea, Borneo, and the lesser island chains. Submarines idling on the surface in shallow coastal waters, unloading supplies at night, are easy targets for PT boats and aircraft.

"Conversely, if not delivering cargo, they are restricted to picket line duty around the main surface battle fleets. At sea, when the Americans find one sub, they know that there are usually a half-dozen more in the same general area. They concentrate their assets on running down the picket line until they have located and sunk them all." Yarizuma stopped before he went too far. "That is my opinion, Honorable Admiral."

"And you would use submarines in a very different way," Yamamoto prompted.

Yarizuma held the admiral's eye. "I am on record as to my conviction that submarines should be used as free-lance hunters, deployed widely and independently, to whittle away at the enemy's supply lines. Concentrating them in one small area in association with a main surface fleet, in the vain hope of eliminating the enemy's entire navy in a single huge engagement, takes away their inherent advantages of stealth and surprise. If the Americans locate one of our battle fleets, they know the subs are there, picketed around it."

He was on dangerous ground here. Yamamoto was a well-known advocate of the old-school approach to naval warfare: win the war at sea with one brilliant stroke. This Tsushima Strait–inspired thinking had cost him the Battle of Midway. American admiral Chester Nimitz had refused to be drawn into a gun-to-gun slugging match with Yamamoto's battleships, and instead had utilized long-range aerial attacks from his well-placed aircraft carriers to sink half the *Japanese* carriers. Yamamoto had been forced to withdraw.

Not for the first time in his life, Yarizuma wondered if he'd spoken too directly. But the admiral, gazing out at the dark waters of the archipelago, looked unruffled.

"You know," he said, "I attended both Harvard and Yale Universities in the United States."

Yarizuma blinked. "I beg your pardon, sir?"

"Yes. In the 1920s, as a graduate student in military-political affairs. A most enlightening experience." Yamamoto looked at Yarizuma again. "Do you speak English, by any chance?"

"No, sir."

"How unfortunate. I do. It has become the dominant business language of the world, and is likely to remain so. You would do well to learn it; we are going to have to deal with the Americans and the British for a long time to come. They are a fact of life."

Yarizuma became aware that he was sweating under his light collar. The admiral's comments seemed vaguely . . . seditious.

"You will recall, back in 1940," Yamamoto went on,

"that I counseled our government *against* entering into a war with the United States. I based this on my first-hand experiences as a resident of that country. I had seen the industrial might of America with my own eyes, and knew that while we could probably achieve some degree of military success against her in the first year of hostilities, we could not possibly win in the long run." The admiral smiled into the night. "Of course, as you know, my counsel was ignored. I was instructed by our political leaders to come up with a strategy to eliminate the U.S. Navy from the Pacific Ocean."

"And did so admirably, sir," Yarizuma interjected, unsure of where this was all going. "The Pearl Harbor attack was a masterpiece of military planning. So was your follow-up plan for Midway. . . ." He winced inwardly, his voice trailing off.

"Ha!" Yamamoto looked genuinely amused. "Pearl a masterpiece? Perhaps. But like all so-called masterpieces, it contained a flaw. The American carriers were not in port, so we did not sink them. And as for Midway—it was a sound enough plan, but my esteemed opponent, Admiral Nimitz, refused to cooperate. He had the incredible luck to place his carriers in just the right position to intercept our main battle fleet with his aircraft, while not having to face our battleships. Astonishing." Yamamoto tipped his head back and looked up at the stars. "It was almost as if he knew in advance what I had decided to do."

"Impossible, sir," Yarizuma said. "Strict secrecy was maintained, and your strategy of drawing in the American fleet was inspired. Nimitz was lucky, that's all."

"He won," Yamamoto said flatly, "and that is all that matters." His voice softened. "You know, I admire him. He is a worthy opponent, calm and disciplined. In an odd way, it pleases me that I am able to respect my opposite number. It makes me try harder. We are almost like brothers, contending." He caught Yarizuma's eye again. "What do you think of that?"

"I'm . . . not sure what to think, Admiral," Yarizuma muttered.

Yamamoto raised his left hand. It was covered in old scars, and several fingers were missing. "Do you know how I got this, Yarizuma?" he asked.

"Uh—no, sir," the submarine captain replied, although he had heard rumors.

"I was wounded while commanding a motor torpedo boat in the Battle of Tsushima Strait," Yamamoto said. "It was my privilege to lose these fingers while making a modest contribution to Admiral Togo's great victory over the Russians."

"A mark of honor, sir," Yarizuma declared immediately.

The admiral eyed him. "Quite. Did you know that Chester Nimitz is also missing the ring finger of his left hand? A service injury, like mine."

Yarizuma shook his head. "I did not know that, sir."

"Yes. A rather astonishing case of parallelism, don't you agree? If I was more medieval in my thinking, rather than being a man whose faith rests largely in science and logic, I would tend to consider it less a coincidence than a sign—a sign that my fate and Nimitz's are inextricably bound together."

Yarizuma's mouth opened, then closed again. Yamamoto's eccentricity was widely considered a harmless side effect of his conceptual brilliance, but this was becoming ridiculous.

The admiral laughed lightly. "Of course, that would be mere superstition, after all."

Yarizuma nodded. "Yes, sir."

Yamamoto faced the submarine captain squarely. "Listen to me now, Yarizuma, and consider my words carefully: *we cannot win.* No—don't look so shocked; my opinion on this, from the outset, has always been crystal clear." He smiled, but rather than pensive his face was now hard, analytical. "The industrial capacity of America is many times that of Japan. She can build aircraft, ships, and submarines much faster than we can. The United States is the world's largest producer and exporter of oil and steel, both vital strategic materials. In Japan, we have none of our own, and formerly bought most of ours from the U.S.

"Long before Pearl Harbor, we tried to cow the Americans into not interfering with us in Asia by signing an alliance pact with Germany and Italy, stating that if the U.S. entered the European war on the side of the British, we would enter on the side of the Axis. We also signed a nonaggression pact with the Russians.

"The Americans—no surprise to me—were not cowed. President Roosevelt responded by stating that the United States would tolerate no further Japanese aggression in the Far East, then promptly froze all Japanese assets in the U.S. and banned the sale of oil and steel to Japan indefinitely. We knew we could not maintain our strength for long under these kinds of restrictions, so we went to war with America."

"Honorable Admiral," Yarizuma said, daring to sound a trifle bored, "I am well aware of recent political history. Is it not true that our successful seizures of oil and rubber resources in the former Dutch East Indies, and our occupation of iron- and coal-producing areas of Manchuria, have more than compensated for the loss of imports from the United States? We continue to build ships, submarines. My own *Sen-Toku* and her sister vessels are tangible evidence of our country's continuing productivity, are they not?"

Yamamoto shook his elegant head. "Too little, too late, I'm afraid. You hear the propaganda, Yarizuma. I see the numbers. Our rates of attrition in combat are too high. The losses we are able to inflict on the Americans and their allies are too low. The Americans are relentless. They are overwhelming us, slowly but surely, by sheer weight of numbers, by sheer volume of manufacturing. As I predicted they would."

Yarizuma could feel his face reddening with anger. "Excuse my presumption, Honorable Admiral," he said, "but how am I to consider your comments as anything other than . . . defeatist?" He swallowed, then went on. "You are saying that our great struggle—*your* great struggle, sir—has been futile from the beginning!"

"Not futile, Yarizuma," the admiral countered. "There has always been a way to accomplish significant gains for Japan without necessarily routing or even holding the Americans at bay. That is to make them pay so dearly for every inch of territory recaptured, for every battle won, that rather than fight a protracted war into the second half of the twentieth century, they will elect to sue for a negotiated peace—a peace that will enable us to hold on to many of our country's newly acquired assets, even if we cannot hold on to them all.

"The harder we fight, Yarizuma," Yamamoto said, "and the more pain we inflict on the Americans *now,* the more favorable will be the lines drawn on the map in the context of the coming peace settlement." His philosophical smile returned. "It's all bargaining, you see. They'll come to the table eventually. No one wants to be at war forever—it becomes too dreary after a while. This applies to Americans in particular: they are a great people, but have a short attention span. We must simply battle them long and hard enough that they will consider it worth their while to talk to us and make compromises for peace rather than continue fighting."

"They will sicken of us long before we tire of striking at them, Honorable Admiral," Yarizuma declared defiantly. "Our spirits are high."

"Mm. Yes, I know," Yamamoto said. "Spirit is something we have plenty of. Unfortunately, we are short of just about everything else. So we must use our abundance of spirit to hasten the Americans' inevitable disillusionment with all this fighting." The admiral's shrewd eyes drifted over Yarizuma's face. "In times like these, unexpected successes—grand gestures, if you like—can have a profound effect on the psyche, the morale, of a nation. I'll give you an example: look at how stunned our own citizens were, however temporarily, when Lieutenant Colonel Doolittle managed to bomb Tokyo. That the far-off enemy, still reeling from the body blow we had administered at Pearl Harbor, could reach out and strike at the heart of Japan—it sent people into a state of shock. And what a psychological tonic for the citizens of the United States! All of a sudden, their spirits were revitalized while ours were shaken. In effect, Doolittle's raid was the reversal of Pearl Harbor."

Yamamoto coughed, clearing his throat, and looked up at the stars again. "I often think, as the Americans become more and more flushed with their own success, that a well-placed grand gesture might remind them of their own vulnerability. Make them conscious of the fact that a war they insist on protracting can travel around the globe and touch them directly . . ." The admiral paused, moving his gaze down onto the flickering lights of the garrison compound below. "What do you think of that, Yarizuma?" he asked, his tone casual. "Say, for example, a full-blown strike against Washington, D.C.? A strike against the beating heart of the American homeland—much as Doolittle's bombers struck at the heart of Japan."

A surge of excitement such as he had not felt in years coursed through Toshiko Yarizuma. "I think it is a noble idea, Honorable Admiral," he said at once. "Plans for its execution should be drawn up without delay."

Yamamoto smiled. "Yes, well, they have been. As a matter of fact, the *Sen-Toku* class of submarines, of which your *I-403* is the first, was designed with this global strike capability in mind. Unfortunately"—he shrugged—"the consensus of opinion at the highest levels of our military-political leadership is that an attack on a major U.S. city would be impractical—more of a futile gesture than a grand gesture. The thinking is that it would only make the Americans more angry than they already are, without actually having any material effect on their ability to wage war in the Pacific. The preference, currently, is for an attack on the Panama Canal, to close it and prevent U.S. naval assets from transiting rapidly from the Atlantic to the Pacific. I do not agree, but even though I am commander of the Combined Fleet, I am still only one voice."

Yarizuma was shaking. "Sir," he said. "A raid such as you describe would be the single greatest blow Japan could strike against—"

"It would take an exceptional commander to lead it," Yamamoto continued conversationally. "A man with utter devotion to the emperor and Japan. A man of long experience and proven ability. A man capable of independent action, of seizing the moment and carrying through regardless of the cost to himself."

"Sir—" Yarizuma ventured.

"Well, it's out of the question for the time being," Yamamoto mused, "but things have a way of changing." He stretched his arms behind his back and stamped his feet. "You know, such a mission might be of interest to a man like you, Yarizuma." He turned and began to move back down the trail. "We will speak of this at a later date. Right now, it is late, and tomorrow I must start a series of long flights to the Solomon Islands. Consider what I have said, Captain. File it away in your memory for future reference."

Yarizuma stepped up beside the admiral. "I will, sir."

Yamamoto looked at him carefully with his shrewd eyes. Then he nodded and smiled.

"Good," he said.

Toshiko Yarizuma continued to stare up at the darkness in his captain's quarters. Admiral Isoroku Yamamoto had departed the next day in his seaplane transport, taking off eastward into the rising sun. One week later, he was dead. Shot down by American P-38 Lightnings that had jumped his transport over the Solomons. One stroke of bad luck, and Japan's greatest warrior was gone.

But he had left Yarizuma with the tantalizing idea of striking at America as Doolittle had struck at Japan— exacting retribution for the criminal bombing of Tokyo by returning the favor on the U.S. mainland. Letting the Americans feel the pain of civilian casualties in their own cherished cities. Letting American families mourn loved ones murdered in their own beds, even as he had mourned.

The longer Yarizuma had thought about it, analyzing the pros and cons in the dark vaults of his megalomaniacal psyche, the more justifiable—the more *essential*—the concept had become. The attack on Pearl Harbor had been a legitimate strike against a military target—the U.S. Pacific Fleet. Doolittle's retaliatory raid, on the other hand, had been a random, strategically insignificant bombing of a civilian center, perpetrated solely in order to spread terror and make the Americans feel better. Claims in the U.S. press that Tokyo's factories and docks had been the intended targets were self-serving lies. Had not his wife and sons died in their own home, in a residential area known only for the beauty of its mature cherry trees?

In the aftermath of Admiral Yamamoto's death, the remaining high-level navy commanders had waffled indecisively, squabbling with the much more politically influential army for the attentions of the emperor and adopting an overcautious, defensive approach to deploying ships and submarines. Island by island, region by region, they had allowed the IJN to be driven back northward toward Japan. While individual islands like Tarawa, Saipan, and Guam had been defended to the death in true samurai fashion, there had been no outstanding *offensive* actions taken—no grand gestures, bold and unexpected, put forth to surprise and stagger the enemy. To inspire the hard-pressed Japanese military and rejuvenate the loyal but war-weary citizenry.

The Admiralty, as had been the case twenty years earlier, was being dominated by dithering old men—afraid to commit Japan's most powerful weapons for fear of losing them. But by not committing them fully they were losing the *war*. Yarizuma's sense of déja vu was almost overwhelming. Here he was again, with the means at hand to strike a fearful blow against the emperor's enemies, being bound by the defeatist policies of an indecisive naval high command.

Toshiko Yarizuma turned over in his bunk in the dark and closed his eyes.

Loyalty was everything. Loyalty and Duty. But his allegiance was to the emperor and Japan, not to a staff room full of bickering little shoguns who exhibited more pessimistic inertia than true fighting spirit.

There would be a grand gesture, and soon. In spite of the admirals and their maundering. Yamamoto had as much as given his tacit permission, hadn't he?

Of course he had.

Chapter
Seventeen

"Lawd Jesus!" DuFourmey yelled, recoiling. "There's another one!"

He yanked his leg out of the ink black water as a large, torpedolike shape, sheathed in a sparkling cloud of green phosphorescence, swept past the partially submerged log on which he was sitting. There was a flurry of spray as a smooth back and dorsal fin, gleaming dully in the starlight from the moonless midnight sky, broke the surface and plunged on ahead of the scudding raft.

"Sharks!" the steward's mate hollered, trying to sit cross-legged on the log rather than astride it. "There's sharks all around us!" The raft bucked over a breaking swell and DuFourmey lost his balance, dropping his split-bamboo paddle.

From behind, Joe Garth leaned forward and slapped one hand between his shoulder blades, steadying him. With the other he scooped up the dropped paddle as it drifted past. The twin-log raft, its palm frond sail pulling hard in the brisk breeze, continued to boil along through the dark waters of the strait—its nine-man crew clinging on, four bodies on one log and five on the other, for dear life.

"Here's your paddle, Henry," Garth called out, slipping the blade under DuFourmey's arm. "Sit with your legs on either side of this log like the rest of us, or you're gonna fall off."

DuFourmey twisted around, pointing at the water. "You seen them sharks in there," he said. "I ain't about to offer them no drumstick o' mine."

Randall, opposite him on the other log, swore audibly. "Shit, they're not sharks, DuFourmey," he shouted. "They're *porpoises!* You've seen them before, swimming at the bow of your ship. They're harmless."

"I ain't never seen no such thing," the steward's mate protested. "I spend my time at sea in the galley or down in the magazine passin' up shells and powder bags! Once in a blue moon I rotate onto a gun crew. I ain't never been close to no por-puss. How I'm supposed to know they ain't gonna chew my leg off?"

A gust of wind carried away Randall's response, and he leaned back against the sudden pull of the vine that was rigged to the starboard edge of the palm frond sail. On the port log, Mulgrew, sitting in front of DuFourmey, did the same. A fluttering sound accompanied the moan of the wind and the rush of the water, and a small section of woven fronds tore loose high up on the sail and whirled off into the darkness. Yomat Dap, who had just repositioned himself on a cross member at the base of the small peeled tree that served as the raft's mast, frowned upward through his smudged face paint at the partial disintegration of his handiwork.

After lying under cover through the steaming heat of their first full day in the cove, dozing and gathering their strength, the nine crash survivors had hauled their makeshift catamaran out of the trees and into the water about two hours after sunset. The wind had picked up at dusk, blowing out of a shifting bank of purple-black thunderheads to the east. They'd erected the mast and sail using a simple arrangement of stout vines and paddled for the mouth of the cove. Once in open water, the freshening wind had caught the sail immediately and begun pushing the raft westward, straight toward the twin-coned island.

At the back end of each log, Horwitch and Foster had been able to steer adequately by leaning into long bamboo sweeps that were lashed to the aftermost cross member.

Now, two-thirds of the way across the strait, both men were feeling the strain of the constant battle to keep the raft from slewing sideways in the running seas. Horwitch, his normally ruddy face pale in the dim starlight, looked over at Foster, who was prying on his sweep with gritted teeth, the muscles of his arms bulging. Like everyone else on the raft he was soaked to the skin, his longish hair plastered to his head and the sides of his neck.

"How goes it, Sergeant?" Horwitch shouted, spitting spume off his lips. "Do you need relief, man?"

"Not bloody likely, Major," Foster rasped. "Not before you." He shot Horwitch a glance. "Sir," he added.

The British officer gave a curt nod. "Carry on, then. Almost there."

"Well, thank you very bloody much for your permission," Foster muttered under his breath. Once again, he threw his weight against the sweep as a following swell overtook the raft and lifted its stern off to one side.

Hooke, seated on the starboard log in front of Randall, took hold of one of the thick vines supporting the mast and stood up. Locking an elbow and a knee around the makeshift shroud, he stared out into the darkness ahead, swaying as the raft rolled in the running seas. His wet shirt fluttered noisily across his back as a hard gust of wind drove the ungainly craft onward, gurgling and sizzling through the black swells.

"How's our track, Mr. Hooke?" Horwitch shouted.

The New Zealander half turned. "Hard to see with no moon, Major," he called, "but I can just make out the silhouette of the island. It looks like the current is pushing us slightly to the south, but we're still on course to make landfall somewhere below the base of the westernmost volcanic cone."

"See any lights?" Randall asked.

Hooke looked again, then shook his head. "Not a one. Doesn't mean anything, of course. With MacArthur's invasion fleet in the neighborhood and Allied planes roaming the skies, all Japanese island garrisons are going to be maintaining a strict blackout after sunset."

"Sure," Randall said. "It's just that sometimes Jap sentries carry lanterns when they're on beach patrol." He glanced over at Garth in the darkness. "Joe and I have seen it, close-up."

Hooke nodded. "I'll keep an eye out as we get closer."

The raft rose up on a large breaking swell. Now, in addition to the moan of the wind and the sloshing of the seas, there was another sound: a deep, continuous rumble that infiltrated the night air like distant thunder.

"What's that?" DuFourmey asked, his eyes darting skyward. "Storm comin'?"

"You might say that," Joe Garth replied. "That's the sound of these waves we're riding over driving into the island's barrier reef."

DuFourmey swiveled, to look back at Garth.

Once again, Garth slapped a steadying hand up between the seaman's shoulder blades. "Stay on the log, Henry," he said. "You don't want to be swimming alone out here."

DuFourmey stared over at Randall. "Who said anything 'bout gettin' over a coral reef in the dark?"

"Nobody," Randall told him. "We've just got to, that's all."

"That coral's sharper'n a Baptist preacher's tongue," the steward's mate lamented. "I done been told about it. Cut a man's ass right up."

Randall looked at him in the dark. "Then you better make sure you stay on your toes and off your ass," he said.

Superior Petty Officer Zenji Kono stepped down into the machine gun nest that overlooked a central section of the island's southern beach. There he paused, taking in the slight form of the young soldier who was nodding over the grips of the tripod-mounted Nambu heavy machine gun. Beside him, curled up in the sand in the fetal position, was his companion sentry, snoring lightly. Kono examined his face in the dim starlight; he looked barely a teenager, and far too small and thin for his uniform.

The petty officer let out a quiet sigh, shaking his head. Pitiful. Just pitiful. Here he was, a ten-year veteran NCO of the *Rikusentai*, on the battle line with an American invasion force hammering away at Leyte just over the horizon—still baby-sitting adolescents masquerading as soldiers. Most of the men in his charge were fairly well seasoned, having seen combat in China and Borneo, but somehow these two youngsters—recent conscripts—had slipped into his unit as replacements. Both were still in their teens—awkward, pimply-faced, and green as grass. Even now, after weeks on the island, they were still unable to function well without a full eight hours' sleep every night. Kono chewed his lip in annoyance. The first thing a soldier learned was how to go without sleep. These two belonged at home with their mothers, not in the *Rikusentai*.

Or at least in the army, not the navy. Both branches of the military were equally represented in the island's mixed garrison, and in Kono's admittedly biased opinion, the caliber of enlisted man was several notches lower in the army. The IJN's Special Naval Landing Forces—*Rikusentai*—were comprised of elite land-fighting seamen, capable of executing amphibious assaults, riverine warfare, and conventional occupation/defensive duties—or a combination of all three—on demand. Some of the army privates, on the other hand, could barely get out of their own way. Thank heaven they were assigned primarily to the medium-artillery and antiaircraft gun emplacements higher up on the shoulders of the twin volcanoes. At least they wouldn't be stumbling around in front of the *Rikusentai* firing positions when the Americans finally came.

Not that that would be much of an advantage to Seamen Second Class Iwao Yoshi and Kiichi Uchino. They would probably be sleeping as the Yankee marines stormed ashore.

Kono's tough, thirty-three-year-old face screwed up slightly as he considered pouring the contents of the two bowls he was carrying on the heads of the dozing sen-

tries. Serve them right, but no. They were what he had
to work with, and the steaming, salty miso soup would
be deployed better in the young soldiers' stomachs than
down their necks. Lucky for them he had a strong streak
of decency running through his hard noncom's heart. He
sighed again. He was going to have to work on that. It
made him a little too soft on his men sometimes.

"Seaman Second Class Yoshi," he said quietly to the
boy nodding over the machine gun. "Please tell me you
are not sleeping on guard duty like your miserable
friend Uchino."

The nodding head jerked upward slightly, but its
owner did not answer.

Superior Petty Officer Kono kicked Seaman Yoshi in
the thigh, not as hard as he could have, with the toe of
his boot. The boy thrashed awake.

"Wha—wha—" he babbled.

"You disgust me, Yoshi," Kono said, and kicked
Uchino smartly in the left calf. The seaman yelped and
scrabbled to a sitting position. "You, too, Uchino."

"Honorable Superior Petty Officer," Yoshi blurted, "I
was not sleeping. I was merely . . . ah . . . resting at my
weapon. And we were taking catnaps in turn, sir . . . as
we have been trained."

"Do you think me an idiot?" Kono growled. He bent
down, scowling at the quaking teenagers, and extended
the two bowls he had brought with him. "Here. Mother's
milk for the worthless runts of my litter, curse you. Will
you never toughen up, by the gods?"

"It does not look hopeful, Honorable Superior Petty
Officer, sir," Uchino mumbled, accepting the bowl and
looking appropriately morose. "I suspect we may be all
but useless." There was a note of dry humor in his sub-
servient tone; Kono, the epitome of the gruff, kindly
noncom, was revered, not feared, by his men.

The petty officer grunted, spat on the sand, and then
yanked his prized sidearm—a genuine nine-millimeter
German Luger—from its holster and leveled it at Yoshi.
Even in the dim starlight, both young soldiers' faces
blanched visibly.

"Do you know," Kono stated, "that I could summarily execute both of you on the spot for sleeping on guard duty? As a matter of fact"—he pulled back the pistol's cocking mechanism—"I don't know why I don't do it right now and save myself a lot of exasperation in future."

The two young soldiers sat frozen, their soup bowls halfway to their lips.

Kono released the weapon from full cock, lowered it, and put it back into its holster. Then he sat down on the edge of the gun pit and regarded the two seamen. "This is not a matter to be taken lightly," he said. "You may nap in shifts while on MG duty until such time as an enemy presence is reported in the area. You may *not* both sleep at the same time. If I catch you at it again, I will not deal with you myself. I will report the matter directly to Lieutenant Commander Ogaki." He paused to let the effect of his words sink in. "I think you will agree that his reaction to your dereliction of duty will not be as benevolent as mine."

Yoshi and Uchino swallowed hard, genuinely frightened. Ogaki, the commanding officer of the island garrison, was a notorious martinet, a man quite willing to use severe corporal punishment to discipline his troops. Just the previous week, the entire company had been turned out to watch an army cook receive a prolonged beating with a bamboo cane on his lower back and buttocks, strung up to the parade ground flagpole with his trousers pulled down around his ankles. His transgression had been to accidentally break a second teacup from Ogaki's personal collection of fine English china.

The man had been nearly crippled, but Ogaki had permitted him only forty-eight hours in the garrison infirmary before ordering him back to kitchen duty, bleeding welts and all, under threat of further punishment. With that kind of incentive, the cook had somehow mustered the strength to comply.

"We will both be awake in the future, Honorable Superior Petty Officer," Yoshi promised. Beside him, Uchino nodded, slurping soup.

"Mm," Kono grunted. "We'll see." He fished in the breast pocket of his shirt for a cigarette.

"Honorable Superior Petty Officer," Uchino said, "I have a question."

Kono lit the crumpled cigarette with a match. "Mm."

"May I ask where you got the German pistol? It is beautiful, sir."

The tough petty officer almost smiled. "In Burma," he said, "during the invasion of Rangoon two years ago. I took it from the body of a British colonel I killed with a hand grenade on the steps of the abandoned American embassy." He retrieved the pistol from its holster and held it up. "You can't see it in this light, but it's engraved in German, right here." He traced a finger along the steel spine of the handgrip. "I had it translated. It says, *'To Hans, from your brother Karl. May this keep you safe.'* " Kono scratched his chin. "A gift from one German brother to another, obviously. And obviously, it didn't work, since it was in the belt of an English officer half a world away from Western Europe. I imagine the British colonel took it from the body of the German it belonged to during an earlier campaign, much as I took it from him."

"It makes you think," Yoshi said agreeably, "though I'm not quite sure of exactly what."

Kono grunted again and put the pistol away. "I'll tell you what it should make you think of, boy. It should make you think of two dead men, each of whom lost this gun in turn, and who were both probably better soldiers than you or your ridiculous friend." He glared at Uchino for a moment. "So if I were you, I would attend to my duties, improve my performance, and above all *stay awake* when manning my machine gun. Or I wouldn't hold out much hope for my continued happy existence in the *Rikusentai,* even before the Americans get here."

He blew a short puff of cigarette smoke and stalked out of the Nambu nest into the breezy, humid darkness.

The raft scraped over the outermost coral heads of the barrier reef just before one o'clock in the morning, driven onward by running five-foot swells that steepened as they traversed the shallow water and then broke into the lagoon beyond. The fresh breeze no longer propelled the crude vessel. In order to maintain a low silhouette, Dap, Randall, and Garth had cut down and discarded the mast and sail halfway through the final mile of the crossing.

Now the nine men paddled furiously through the heaving black water, their drawn-up feet scant inches from the razor-sharp coral immediately beneath them. A swell lifted the raft, turned it sideways, and dropped it. The two big logs hit the reef with a crash, all but throwing the paddlers off their perches. Before the shaken men could catch their breath, the next swell lifted them off the reef, slewing the raft sideways even farther.

Randall, clinging to the starboard log like a limpet, looked down into the wave trough. A giant dome of brain coral appeared, pale and corrugated, in the surging black torrent. He began to yell a warning as the raft dropped again, but was cut off as the log he was straddling struck the exposed coral head with tremendous force.

The thick log snapped in two like a dry stick broken over a knee. Randall was catapulted into the air and landed flat on the water on his bad rib. The stab of pain drove the breath from his lungs. He floundered to a vertical position, tried to stand—but the water was too deep. A wave broke over his head, smothering him. He clawed his way upward through the swirling underwater blackness, chest burning. He found the surface, threw his head back, and gasped in a ragged breath. Out of the corner of his eye he saw the next breaker coming. He ducked under it . . . came up . . . sucked in more air. . . .

"Charlton!" The voice was Joe Garth's. *"Over here!"*

Randall spun around 180 degrees. Fifteen feet away, the damaged raft was bobbing, a low silhouette topped by the vague outlines of those who had not fallen off upon impact with the coral head. All at once Randall realized where he was: in the calmer waters of the inner lagoon. The breaking swells had driven vessel and men completely across the reef.

His injured side still throbbing, Randall kicked over to the wallowing raft. The starboard log had splintered in half at midpoint, and all but a few cross braces were broken and dangling. But it had served its purpose. They were across the strait, within easy distance of the destination island's beaches.

Randall felt a hand under his upper arm, lifting, drawing him in to the nearest log. "You all right, L.T.?" Joe Garth asked. "Easy, now. Get your wind back."

Randall nodded, taking slower breaths. He hadn't realized he'd been panting so hard. The knot of fear that had been tightening in his stomach as they'd passed over the reef began to subside rapidly. Like so many times in the past, it was good to hear Joe's low, steady voice absorb some of his calm.

"Ev-everybody here?" Randall inquired. Hell, he was a lieutenant, supposedly a leader. He could at least act the part.

"All present and accounted for, Lieutenant Randall," Horwitch called softly, "now that you're here. Are you injured, sir?"

Randall grunted. "Banged my bad rib."

"I assume you can carry on," Horwitch responded.

Randall looked across the log and located the major's broad-shouldered silhouette in the darkness. Pushy, this Brit.

He spat salt water. "You assume correctly, Major," he said.

If Horwitch caught the coolness in Randall's reply, he didn't show it. Rather, he cleared his throat and sat up straight on the log, looking at the beaches.

"All right," he declared. "Everyone into the water and start kicking. We'll push toward that outcropping of rocks over there to the left. No more talking. If anyone's on that beach, we don't want them alerted. Understood?"

"Understood," came the collective reply.

"Splendid, then. Let's go. Put some effort into it, gentlemen."

At the forward end of the intact log, Foster nudged Mulgrew as they began to kick. "Bloody prancer," he grumbled quietly.

"Did you hear something?" Seaman Second Class Yoshi asked Seaman Second Class Uchino, as he passed him a postsoup cigarette.

"What?" Uchino said, taking the butt. "When?"

"Just now."

"Well . . . *what?*"

Yoshi looked at his companion in irritation. "What do you mean, 'what'? A sound, just now—what do you think? Did you hear it or not?"

Uchino leaned back on one elbow in the sand and blew a long stream of smoke, regarding Yoshi with all the nineteen-year-old sagacity he could muster. "I didn't hear anything, Iwao. Why don't you tell me what your sound sounded like."

Yoshi craned his neck and looked out over the lip of the gun pit at the black sky and sea. "Oh, I don't know. A faint cry, like a—a shout, or something."

"A seagull, most likely," Uchino declared. "Or perhaps a worker back at the sub pen dropping a ball peen hammer on his toe."

Yoshi peered intently into the dark gloom. Offshore, the breaking surf continued to pound the outer reef with a constant, rhythmic rumbling.

"It didn't sound like a seagull, Kiichi," he said, looking fretful.

"Oh, sit down," his friend told him, "and have some of this horrible cigarette before I smoke the whole thing myself. The Americans will be here soon enough, and when they come, you won't have to guess at sounds to know they've arrived."

Yoshi sighed and slumped back down beside the machine gun. He looked at Uchino briefly, then extended two fingers to take the cigarette.

"I suppose you're right," he said.

Chapter Eighteen

Very slowly, Joe Garth raised a hand and wiped a trickle of sweat away from the corner of his right eye. He stood otherwise motionless in the deep shadow next to a large teak tree. The Japanese were all around, salted throughout the jungle. In machine gun nests, mortar pits, and artillery emplacements. All but invisible to any assault force invading from the sea.

As slowly as he'd raised it, the UDT man lowered his hand. The crash survivors would never have made it this far without the superlative stalking skills of Yomat Dap, who was leading them into the highlands. Garth, walking second point, had thought he knew how to move silently over terrain. The Dayak headhunter had put him to shame. Not that Garth had made a sound or attracted any attention—it was simply that while he was stealthy, Yomat Dap was . . . *invisible*.

Five minutes earlier, Dap had drifted like a wisp of ether to the very edge of yet another narrow footpath through the jungle, then halted. Twenty feet behind him, Joe Garth had stepped into cover next to a small thicket of bamboo, watching and listening. There'd been the scuffing sound of a boot, the brief flash of a hand lamp. Garth had brought one of his .45 automatics up to his cheek, the metal of the slide cool against his damp skin. Down the trail had come a Japanese infantryman, heading straight for Yomat Dap, who had no cover and no time to move away.

Garth had sighted the pistol on the enemy soldier's head, tracked him along as he'd approached Dap. *Any moment now . . . any moment . . .*

The infantryman had walked confidently through the jungle, head up, paying attention to his surroundings— right past where Garth had last seen Dap and on down the trail, without a break in his stride. Garth had blinked and searched the shadows for the Dayak, but even his keen hunter's eyes had not been able to pick him out. Incredible. The man had not had time to move, and yet he was no longer there. Cautiously, Garth had stepped out from cover, placing his feet without making the slightest sound, and eased up to the edge of the path.

No Yomat Dap. Only shadows and starlight.

"Hssst!"

The sound had been right in his ear. Startled, Garth had jerked his head to the left. The empty shadow beside him had loomed an inch or two closer. There'd been a rustle of headdress feathers, a pale grin of filed teeth. Dap had not moved. He had been there all along.

There had been no cover, and no attempt by Yomat Dap to find any. He had simply become part of the landscape.

Watching the Dayak continue his stalk up the jungled slope, Joe Garth wiped another trickle of sweat from the corner of his eye. In his entire life, he had known only one other person capable of vanishing instantly into his surroundings with such ease—his Apache grandfather. Even as a boy of nine, he would not have believed it if he had not seen it with his own eyes.

The old Chiricahua named An-oh-neh had been his mother's father, and as a young man had been a trusted adviser to the great Apache chiefs Mangas Coloradas, Cochise, and Victorio, as well as an oddly charismatic warrior-shaman named Goy-ah-kleh. Joe Garth had never heard his grandfather refer to this last man by his more famous name, Geronimo.

Once, An-oh-neh had lived, hunted, and fought with his Apache brethren in a vast area of desert badlands stretching from southeastern Arizona to western Texas. Carried on a guerrilla war with Mexican army regulars, blue-coated U.S. cavalry, and white settlers alike. He had been young and strong then. But when his daughter's son had known him, he had been old and gray and bowlegged and beaten—more than eighty years of age and worn down to a virtual stick figure of a man by nearly six decades of the U.S.'s war to wipe out the red man.

Old Ano, as he'd been called by the townspeople in and around Laredo, had been regarded as something of a comic figure, an aging remnant of a long-defeated tribe who had somehow escaped confinement on a reservation—probably because his daughter had married a white Texas Ranger—and who regularly refought old battles on the outskirts of town at midnight at the top of his voice, clutching a bottle of rotgut whiskey. Harmless and hopeless, the white citizenry had said. A creature to be laughed at and perhaps pitied.

But to Joe Garth, he'd been the embodiment of his mother's heritage—a walking encyclopedia of Apache culture and myth, survival and warfare skills. Many times during his boyhood, the two of them had gone off into the hot, arid badlands alone, with nothing but the clothes on their backs, only to return a week later—well fed, well rested, and none the worse for wear. Joe Garth's father had publicly frowned at these expeditions, but secretly approved. Joe's mother had simply looked at her father in fond despair and contented herself with a few halfhearted remonstrations. Old An-oh-neh had usually giggled at the devilment he'd caused and gone off to find another bottle of bad whiskey.

It had been on one of these impromptu pilgrimages into the backcountry that Joe Garth had witnessed his grandfather vanish into thin air, in broad daylight.

They'd encountered a small-time rancher named Amos Blankenship and his lead hand—a rough-looking type called Nevada—who'd happened to be passing through the area on horseback.

Joe Garth blinked into the humid darkness of the Philippine jungle, watching as a Japanese soldier in a mortar pit less than forty feet away took off his helmet and scratched his head. The boyhood memory continued to replay itself in his mind's eye. The incident with Blankenship and his lead hand was still as vivid as if it had happened yesterday.

"Damn!" the rancher had said, reining in his horse. "Almost didn't see you there. You're Captain Samuel Garth's boy, ain't you? The Texas Ranger." He chewed his tobacco for a moment, then snapped his fingers. "Got it—*Joe*. Joe Garth." Another pause. "I declare, son— you ain't no bigger'n a two-finger pinch of coyote shit. Not even ten years old, I'll wager. What the hell are you doin' runnin' around out here with that drunken old Injun for?"

"He's my grandfather," Joe said, bristling.

Blankenship smiled. "Whoa, son. Simmer down. I don't mean nothin' by it. It's just that you're an awful long way out in this godforsaken desert with no horses, no water, no guns, and only a half-crazy old Injun souse for company. You want to ride along with us? Get on home?"

Joe shook his tousled head. "No, sir, Mr. Blankenship. I am home." He stepped back beside his grandfather, who put a leathery brown hand on his shoulder.

Nevada looked the old Apache up and down, taking in the long gray hair bound by a faded red headband, the dark, wrinkled skin stretched over high cheekbones, the cheap blue calico trade shirt, the bowed legs encased in moccasins and leggings. The white man's face seemed to go slack and his dark eyes became duller, more cruel.

"I don't like Injuns," he said. "Specially Apache."

Blankenship looked at him uneasily. "Steady now, Nevada. Ain't no need to get unpleasant. This old drunk is Sam Garth's father-in-law. Believe you me, that's one Texas Ranger you surely don't want comin' after you."

Nevada spat. "What the hell do I care 'bout a white man who sires some half-Injun whelp? Time was, not so long ago, Apache scalps brought a gov'mint bounty of twenty-five dollars, each one! Now, I ain't gonna trouble the kid, even if he *is* part savage—but how bad do you think anyone's gonna miss one old drunk Injun?"

"Make them look away, boy," Joe Garth's grandfather whispered under his breath in Chiricahua. *"Just for a moment."*

Joe didn't hesitate. He dashed forward between the two horses, slapping their noses and making them jink sideways in alarm. Both riders were nearly unseated.

"What the—Goddamn, son! What the hell you think you're doin'?" Blankenship yanked at his horse's reins to bring it under control.

Beside him, Nevada cursed more fluently as his mount stumbled over a barrel cactus, bucking.

Joe, who'd run about twenty feet past the horses, picked up a handful of gravel and flung it at the two riders. "Leave us alone!" he yelled.

There was a metallic snick as Nevada drew his pistol and cocked the hammer. "Goddamned whelp," he snarled as Joe bent down to grab another handful of pebbles.

Blankenship's hand clapped onto his shoulder in an instant. "Have you done lost your mind? Put that thing away! What're you gonna do, shoot Sam Garth's kid?"

The man's coarse face worked for a moment as he glared at the skinny, dark-haired boy brandishing the fistful of stones. Then he cut his eyes sideways at Blankenship and jerked his horse's head around. "No, boss. I ain't gonna shoot the kid. But I am gonna kill me a dirty Inj—"

His words faded as he looked this way and that over the barrel of his revolver. Where the aged Apache had been standing, there was now only an empty plain of hot sand and scrubby weeds, dotted by innumerable red brown sandstone boulders—none of which was large enough for a man to hide behind.

Nevada spurred his horse forward a few steps.

"Where'd that old bastard go?" he shouted. He wheeled the animal around, his pistol tracking over the barren landscape. "He's hidin' behind somethin', dammit! There! That big rock over there!" He aimed the revolver and squeezed off two shots. "Show yourself, you old snake-eater!"

Chips flew off the dome-shaped lump of sandstone as the slugs struck. A few seconds later Nevada was circling the rock in frustration, finding nothing. He spurred his horse back toward the roadway. Blankenship was sitting in the saddle with his own pistol resting across the horn as he watched him patiently.

"Just stay there, son," he muttered to Joe, "and drop them stones. We'll be movin' along presently."

Nevada eyed the ground as he neared the road. "Where's his tracks? He got to have left tracks!"

But there was nothing. Only a cluster of moccasin footprints where An-oh-neh and his grandson had first stood when confronted by the two riders.

"Goddamn it to goddamned almighty hell!" Nevada bellowed, furious. He emptied his pistol at the surrounding rocks. The slugs ricocheted off the rounded sandstone, throwing more chips. Gradually, the sounds died away.

"Are you through blasphemin' now?" Blankenship inquired. Nevada blinked at him uncertainly, sweating and panting. "If so, let's go. That is, if you want to keep your damn job."

The rough-looking cowhand licked his lips, then stared over at Joe Garth and scowled. "You little—" he began.

"I mean now, Nevada!" Blankenship barked, cocking his pistol without lifting it from his saddle horn. "And if you don't understand what *now* means, you can clean your gear out of the bunkhouse when we get back tonight and get the hell off my ranch! *Comprende?*"

"All right, all right," Nevada said. With a last dirty look at Joe, and a vicious jerk of the reins, he yanked his horse's head around and spurred the animal off down the road.

Blankenship holstered his Colt and smiled down at

Joe. "Tell your grandfather we didn't mean nothin' by it," he said. Then he touched the brim of his battered Stetson and cantered after his lead hand.

Joe waited until the two men were several hundred yards down the road before dropping the handful of pebbles and walking over to the cluster of footprints where his grandfather had last stood. He'd seen what had happened behind the backs of Blankenship and his hired hand, seen where his grandfather had gone, but to his amazement could not now pick the old man out of the boulder-studded landscape, though he knew him to be no more than spitting distance away.

"Grandfather," he called in Chiricahua, his eyes roving over the barren ground. *"They're gone. Where are you?"*

There was a wheezy giggle, and a small brown boulder less than a dozen feet to Joe's right unfolded itself and stood up, shedding sand and dust. An-oh-neh shook out the shirt he had bunched in his hand, chuckling deep in his throat, and repositioned his headband around his tangle of long gray hair.

As soon as Blankenship and Nevada had focused their attention on Joe, the old Apache had sprung sideways and taken three great bounding leaps off three small boulders, stripping off his calico shirt and headband as he'd done so. He'd made absolutely no sound. He'd left no footprints. At the fourth leap he'd tucked his legs, clothing, and arms under him and hit the sand in a crouch next to a scraggly ball of dead sagebrush. With his red-brown back—exactly the same color as the surrounding rocks—hunched into a curve, his head tucked into his shoulder, and the foot-high tangle of sagebrush breaking up the outline of his body, he'd been indistinguishable from the thousands of small sandstone boulders littering the desert plain.

Nevada had been no more than fifteen feet away from him, but he'd been looking for an old Apache in a blue calico shirt and red headband, not a single red-brown rock in a sea of red brown rocks.

"Even I couldn't see you, Grandfather," Joe said, still

speaking in the Chiricahua tongue, which the old man preferred. *"How could you disappear so completely?"*

An-oh-neh smiled. *"When the white men were looking for me,"* he said, *"they expected to see two things: an old Indian, and the same thing they had been seeing all day long—a desert full of brown boulders. I became the second thing they expected to see—yet another boulder—and so was invisible to them as the first thing."*

Joe's dark eyes widened in delight. *"Can you teach me how to become invisible like that, Grandfather?"* he asked breathlessly.

The old Apache smiled again, his leathery face dissolving into a mass of wrinkles. *"As of today,"* he said, *"you already know."*

Because another Japanese soldier was coming down the narrow footpath, Joe Garth did not attempt to brush a third trickle of sweat from his brow. His grandfather had been right, of course. All one needed to know was how to become what the enemy was accustomed to seeing every day—and consequently there would be nothing to catch his eye. He'd used the crouching trick before, most recently on Beach Black during the midnight reconnaissance of Leyte. Being covered in a layer of sticky grease and having time to roll in the sand and scoop some along his body had helped, but the principle was the same.

Yomat Dap, like An-oh-neh, was a master of blending into the natural environment, Joe Garth realized. Becoming shape or shadow, leaf or wood, rock or soil, as the need arose. And so was he.

That was why, thirty seconds later, when Superior Petty Officer Zenji Kono strode down the path to check on two more of his soldiers in another gun emplacement, he did not see the tall half-Apache American—impersonating an empty shadow beside a small thicket of bamboo—whom he could have reached out and touched in passing.

Chapter Nineteen

"My *Seiran* pilots—for your country and your emperor—are you ready to die?"

"*Yes, sir!*" the three young flight lieutenants chorused, standing at ramrod attention in front of Captain Toshiko Yarizuma.

"My *Kaiten* pilots—for your country and your emperor—are you ready to die?"

"*Yes, sir!*" the three young navy ensigns shouted, outdoing their aerial counterparts.

Yarizuma gave a single grim nod and turned to the seventh man standing before him. "Lieutenant Yagi, my *Ohka* pilot—for your country and emperor—are you ready to die?"

"*I am, sir!*" Yagi barked, staring at the bulkhead above the *Sen-Toku* commander's visored cap.

Once more, Yarizuma ran his eyes over the young warriors standing across the table from him in the giant submarine's cramped officers' mess. In keeping with his chosen command demeanor, his face had a preternatural serenity—a kind of deadly calm that suggested both utter competence and the blank single-mindedness of a zealot. He bent forward stiffly at the waist, barely creasing his immaculate dress uniform, and picked up a small crystal glass of sake. Holding it out in front of him, he waited until the seven junior officers had done likewise, then declared: "Long live the emperor!"

"Long live the emperor!" came the response.

Yarizuma ceremoniously tipped back his head, swallowed the sake, and set the glass down on the mess table with a loud rap. The young officers duplicated his actions, rapping down their glasses with gusto before coming back to attention.

"My young brothers-in-arms," Yarizuma said, looking each man in the eye in turn, "we gather once again to celebrate and renew our commitment to Japan's great struggle. As the day of our grand gesture—and the hour of your supreme sacrifice—grows nearer, I know that your warrior's resolve only strengthens with the passing of time. I am confident that as you meditate and reflect upon your sacred duty, you continue to draw strength from the loyalty of your comrades, the love of your families, the benevolence of His Majesty Emperor Hirohito, and the glorious example of the heroes who have preceded you in death to the Shrine of Yasukuni."

"Tenno heika banzai!" Yagi shouted out, overcome with emotion, the strong sake coursing through his bloodstream.

Not to be outdone, the other six cried the common wartime slogan, "May the emperor reign for ten thousand years!"

A smile played at the corners of Yarizuma's hard-set mouth. An essential part of his job as commander was to maintain the unquestioning, fever pitch enthusiasm of his young *tokko* pilots. Sake and slogans could be relied upon to help do just that, for, like all twenty-year-old soldiers since time immemorial, each of them had a desperate need to prove his courage, to be elevated in the eyes of his peers. Each and every one already believed he was immortal, as the young always do. And there was one other common characteristic—a characteristic that Yarizuma was careful to nurture and exploit: each young suicide pilot, deep down, had an overwhelming need to feel *special*, part of an elite. It was with these regular private meetings-cum-celebrations that Yarizuma catered to this need as the weeks passed, and so kept the blade of the sword with which he would soon strike at the enemy—his small *tokko* corps—honed to a razor's edge.

"My young comrades," Yarizuma said, "I bid you recharge your glasses and drink another toast with me—this one to our honored fallen commander of the Imperial Japanese Combined Fleet, Admiral Isoroku Yamamoto. May he dwell in peace at Yasukuni even as he watches us carry on in his glorious footsteps!"

He refilled his sake glass from a crystal flask, turned to the formal picture of Yamamoto on the bulkhead, and raised it. "Banzai!" he declared, and gulped it down.

"Banzai!" the young pilots shouted, draining their glasses.

Yarizuma set his glass down again. On the table before him was an array of edible delicacies, rare in wartime, but available more often than not to members of the submarine service. A variety of cooked and raw fish, fresh vegetables such as daikon, pickled seaweed, and even *kachi kuri*—the peeled "victory chestnuts" traditionally served to promote success in an upcoming endeavor. Yarizuma opened his hands over the feast in a gesture of invitation.

"Be seated," he said, "and indulge yourselves. Let us eat, and drink, and talk of the great things to come."

Six of the *tokko* pilots began to sit, but Yagi raised the glass he'd already refilled a third time and held it out at arm's length. "One more toast," he declared loudly, sweat sliding down his flushed cheek. "This one to our beloved leader, Captain Toshiko Yarizuma." The other pilots, taken off guard, scrambled back to their feet and hurriedly refilled their glasses. "You inspire us with your example, Honorable Captain. May we all prove ourselves worthy of your leadership at the crucial hour! *Banzai!*"

"Banzai!" the young pilots cried, their blood now thor-

oughly overheated by the powerful liquor. *"Yes, Honorable Captain! Banzai! Well said! Banzai!"*

Yarizuma, sitting now, favored them all with a benevolent smile and indicated again that they should take their seats. He didn't think much of Lieutenant Yagi's ability to handle alcohol—but then, emotional reactions were what he was cultivating for the present. Let Yagi and the other pilots prop up their frail young egos with outbursts of enthusiasm and declarations of heroic commitment. Let them prop *each other* up. Slogans were free. Sake was cheap and plentiful. It was courage that could be in short supply.

Yarizuma let them fill their bellies with the excellent food, brag to each other about who would be first to strike at the enemy, who would deal the most lethal blow—and empty the half-dozen flasks of sake on the mess table. He participated lightly in the conversation, confining himself to a wise smile here, a patient nod there, a brief comment that inevitably led to a renewed outburst of youthful, alcohol-fueled chatter.

When the eyes of his *tokko* pilots were red and slightly glassy, and their speech was beginning to slur—but not too much—he clapped his hands for the orderly to bring pots of strong tea and then cleared his throat for attention. The boisterous young men fell respectfully silent, squaring their shoulders and trying to look more in command of their faculties than the sake they had consumed would allow.

"My fellow samurai," Yarizuma began, for being called such always flattered his young pilots to the depths of their souls, "this is a special day. We band of warrior brothers, bound together by our shared sacred duty to emperor and country, will now share yet another bond . . . one uniquely ours at this particular point in history."

He reached beneath the table and produced a single sheet of paper. Placing it facedown in front of him, he put his right hand on top of it, his left over his heart. His face was composed, serene, his voice low and grave:

"I reveal to you now the exact nature of the great

task with which we have been charged—and from whom
the order comes. Truly, we are blessed, my fellow
samurai—for this is the final and most profound directive from the greatest warrior of Japan's modern age.
And it is only we—we stalwart eight—who have been
entrusted with this most vital undertaking."

Yarizuma paused, letting the words sink in . . . letting
his deep gaze drift from man to man. The young pilots
gaped at him, shaking with alcohol and adrenaline.

"Lieutenant Yagi," the *Sen-Toku* commander said,
"you will have the honor of reading this letter aloud to
the rest of the company." He reversed the paper on the
tabletop without turning it over and pushed it toward
Yagi.

His face flushing purple, Yagi picked up the single
sheet, swallowed to steady himself, and began to read:

> *April 12, 1943*

> *To Captain Toshiko Yarizuma, commander,*
> Sen-Toku I-403:

>> *I refer you to our conversation of several days
>> ago, which took place during my inspection
>> of your submarine pen and support facilities on
>> Island No. 12863 in the western Philippines.*
>> *We spoke of the ever-growing need for a
>> "grand gesture"—an attack so bold and dar-
>> ing, so crippling to the enemy's confidence, that
>> the Americans and their allies would reel be-
>> fore it, and our indomitable but weary people
>> have their spirits rejuvenated.*
>> *I said during our conversation, Captain Yari-
>> zuma, that I thought you might be just the
>> man to carry out such an attack. A man capable
>> of independent thought and action. A man
>> prepared to take great consequences upon him-
>> self, to undertake the most difficult of missions
>> under the most trying circumstances, in order to
>> advance the interests of emperor and empire.*

*I have searched my soul, and come to the con-
clusion that you are. Not only are you the
correct man for the task; you also have at your
disposal the appropriate weapon. The Special
Submarine I-403 has the range to travel around
the world to the east coast of the United States,
and the armament to launch an effective attack
once there. No doubt you may be able to increase the Sen-Toku's strike capability in the
months to come, as new technology continues
to become available.*

*I hereby authorize you, under this most secret
of orders, to conduct an independent operation of your own devising against one or more
key population centers on the United States
mainland, Atlantic littoral. I urge you to proceed
as we discussed—Washington, D.C., being the
target of preference—but leave the details up to
your discretion.*

*This order will receive no support from Admi-
ralty high command, as they will not know of
its existence. They would never agree with it
anyway—again as you and I discussed. Only
you and I, Toshiko Yarizuma, will know of the
task you undertake. Therefore, provision
well, and maintain complete radio silence after
you depart the Island No. 12863 sub pen.
You will have no help once you begin, and once
you do put out to sea in contravention of
existing deployment orders, there can be no
turning back.*

*Also choose well your comrades in this en-
deavor: those officers who will help you see
the Sen-Toku safely across the vast oceans of the
world, and those brave heroes—those pilots of
Kaiten and Seiran and Ohka—who will ultimately strike the actual blows for our emperor
and nation. Remember, Yarizuma: only the best
and the bravest of our young warriors can be*

*relied upon to carry out so vital a mission. Again
I say, choose well.*

   With utmost respect,

   *Admiral Isoroku Yamamoto
   Commander, Imperial Japanese Combined
Fleet*

There was complete silence in the mess hall as Yagi
finished and let the paper slip gently to the table from
trembling fingers. Yarizuma pushed back his chair, rose
slowly to his feet with great dignity, and picked up the
letter. Holding it up and reversing it so that all could
see the inked signature of Isoroku Yamamoto, he once
again caught the eye of every man in turn.

"Look around you, my samurai brothers," he said.
"As anyone can plainly see, I could not have chosen
better."

There was a muffled gasp—and then, instantly, all
seven young pilots were on their feet, Yagi in the lead,
snapping to rigid attention, tears coursing down their
faces.

"Banzai!" they shouted in a delirium of emotion.
"Banzai!"

Yarizuma opened his arms in a fatherly gesture, his
face as placid as the surface of a mountain lake. "My
samurai," he intoned.

"Banzai!" the young men shrieked, over and over.
"Banzai!"

Ensign Hajimi Ona—about a dozen shots of sake past
his usual limit—wobbled his way forward along the *I-
403*'s narrow starboard passageway. Unlike most submarines, the giant *Sen-Toku* had not one but two internal
pressure hulls—immense steel cylinders welded together
side by side to create a horizontal figure-eight cross section. The external hull and superstructure were for
streamlining, fuel tankage, and buoyancy control only.

Ona stopped beneath the small ladder and hatch that provided access to his *Kaiten,* mounted directly overhead on the submarine's foredeck. Blearily, he gazed up at the circular metal hatch and dogs, then took hold of the ladder and began to climb. He nearly lost his balance halfway up—the sake was making things spin—but managed to wedge his shoulders into the short, tubular access trunk. Undogging the hatch and pushing it back, he squeezed himself up into the *Kaiten*'s cockpit-sized, single-seat control room.

Settling into the pilot's chair, Ona reached over his head and switched on the only source of light in the impossibly tight space: a small battery-powered lamp. The cold metal sides of the cockpit glistened with condensation in the dull glow of the lamp's single bulb. The gauges of the simple instrument panel—gyrocompass, clock, depth indicator, fuel reserve, and engine oxygen pressure—were fogged over, unreadable.

Slowly, Ensign Hajimi Ona reached out and began to rub the condensation from the gauge faces with his thumb. It was in this cold, claustrophobic little space that he was destined to die.

It worried him that the thought of dying at age twenty frightened him. This was inexcusable. The other two *Kaiten* pilots—Yonehara and Wada—were utterly at ease with the fate they had chosen—always relaxed, joking, high-spirited. He, on the other hand, had been dismayed to discover that he had to work hard to keep his brave face on. Although like every other *tokko* combatant in the Japanese military, he was a volunteer, and although he believed in honorable death and Yasukuni and *kami* reincarnation, he did not believe in them firmly enough, apparently, to stop the perpetual dryness of his mouth, the persistent slight tremors in his hands, or the terrible night sweats that had plagued him since his graduation from the *Kaiten* training base at Otsujima in Japan's Tokuyama Bay. Sometimes it was all he could do to emulate the endlessly brave, cheery demeanor of Yonehara and Wada in front of the *I-403*'s crew, and so not give for an instant the impression that he was committing the unpardonable sin of losing his nerve and falling out of rank with his *tokko* comrades.

Ona rubbed the last gauge free of condensation. That would be the worst fate of all: to be the one whose courage failed him at the crucial moment. Far, far worse than dying. Such disgrace had no remedy—and it would fall upon not only him but his entire family.

So, once again, he sat in his *Kaiten*, the vehicle of his own destruction, and endeavored to make friends with it—to take it into his soul and become one with it. To love it and what it could do for his emperor and nation.

The *Kaiten* was a modified "Long Lance" torpedo— a weapon that in its earlier form had been launched unmanned by surface ships at enemy targets from great distances. Though at seventeen meters in length and more than a meter in diameter the *Kaiten* was somewhat larger than the Long Lance, it retained most of the original oversized torpedo's design characteristics, including its wakeless liquid-oxygen engine. It was capable of submerged speeds in excess of forty knots, and packed a ship-killing one-and-a-half-ton warhead.

Ona rested his right temple against the cold, wet steel of the *Kaiten*'s side. His celebratory drunkenness was slowly evolving into a monumental hangover. The chilled metal felt good against his skin. He closed his eyes and began to run his hands over the *Kaiten*'s controls—a blind drill from the training days at Otsujima—and went through their various functions in his mind.

He would regulate the supply of liquid oxygen to the engine—and thus the speed the weapon could develop— with the oxygen flow valve above and to his right. He would manipulate the rudder, which provided port and starboard directional control, with the steering lever at his right knee. He would maintain the proper depth using the external diving planes. The lever controlling them was to his left, at shoulder level.

Ona moved his head away from the side of the *Kaiten* and let it loll back, keeping his eyes closed. Directly overhead was the lever that started the engine. There. Another valve would allow him to admit seawater to the trim tanks, compensating for the weight loss of fuel and liquid oxygen as it was consumed: the valve was on his left, just below the diving-plane lever.

The short, single-eyepiece periscope could be extended and retracted by rotating a small brass hand crank. There it was on the right, just below the oxygen-flow valve. But during an actual attack, he would resist the temptation to raise the periscope, to visually confirm his target, until the final thirty seconds before impact. This to prevent enemy gunners from spotting the trailing white "feather" of an exposed scope head approaching at high speed. He would navigate toward the target underwater using only gyrocompass and stopwatch, taking as his reference point the final range and bearing relayed to him by Captain Yarizuma before detachment from the mother sub.

He rolled his head to the left and placed his opposite temple on the cold steel plate of the *Kaiten*'s hull. The throbbing was getting worse. Why had he drunk so much sake? Because everyone else had, that was why. And it was better to be sick than be excluded.

He had always had difficulty with the navigation problems while in training at Otsujima. Mathematics and geometry were not his strong points. But he had persevered, passed the field tests. It worried him now that he felt unsure of his ability to execute a blind compass attack. But he had managed well enough to be graduated from Otsujima with relatively high marks, so he would probably be able to manage once more, when it really counted, if he kept calm.

He had not had as much difficulty with navigation at Otsujima as his best friend, Isamu Matsura, whose ashes now lay in a small cedar box beneath the *Kaiten*'s seat.

Hajimi Ona let out a deep sigh and tried to push the painful memory from his mind.

If only his head would stop throbbing.

In the great watertight hangar next to the *Sen-Toku*'s offset conning tower, Flight Technician Kameo Fujita lay across the horizontal tailplanes of the *Ohka*, gasping for breath. Over him stood a very drunk, very animated Lieutenant Sekio Yagi. Yagi had just broken his usual pattern—instead of upbraiding Fujita with verbal abuse and an open-handed blow or two to the face, he had chosen this time to punch the sullen tech unexpectedly in the solar plexus with his closed fist. Fujita had collapsed, retching in pain.

"You are a disgrace, Fujita!" Yagi screamed. "Reprehensible! I ask for a vital modification to my aircraft and you deliver only half measures and excuses!"

Fujita opened his mouth in an attempt to speak, face contorted with effort, but no sound came out.

"*Range!*" Yagi shrieked, shaking his balled fist in front of him. "I must have *range!* You promised me you would do it!"

Kameo Fujita managed to push himself partly upright. Still gasping for air, he shook his head. "Hon-Honorable Lieutenant," he croaked, "I said . . . I would try."

His contrary answer only enraged the alcohol-soaked Yagi more. "*Insect!*" he roared. "*Insolent shit heap! Get out of my sight!*"

Fujita slipped off the tail of the *Ohka* and staggered away, holding his stomach. Just before he eased himself down through the access hatch that led from the hangar into the main hull of the submarine, he turned and glanced back at Yagi through a fog of pain. The lieutenant was standing beside his *tokko* weapon with his hands clasped behind him, his pose as arrogant and self-satisfied as ever. Fujita was now quite sure that he had never hated another person so much in his entire life— unless it was the senior engineer at Mitsubishi who had ruined his career with false performance evaluations and then reported his dismissal to the recruitment board of the Imperial Japanese Navy.

Fujita coughed as he descended the hatch ladder, certain he could taste blood. He wondered briefly if the lieutenant's blow had ruptured one of his internal organs. Yagi and that cursed engineer were two of a kind—so smug, so superior, so contemptuous of a man with genuine talent such as him. And now this new abuse—unwarranted, painful, and quite possibly life-threatening. It was unbearable.

Unbearable.

An aerial *Kaiten*, Yagi was thinking, his brain sour with sake. That's what my *Ohka* is, in essence. It even looks like a torpedo with stubby wings and a tail. Complete with warhead. But instead of a propeller in the back it has a rocket engine and a jet engine, and instead of a periscope it has a cockpit windscreen.

He touched the navy blue paint of the *Ohka*'s fuselage with the tips of his fingers, ran them over the American star insignia emblazoned on the side of the aircraft just behind the cockpit. He rubbed slightly, and his fingers came up blue. A smile spread across his face as he looked at the stains. On the crucial day, with any luck, he would find a rainsquall to fly through, thus giving his martyrdom a glorious finishing touch.

At least the malingering Fujita had managed to add another twenty-five miles of range to his *Ohka*. It was not the fifty he'd asked for, but it would help.

He thought again of Admiral Yamamoto's directive, of Captain Yarizuma's speech in the mess hall, and felt hot tears of patriotic pride well up in his eyes once more. The surging emotion in his chest was almost painful. He placed both palms on the fuselage of his *Ohka*, bowed his head, and let the powerful feelings carry him away.

Away to glory.

In the privacy of his cabin, Captain Toshiko Yarizuma sat on the end of his bunk and stared at his reflection in the mirror of the little personal Shinto shrine. They would be ready, his *tokko* pilots. The letter from Admiral Yamamoto, complete with inked signature, had sealed their commitment. The moment could not have been more dramatic had he produced a document signed by Jimmu Tenno—the original divine emperor of Japan—himself.

Yarizuma looked down at the letter in his hand, folded it, and placed it upon the shelf below the shrine mirror. The young were so malleable . . . so *gullible.* So willing to believe what they were told, as long as it was what they wanted to hear.

At the time of his death in the skies over the Solomon Islands, Admiral Isoroku Yamamoto had heard of *Kaiten* only in the context of a bizarre proposal by two fanatical junior naval officers, Sublieutenant Hiroshi Kuroki and Ensign Sekio Nishina, to develop a manned *tokko* torpedo. Yamamoto, a humanist, had flatly refused to even consider the idea of an intentionally suicidal weapon.

The great warrior admiral had seen only prototypes of the agile *Seiran* attack aircraft, and expected that they would ultimately be deployed as conventional fighter-bombers. Although he had heard of both American and Japanese pilots—usually wounded and dying—intentionally crashing their aircraft into enemy ships and planes in the heat of battle, he had never endorsed the kamikaze concept. And he had never had even preliminary knowledge of the piloted, rocket-powered flying bomb called the *Ohka.*

So he could not very well have made reference to these suicide weapons in a letter. He had met his death long before Japan's military situation had deteriorated to the point where the adoption of *tokko* techniques and weapons merited serious consideration. And Yamamoto, above all, was a samurai—*One Who Serves.* For all his warrior spirit, he was loyal—too loyal—to the hierarchy of which he was a part. He would not have sanctioned the idea of a long-range attack against Washington, D.C., without the consent of the rest of the Japanese Admiralty. He would never have instructed those under his command to go against existing deployment orders.

Yarizuma blinked at his placid visage in the mirror. Circumstances had changed, and so, too, probably, would have the opinions of Isoroku Yamamoto. Who could say for certain? But the revered admiral was beyond such mortal considerations now.

That was why it had been necessary to forge the letter he had presented to his young *tokko* pilots. Why it had been necessary to copy the inked signature from the personal note of sympathy Yamamoto had left with him concerning the loss of his wife and sons in the Doolittle raid, the day the admiral had departed Island No. 12863 for the Solomons.

Yarizuma blinked again at himself in the shrine mirror, slowly . . . calmly.

Yamamoto, the consummate samurai warrior, would have understood the deception—would have understood the need to keep the passions of the young suicide pilots at full simmer.

He would have understood the need to keep the blade of the sword honed to a razor's edge.

Wouldn't he?

Blink.

Of course he would have.

"What the hell is that thing?" Randall muttered, wide-eyed.

"Bad news," Joe Garth whispered in reply.

It was one hour after dawn. The two UDT men were lying in the grass behind a ridge of black lava, high up on the northwestern shoulder of the island's northernmost volcanic cone. The rest of the company—Horwitch, Foster, Mulgrew, Hooke, Dap, Matalam, and DuFourmey—lay motionless on either side of them, taking in the daunting scene several hundred feet below.

The northern coastline of the island jogged inward to form an enclosed, banana-shaped bay perhaps four miles long by a half mile wide, connected to the sea by a narrow pass no more than a hundred yards across. The shores of the bay were lined by cliffs of coral rock and black lava, ranging in height from less than 10 feet above sea level near the pass, to in excess of 150 feet at the bay's opposite end. The waters of the inlet were fairly deep in the center, a rich cerulean blue even in the moderate light of dawn, shallowing to a pellucid green along the rocky shoreline.

The highest cliffs were the result of a massive outflow of magma from the northernmost of the two volcanoes.

At some time in the distant past, a huge snaking river of molten rock had wended its way down the side of the mountain and met the sea, eventually cooling into the great bulwark of black lava that dominated the head of the bay. Wind and wave action had carved a huge natural grotto into this mass of rock—a grotto that had clearly been expanded and reinforced by the efforts of man.

Lying well back inside this deepwater sanctuary, sheltered from observation by overflying aircraft but clearly visible from the crash survivors' relatively low angle, was the largest submarine any of them had ever seen.

Part Three

Chapter Twenty

The sub seemed to lurk in the shadows of the cavern like some monstrous gray eel, waiting patiently for something to pass at which it could strike, Randall thought. Waiting for prey.

It was a fearsome thing, in terms of both its sheer size and the unfamiliar, complex design of its superstructure. Randall felt the ever-present ball of fear stir in the pit of his stomach, his heartbeat quicken. An aura of pure lethality came off the enemy sub like an invisible glow.

Joe Garth nudged his shoulder, pointing through the grass. Randall followed his finger, looking down at the jungle at least two miles eastward along the shore from the grotto and several hundred yards inland. At first he could see nothing. . . . Then his eye caught movement. Gradually, a series of bamboo huts took shape in the confusion of foliage, obscured beneath a series of interconnected camouflage nets. The movement continued, flitting through patches of shadow and sunlight. It was a khaki-clad Japanese soldier, walking rapidly across the grounds of a large concealed compound with his rifle slung over one shoulder. Behind him scurried two unarmed men in ragged, gray-white clothing, carrying shovels. Civilian laborers, Randall guessed.

He turned his attention back to the submarine, willing his heartbeat to slow. For the first time, he noticed a trio of short wooden docks extending out from shore opposite the camouflaged buildings, partly hidden by overhanging palms. More nets covered a handful of small bamboo huts behind the docks, as well as what looked like the stacked drums of a gasoline dump. A couple of thirty-foot utility launches, also draped with camouflage nets, were grounded on the small beach, along with several dugout canoes. Tethered alongside the nearest dock, bobbing gently on the minimal swell, was one of the navy blue, American-marked seaplanes that had attacked and sunk the hapless PT boat two days earlier.

Lying awash next to the remaining docks were two long black objects that resembled immense torpedoes, except for a slight bulge—like a shrunken conning tower—amidships. In front of one, a small floatplane bearing conventional Rising Sun insignia was moored. As Randall watched, a man appeared on the farthest dock, stepped onto one of the strange craft, and opened a hatch on top of its bulge.

"A type of miniature sub, I'd guess," Finian Hooke said, adjusting the focus on his compact binoculars. "Similar to the ones that tried to infiltrate Pearl Harbor on the morning of the December seventh raid . . . but even smaller and of a very radical design." He paused, frowning. "Interesting. They look like great . . . bloody . . ."

"Torpedoes," Randall said. "That's just what I was thinking."

"Hmm." The New Zealander stared for a few seconds more, then shifted the binoculars to the moored seaplane. "That's definitely one of the attacking planes we saw. Complete with American star and blue paint job."

"Not a lot of personnel visible down there," Horwitch said, crawling up next to Hooke. "Not on the docks, at any rate."

"There are actually quite a few men moving around under the trees and netting," Hooke told him. "They appear to be conscientious about avoiding activity out in the open."

"That suggests good discipline," Horwitch said. "Someone's drilled the habit into them."

"More than likely." Hooke moved the binoculars over to the grotto. "That, my friends, is one gigantic submarine."

"Ever seen anything like it before?" Joe Garth inquired.

"Never."

"What kind of detail can you see?" Horwitch asked. "Any specific weaponry?"

"I can see a partial letter-numeral designation painted on the conning tower. *I-4-0* something . . . the rest is blocked by what seems to be a loose tarpaulin." Hooke chewed his lower lip. "Give me a moment to take a good look."

The New Zealander examined the sub at length, moving his binoculars a fraction of an inch at a time. It occurred to Randall that as a coast watcher, hiding in the jungles of occupied islands and reporting on Japanese ship and aircraft movements day after day, Hooke must have developed his powers of organized observation to a considerable degree. His assumption was confirmed a minute later when Hooke began to recite a litany of specifics in a low, practiced monotone.

"Overall length, approximately four hundred feet. Top of conning tower superstructure to waterline, at least thirty-five feet. Three antiaircraft gun mounts, light to medium caliber, multibarreled. The conning tower is not centered directly on the vessel's midline; rather, it is offset to port, alongside a large horizontal tubular structure approximately one hundred twenty feet long and at least twelve to fifteen feet in diameter, occupying the starboard half of the amidships area. There is a large watertight door—a giant hatch—in the forward end of this tube. Extending from the hatch almost all the way to the bow is what appears to be an aircraft catapult ramp, sloping very slightly upward, following the sheer line of the hull. The ramp is perhaps . . . one hundred thirty feet long."

Hooke lowered his binoculars for a moment. "That submarine," he said, "is far and away the largest I have ever seen. Not only is it long—it has massive volume. I estimate its displacement at well over five thousand tons."

"What that mean?" DuFourmey asked. "What's all that gobbledygook?"

"The largest American submarine in existence," Hooke said, "is the USS *Argonaut*. This Japanese sub is at least sixty percent larger."

"Wait a minute, wait a minute," the black seaman persisted, his agitation growing. "How you know how long that sub be? How high the—the—*conning* thang is? You just guessin', same as us!"

Hooke raised the binoculars to his eyes again. "Comparative sizing," he explained. "When you need to estimate the dimensions of an unfamiliar object at distance, you look for a familiar object close to it. In this case, that aircraft tied to the dock below us." He pointed down through the grass. "It suddenly has a man standing on its starboard wing—convenient. Taking him to be of average height, I estimate the length of the fuselage to be in the neighborhood of thirty-eight to forty feet. Now, on the foredeck of that large submarine, there is currently an operation under way which those of you without binoculars cannot see. A collapsible crane is hoisting another of these attack seaplanes aboard."

Hooke cleared his throat. "There are a number of men standing on the foredeck, guiding the plane inboard. They give some idea as to scale. But the best indicator is the seaplane. It is suspended immediately beside the submarine, and is large enough to provide a good comparison. Since I have determined it to be forty feet long, I estimate that it would be possible to line up five such planes nose to tail from bow to conning tower. Similarly, another five planes could be lined up from conning tower to stern. That makes ten forty-foot planes in total. Therefore, the submarine is somewhere around four hundred feet long."

The New Zealander looked over at DuFourmey, smiled thinly, and went back to adjusting his binoculars.

"Shee-it," the steward's mate said.

"Please continue with the pertinent details, Mr. Hooke," Horwitch rasped, glaring at DuFourmey.

"Certainly, Major," Hooke said. "Something else interesting: there is an object secured to the foredeck just to one side of the aircraft catapult. It looks exactly like the two torpedo-shaped craft tied to the dock below us. It is sitting in a cradle, and is held in place by metal retaining bands. I estimate it to be approximately fifty feet in length, perhaps a yard in diameter. There appears to be a short tube extending from the belly of the craft to the deck immediately beneath."

"An access tube," Garth said. "Suppose that *is* some kind of minisub. The tube might be a way to enter it directly from the interior of the primary submarine."

"Reasonable," Horwitch grunted, nodding.

"There is another such cradle on the afterdeck," Hooke announced. "Empty. But I can make out a small hatch between the support uprights."

"So we've got a giant submarine that carries American-marked attack aircraft and two or three minisubs that look like great bloody torpedoes," Foster growled. "And we've got a sub pen and personnel to support it, and a dug-in garrison of soldiers to defend the whole shooting match." He hawked phlegm and spat into the grass. "Perfect. What bloody else?"

"Not just any soldiers, Web," Mulgrew remarked. "You get a good look at 'em when we were sneakin' through the positions last night? I did. Some are regular army, but more than half are bloody *Rikusentai,* mate."

"Riki-tiki-*what?*" DuFourmey said.

Foster scowled at him. "Keep your perishin' voice down, Yank. Where the hell d'you think you are, in a bloody Queensland pub?" He jabbed a big finger at the

black seaman. "*Rikusentai*—Jap marines. Fokkin' good
soldiers, mate. Tangle with 'em and you'll know you're
in a fight.''

DuFourmey gulped and twisted around to look at the
jungle behind him.

Randall looked at Horwitch. "I wonder what their
strength is, Major."

The British officer stroked his mustache, his brow furrowing. "Judging by the distribution of the forces we
penetrated last night, and assuming they're spread out
in similar fashion over the rest of the island . . . I'd say
at least fifteen hundred men. Maybe more if there's a
secondary garrison based on the other side of that farthest volcano."

Mulgrew sighed and rolled over onto his back, draping
an arm over his eyes. "Wonderful."

Horwitch ignored him. "Even fifteen hundred men can
be dealt with if they're all running in circles and shooting
in the wrong direction. The element of surprise is a powerful advantage."

As one, the other eight crash survivors turned and
looked at him. No one spoke for several seconds.

"Major," Mulgrew said finally, "beggin' your pardon,
sir. We came over here to have a look-see and evaluate
the enemy's setup and strength—maybe do a little damage to him if the odds were halfway even. That's what
we all agreed the other day. Well, we've just done that,
sir, and he's bloody well set up and he's bloody well
here in strength! Now, I'm for killin' as many Japs as
possible, just like the next bloke—but there ain't a hope
in hell that the nine of us can wipe out an entire garrison
of Jap army troops and navy *Rikusentai*!" The swarthy
corporal licked his lips nervously as Horwitch's ice-blue
gaze bored into him. "I say the best thing we can do is
to pull back into the highlands, reconnoiter on the sly
for another day or two, then slip the lines on one of
those launches down there and make for Minglaat or
Leyte, island-hoppin' at night. We present our report,
and the flyboys come and blast this place to hell—that
fokkin' sub included, sir!"

"That sounds like the smart play to me, Major," Foster chimed in, "puttin' it in Yank terms, sir."

He fell silent as Horwitch's cold eyes drifted from Mulgrew's and locked on to his.

"Your insight is noted, Sergeant," he said. "Yours as well, Corporal." His teeth were set, jaw jutting out. "Unfortunately for you both, the combined British Commonwealth and Allied military has not yet degenerated into a democracy. Tactical decisions will be made by the officer in command—me."

He turned to address the group as a whole. "As I explained not more than two days ago, this is now a functional combat unit, and as ranking Allied officer I am well within my rights to issue orders to both Commonwealth and American personnel. The civilian members of our company are free to do as they choose, but they have indicated quite clearly that they wish to act in concert with the rest of us." Horwitch stabbed a finger in the direction of the grotto. "The island garrison I am not particularly concerned with. The soldiers are not going anywhere. But a submarine of that size represents a unique and mobile threat to all seaborne Allied assets in this area—and indeed the entire western Pacific. The aircraft associated with it have already destroyed one American PT boat, and if its commander and crew intend to continue attacking Allied targets under the guise of false markings, as I'm sure they do, the havoc they could cause before they are finally hunted down might well be astronomical." He paused, the set of his face grim. "We are obligated to do something about that, gentlemen."

"It's a hangar," Hooke said suddenly.

All heads turned toward the New Zealander, who had resumed scanning the sub pen with his binoculars.

"What's that again?" Randall demanded.

Hooke tweaked the focus on the glasses. "It's a hangar," he repeated. "That long, broad tube alongside the conning tower with the huge watertight door in its forward end. It's a deck-mounted, underwater aircraft hangar." He looked at Horwitch and held the binoculars out to him. "They're putting the seaplane they were lift-ing with the collapsible crane inside it right now."

The major took the glasses and stared through them for the better part of thirty seconds. "By the devil," he muttered. "The wings fold back along the fuselage. So do parts of the tail."

"And the floats come off as well," Hooke said. "That's how they get an aircraft with a forty-foot wing-span into a tube only twelve feet wide."

"Bloody hell," Foster said, crouching next to Hor-witch. "How many planes can they fit into that damned thing?"

Hooke chewed his thin lip. "A one-hundred-twenty-foot hangar divided by a forty-foot aircraft fuselage," he said. "I make it at least three—perhaps more, depending on how they're crammed in."

"And the sub can travel to any location," Garth said, "surface, roll the planes out of the hangar, extend their wings, and fire them into the air off that catapult."

Hooke nodded. "Exactly."

"Hell," DuFourmey cut in, "it's like an underwater aircraft carrier, you know? You can't even see it comin'. What's to stop it from sailin' off to San Francisco or Sydney—or even Pearl again—and sendin' them planes to shoot up or bomb the center of town?"

Joe Garth and Randall looked at him.

"Nothing," Garth said. "Nothing at all."

Chapter
Twenty-one

"Are you certain you want to do this, Mr. Matalam?" Major Horwitch stood before the Moro guerrilla leader, stroking his ginger mustache with two fingers and frowning, his arms crossed. The company had withdrawn from the lava overlook into the cover of a small copse of broadleaf trees. As Salih Matalam handed his tommy gun and ammunition bandoliers to Horwitch, the other seven men knelt in silence in the sun-dappled shade, watching.

"I do it, Major," the Moro said. "We need information—location of troops, weapons, best way to approach submarine pen." He grinned, unarmed now, holding out his open hands. "I look like civvy laborer, eh? Good little coolie." He shot Mulgrew a wry glance.

The sardonic corporal took in Matalam's grass sandals, ragged black pants, and camouflage shirt. Slowly, he made a circle out of his thumb and forefinger. "The very bloody picture, mate. Except for the camo blouse."

Matalam stripped it off, exposing a worn, light-colored garment resembling a sleeveless undershirt. Carefully, he folded and rolled the camouflage shirt, and held it out to Mulgrew. "You hold for me, please, Corporal," he said, smiling.

Mulgrew balked for an instant. Then he made up his mind. "Sure, mate," he said, taking it. "Be careful down there. Keep a low bloody profile, eh?"

Matalam nodded briefly. "Yes. Thank you." He pulled a long strip of beige cloth from his pants pocket and wrapped it quickly around his head. "Sun hat for poor worker," he said.

He raised a hand, looking around at the other members of the company, then turned and trotted off into the jungle, padding along softly like a cat. In twenty seconds he was out of sight.

"What do we do now, Major?" Randall inquired, wiping sweat off his brow.

Horwitch rubbed his brow, then squatted and sat down with his back against the thick trunk of a palm tree.

"We wait," he said.

Lieutenant Commander Eiju Ogaki strode—or rather waddled—across the open compound between his command post and the bamboo hut that served as his personal quarters, and slapped his riding crop against the left leg of his cavalry breeches. It was hot under the camouflage netting that hung twenty feet overhead, strung between hut roofs, the central flagpole, and perimeter trees—too hot for the old-style horse soldier's trousers and high boots the commander of the island garrison favored. Whenever Ogaki found it necessary to move around during the heat of the day, the sweat literally poured out of his pudgy body, ran down his legs, and pooled in his boots. The well-worn leather had become so impregnated with fermenting perspiration that his orderly, who was responsible for polishing the boots each and every night, had given him the unflattering, behind-the-back nickname *Kusai Ashi*—literally, "Stink Foot." No one in the garrison, however, had yet been foolish enough to refer to Ogaki as such when he was within earshot.

Eiju Ogaki may have been garrison commander of Island No. 12863, in charge of both Navy *Rikusentai* and army artillery troops, and a military careerist with some fifteen years of service behind him, but he was still little more than a garden-variety bully—a middle-management tyrant who delighted in terrorizing those beneath him and fawning on those above. The structure of the newly expanded IJN and his obscure position within it appealed to him. He had been given his own little island kingdom—complete with subjects—and on it he was absolute ruler. Ogaki the Great. Ogaki the Wise. Ogaki the Terrible.

Ogaki the Disciplinarian.

He puffed himself up, doing his best to glower like an angry god, as he approached the three *Rikusentai* standing at attention next to the parade ground flagpole. He succeeded only in appearing fat and bad-tempered.

"Stand fast, boy," Superior Petty Officer Zenji Kono hissed out of the corner of his mouth to Seaman Second Class Iwao Yoshi. "Like a tall pine. No flinching."

The warrant officer standing just in front of Kono—a slender, self-righteous type named Soemu Tanabe—half turned and scowled over his shoulder at the barely audible whispering, then snapped back to attention as Ogaki drew near. Stepping forward smartly, he saluted.

"Honorable Lieutenant Commander," he announced. "It is my duty to report the dereliction of duty of Seaman Second Class Yoshi."

Ogaki stared at the smooth-faced young soldier with small, piggy eyes. "Proceed."

"Last night I overheard Superior Petty Officer Kono, in the course of his usual evening inspection rounds through the southeastern machine gun positions, warn Seaman Second Class Yoshi not to fall asleep at his post. That such a reprimand should even be necessary I found to be alarming, and so, after Superior Petty Officer Kono left, I waited perhaps ten minutes and then approached Seaman Yoshi's position. There I found him asleep, slumped over his Nambu. His comrade, Seaman Uchino, was also asleep—but as he was not manning the machine gun I took him to be the soldier in rest rotation, and therefore did not see a basis for charging him with dereliction as well."

Meddling bastard, Kono thought. A walking book of regulations.

"The charge is sleeping on guard duty, Honorable Lieutenant Commander," Warrant Officer Tanabe stated. "I swear to it."

Lieutenant Commander Ogaki immediately recognized in Tanabe a personality trait that he himself shared—a cold-blooded willingness to steer credit toward himself by pointing out to his superiors the occasional human lapses of those around him. He felt a surge of revulsion for the warrant officer, largely because he possessed enough self-awareness to be cognizant of the uncomfortable fact that one is least able to tolerate in others what one dislikes most about oneself. Listening to the blatantly sycophantic Tanabe was like having a mirror held up to his own small, mean character.

He glanced at Tanabe in distaste, then shifted his stare back to Yoshi and stepped forward, his hands clasped behind him, riding crop twitching the air. "Is this true, Seaman Yoshi?" he inquired in harsh, clipped tones.

Yoshi drew a deep breath and nodded. *"Hai*, Honorable Lieutenant Commander!" he sounded off.

Ogaki brought the riding crop around like a lash and cracked it across Yoshi's left ear. The young soldier gasped in pain and staggered sideways, dropping his bolt-action Arisaka rifle in the sand.

"Remain at attention!" Ogaki screamed. *"Pick up your rifle! Remain at attention!"*

Tanabe smiled.

"PICK UP YOUR RIFLE!"

Yoshi false-started several times, trying to follow Ogaki's confusing and contradictory string of instructions. Finally he snatched up the Arisaka, clamped it to his side, and came back to attention. A thick red welt glistening with a hairline streak of blood ran from his ear to his left cheekbone.

The fat little commander moved in closer, his face purple and beaded with sweat from the effort of shouting. He poked Yoshi in the chest with his riding crop.

"I am a disciplinarian," Ogaki announced, "but I am not unreasonable. You are one of the new replacements, yes?"

"H-hai, Honorable Lieutenant Commander!" Yoshi replied.

"Very well," Ogaki went on. "I cannot have my men sleeping on guard duty. However, in this case, I am prepared to be lenient. Superior Petty Officer Kono!"

"Sir!" Kono barked, stepping forward.

"Seaman Second Class Yoshi will serve three days of punishment detail with the civilian laborers who are digging additional antiaircraft emplacements into the rock above the submarine pen. Half rations and water, as well. You will escort him to the work site immediately and put a pick in his hands."

"Yes, sir!" Kono acknowledged, and spun on his heel to face Yoshi. "Seaman Yoshi! To your left . . . *turn!*" The young soldier spun and stamped a heel. "By the left . . . quick—*march!*"

The two *Rikusentai* moved off quickly toward the far end of the parade ground. Kono eyed Tanabe in passing. A smile was still curling the corners of the warrant officer's mouth. Kono gave him a look so withering that the smirk faded instantly from his face.

"Warrant Officer Tanabe," Ogaki said. "Dismissed."

The obsequious minor officer lingered at attention, opening his mouth as if to speak—but Ogaki turned on his heel and strode away toward his quarters. Tanabe would not receive any approbation from him for his malicious informing. Besides, the little commander was hot and itchy in his woolen cavalry uniform and found himself craving his daily bath—a pleasant diversion at a private location about halfway along the bay, where a tiny waterfall of freshwater cascaded into a basin of salt water. The idyllic, out-of-the-way spot was concealed by a dense stand of palm trees and bamboo, and Ogaki had

ensured its privacy by issuing a standing order that no
one was to venture within five hundred yards of it, on
foot or by boat.

Command had its privileges, and a civilized man
needed his luxuries.

"How is it, boy?" Kono asked, touching the vicious
welt on Yoshi's cheek as the two of them trudged up
the hillside path toward the work site. "He really laid
into you."

"*Ow!* Honorable Superior Petty Officer, it stings considerably," Yoshi replied.

Kono grunted, scowling in sympathy. "When we get
up closer to the labor detail, I'll clean and dress it for
you," he said gruffly. "Curse that sniveling toady Tanabe. He had no business checking up on my boys like
that after I'd made my rounds."

"Honorable Superior Petty Officer," Yoshi said, "I
deserve this punishment. I fell asleep over my machine
gun again, in spite of your warning. Warrant Officer Tanabe was quite right to report me to Lieutenant Commander Ogaki." Kono looked at him; the boy was trying
to be brave, and doing not a half-bad job of it. "I feel
humbly fortunate that I received only a single blow and
three days' hard labor as my penalty. As you said, I
might have been shot."

"And three days on half rations and water," Kono
reminded him. "Don't forget that. Your head will be
spinning after two days of hoisting that pick in the sun,
dehydrated and undernourished. Pace yourself." He
scowled again. "And don't give Tanabe so much credit.
A man can technically be right and still be a complete
asshole. People in command are supposed to use their
discretion when dealing with lapses in discipline. He
didn't have to bring Ogaki into it; he could have dealt
with you himself."

"He must have felt compelled to keep the commander
apprised of the integrity of the frontline defenses,"
Yoshi offered, wincing as he touched the welt on his
face. "My failure created a weak point, sir."

Kono stopped walking as they reached the crest of the hill and unsnapped the flap of the first-aid pouch on his belt. "Stop being so noble, boy," he growled. "Tanabe informed on you in order to put a feather in his own cap, and for no other reason. He tries to create petty advancement for himself by telling tales on his own men, curse him. This is not the first time he's done it, believe me. And it will catch up to him someday."

"Yes, Honorable Superior Petty Officer," Yoshi said, squirming a little as Kono began to dab at the stripe on his face with a disinfectant swab.

"Hold still, hold *still*. By the gods, you are a lot of trouble. . . ."

After returning to his personal hut, stripping off his sweaty uniform and boots, and donning a black silk kimono, Lieutenant Commander Eiju Ogaki set off on the narrow jungle path that led along the edge of the bay and down to the hidden bathing cove. He took with him a toiletry kit containing jasmine scent and cherry-blossom wash. In the fetid heat of the jungle, he'd found to his dismay that his own body odor sometimes offended *him*—particularly that of his feet. Thank heaven no one else ever noticed; he'd have been a laughing-stock.

It took a good twenty minutes to reach the thick grove that concealed the bathing pool and waterfall, and another five to pick his way through the growth to the water's edge. But it was worth the effort. The tiny cove looked as if it had been created by the best landscape gardener in Japan. It consisted of a clean, rocky pool of emerald-tinted salt water, as clear as fine sake, surrounded by lush greenery and disturbed only by the soft plattering of a freshwater waterfall, twice the height of a man, which poured steadily out of the jungle to blend with the sea. A true feast for the eyes.

Upon reaching the pool, Ogaki stripped off the kimono and lowered his pale, bloated body into the water. At one time, it had bothered him that his belly had grown so large that he could not see his own genitals, but he rarely thought of that now. He had been married for more than twenty years to a woman he'd never really found attractive or even liked, so sex—on the few occasions he was home, anyway—was far less important than food. When he wanted physical release, there were always the Filipino comfort women in the barracks bordello at the far end of the island. Rather worn and weedy-looking, but they filled the need adequately—if not enthusiastically.

"Ah, there you are, Fish," he said aloud, rubbing brine up his arms. Lurking in the shadow beneath a nearby overhanging log was a medium-sized barracuda, sculling its transparent fins and looking up at Ogaki with cold, swiveling eyes. It gaped momentarily, showing rows of teeth like fat white needles.

Ogaki was not concerned because he was accustomed to seeing the resident three-foot-long fish in the pool, and knew that it would not attack anything as large as a man unless stimulated by thrashing movement or blood in the water. Occasionally, when he was through bathing, he'd swat a large dragonfly out of the air and toss it onto the surface of the water just under the overhanging log. The insect would give a crippled twitch or two, and the barracuda would strike like a bolt of lightning. A violent splash—and the dragonfly would be gone. By the time the ripples settled, the barracuda would be back beneath the log, sculling.

"I know you would not bite the hand that feeds you, Fish," Ogaki said. He moved under the little waterfall, relishing the cool freshwater as it cascaded onto his head and shoulders.

Bliss.

He was enjoying the sensuous feeling of the water sheeting down his body, his mind starting to wander off into thoughts of the chubby new teenage comfort woman who had been brought to the island on the most recent supply barge from Luzon—when something struck him a tremendous blow in the solar plexus. He buckled at the waist, nearly retching up his breakfast, and a hard hand clamped onto the back of his neck. Simultaneously, his legs were kicked out from under him, and he was thrust face-first down into the pool. Only the fact that the blow had paralyzed his diaphragm prevented him from breathing in seawater and starting to drown immediately.

He tried to scream, to struggle, but was pinned to the pool's rocky bottom like a minnow beneath a boot. Unable to inhale water with his breathing center paralyzed, he was not drowning. He was suffocating.

The horrible choking sensation increased as his brain began to shut down. The dark, whirling vortex of tunnel vision closed in tighter and tighter until at last—with a final agonized shudder—he blacked out completely.

When he came to, he was standing in thigh-deep water beneath the overhanging log, his arms stretched straight out from his shoulders along the mossy wood and tied at the elbows and wrists with tough vines. Something foul-tasting was crammed into his mouth, held in place by what felt like a strip of cloth wrapped around his head and running between his teeth. His chest and head ached as if they were on fire.

Ogaki blinked salt water out of his eyes and tried to focus. Gradually, the details of his surroundings took shape. There was the familiar vegetation that ringed the bathing pool—palm trunks and green bamboo. Exotic tropical blossoms nodding here and there in the verdant tangle. And something else . . .

A man was sitting on his haunches directly opposite him, on the shoreline atop a large coral rock. He was less than six feet away, his eyes even with Ogaki's, staring. A large, floppy-brimmed bush hat shaded his narrow face, which was peppered with graying stubble. He was tall and thin, with broad, bony shoulders, narrow hips, and long legs. The sleeves of his olive green shirt were rolled to the elbows, exposing forearms comprised entirely of whipcord muscle and sinew.

The man was of European extraction.

Ogaki struggled, doing little but stirring the water around his legs. He made a gurgling sound. The gag barely allowed him to breathe, much less talk.

The man was smiling now, long white teeth gleaming behind thin lips. His eyes were like those of the barracuda that lurked somewhere nearby—bright, alert, and as cold as spheres of black ice. Ogaki blinked helplessly as the man raised a finger into the air, gestured. . . .

There was a sudden, excruciating pain in his right hand. He squealed behind the gag and thrashed violently, jerking his head sideways to see what had bitten him.

Sitting astride the log, about three feet away, was a naked apparition with a spray of black feathers where its hair should have been, and the black, red, and white painted face of a demon. It grinned, showing pointed teeth. As Ogaki shrank away, eyes bugging, the apparition held out a long sword toward him, the blade level with the surface of the water. Lying across its tip was Ogaki's little finger, which the sword had just sliced off.

The garrison commander of Island No. 12863 squalled again deep in his throat and yanked at his bonds, half crazed with pain and fear. To no avail.

"Now that I have your attention," Finian Hooke said in Japanese. . . .

Chapter Twenty-two

"I have not seen you before, friend," the Filipino laborer next to Salih Matalam muttered in Tagalog, lifting his sledgehammer for another swing. He brought it down on the black lava rock with a grunt, closing his eyes as shards and dust flew.

"No, friend," the Moro answered smoothly. "I came in last night on a supply boat from Mindanao, and was landed at the . . . far end of the island." He paused, waiting.

"Ah, you mean at the western barracks," the laborer said. "Where the airstrip is being constructed."

Matalam smiled and swung his pick. "Yes, exactly. But it was dark, and I did not notice an airstrip."

"Well, that is not surprising, friend," the laborer grunted, "since it is little more than a slash in the jungle right now. But you must have noticed the other labor gangs camped near the boat dock, and the bulldozer sitting under the trees nearby."

"Yes, of course."

"That bulldozer has been broken down for a month now," the Filipino said in disgust. "So they push us twice as hard. Just be grateful you're not assigned to that end of the island. The men there have had to clear all the growth from the airstrip by hand."

"Almost as tough as breaking rocks," Matalam remarked with a grin, bringing his pick down again.

"Truly."

They were standing on top of the great hump of black lava that formed the western end of the little bay. Beneath their feet, protected by seventy-five feet of solid volcanic rock, lay the giant submarine, snug inside its reinforced grotto. Surrounding them were at least two hundred other civilian laborers, swinging picks and sledgehammers; sweating and grunting and chattering to each other under the watchful eyes of several dozen Japanese soldiers, who patrolled through their midst with rifles cradled in their arms. Overhead, the sun burned down through a clear blue sky wheeling with seabirds, sending a million diamondlike sparkles dancing off the azure waters of the bay.

"What happens beneath us, friend?" Matalam inquired casually. "Did I see a great vessel lying in a cave when I climbed the hill to join the work crew?"

The laborer jerked his head up, looking for the nearest Japanese. "Shh!" He lowered his head again. "It is not permitted to speak of the submarine pen. The soldiers become angry, sometimes violent."

"Oh," Matalam responded humbly. He dug with his pick for a moment. "I am sorry—I am new. I did not know. I do not wish to bring trouble upon you."

They worked together in silence for a couple of minutes more. Then the laborer moved close to Matalam again. "It is not permitted, but I will tell you anyway," he said, his voice low but defiant. "I will tell you of this and other things."

The Moro smiled. The man had wanted to talk. Sometimes polite silence was as effective as a direct question.

"I am listening, friend."

The man glanced around quickly. The nearest soldier was loitering thirty feet away, his back to them. "The Japanese are full of contradictions, friend," the laborer muttered, "as you doubtless know. They came to our villages, our towns, and declared themselves to be our liberators—freeing us from the oppressive influence of the imperialist Americans. Then they informed us that all able-bodied men had to assemble and work as forced labor—or terrible harm might befall our families and homes.

"Myself, I had not noticed that I was particularly oppressed by the Americans. I came and went as I chose, sold the fruits and vegetables I farmed, and was able to provide for my family. No one ever troubled me—in fact, the soldiers on leave often came through our village and spent money, buying food, drink, and various goods. Quite regularly, a truck with an army doctor and several medics would stop by to provide free medical care. They told us that this was a gesture of goodwill from General MacArthur, who at that time—just before the war—was helping our then President, Manuel Quezon, rebuild the Philippine Army. Surely you remember." The laborer slammed his sledgehammer into a knob of rock, paused, and spat angrily. "And then the Japanese drove them out of the Philippines, and everything changed. Our 'liberators' turned out to be far worse than our 'oppressors.' "

"You speak truly, friend," Matalam agreed. "And so—like me—they brought you here, far from your home and family, to work in support of this island's submarine operations." He looked around at the sea of sweating bodies, the flurry of rising and falling picks and sledgehammers. The *whack-crack-whack* of steel on stone was deafening and continuous. "It must make you angry, to be so ill used. It does me, and I have not been here nearly as long as you. . . ."

"Ha!" The laborer shot him a caustic glance. "For five months I have been on this dismal little blot of an island, breaking up rock here and moving it there for these accursed Japanese. Although they claim we are not prisoners, we are not permitted to stop working, or leave, or—"

"Indeed, you must possess the tenacity of a water buffalo to have endured for so long," Matalam cut in carefully. "A feat of strength and will that I can only hope to duplicate." The laborer beamed, pleased. "And in that time, I suppose, the Japanese have driven you to distraction with their comings and goings, their deployments and redeployments, their usual incessant shuffling of men, weapons, ammunition, supplies. . . ."

The laborer rolled his eyes conspiratorially. "Ah! You do not know the half of it, friend," he said. "The ammunition I have moved, the gun pits I have dug, the constant drills and exercises I have seen and heard on land and out on the bay—particularly involving that miserable submarine—"

Matalam cracked the point of his pick down on the black lava rock and stood up to wipe his brow, leaning in close to the other man as he did so.

"I recognize you for that rare being, a truly observant man, friend," he said under his breath. "Share with me everything—will you not?—so that I may know my surroundings and endure my time here half as well as you."

Up on the shoulder of the volcano, in the copse of broadleaf trees, Major Harold Horwitch was fuming.

"I did not authorize any further reconnaissance!" he seethed, keeping his voice low despite his anger. "Mr. Matalam was the one chosen to gather intelligence during daylight hours because he stood the best chance of blending in with the Filipinos and Japanese. A white man or even a—a Negro is too apt to be spotted, what with all the Japanese scattered about!" He glanced peremptorily at DuFourmey. "I expected more responsible conduct from Mr. Hooke and his Dayak friend."

Randall looked down toward the bay. "I didn't even see them leave, Major. None of us did. One minute they were here, the next—gone." He shaded his eyes with his hands, squinting. "Fat chance of picking them out down there now."

"You'd better bloody well hope you don't," Foster drawled from under his bush hat, which he'd placed over his face. He was lying flat on his back on a fallen palm frond, hands locked together over his stomach, his Sten gun wedged up under his left forearm. "If you can see 'em from up here, mate, the Japs sure as hell are going to spot 'em down there."

"Blast it," Horwitch growled. He moved up beside Garth, who was looking out in the direction of the submarine pen. "I don't suppose you can pick out Matalam in that bunch, eh?"

"No, sir," Garth replied. "There have to be at least a couple hundred men digging on top of that lava hill. They all look the same. Even with Hooke's binoculars I'd be hard-pressed to tell them apart."

"Bugger." Horwitch spun on his heel, pacing. "Listen to me, all of you. We will wait until one hour after sundown for Mr. Matalam to return. If Mr. Hooke and Mr. Dap show up in the interim, so much the better. Hopefully they will have information to add to Mr. Matalam's that will justify the danger they've put us all in by traipsing off on their own. In the unlikely event that Mr. Matalam does not return, we will proceed with an organized reconnaissance of our own, as best we can. Specifically, we are looking for the most effective way to take out that sub, which may involve capturing a nearby artillery emplacement and cranking off as many rounds at it as we can before the Japanese figure out what's going on. It may involve creating a diversion of some kind, as well as setting up one or more fields of fire along the land approaches to the sub pen. We want to bottleneck the Japanese when they try to rush our positions, and to do that we need to find the best vantage points at which to set up heavy machine guns."

"Beggin' pardon, sir," Mulgrew asked, lying back beside Foster with a stalk of grass between his teeth, "just where are these heavy machine guns comin' from?"

"We'll capture them," Horwitch told him. "And all of this preparation for battle stems from good reconnaissance—so get ready to move around in the jungle tonight, gentlemen." He paced off toward the far edge of the little dell, frowning.

Mulgrew put his forearm over his eyes. "Wonderful," he said.

"Do I detect a hint of sarcasm, Corporal?" Randall inquired, settling back on an elbow.

"Bloody right you do," Mulgrew said. "You didn't hear him mention anything about how we're gettin' out of here alive, did you?"

"Fokkin' Mad Harry," Foster muttered. "He's in his element, and no mistake."

"Who?" Randall asked.

Foster picked his hat off his face and looked for Horwitch. The British major was a good forty feet away, peering through the foliage at the Japanese positions below. "Oh, that's right," the Aussie sergeant said quietly. "You Yanks wouldn't know about the legendary bloody Horwitches."

Randall glanced at Joe Garth, then back at Foster. "Enlighten us, why don't you?"

Foster cut his eyes at the major again, then cleared his throat and continued in a low voice: "That's Major Harold 'Mad Harry' Horwitch. Queen's Rifles, Black Watch, Scots Guards—you name the unit, he's been associated with it. A bloody war machine. And if that ain't enough, he's got a fokkin' brother—Colonel Michael 'Mad Mike' Horwitch, who comes with his own never-endin' list of units and campaigns."

"Those two buggers have been gettin' soldiers servin' under 'em killed in the name of the bloody British Empire for over twenty years," Mulgrew grunted. "Afghanistan, Kashmir, Ceylon, Burma, Palestine, the Sudan . . . wherever."

"Yeah?" Joe Garth said. "Is that a fact?"

"That's a fact, mate," Foster growled.

The UDT man looked over at Horwitch's broad back. "Do they get the job done?"

Mulgrew paused before answering. "Oh, sure, mate," he muttered. "They get the job done, all right. And that ain't all they get. They also get medals, and press headlines, and dinner with the fokkin' Lord High Pompity Poofter at Buckingham Palace. But the poor bleedin' enlisted sods that fight for 'em—that'd be us, see—they just get one thing . . . *dead*."

"All I asked you," Garth replied, "was if Horwitch can get the job done. Yes or no."

The corporal lifted his arm off his eyes and looked at the UDT man, taken aback by his bluntness. Garth wasn't smiling, and his expression informed Mulgrew that his constant sardonic commentary was wearing thin.

"Can he get the job done?" Joe Garth repeated quietly. "Yes or no?"

Mulgrew put his head back down and repositioned his arm across his eyes. Then he grinned, still chewing the stalk of grass.

"Yes," he said. "The bastard bloody well can."

A glittering school of tiny tropical fish had gathered around Lieutenant Commander Ogaki's legs, attracted by the scent of the blood dripping steadily into the water from the stump of his little finger. The yard-long barracuda lurked just beneath the surface about six feet away, stimulated.

The throbbing of his hand was intensely painful, but Ogaki was less concerned with that than he was with the razor-sharp edge of the long sword that was pressed up against the base of his scrotum. It was as a consequence of the sword's placement that he had not cried out for help when the gag had been removed, permitting him to cough out the ball of wet moss that had been jammed into his mouth.

"As an individual who appreciates horses," the white European had said prior to loosening the gag, "I'm sure you are familiar with the procedure known as *gelding*." He'd smiled and brought a finger to his lips. *"Shhhhh."*

Ogaki had taken his advice.

Now, twenty minutes after the gag had been removed, the Japanese garrison commander continued to answer the European's questions in a low, halting voice, periodically taking time to whimper as the pain in his hand surged and ebbed. All the while, the feathered apparition with the grinning, demon-painted face remained perched on the log just above him, holding the sword so that its blade reached under his bulbous stomach and contacted his genitalia.

"You have been most cooperative, Lieutenant Commander," Hooke said, his Japanese accented but fluent. "Tell me more. The longer you keep talking, the longer you keep your testicles. And if what you say *really* pleases me, you may even live to enjoy them again."

"What—what more can I tell you?" Ogaki moaned. "I have given you my—my garrison strength and disposition, my general . . . defensive plan for the island. I—I have given you . . . details of the . . . gun emplacements surrounding the submarine pen." He moaned again, shaking his head. "My honor is gone . . . gone."

"Which would you rather lose?" Hooke asked him. "Your honor or your balls?"

Ogaki stared at him, horrified.

"Come now," Hooke urged, his voice unnaturally calm, "you must have some other little tidbit you can dredge up for me." He nodded to Yomat Dap, who twitched the blade of his parang just enough to make Ogaki flinch. "Dig deep, *tomodachi*. Some more about the submarine."

"I—I have told you," Ogaki whined. "It launches attack aircraft and *tokko* manned torpedoes. It has . . . great range." He hesitated. "I am not a submariner. . . . What more can I—"

He gave a strangled yelp as Yomat Dap drew the blade upward a quarter of an inch.

"There—there is . . . s-something I know," Ogaki blurted, tripping over his words in panic. "Yarizuma, the captain—he told me. We had s-sake together one night. He drank a little too much . . . began to brag—could not help h-himself. Swore me to . . . secrecy."

"Yarizuma," Hooke repeated. "That is the name of the submarine captain?"

"Of—of the *I-403,* yes," Ogaki replied. "He said that Admiral Yamamoto had entrusted him with a s-sacred . . . mission that would . . . stand the Americans on their heads."

"Indeed," Hooke said. "And what was that mission to be?"

The garrison commander rolled his head in misery and then blinked up at the New Zealander. "To launch an aerial *tokko* attack against Washington, D.C."

"That was to be Yarizuma's mission when he departed this base?"

"Y-yes."

Hooke sat back on his haunches on the rock, his sinewy arms resting on his knees, and fixed his shivering prisoner with a dark, heavy-lidded stare. Then he motioned to Yomat Dap. The Dayak let the parang drop away from Ogaki's groin.

The lieutenant commander lifted his head again as Hooke stepped down into the water and waded toward him. "Th-thank you for removing that sword," he croaked. "My hand. . . ."

Hooke stared into his eyes. "How many innocent people have you killed over the past several years, Ogaki?" he asked. "How many laborers bayoneted or shot?"

The garrison commander looked confused. "I personally? None. Of course, there have been some—some necessary killings . . . in order to ensure the ongoing compliance of the workers. . . ."

Hooke moved in very close.

"My wife's name was Liu," he said. "My daughter's name was Kim."

"What?" Ogaki muttered.

In that instant, Finian Hooke swung the coconut-sized chunk of coral rock he had been concealing behind his back. It struck Ogaki's head just above his left ear, crushing his skull. The pudgy Japanese went limp, shuddered, and died, sagging on his bound arms.

Hooke heaved the bloodied rock out into deeper water, then pulled a jungle knife from his belt and cut Ogaki down. The slashed bonds he tossed into the jungle. Then he took the body by one arm, dragged it facedown over to the waterfall, and draped it across a partially submerged shelf of bleached coral. Scooping some of the gore off the side of the corpse's head, he smeared it on a spur of rock that jutted out beside the freshwater cascade, then washed his hands.

"Accidents will happen, brother," he said to Yomat Dap in the obscure Malayan dialect of coastal Borneo. "Even when doing something as simple as taking a bath."

"Indeed, brother, they are unavoidable," Dap replied. He grinned, his filed teeth flashing, and slid off the log into the water.

Thirty seconds later they melted into the jungle together, Yomat Dap taking the lead. In the idyllic little bathing pool, the yard-long barracuda sculed closer to the body of Eiju Ogaki, twitching its toothy head, following to its source the dilute blood trail that was perfuming the water.

Chapter
Twenty-three

Hooke and Dap had returned to the copse of trees just after sunset, followed thirty minutes later by Salih Matalam, who had slipped away from the laborers' encampment without difficulty, cutting a pair of ground-run phone lines as he went. To the delight of the other members of the company, Matalam had arrived lugging a sack of dried fish and a five-gallon jerrican of freshwater, stolen from a field kitchen. Other than scavenged fruits, it was the first solid food any of them had had since finishing off their survival rations on the crash site island.

The whispered discussion that ensued after their meager feast continued for nearly three hours nonstop, and included a wealth of detailed information from both Hooke and Matalam. Three incontestable facts emerged. One, the Japanese still had no idea they were on the island. Two, the garrison strength was only half of what it had been as recently as two months earlier—six hundred of the original twelve hundred troops had been transferred out to reinforce neighboring islands. And three, the giant submarine, once it departed its pen, was almost certainly bound for the United States for the express purpose of launching a suicide attack on Washington.

"I wouldn't bloody well have believed it if I hadn't seen that fokkin' thing with my own eyes," Foster grumbled. "I never knew a submarine like that even existed." He looked at DuFourmey. "You were right, mate. A bloody underwater aircraft carrier."

"And then some," Hooke said, chewing on a piece of dried fish. "Ogaki was very informative about its mission and capabilities, once we insisted. I imagine its crew will find a use for those manned torpedoes while they're haunting the open end of Chesapeake Bay, too. There are a lot of ships around there. Plenty of targets."

"They are called *Kaiten*," Matalam put in. "Piloted by one man. They are supposedly secret weapon, but secret cannot be kept forever on a small island with so many people on it. The laborers have seen them practicing attack runs in the bay many times, and heard soldiers talking about them. The laborers say that is why they are not allowed to leave. The Japanese think they know too much about these *tokko* weapons, and the submarine that carries them."

Randall scratched the stubble on his chin. "Practice runs, eh? Is that why two *Kaiten* were in the water by the dock? So the pilots could take turns doing drills?"

Matalam nodded. "The worker I talk to say yes, Lieutenant. Sometimes all three *Kaiten* have been seen in bay, making high-speed attacks from many different directions on large cloth buoys full of air."

Horwitch raised his eyebrows and glanced from Matalam to Hooke. "While you were away, the Japanese motored one of the two *Kaiten* at the dock over to the sub and loaded it onto the foredeck, using a big industrial block-and-tackle rig that runs on a track in the ceiling of that grotto. Obviously, the small collapsible aircraft crane they have on board can't handle a load that size. They did use it to pick up that last U.S.-marked attack seaplane about an hour later and stow it in the watertight hangar."

Randall kept scratching his chin. "I wonder if the warheads on those manned torpedoes are armed . . . or if they have to be fused manually before being launched at an actual target."

"I ask my worker friend that," Matalam replied, "and he say that one time he overhear two Japanese sailor men talking—say that they worried about hoisting *Kaiten* because if they drop it on its nose, the warhead maybe go off."

"A crush fuse or impact pistol," Horwitch declared. "Drive it into anything solid and *bang*—it detonates."

Randall cleared his throat. "Suppose someone was to get aboard that last *Kaiten* and pilot it into the side of the submarine. Say while some of us were creating a diversion."

Everyone looked at him. "What?" Horwitch demanded. "And intentionally get himself killed? We've just established that the *Kaiten* is a suicide weapon."

"Well," Randall said, "I was thinking of jumping clear with time to spare."

Everyone blinked and looked at him again, this time as if he'd gone crazy. Including Joe Garth.

"L.T.," Garth said carefully, "the front of that *Kaiten* is big enough to hold two thousand pounds of high explosive . . . probably more. Even if you managed to bail out with two or three hundred yards to go, the shock wave from the explosion would kill you. You know that." His voice got quieter. "You know that from Saipan and Guam and Peleliu. You know it from Leyte . . . from Beach Black."

His dark eyes searched Randall's face. For the first time in several days, he noticed how bone weary his friend looked—how careworn and used up. But in spite of that, Randall smiled.

"That's why I thought I'd tie one of those small dugouts down there to the conning tower on a short tether and tow it behind me," he replied. "I'll cut the canoe loose just before I jump, and then climb into it. If I'm out of the water, the shock wave can't kill me." He kept his tired eyes steady on Joe Garth's. "Just like Beach Black."

Horwitch made a dubious growling noise deep in his throat. "What makes you think you can even figure out how to pilot that blasted thing?" he demanded. "Steer it . . . or even start it up?"

"How hard can it be?" Randall countered. "It's a disposable, one-time-use weapon, so everything inside is bound to be pretty basic. It's a manually controlled torpedo, so it'll have stern propulsion and left and right rudder controls. It's already floating, and I'm not going to try to submerge it, so I shouldn't have to worry about diving planes or ballast tanks."

"If you're runnin' on the surface, mate," Foster said, "you'll be in plain view of all those gun positions scattered around the bay. You'll make a juicy target."

"They won't have time to stop me," Randall replied. "It can't be more than two or three miles from the docks to the mouth of that grotto. Even if all I can manage is, say, eight knots—it'll only take twenty minutes or so to reach the sub. Besides, you'll be engaged in some business of your own, won't you?" He smiled and shifted his gaze to Horwitch.

"Bloody right we will," the major said. "Myself, I favor quietly taking out the gun crew on that pedestal-mounted one-hundred-fifty-millimeter howitzer over there on the peninsula that separates the bay from the ocean—the one that may have a clear shot into the sub pen if we can depress the cannon muzzle far enough. It's a defensible position, one that gives us a wide range of fire over the entire bay. We can probably neutralize some of the other guns nearby that may try to zero in on the *Kaiten*. And it gives us another means of destroying or at least crippling that sub, if for some reason the *Kaiten* doesn't do the job."

"Can I tell y'all somethin'?" DuFourmey said.

Horwitch rubbed his mustache with two fingers, then nodded. "Have your say, Steward's Mate."

DuFourmey rolled his eyes at him. "Well, *thank you*, Majuh, suh," he declared, purposely exaggerating his Deep South accent. "Sho' do 'preciate you lettin' me put in mah two cents' worth." He paused, dropping the act. "Y'all gone *crazy!* We gonna attract every damn Jap on this here island and end up trapped in a losin' gunfight out on that skinny little strip of land!" He pointed out at the peninsula, now little more than a slightly darker mass in the darkness of late evening. "I like a good roll of the dice as much as any gambling man. But when I shoot craps, I don't play to *lose*. So why ain't nobody talkin' about how we gonna get outta here *alive*?"

"Well, Steward's Mate," Horwitch said immediately, "I thought you'd take care of that end for us."

"Say what?"

"Yes." The major turned his icy stare on the black seaman. "I thought that since you have such an aversion to combat, you could slip down to the beach below while the rest of us are engaging the enemy, and snatch one of those utility launches without being seen. Be our 'getaway driver,' to use an American expression."

"Where . . . where I'm supposed to go with it once I get it?" he asked, warily.

"Simple," Horwitch told him. "All you have to do is pilot the boat out through the mouth of the bay and around to the seaward side of the peninsula. That'll put you on the ocean side of the gun emplacement we're going to take, which is another of the reasons I chose that one and not some other. It has a back door—an escape hatch."

"Thank bloody Christ," Mulgrew breathed. "That's the part I was waiting to hear."

Horwitch eyed him. "Relax, Corporal. I don't make a point of getting my men killed if I can avoid it, despite what the rumor mill says."

Mulgrew stirred uncomfortably. "Er . . . yes, sir."

"Major," Joe Garth said, "I'll be accompanying Lieutenant Randall. It's going to take two men to check out one of those *Kaiten* things, cast it off, and get it under way." He grinned at Horwitch, his teeth pale in the darkness. "Besides, this is classic UDT work—stealth approach by water. Right up our alley, sir. As you're well aware, we've done it many times before, the lieutenant and I."

Horwitch nodded. "You feel a swimming approach is best?"

"I'd suggest it," Hooke offered quickly. "Yomat Dap and I found it relatively easy to pick our way through the Japanese positions about halfway down the bay. If you follow the shoreline from the waterfall pool back toward the docks, it should be no problem to remain unseen. The trees and brush overhang the water and provide concealment."

Garth grinned again. "Then that's it. We'll slip through the Jap lines where they're thinnest, enter the water at that little pool, and swim up on the *Kaiten*. Like I said—real bread-and-butter UDT work."

"How will you get around the bay to join us for the escape?" Horwitch asked. "All hell will be breaking loose on shore."

Garth shrugged. "Lieutenant Randall will have the bailout canoe; he can paddle over to the peninsula. If I can't steal another one, I'll swim. Or would you rather I stayed to help Henry grab the escape launch?"

The major shook his head. "You'll have enough to concern you. Mr. Matalam, I'd like you to accompany Mr. DuFourmey to the launch, if you agree. You have the stalking skills to get past any soldiers you run into."

The Moro guerrilla nodded without hesitation. "I do it, Major."

"Sergeant Foster, Corporal Mulgrew," Horwitch said. The Australians looked up. "You two go together like fingers on the same hand, and I have no doubt that you are accustomed to fighting like that as well. Mr. Matalam has pointed out to us the two machine gun nests that protect the single land approach to the peninsula. If you took out the lower one, then occupied the one higher up, you'd have a field of fire that includes the open end of the slot canyon through the lava dome above the sub pen. Anyone trying to assault the peninsula by land has to follow the trail through that canyon. You could easily bottleneck the Japanese there for hours."

"No flanking maneuver possible, either," Matalam added. "Slopes steep and thick with jungle, and only other approach is over top of lava hill where laborers dig today. Completely exposed—easy to sweep clean with heavy machine gun."

Mulgrew's lean face creased into a flinty smile. He put a crumpled cigarette into his mouth, then handed one to Foster. "Just like the bloody Kokoda Trail, eh, Web?" he said.

Foster took the smoke and with the lighter Mulgrew held out, he lit it, carefully shielding the flame with both hands. "Better than Kokoda, Mick," he grunted. "At least this time we won't be fighting while we're backing up." He looked Horwitch in the eye and nodded. "We'll do it, Major."

"Excellent," Horwitch said. "The three of us, along with Mr. Hooke and Mr. Dap, will capture the howitzer emplacement first—quietly. We should be able to take out the remaining gun positions on the peninsula, and perhaps a couple on the opposite shore. Then, in the initial confusion, you and Corporal Mulgrew will assault and neutralize the two Nambu nests, man the uppermost one, and hold off the Japanese counterattack when it comes from the mainland."

"For a while, anyway," Mulgrew remarked. The note of cynical resignation in his voice offended no one. It seemed entirely appropriate.

Silence fell over the group. The men sat or reclined in the humid darkness of the copse, each gazing at the ground and trying to digest what he had to do. Overhead, a night-flying seabird drifted past, a black wisp scudding before the stars, and let out a long, mournful cry.

"This gonna turn out bad," DuFourmey said resignedly, to no one in particular. "I can just feel it."

His comment elicited no response. Another minute or so passed before Randall spoke up. "When do we go, Major?"

The British officer examined the luminous dial of his wristwatch. "It's twenty-one hundred hours right now. We'll start to move at oh two hundred . . . deep in the wee hours of early morning, when the Japs are at their groggiest."

"We hope," Mulgrew said around his cigarette. He inhaled, and the tip glowed red in the darkness.

"I'm happy," Foster muttered, settling back, and pulled his battered bush hat over his eyes. "We get five hours of sleep before we have to go to bleedin' work."

"Ain't nobody worried 'bout this?" DuFourmey whispered, aghast.

Foster crossed his booted feet and slapped at a mosquito that had landed on his chin.

"No point, mate," he replied from beneath the brim of his hat. "No point at all."

The IJN doctor wiped his hands on a bloodstained towel and shook his head. "Very nasty," he said to Warrant Officer Soemu Tanabe. "The left side of the skull is completely crushed, with considerable damage to the proximal brain tissue. A tragic accident. He was dead before he hit the water."

The two men were standing in the infirmary of the garrison compound, looking down at the pale, flaccid corpse of Lieutenant Commander Eiju Ogaki, which had been laid out on an operating table. Hovering in the background, smoking and whispering, were the soldiers who had carried the body up from the bathing pool.

"Are you sure he didn't drown?" Tanabe demanded. "We found him floating facedown beside the waterfall."

"Dead before he hit the water," the doctor repeated. "There is no water in his lungs. He was not breathing. The massive wound to the head shut down all bodily functions instantaneously." He snapped his fingers. "Like *that*."

Tanabe shook his head, more in bewilderment than sympathy. "When he didn't return from his morning bath for more than four hours, I became concerned. I went to look for him with a small detail, and found this. . . ." His voice trailed off.

The doctor looked at him sideways. "Of course, there's no doubt as to what must have happened . . . is there?"

The warrant officer snapped to as if coming out of a daydream. "Absolutely not!" he declared. "There was blood and tissue on an outcropping of rock right beside the waterfall where Lieutenant Commander Ogaki was known to bathe. The footing is very treacherous—smooth and slick with moss. It's obvious that he slipped, fell, and struck his head on the jutting rock. The men who accompanied me to the pool will corroborate this, and my official report will read as such."

"And this?" The doctor gestured at Ogaki's right hand. It was mangled and shredded, as if it had been fed into a mechanical hopper. Several fingers were missing.

"There was a large barracuda in the pool," Tanabe said. "It became excited by the smell of blood and attacked the body—by chance concentrating on the hand."

"Mmm," the doctor mused, poking at the damaged extremity. "Multiple bites . . . three fingers gone . . . a fair amount of tissue loss up the forearm to the elbow. Look here: the cut is so clean at the base of the little finger, it could have been done with a scalpel."

"That's a barracuda for you, sir," Tanabe said confidentially. "Have you ever seen the teeth and jaws of one close-up? Like living shears."

The doctor shuddered and shook his head. "No, I haven't, Warrant Officer, and I don't care to." He backed away from the table. "Cover him up," he told one of the soldiers. "Use that sheet over there."

"Hai!" the trooper responded, stepping forward.

"A shame, sir," Tanabe said, showing what he estimated to be an appropriate amount of respectful remorse, though in reality he felt none. The doctor was a ranking officer.

"Quite," replied the doctor, despite the fact that he had always considered Ogaki a disgusting pig of a human being. "Have you contacted Lieutenant Harada on the other end of the island? Command of this garrison has now fallen to him."

Tanabe glanced down at the bulbous, lifeless form beneath the damp sheet. "Yes, sir," he said. "I've dispatched a runner. As you know, because of the proximity of the American forces on Leyte, we are observing strict radio silence. In addition, the ground phone lines were accidentally cut by the workers this afternoon, and are not yet repaired."

"Hm," the doctor grunted. "Disrupted communications—the bane of military existence. Well, as long as he gets the word. I'm sure he'll be delighted to learn that he's suddenly ascended to the throne of this wretched little piece of real estate."

Chapter
Twenty-four

It is in dreams that the most cherished desires and darkest fears of men bubble up out of the subconscious to commingle, for a while, in the netherworld between the blankness of deep slumber and the groggy first perceptions of awakening. By random concurrence, by accidental synchronism, in a single hour on the night of October 30, 1944—sixteen men whose fates were irrevocably intertwined occupied that netherworld of sentient sleep at the same time.

Toshiko Yarizuma stood before his wife and sons beneath a mature cherry tree heavy with fresh pink-and-white blossoms. He reached up over Nima's head to pick one, thinking of placing it in her hair—but just as the tips of his outstretched fingers were about to touch it, it burst into flame. When in confusion he dropped his eyes back to his family, he was confronted with four blackened, grinning corpses, wreathed in fire.

Harold Horwitch was running across a frost-rimed rugby pitch at Yorkshire Boys' School, ball in hand, his brother, Michael, keeping pace just off his right flank. All eyes were on him, including those of Prime Minister

David Lloyd George, visiting for the day. An opposing
tackler lunged in, followed by two more. Horwitch
dodged, spun, and tossed the ball toward Michael in a
perfect lateral feed. But his brother wasn't there.

Hajimi Ona stared in horror as the *Kaiten* of his best
friend, Isamu Matsura, badly off course on its initial
training run in the chilly waters of Tokuyama Bay,
slammed into the side of an attending tugboat, crushing
its tiny conning tower. As it sank, he could hear Isamu,
trapped within, screaming to him for help. But he could
do nothing. Nothing but burn in the overwhelming sense
of shame that accompanied the equally overwhelming
sense of relief that it was his best friend who was drowning, and not he.

Charlton Randall was standing knee-deep in roiling
water on top of a barely submerged reef, watching
Fitzgerald—not so far off, it seemed—pump his arms up
and down above his head, smiling sadly under his carrot
red hair, and disappear behind a massive series of
aquatic explosions. Stricken, Randall turned to look for
help—and there was his father, shaking his head in mute
contempt. He turned the other way—and there was his
mother, her patrician face pinched, ever dissatisfied, ex-
uding silent reproach. He looked back toward the explosions, and every dead member of his UDT squad was
there, standing knee-deep around him in a semicircle—
Fitz, McNab, Bartlett, and Drexel—their flesh torn and
white and rotten, their eyes nothing more than empty
black holes . . . yet brimming with accusation.

Sekio Yagi was riding through the gates of Yasukuni
atop his *Ohka*, waving to the throngs of people who
were showering him with cherry-blossom petals, cheering
wildly as they did so. Just ahead in the near distance
rose a golden palace where the other *kami* warrior heroes dwelled, waiting to welcome him as one of their
own.

Finian Hooke was watching as his wife Liu's desperate, pleading eyes vanished beneath a mass of heaving,
khaki-clad male bodies. Then he heard his daughter
scream for him. He saw the hard-eyed Japanese para-

trooper grin into his face—felt the bayonet sink into his abdomen. And then everything happened all over again.

Kameo Fujita was struggling to reset an altimeter in the cockpit of Lieutenant Sekio Yagi's *Ohka*. His fingers felt like balls of rubber, and he was fumbling, fumbling. Yagi stood over him, shrieking vague threats. With every clumsy movement, every misstep, Yagi would scream anew. Fujita could hardly stand it. But he knew that if he could just get the altimeter reset, all would be well and Yagi would cease troubling him.

Henry DuFourmey was riding in a streetcar, sitting on a bench seat at the very rear. The vehicle was full, and every other person on it was white. They had all turned in their seats and were staring back at him.

Zenji Kono was trying to keep his boys moving. It was a bayonet attack, a desperate charge through withering enemy fire, and despite his shouted encouragement they were faltering. One would go down, then another and another. Kono thought they were hit, but each time he knelt down beside a prostrate soldier and rolled him over, he found that the boy was not shot, but sleeping.

Web Foster was in his favorite cattlemen's bar in the dusty outback town of Didgeree, Australia. The beer was cold and there was plenty of it flowing out of the taps, because every single cow on the six small ranches he and his five closest mates owned had calved on the same day, and every calf had lived.

Iwao Yoshi was dreaming of sleeping—but in the dream, whenever he began to nod off, some loud individual with a warrant officer's stripes on his sleeve batted him awake and thrust a pick or shovel into his hands.

Mick Mulgrew was winning. The dice kept bouncing off the bamboo wall of the little hunters' hut in the Owen Stanley Mountains and coming up seven-eleven, time and time again. The wad of cash in his left hand was becoming so fat he could barely get his fingers around it. He blew on the dice for luck and threw again. Seven-eleven, by God. He was going to be able to retire on this one game. But the rattle of small-arms fire was growing louder on the rain-soaked Kokoda Trail outside, and the frantic shouts of running men were beginning to interfere with his concentration. The Japanese were coming again. Just his luck. They were going to ruin his streak.

Kiichi Uchino was trying to get the attention of a girl he had known since childhood. But she was coy and giggled behind her hand, flashing her dark eyes now and then and pretending to be shocked at his forwardness. He thought he had never seen another human being look so attractive.

Salih Matalam was practicing the *balisong* with his father, moving through the balletlike training sequences of the martial art like the older man's mirror image, trying to handle the flickering, glittering blade with half the delicacy and precision sixty-seven-year-old Kivat Matalam displayed. One day, perhaps, if he was diligent, he would achieve his father's level of skill. The song of the knives chattered gently in his ears.

Soemu Tanabe was stepping up to take command of a *Rikusentai* regiment. Behind him, dismayed and overawed, were the dozens upon dozens of men he had outwitted, outperformed, and outmaneuvered in order to achieve his advancement. Look at them back there, stupefied at their fate, left in his dust like so much loose change. A fool's due was to be used, bypassed, discarded, and laughed at by his betters. The thought gave him a surge of pure glee.

Joe Garth was sitting cross-legged at the edge of a red-brown canyon, his Apache grandfather by his side. Together they were watching the sun set behind a jagged horizon of purple-and-gold badlands. The sky was the fiery crimson color of a cactus rose.

Yomat Dap, on watch, did not sleep.

Chapter Twenty-five

Lieutenant Chimaki Harada strode along the narrow jungle path as quickly as his tired legs would carry him. In the pitch darkness of early morning, the small hand lamp he brandished barely illuminated the winding, overgrown route ahead. He glanced at his watch—two A.M.—an ungodly hour to be called on to assume command of the garrison. Ogaki might have obliged him by having his fatal accident just after breakfast.

He stumbled over a chunk of lava, cursing. The path had led out onto an uneven plain of broken rock: the lava dome upon which additional gun pits were being dug by the island's eastern labor gang. Harada paused to wipe sweat from his forehead. The battery of his hand lamp was failing, and he turned the unit off. Just beyond this dome, past the entrance to the narrow cleft in the lava that led around the end of the bay to the north-shore peninsula, there was a wider trail that would take him down to the main garrison compound.

The *Rikusentai* lieutenant spat on the ground in annoyance. A seven-mile walk, from the opposite end of the island. If the engine of the single utility launch he'd had at his disposal hadn't been out of commission, he'd have been here a lot sooner, and with a lot less effort. He was going to assume command formally—then use what was left of the night to get some *sleep*.

The trail down past the entrance to the canyon was littered with rock shards, and he proceeded in the dark with caution, mindful of twisting an ankle. The entrance to the thirty-foot-deep cleft was just coming up on his left. It was at that moment he saw four human shapes emerge from the jungle and begin to walk toward the opening.

"Matsu, Rikusentai," he called. "It's Lieutenant Harada. I'm looking for Warrant Officer Tanabe."

The four dark figures froze in place. They did not acknowledge him.

"Did you not hear me?" Harada said, striding forward. "I am—"

Something stung the back of his neck. A bee, he thought, shocked, or a wasp . . .

He blinked. The world seemed to be turning ninety degrees. And he felt the strangest sensation throughout his entire body. A feeling of . . . disconnection.

Something was pressing against his cheekbone . . . a vertical surface of dirt and gravel.

Most curious . . .

Yomat Dap pulled the three inches of spearhead he'd just shoved through the back of the Japanese officer's neck free and nudged the prostrate man with his toe. No response. The enemy lieutenant's spinal cord had been cut between the first and second cervical vertebrae, as cleanly as if he'd been guillotined.

"Is it done, brother?" Finian Hooke whispered in Dap's dialect, crouching in the darkness beside Horwitch, Foster, and Mulgrew.

Yomat Dap nodded. "This one has departed, brother."

"What the devil did you two just say?" Horwitch hissed.

"The Jap's dead, Major," Hooke told him, switching to English.

"Any more of the buggers traipsing around in the dark nearby?"

"Just before Yomat Dap stepped away from us, he told me this was the only one."

"Good." Horwitch paused, looking around. "Let's stuff his body in this crack over here and get a bloody move on."

Foster and Mulgrew crept forward immediately and hoisted the dead man between them. Crouching, Horwitch pushed back the brush that partly covered a deep, two-foot-wide fissure in the lava and gestured with his pistol. The two Australians rolled the corpse into the gap; it fell and wedged itself about six feet down. Horwitch dropped the brush back over the crevice and turned toward the canyon entrance.

"All right, then," he whispered, his voice taut with strain, "let's go."

The waters of the bay were warm, Randall thought— far warmer than those of Leyte Gulf. That was a good thing. After the debacle at Beach Black when he'd drifted offshore for days on end, the cold had all but paralyzed him. No such problem here, even barefoot and stripped to the waist.

He and Garth breaststroked silently along the shoreline beneath a continuous tangle of overhanging brush. Earlier, led by Salih Matalam, they had found it a simple matter to slip through the Japanese defenses and locate Ogaki's bathing pool. The sole concern had been DuFourmey, who seemed incapable of placing his feet without making some kind of noise. But they had not been discovered, and had split up in a small ravine about a hundred yards past the main line of defense—Matalam and DuFourmey heading westward toward the garrison compound, Randall and Garth moving down through the jungle toward the faint sound of the waterfall.

Now, gliding along through the oil black water, their

luck seemed to be holding up almost too well. Joe Garth watched Randall carefully, staying close. He didn't trust the suddenness with which his friend had volunteered to pilot one of the *Kaiten* into the side of the submarine, or the expression of detached calm that seemed to have settled over his perpetually troubled face. Something had changed.

"Okay, L.T.?" he whispered, bumping shoulders with him.

Randall smiled beneath his tired eyes. "Yeah, Joe. Just fine. Look. There's the first dock."

Garth began to scull in place. "I see it." He glanced at the overgrown bank. "Let's stay right up against these mangrove roots, underneath the brush. We'll have cover the whole way."

"Roger that," Randall said.

Garth moved into the lead, picking his way along the shoreline fringe. He could feel the fish disturbed by his passing fluttering against his legs—gray and mangrove snappers, most likely. He hoped there were no moray eels or stingrays.

A one-gallon can was caught in the roots just ahead. He drew abreast of it, investigated. The discarded tin had contained heavy black grease. A thought struck him, and he scooped up some of the thick residue on the ends of two fingers.

"Grease," he whispered to Randall. "We can black ourselves down."

He wiped some of the lubricant onto Randall's face, then smeared the remainder on his own. "Spread it around some," he coaxed. Randall did so, effectively dulling down the pale gleam of his Anglo-Saxon complexion.

They took another minute to smear more grease on arms and torsos, then wiped their hands on overhanging leaves and resumed their slow advance toward the dock. Ten feet out from shore, a small needlefish leaped out of the water and reentered with a light slap, sending a delicate pattern of concentric ripples shimmering across the glassy black surface. The only other sound was the low, continuous hum of generators that emanated from the submarine pen at the head of the bay.

"Barnacles and sharp coral," Garth muttered to Randall as he touched the first piling. "Don't cut yourself."

"Okay. See anybody?"

"Not yet."

It was dank and shadowy under the dock, the air heavy with the stink of creosote and decaying sea growth. They trod water in silence, moving from piling to piling, hardly daring to breathe as the *plok . . . plok . . . plok* of moisture dripping from the overhead planks marked the passing seconds like the ticking of a clock.

The *Kaiten* now lay beside them—fifty-plus feet of tubular black steel, like a giant sewer pipe—floating next to the coral-encrusted pilings with only its small conning tower and two or three inches of its uppermost hull extending above the brimming surface of the water. There was a creaking sound as the thick manila line securing the bow tightened slightly, then slackened again.

Randall was pleasantly surprised. Normally, his heart would have been hammering in his throat. He would have been looking around constantly for the men in his squad, worried about them, worried about the mission. Fear—of letting his men down, of not measuring up as a leader, of not achieving the objective—would have curdled into its familiar leaden ball in the pit of his stomach.

But not this time. This time there was only Joe Garth beside him, and no one else. He did not have to worry about getting anyone killed, because Joe was indestructible—and the rest of his squad was already dead. It was impossible to get your friends killed twice.

He was free.

Water continued to drip from the dock above, keeping time in the foul-smelling darkness like a metronome.

Randall caught Garth's eye and smiled. "I'm going to climb up on this thing and pop the hatch," he whispered, his voice very calm. "Why don't you swim back to the rudder and give me a quiet tap on the hull when you feel it move?"

Garth examined his friend's face in the darkness. "Okay, L.T.," he said warily. "Be careful. Try not to make any noise, huh?"

"You bet."

"You sure you don't want any help?"

"If I need help, I'll come and get you."

Once more, Garth paused to scrutinize Randall's expression. Then he began to move backward along the *Kaiten*'s hull. "Okay, Charlton."

Had the *Kaiten* been floating higher out of the water, climbing up on top of it would have presented a problem, as its streamlined hull had no footholds or handholds. But since it was nearly awash, Randall simply dragged himself up onto the curving steel plate, straddled it, and then crouched beside the conning tower, keeping it between him and the landward end of the dock. The manila lines creaked once more as the immense torpedo eased away from the pilings in response to his added weight.

He looked toward shore, past the light floatplane tied to the dock behind the *Kaiten*, and examined the dark huts beneath the nodding palms . . . the rows of stacked fuel drums back in the jungle to the right . . . the narrow strip of beach with its handful of dugout canoes upturned above the high-tide mark . . . the two utility launches grounded at the waterline. Briefly, he hoped that DuFourmey would have the presence of mind to steal the boat with the most fuel in its tanks—then reassured himself with the thought that Matalam, if he accompanied the steward's mate all the way to the beach, would certainly see to it.

As far as he could tell, there was no movement on land within several hundred yards of the dock. He turned and looked across the dark bay at the mouth of the sub pen. A faint glow came from deep within it, as if from a hidden reservoir of molten lava or the fires of some great subterranean forge. The giant submarine lay silhouetted at its concrete mooring bulwark, dimly backlit by a soft orange gleam. The humming of generators continued to pulse out over the bay.

Odd, Randall thought, that the Japanese would be

careless enough to let even a small amount of light spill out of so important an installation, with the Leyte invasion fleet so near and the skies soon to be full of American and Allied warplanes.

He saw Joe Garth lurking in the water at the rear of the *Kaiten* and nodded to him, getting a nod in return. Then he leaned over the top of the conning tower, grasped the narrow handle at the edge of the circular steel hatch, drew a deep breath, and pulled.

The hatch was heavy, but it swung up without a sound. Gingerly, Randall laid it all the way back. The inside of the *Kaiten* was completely dark—a narrow vertical tunnel in the top of the conning tower with no visible bottom. But as the hull was barely a yard wide and the conning tower less than two feet tall, it could not be more than five feet down to what he imagined must be the control cockpit.

With a last nod at Garth, he maneuvered himself into the hatchway with his weight on his arms, found a foothold, and slipped inside.

It was a tight squeeze for a six-footer with wide shoulders, but he managed it. The interior of the *Kaiten* was absolutely pitch-black—a complication he'd failed to anticipate—and as disorienting to the touch as a Rube Goldberg contraption. In addition, the cockpit space seemed impossibly tight, as if it had been constructed for a midget rather than a full-sized man.

Alarmed at his inability to make sense of the *Kaiten*'s interior, Randall knelt down and began to feel along the side and bottom hull plates. His fingers found a confusing array of hoses, valves, tubes, and levers . . . and then what was undoubtedly the pilot's seat. With a silent exhalation of relief, he twisted his body around and sat down.

The seat was uncomfortable, like a hard, low-backed chair with no legs. Randall felt around some more. His fingers discovered the lower housing of a simple periscope, its single rubber eyepiece positioned directly in front of his face. All around him in the darkness were more handles, levers, and valves.

He sat still and thought for a moment, feeling quite calm. The air inside the *Kaiten* had a rancid, metallic quality, a combination of grease, rust, human sweat, and mildew—the latter two of which seemed to be coming from the filthy canvas pads lining the pilot's seat. Randall put the stench out of his mind and focused. Would a Japanese operator have to bring a portable light in with him each time he boarded the *Kaiten?* Or . . .

On a whim, he reached over his head. His fingers fell immediately on the small battery-powered lamp secured to the steel plate. He found the switch, clicked it on. A soft yellow glow promptly bathed the cockpit interior.

Randall smiled to himself. That was better. He inspected the large hand levers on either side of the pilot's chair, noting the cable attachments that ran astern from their lower ends. Likely candidates for rudder control. He laid hold of the right-hand lever and pulled it.

Tap tap tap.

The soft knocking of Garth's pistol butt on the hull plates confirmed the lever's function. Randall pushed it forward again.

Tap tap tap.

Perfect.

He surveyed the cockpit controls again, item by item. As he'd imagined, the layout was relatively simple. By starting with the obvious and working through a logical process of elimination, it was possible to identify the basic function of nearly every piece of equipment. He would not need to worry about most of them, however. Fire up the propulsion plant and steer left and right—that was it.

On his left, the dive plane lever, most likely, he judged by the attached cables. He moved it slightly, then released it. Leave it where it was, unless the *Kaiten* tried to nose down once it started moving. In front of him, below the periscope housing, a simple instrument panel. He recognized a compass and a clock, but the other three gauges—scribed with Japanese characters—were a mystery. Probably something to do with engine function . . . perhaps rpm, temperature, or fuel capacity. It didn't matter. If he got the thing started, it wouldn't be running long enough to develop an engine problem.

He touched the little brass crank at his right knee, moved it a quarter turn. The shaft above the lower periscope housing extended upward a few inches. Since he wasn't submerging, he wouldn't be using that, either. He put his eye to the rubber skirt of the eyepiece, pulled down the small shears on either side of it, and rotated the periscope to the left. The dark contours of the peninsula on the opposite side of the bay moved horizontally across the viewing field until the faint orange glow of the sub pen appeared.

Only one thing left to figure out . . .

"Psst! Charlton!"

Joe Garth's urgent whisper came down sharply through the open hatch. Randall leaned forward around the periscope housing, twisting his neck to look upward.

"Hey," he said softly.

Garth's grease-blackened face was suspended over the edge of the hatch trunk, dripping with seawater. "How's it going down there?"

"Good. I think I understand most of it."

"Glad to hear it." Garth glanced up quickly, his eyes searching the shoreline, before continuing: "The first control you moved was the vertical rudder. The second was the horizontal diving plane." He brushed water out of his eyes. "This damn thing really is nothing but a monster torpedo. It's got two big propellers in the back, mounted one behind the other. The blades are angled in opposing directions."

"Counterrotating screws," Randall said. "They keep it running straight. No torque."

"How 'bout that?" Garth scanned the shoreline briefly again. "If you're ready to go, I'm going to swim over and grab one of those dugouts . . . tie it up to the conning tower before I cast you off."

Randall nodded. "Just one thing I haven't discovered yet: how to start the engine."

"What's that?"

"I said, there's just one thing I haven't discov—"

"No, no," Garth hissed, pointing. "I mean, what's *that*?"

Randall twisted around farther, craning his neck. Above and behind him was a small lever with a bright red handle. Attached to it and extending aft were rods that looked very much like engine linkages.

He reached back over his shoulder and palmed the lever. "I guess this is what fires it up," he said. "If it's not the self-destruct mechanism."

"Don't jinx us, L.T.," Garth told him. "I'm going for that canoe." He disappeared from view, leaving the circular hatch opening empty but for black sky and a few stars.

Randall reached over his head and switched off the lamp. The stars were beautiful, like diamond chips in a bed of black velvet, and a soft breeze was beginning to waft down the open hatch, diminishing the odor of sweat and mildew. He ran his hands over the controls once more, fixing their respective locations in his mind.

There was one other thing he wasn't yet sure he'd found: the throttle. There were no pedals (that would have been too easy) and no obvious levers besides the directional controls. There *was* an oddly shaped valve just below the dive plane lever, with high-pressure steel tubing plumbed to it and running back toward the engine. If the *Kaiten* fired up when he pulled the red lever, he'd try adjusting that valve to see if it somehow controlled the vessel's speed. He had some distance to cover between here and the sub pen—at least a couple of miles. He assumed that the *Kaiten* would take off rapidly from the dock once the engine caught. Being little more than a giant torpedo, it would have no transmission and only one gear: forward.

He tipped his head back and closed his eyes, breathing in the ocean air and listening to the silence that he knew would not last much longer.

Chapter
Twenty-six

At the base of a small outcropping of rock, concealed in the jungle about fifty yards above the trail that led from the garrison compound up to the lava dome, Salih Matalam and Henry DuFourmey lay in a shallow cave behind a fallen palm trunk. Immediately below them was an antiaircraft artillery emplacement—a sandbagged pit fifteen feet in diameter containing a bulky, pedestal-mounted light cannon with three barrels canted up toward the sky at a steep angle. There were two soldiers manning it, both asleep on cots beneath thin layers of mosquito netting.

Matalam brought his lips close to DuFourmey's ear. "Twenty-five-millimeter antiaircraft, antitank gun," he whispered. "Triple-mounted, full automatic fire. Gas-operated, air-cooled, three-hundred-and-sixty-degree rotation. Model ninety-six."

"Model ninety-six, eh?" DuFourmey hissed back. "Damn, I'm glad to know that. I was afraid I wouldn't never find out what model it was. Must be kinda like the twenty-mil gun I rotate onto once in a while back on board ship." He shot the Moro guerrilla an incredulous glance. "For someone who don't speak much English, you sure rattled them numbers off pretty good."

"Japanese weapons I know," Matalam muttered. "I study U.S. War Department field handbooks on Japanese equipment—memorize all spe-speci-*specifications*." He considered for a moment, then shook a finger at the complicated-looking weapon. "I like this one. Excellent position." He slid DuFourmey a sideways glance. "You have firing time on gun like this one, eh? Good, sailor, *good*. Because I think we borrow it soon."

DuFourmey put his head down on his forearms. "Lawd help me."

Matalam looked at him, his brow furrowing. "Lod? What is lod?"

"*Lawd*, you heathen," DuFourmey hissed nervously. "The Good Lawd, God Awmighty."

Matalam pondered for a second or two, then dismissed the matter and resumed his careful examination of the jungle below. Silence filled the cave. After a full minute, Matalam touched DuFourmey on the wrist and pointed at the docks. "Light. See?"

The faintest glow was coming from the open hatch of the *Kaiten*. Matalam moved his finger to the sand strip where the two launches were beached. DuFourmey rubbed his bleary eyes and focused. A dark figure was dragging a dugout canoe across the sand toward the water.

"That them?" the steward's mate inquired.

Matalam gave a silent nod. Then he pointed into the jungle about a hundred yards behind the beach.

"*What?*" DuFourmey hissed, annoyed.

"Fuel drums," Matalam whispered. "Very many."

DuFourmey looked at him, blinking and waiting, the incredulity of his expression intensifying with each passing second.

"*So?*" he demanded finally, when Matalam did not elaborate.

The Moro just smiled. "You make ready to follow me, my friend," he said.

*   *   *

Warrant Officer Soemu Tanabe pushed the curtain of mosquito netting aside and sat up on the edge of the bed. He'd slept longer than he'd intended—the mattress in Lieutenant Commander Ogaki's personal quarters being top quality, of course. The deceased garrison commander had been very adept at taking care of his own comforts, though he had shown little regard for those of his men. Tanabe knew the mind-set: for certain officers, a degree of luxury in the field was a privilege of rank; the average soldier could exist on the bare necessities. Not a policy he was opposed to, frankly, as a man on his way up the ladder.

He looked at his watch as he pulled on his boots. Three ten in the morning. Harada should have arrived at the camp an hour ago. A briskly walking man could travel the length of the island in two and a half hours, and the senior lieutenant would have received word of Ogaki's fatal misadventure more than four hours earlier. Tanabe rose to his feet and belted on his pistol and officer's sword. It was unlikely that Harada would have gotten lost in the dark, for the trail was easy to follow. Late as he was, it was much more likely that he'd sprained an ankle on the rocky terrain.

Tanabe put on his cap and walked to the door of the hut. Outside, he paused to light a cigarette and glance at his watch again. Three fifteen. He would give Harada until three thirty to show up, then organize a search detail.

He blew smoke and began to stroll across the compound. The open parade ground between the supply and barracks huts was nearly as dark as the surrounding jungle, due to the camouflage netting suspended above it. The air tended to get trapped under the nets and become very humid and stale.

Wanting to feel a breeze, Tanabe headed for the docks.

He looked up the main trail as he emerged from the line of palms bordering the beach. Still no sign of Harada—or any returning messenger. Maintaining radio silence was a major inconvenience, and the ground phone lines would not be repaired until the break was located at first light. So, in the meantime, *he* was the de facto garrison commander of Island No. 12863. The thought gave him a warm, empowered feeling.

He gazed past the floatplane tethered to the nearest dock, past the small conning tower of the *Kaiten* moored behind it, and examined the dim orange glow illuminating the mouth of the submarine pen. Metalworkers were still burning large sections of external decking off the aft third of the *Sen-Toku*, making room for another *Kaiten* mounting cradle. Tanabe didn't like the amount of light escaping from the cavernous opening; if he'd been in a position to do so, he would have ordered the captain of the submarine to halt work until morning. But the *Sen-Toku* commander was a law unto himself aboard his own vessel and within the confines of the sub pen.

He looked out toward the end of the dock. The bay was beautiful on a clear night such as this, with balmy breezes rippling the black surface like—

Movement caught his eye. He blinked in surprise as a tall, broad-shouldered man, stripped to the waist and muscled like an athlete, emerged from the water at the rear of the *Kaiten*. Streaks of dark slime covered his upper body. He began to pad forward along the top of the hull, dragging something behind him . . . a length of rope. As Tanabe watched, standing on the landward end of the dock, the man halted at the conning tower and proceeded to secure the rope to an available pad eye.

Then the head and shoulders of a second man appeared, illuminated by a faint yellow glimmer from within the *Kaiten*. He, too, was shirtless, and, like his comrade, was covered in streaks of dark slime. He twisted in the tower's open hatch, whispering to the man who had come out of the water.

Something was very wrong here. Instinctively, Tanabe began to walk forward, slowly at first, then increasing his pace. These seamen—they were too tall, had a body language and physical profile that looked foreign to him. And the last *Kaiten* was not to be loaded onto the *Sen-*

Toku until much later in the day, after its support bracket had been welded in place.

The thumping of his boot heels on the dock became louder as his stride quickened. He felt for the pistol at his waist, unsnapped the holster flap. His mind was awhirl—filled with burgeoning comprehension and alarm. . . .

Abruptly, the man standing beside the conning tower looked up, straight at him.

"Stay where you are!" Tanabe shouted. *"Identify yourselves!"*

In one smooth motion, Joe Garth pulled his .45-caliber automatic from the waist of his trousers, leveled it, and fired at the enemy soldier who'd suddenly appeared out of nowhere. The slug clipped Tanabe's left cheekbone, knocking him flat on his back. Stunned, the warrant officer rolled to the opposite side of the dock, taking cover behind a low stack of wooden planks. He began to shriek in rapid-fire Japanese.

"If you're gonna start this thing," Garth said matter-of-factly to Randall, "now would be a good time."

He ducked behind the conning tower as Tanabe finally brought his eight-millimeter pistol to bear over the planks and loosed off several shots. The slugs pinged off the metal skin of the *Kaiten* as Randall dropped down to the pilot's seat. Garth waited for the fusillade to ebb—then peered carefully around the side of the conning tower. The injured officer was still screaming in Japanese. Back under the trees, in the vicinity of the main compound, hand lamps were beginning to wink on.

Garth raised his automatic, braced his wrist against the conning tower, and fired once. The slug hit the sole of Tanabe's right boot, which was protruding from the near end of the plank stack, and blew off his little toe. The string of shrieked orders became an incoherent shriek of pain.

"Cut me loose, Joe!" Randall called up through the hatch. "I have a feeling this thing's going to take off once I start the engine! No gears!"

"Right." Garth took a deep breath, eyeing the planks, and dashed down the after portion of the hull to the lone cleat that held the stern line. With a quick motion, he threw the rope off. The Japanese officer's pistol came up over the planks again, and Garth put four rapid shots into the wood to keep the man's head down. He made it back to the conning tower, fired his remaining shots, then sprinted for the *Kaiten*'s bow. A quick tug freed the forward line, as well. He scrambled back behind the conning tower as the wounded officer got off another half-dozen rounds in his direction. But Tanabe was too awash in adrenaline to have a steady gun hand, and all the shots went wild.

"You're free!" Garth called into the hatchway, slapping a fresh clip into the handle of his automatic. Fast-moving shapes were starting to materialize under the darkened palms on shore.

Randall pulled the red-handled lever.

Instantly, a high-revving whine filled the air. The *Kaiten* shook violently under Garth's feet. At its stern, the counterrotating propellers began to churn the black water into pale foam.

Garth staggered as the *Kaiten* slid forward, water washing over the semisubmerged hull and up against the conning tower. Only a quick hand on the rim of the hatch saved him from going over the side. Six feet to starboard, the dock pilings ticked by—and then the *Kaiten* was past the end of the pier and surging out into the bay.

Clawing his way around to the lee side of the conning tower, Garth looked astern. At the end of its forty-foot tether, the dugout canoe was trailing along in the giant torpedo's wake. The dock was beginning to swarm with soldiers, some bringing rifles up to the firing position.

The sound of small-arms fire was almost lost in the high-pitched hum of the *Kaiten*'s engine. A few skiffs of water popped up to either side of the accelerating vessel as a handful of bullets missed their mark. Garth crouched behind the conning tower, trying to make himself small. Spray began to fly over the open hatch as the great torpedo creamed along through the black water, briny foam sizzling past it on either side.

"Joe!" Randall's faint yell came up from the control cockpit. *"Bail out now! I'm heading for the sub pen!"*

Warrant Officer Soemu Tanabe had regained his feet, although he was limping badly and missing a nickel-sized chunk of his left cheekbone. Blood kept pouring into his mouth and making it difficult to speak. Still, he continued to scream orders, waving his pistol in the air.

"Infiltrators!" he bellowed. *"Sabotage! Kill the men on the Kaiten!"* The soldiers continued to get off scattered rifle fire, although some were clearly confused by Tanabe's instructions to shoot at one of their own vessels. More *Rikusentai* were arriving by the minute, looking for but not seeing the enemy. Tanabe gnashed his teeth and began to wave the soldiers back onto the beach with his pistol. *"Take the launches!"* he screamed. *"Chase down the Kaiten!"*

"Chase down a *Kaiten?*" a nearby corporal echoed. "Impossible!"

Tanabe ignored the man and continued to hobble toward the beach, herding men as he did. *"Alert the gunners on the slope!"* he shouted to the troops still emerging from the trees. *"The order is to open fire immediately on the Kaiten! It must not be allowed to leave the bay!"*

In the chaos of milling bodies, a young soldier stepped up close to him. "Honorable Warrant Officer, sir!" he shouted. "The *Kaiten* is not trying to get out of the bay. It is heading for the submarine pen!"

Tanabe stopped in his tracks and stared toward the illuminated grotto. *"What?"*

"The *Kaiten* is—"

"Fire," Salih Matalam said softly, rubbing between his fingers the blood of the two artillerymen he'd just knifed.

As he'd been instructed, DuFourmey squeezed the triggers of the twenty-five-millimeter antiaircraft cannon,

the triple barrels of which were now depressed well
below the horizontal and pointing down the slope
toward the beach.

*BAMBAMBAMBAMBAMBAMBAMBAMBAM-
BAMBAMBAM* . . .

The stream of high-velocity shells tore through the
dark foliage of the night-shrouded jungle, tracer rounds
flickering like ribbons of green fire, and hammered into
the gasoline drums stacked just to the west of the garrison compound and boat docks.

The fuel dump went up with a huge initial explosion
that killed the fifty-odd *Rikusentai* within seventy-five
yards of it outright, severely flash-burned a hundred
more, and knocked the rest of the soldiers on the beach
and dock off their feet. Immediately thereafter, individual drums began to detonate like giant firecrackers,
blasting into the sky atop boiling columns of orange
flame. The massive primary fireball continued to roll up
toward the stars like a miniature sun, seething with
incandescent-red heat. The entire western end of the bay
was bathed in an unearthly glow.

Across the surreal seascape of flame-colored water the
narrow black silhouette of the *Kaiten* slid, gathering
speed.

Chapter
Twenty-seven

On the far side of the bay, on the ridgetop of the darkened peninsula, the four men of Artillery Position Number Seven, still groggy with sleep, stood around the pedestal of their 150-millimeter howitzer and gaped at the fiery spectacle on the opposite shore. As they watched, green tracers continued to flicker down from what they knew to be an antiaircraft emplacement toward the exploding fuel dump. It had to be an enemy night assault of some kind, not an accident—otherwise, what were the antiaircraft gunners firing at *on land?*

Corporal Iro Sakamaki, in charge of the howitzer crew, was the first to react rationally. Running to the opposite side of the sandbagged gun pit, he seized a field telephone and began to crank the handle that powered its small internal generator.

"This is Position Number Seven calling," he said urgently. "Respond, please! Position Number Seven requesting information regarding explosions at primary fuel dump and accompanying gunfire. *Moshi-moshi?* Hello? *Hello?*"

"Sayonara," Mulgrew growled, reaching over the low

wall of sandbags and sliding seven inches of his stiletto into the soft spot just behind Sakamaki's left ear. The point of the double-edged blade passed through the Japanese corporal's brain stem. He went rigid and died with a quiet gasp, still clutching the telephone receiver.

"Honorable Corporal," one of the remaining three artillerymen called, "there is something in the bay, approaching the submarine pe—"

His words were cut off as Foster's huge, tattooed arm hooked itself around his neck from behind. The soldier was lifted off his feet as the big Australian flexed his muscles, bore down, and wrenched. There was a sound like chicken bones cracking, and the artilleryman went limp.

Foster tossed him aside like a rag doll and spun around, looking for the other two Japanese. One was lying across the support pedestal of the big cannon, his throat cut. The other was kicking wildly at Finian Hooke—who was lunging at him with a drawn knife—while trying to extract his head from the smothering forearms of Major Harold Horwitch.

Hooke stabbed, missed—and before he could draw back for another strike, the wiry Japanese twisted sideways in Horwitch's grip, punched his closed fist back into the bigger man's groin, and sank his teeth into his right wrist. Horwitch buckled, and the artilleryman squirmed free. He staggered sideways with bulging eyes, Hooke in hot pursuit, and opened his mouth to yell.

"*Tasuk*—" he began. There was a wet, shearing sound.

The artilleryman's chin sagged forward onto his chest . . . and then his head dropped off his shoulders. It hit the ground with a hollow thunk. His decapitated body seemed to fold in vertically on itself, collapsing over an ammunition crate.

Yomat Dap stalked forward out of the darkness, his bloodstained parang swinging in his right hand. His file-toothed grin was ear to ear. He bent down, picked up the dripping head by its hair, and looked it over, nodding approvingly. Its eyelids were still fluttering. The others, including Finian Hooke, simply stared. Even the dour Mulgrew was taken aback.

"Jesus bloody Christ," he muttered.

Dap carried the head over to the lone candle lantern in the gun pit and set it upright on a nearby sandbag. Then he brushed the straight black hair up off the forehead of the grisly trophy, smiled again, and began to wipe the blade of his parang on an empty rice sack.

"Good thing we cut those field-phone lines we found running through the slot canyon," Foster said, breathing hard. He gestured at the body of Corporal Sakamaki, slumped over with the telephone receiver still clutched in one hand. "Think he got through to the other artillery positions on this side of the bay?"

"It won't matter in a minute," Horwitch said, cranking rapidly on the flywheel that rotated the big gun on its pedestal. "Get on that other wheel, Sergeant. Depress the muzzle toward that first emplacement we passed on the way in."

"Yes, sir!" Foster replied, stepping up beside the cannon.

"Corporal Mulgrew!"

"Sir!"

"Break open the breech of this weapon. Prepare to load. Shell first, then gunpowder packet."

"Yes, sir!" Mulgrew went into motion, disengaging the gun's breech locks and swinging the heavy rear block open. "Don't have much experience with artillery, Major."

A grim smile formed beneath Horwitch's mustache. "That's quite all right, Corporal. I do."

"Yes, sir."

The muzzle of the cannon was now pointing back along the ridge of the peninsula, almost parallel to the ground. Horwitch stepped behind the howitzer, sighting along the top of its barrel.

"Down a hair more, Sergeant," he said.

"Sir!" The flywheel spun in Foster's hands; the cannon muzzle dropped another inch.

"Good!" Horwitch exclaimed. "Perfect."

The open rear block had a short concave track on which a shell could be placed and rammed into the breech. Mulgrew picked up a ramrod and looked at Horwitch questioningly. "Which shell, Major? There are four separate stacks here, and all the tips are painted a different color."

"Use the shells with the red tips," Horwitch instructed. "High explosive with impact fuses—they detonate when they hit something. The others have three different types of altitude fuses for antiaircraft work. They explode when they reach a certain height, depending on the fuse's preset."

"Here, Mick," Foster grunted, passing a red-tipped shell to Mulgrew. The swarthy corporal took it gingerly and slid it into the cannon's breech.

Horwitch opened a large metal box beside the mounting pedestal and lifted out a short, cylindrical package the same approximate diameter as the shells. It was tightly wrapped in gray cloth, and looked like nothing so much as a small wheel of cheese. He moved around behind the cannon and set the package on the concave track at the mouth of the breech.

"Ram it up behind the shell," he ordered.

Mulgrew did so. "Gunpowder, sir?"

"Correct," the major said. "All right, then."

He slammed the breech shut and locked it. Then he sighted along the cannon barrel once more. "Point-blank," he declared. "A flat-trajectory shot." He glanced back at Foster and Mulgrew. "Just before I fire this gun," he said, "turn your backs to it, put your hands over your ears, and open your mouths—or the concussion will rupture your eardrums." He looked across the emplacement at Finian Hooke, who was staring out at the bay with his compact binoculars. "Did you hear that, Mr. Hooke?"

"I did," Hooke replied without turning. "And I already told Yomat Dap as much."

"Excellent." Horwitch took up the howitzer's firing lanyard in one hand. "Everyone stand by. There are two heavy guns on this ridge besides this one, and we're going to try to take them both out. That means some precise aiming and fast reloading, gentlemen."

"Don't forget those two bloody machine gun nests near the slot canyon," Mulgrew put in.

Horwitch smiled his hard smile again and twitched the firing lanyard between his fingers. "No, Corporal," he said, "we're not about to do that."

"I want runners heading for every gun position at this end of the bay!" Tanabe screamed at the small crowd of soldiers who had taken cover with him behind the supply hut near the easternmost dock. The warrant officer was literally frothing at the mouth. *"Go now, damn you! The order is to fire on the Kaiten! It must be stopped!"*

"Hai!"

"Hai, Honorable Warrant Officer!"

"Hai!"

A half-dozen *Rikusentai* broke away from the group and dashed into the trees, fanning out. Desperately, Tanabe spun and gazed out across the water at the slim shape of the *Kaiten*—still heading toward the grotto mouth at medium speed.

A fresh eruption of fuel drums shook the air, causing Tanabe and the remaining men to flinch closer together behind the supply hut. As the fiery explosions continued, another long burst of green tracer fire from the renegade antiaircraft gun on the slope above raked across the beach and the dock area, churning sand and splintering wood. The several hundred soldiers who had responded to Tanabe's initial cry of alarm had managed to move off the open beach, but were now pinned down in the trees between the garrison compound and the exploding fuel dump. The steep terrain did not allow them to move toward the gun position that had inexplicably targeted them, for they would expose themselves to its direct fire.

"Retreat along the shore!" Tanabe shrieked. *"Work up along the slope and flank that gun! Move, you cowards, move!"*

The *Rikusentai* within earshot, who were anything but cowards and had simply been awaiting a coherent order,

began to rise a few at a time and pull back into the
shadowy mangroves east of the dock. Ribbons of green
tracer flashed down from the gun position on the slope
in response to their movements. Fuel drums continued
to explode, filling the night air with waves of heat,
flashes of weird orange light, and the stifling stink of
burning diesel.

"Fire on the antiaircraft gun!" Warrant Officer Soemu
Tanabe yelled. *"Return fire! Return fire!"*

Henry DuFourmey was sweating so profusely, sitting
in the gunner's seat of the twenty-five-millimeter cannon,
that he could barely see for the sting of salt in his eyes.
Fresh motion caught his attention near the foot of the
farthest dock and he depressed the triggers of the
weapon yet again.

*BAMBAMBAMBAMBAMBAMBAMBAM-
BAMBAMBAM!*

The rapid-firing machine cannon spat out another long
volley of flashing green fire, its three pneumatic-recoil
barrels punching in and out like fists. The trees and un-
derbrush near the docks disintegrated in a whirlwind of
shredding foliage. DuFourmey cackled aloud, delighted
at the weapon's brutal power. Any living thing it hit
died; *everything* it hit was instantly chopped to pieces.

Then his natural paranoia reasserted itself and he
glanced fearfully over his shoulder at the dark jungle
behind and to either side of the gun pit. The Japs would
work their way up to within grenade-throwing range
sooner or later, and he didn't want to be here when
they did. Then he thought about mortars, and the other
heavy weapons positioned on the slopes nearby. A
fresh flood of perspiration broke out on his forehead
and he squinted through the cannon's sight again,
searching for another target. Above the riot of exploding fuel drums directly below him, he could just make
out the small, dark silhouette of the *Kaiten* slipping
through the orange-tinted wavelets on the bay toward
the sub pen.

He was so frightened that he could hardly force himself to remain in the gunner's seat—but every time he fired the cannon and watched the jungle disintegrate, the enemy soldiers tumble and scatter, he felt such a surge of exhilaration that he forgot to give in to his fear and flee into the undergrowth. He was invincible at the triggers of this weapon—king of the goddamn hill.

DuFourmey spotted half a dozen soldiers running in single file along the western edge of the beach. Swinging the twenty-five-millimeter around, he opened fire.

BAMBAMBAMBAMBAMBAMBAMBAMBAM-BAMBAMBAM . . .

He wished Matalam would return soon, so he could get the hell out of here.

Warrant Officer Soemu Tanabe was struggling up the slope immediately behind the garrison compound, cursing with the pain of his injured foot. All around him were *Rikusentai*, stalking forward through the jungle in a loose skirmish line. He had ordered every last man in the compound, including the noncombatant radio-decryption officers and cooks, to join the push toward the renegade antiaircraft gun that was doing so much damage. *Saboteurs,* he thought, his mind reeling with pain and fury. *Or shock troops. Perhaps dropped by parachute . . . or landed by submarine . . .*

A burst of light machine gun fire shattered the night up ahead and to the left. A chorus of screams echoed back through the jungle.

"American marines!" a Japanese voice shouted. *"Hundreds of them! Watch the flank above!"*

"Take cover!" Tanabe shrieked, crouching behind a tree trunk. *"Up the slope to the left! Suppressing fire! Suppressing fire!"*

A cacophony of rifle shots reverberated through the foliage as the *Rikusentai* within hearing distance of Tanabe's order hit the ground and fired blindly up the steep incline. Tanabe emptied his pistol into the darkness. Seconds later, there was another stuttering burp of machine gun fire to the right and below him, followed by more screams.

"They're attacking from below and behind!" someone yelled. *"Watch out! Watch out! They're coming!"*

"Reverse your fire!" Tanabe screamed, terrorized. The darkness and the noise and the pain in his face and foot and the closeness of the jungle were overwhelming. *"Fire down and back to the right! Fire down and back to the right!"*

Confused, yet trained to obey without question, the *Rikusentai* above and below him swung their rifles around 180 degrees and opened up. The ensuing volley went on for several long seconds before Tanabe realized, to his horror, that his order had caused the men on his left flank to fire down into those on his right. The jungle echoed with fresh screams of agony.

"Stop, stop!" he shrieked, waving his hands as high as he dared, as Arisaka 6.5-millimeter rifle bullets zinged past him. *"Cease fire! Cease fire!"*

The shots ebbed away, becoming intermittent. Twenty feet in front of Tanabe, a *Rikusentai* soldier in helmet and combat tunic burst out of the undergrowth and gestured wildly at the dozen-or-so men on Tanabe's immediate left flank.

"Follow me!" the soldier shouted. *"We can split them in two! I've found a gap!"*

The *Rikusentai* infantrymen responded without hesitation. The soldier waited just long enough to make sure he was being followed, then ducked back into the brush.

Tanabe rose to his feet, preparing to urge the men behind him to move forward. He opened his mouth to shout an order . . . then paused. The soldier who'd burst from the jungle had been carrying a submachine gun with a round, drum-style magazine. Imperial Japanese Army and Navy land troops *had* no light, handheld submachine guns of any description. Only rifles and pistols.

He sagged back down behind the tree trunk as the hammering rattle of the submachine gun reverberated through the jungle once more, just ahead of him. More strangled screams—very close—reached his ears.

A great rage at being so easily deceived surged through him, and he rose to his feet with an incoherent

cry. Ripping his officer's samurai sword out of its scab-
bard, he waved it in the air and turned to face the remaining men behind him. Random rifle shots continued
to crack off up and down the decimated skirmish line.

"Charge!" he shrieked. *"For the emperor and Japan,
charge! Banzai!"*

Most of the men rose from the jungle floor and began
to run forward as Tanabe turned and strode toward the
hole in the foliage where the submachine-gun-carrying
soldier had disappeared. One man didn't. As intermittent small-arms fire continued to pierce the night, a cook
named Nobuo Inaba—the man who had received a brutal flogging as a result of Tanabe's informing on him to
Ogaki about the breaking of a second of the garrison
commander's prized teacups—raised his rifle, sighted
carefully, and under cover of darkness shot the warrant
officer through the back of the head.

Chapter
Twenty-eight

Horwitch yanked the lanyard.
BLAM!

The concussion of the 150-millimeter howitzer's firing shook the surrounding palm trees and lifted a cloud of dust from the ground. Foster, Mulgrew, Hooke, and Dap, standing ten feet away from the gun pedestal with their backs turned and hands clapped over their ears, felt as though they'd been walloped by a breaking wave. The force of the blast rattled their spines and sent bolts of pain shooting up through the soles of their feet.

Less than three hundred yards away, a seventy-five-millimeter gun position on top of a small rise in the peninsula's central ridge exploded in a flash of white-orange light. A rapid series of secondary detonations followed with white-phosphorous fragment trails shooting out at all angles into the night sky.

"Ha-*haaaaa!*" Mulgrew exclaimed. "That's fokkin' *beautiful!*"

"Get back on this elevation wheel, Sergeant Foster!" Horwitch barked, cranking furiously on the cannon's rotational flywheel. The long barrel swung slowly around, cordite smoke trailing from its muzzle. "Depress another fifteen inches; we're hitting that three-inch naval gun next. Corporal Mulgrew! Reload with HE! Hurry up, man!"

"Sir!" Mulgrew hustled around to the back of the howitzer and broke open the breech.

"Mr. Hooke!" Horwitch called. "Where is the *Kaiten* now?"

Calmly, the New Zealander focused his binoculars. "Still heading for the grotto, Major," he said. "Two-thirds of the way there."

"Is our escape launch making for the mouth of the bay yet?"

Hooke searched briefly. "No. Both launches are still on the beach."

"That ain't bloody good," Foster panted, spinning the elevation flywheel.

"No," Hooke replied, "but the antiaircraft gun isn't firing at the docks anymore. So Matalam and DuFourmey have probably left."

"If they're not dead," Mulgrew grumbled. He rammed another charge of gunpowder in behind the HE shell and closed the breech block. "Ready, Major."

"Good," Horwitch said. "Stand by."

A distant detonation, sharper and more compressed than the explosions from the fuel dump, suddenly echoed across the dark waters of the bay. There was the screech of an incoming shell, then a second detonation, much louder. The air shook.

Hooke brought the binoculars back up to his eyes in time to see the remnants of a geyser of water cascade back down to the surface of the bay, just behind the speeding *Kaiten*. "Bad news," he announced. "At least one of the gun emplacements on the far slope has gotten the word to fire on the *Kaiten*."

Horwitch let go of the rotational flywheel and sighted along the howitzer's barrel at his next target, a large naval gun some 250 yards away. "Try to spot the weapon tracking the *Kaiten*," he told Hooke. "Point it out to me after their next shot." To Foster, "Depress just a hair more, Sergeant."

"Yes, sir," the big Aussie said, cranking.

Superior Petty Officer Zenji Kono ducked under his helmet as the hand grenade he'd just lobbed through the trees into the twenty-five-millimeter antiaircraft emplacement went off with a muffled bang. As soon as the shrapnel had shredded its way through the foliage above him, he sprang to his feet and charged along the slope toward the wall of sandbags bordering the gun pit. Just behind him ran Seaman Second Class Kiichi Uchino, along with two dozen other *Rikusentai* enlisted men.

Kono was firing from the hip as he vaulted over the sandbags, working the bolt of his short Arisaka carbine with an expert's speed. Uchino jumped over the low bulwark a second later, caught a toe, and landed heavily on his shoulder at the petty officer's feet. Kono drove onward, searching for an opponent into whom he could plunge his carbine's bayonet. Then he pulled up short, breathing hard.

The gun emplacement was empty. Around the automatic cannon, ejected brass shell casings were ankle-deep and smoking, as were the weapon's three muzzles. The barrels were so hot that when Kono spat on one, the saliva sizzled. But whoever had inflicted so many casualties on the *Rikusentai* on the beach and the docks, firing down continuously for nearly a quarter of an hour, was gone . . . and could not possibly be *long* gone.

Kono whirled, swearing. "Spread out in a running skirmish line!" he shouted. "They can't have gone up the slope from here—it becomes too steep! Flush them through the trees toward the peninsula trail! *Move, boys, move!*"

He spun again, took three running steps, hurdled the sandbag wall on the opposite side of the gun pit, and disappeared into the darkness of the encroaching jungle.

*   *   *

"I cain't make it!" DuFourmey gasped, stumbling through the palm trees at the base of the slope. *"I'm all done in!"*

Matalam, still clad in Japanese helmet and battle tunic, seized him under the upper arm and lifted. "You come!" he hissed. "You drive boat around to far side—"

"I cain't," the black seaman wheezed. *"Lemme rest."*

"You come!" Matalam barked. "Or Japs kill you here!"

"Oh, Jesus," DuFourmey wailed. *"Oh, Jesus, oh, Jesus . . ."* But he kept staggering forward.

"If you have breath to pray," the Moro told him, "you have breath to run. *Run!*"

They continued to trot toward the beach through the shell-torn trees, stepping over the numerous bodies of Japanese soldiers DuFourmey had killed with the twenty-five-millimeter antiaircraft gun. Nearby, the fuel dump continued to burn, its flames casting an eerie radiance through the blackened palms. The jungle floor beneath their feet turned from leafy humus to sand as they neared the open beach. Matalam halted, peered ahead— then pulled DuFourmey into the sheltering foliage of a large pepperbush.

The Moro bent down, rummaging. He came back up with a *Rikusentai* helmet. A small white flower had been hand-painted on its front. DuFourmey looked down. A Japanese soldier was lying twisted on the ground at an awkward angle. He had been cut in two at the waist by cannon fire; his pelvis and legs lay eighteen inches to one side of his torso in a puddle of gore. DuFourmey's gut spasmed, and he nearly threw up on the spot.

Matalam shoved the helmet into his chest. "You put this on!" he whispered urgently. "Take dead man's rifle—keep your face low. Five Japs standing between launches. You follow me now—say nothing! Yes?"

"Jesus Lawd," DuFourmey moaned, donning the helmet.

"Yes?"

"Yeah, Goddamn it, awright!" The steward's mate

stooped down and picked up the dead soldier's rifle. A bayonet was fixed to its muzzle. "I ain't no hand with a long gun, you know."

Matalam turned his full attention toward the launches. "Learn quick," he said simply, and stepped out from behind the pepperbush.

DuFourmey followed, head lowered.

The Moro broke into a trot as he emerged onto the open sand, raising a hand to the little knot of enemy soldiers. "American marines on the upper slopes!" he called out in the same perfect Japanese that had fooled Tanabe and his men in the jungle above the main encampment. "They must have come ashore somewhere on the south coast. I have been ordered to instruct all unattached infantrymen to assemble in the ravine near the garrison compound for a counterattack."

The soldiers hesitated. Two of them began to walk across the sand in the direction of the compound. The other three came forward. The man in the lead, a seasoned-looking corporal with an ugly white scar across the bridge of his nose, frowned as he approached.

"Who are you?" he demanded. "Where did you get that weapon?" He jabbed his chin at Matalam's tommy gun. "And why is your companion wearing my friend Corporal Kanmoto's helmet?" He pointed a dirty finger at DuFourmey, who was keeping his head bowed, and said over his shoulder to his comrades, "Is that not the purple-and-white-chrysanthemum insignia Kanmoto painted on his helmet for luck?"

His angry, suspicious tone made DuFourmey look up. The *Rikusentai* caught one glimpse of his ebony African-American face and went for their weapons.

Salih Matalam was faster. In the blink of an eye he had the Thompson up and firing. The Japanese soldiers danced backward in a death frenzy, sprawling on the sand between the launches. Matalam whirled. The other two *Rikusentai* were mere feet away, lunging in with fixed bayonets. The Moro sidestepped the nearest man, parrying the thrust of the blade-tipped rifle with his submachine gun, and brought the heavy wooden stock of

the weapon around in a vicious chop. The butt caught
the enemy soldier at the base of the skull, beneath the
rim of his helmet. He plowed face first into the sand and
lay still.

"*Hooooo* . . . ," the second soldier said.

He fell slowly off to one side, clutching the barrel of
DuFourmey's rifle—the bayonet of which had transfixed
him from breastbone to spine, emerging a full foot beyond his shoulder blades. DuFourmey, on one knee,
mouth open, let the rifle go as the enemy soldier sagged
to the sand, gasping, and died.

The black seaman looked up at Matalam. "He just
sorta . . . *ran* onto it . . . ," he stammered. "All I did
was push it at him."

The Moro shot him a brief smile. "You see? You
learn quick, Yankee sailor." He pulled DuFourmey to
his feet. "You get in launch. Check *fuel* first. If full—
A-OK. If not, check other boat. Then start engine and
back off beach. Go! *Go!*"

"This shit's crazy," DuFourmey protested. "Goddamned crazy . . ." But once again, he staggered forward. Seizing the gunwale of the nearest launch, he
threw a leg up and over and climbed in.

Matalam knelt beside the bow of the boat and slapped
his last remaining ammunition drum into his tommy gun
as he surveyed the edge of the jungle. The silhouettes of
running men were still flitting back and forth through the
trees, backlit by the fiery glow from the fuel dump.
Somewhere on the slopes to the east, a large-bore artillery piece fired with a thunderous *BOOM*. A high-
velocity shell screeched overhead. Matalam twisted, trying
to follow its trajectory, and saw it hit the surface of the
bay just in front of the grotto, its detonation sending up
a huge fountain of spray. He was sure he could make
out the thin shape of the *Kaiten* nearby, and prayed that
the shell had not been too close.

When he looked back toward the tree line, the Japanese soldier he had struck in the back of the head was just
staggering into the arms of a dozen or more *Rikusentai*
who had suddenly materialized out of the jungle shadows.

The man pointed back at the launches, yammering in a high-pitched voice even as his knees buckled.

"She's got plenty o' fuel!" DuFourmey shouted from inside the boat. "But I gotta figure out how to get her fired up before we can back outta here!"

In a flash, Matalam knew what he had to do. The launch had to make it off the beach. It was the only chance all the other members of the company had to escape the island. The enemy soldiers would charge in force in a matter of seconds, overwhelming whatever resistance the Negro American and he could put up, and that chance would be lost.

In 1904, eight years before he was born, his uncle Vatu Matalam had knelt in the midnight jungle outside a U.S. Marine Corps encampment on the Philippine island of Mindanao and prayed to Allah for courage and strength. Then he had stripped to a loincloth, and two of his closest friends had wrapped his biceps, elbows, wrists, thighs, knees, ankles, waist, upper chest, and even his genitals with thin strips of silk—so tightly as to impede the circulation of blood. This to prevent him from bleeding out too quickly upon taking wounds.

He had inhaled a handful of finely ground stimulant herbs and thanked his friends for their comradeship and assistance. Then he had picked up his kampilan—a slender, three-foot-long broadsword—in his right hand, and his kris—an eighteen-inch-long, serpentine-bladed dagger—in his left, and run silently at full speed through the trees toward the American camp.

Vaulting the barbed wire on the encampment's perimeter, he had surprised a handful of marines loitering around a small cooking fire. He had beheaded two and mortally wounded another before racing deeper into the camp, singing the praises of Allah. The marine field commandant had emerged from his tent in his underwear, brandishing a pistol. Whirling like a dervish, Vatu Matalam had beheaded him as well—at that point receiving his first wounds: three Krag-Jorgensen rifle bullets (manufactured by the Randall Munitions Company of Long Island, New York) in his shoulders and upper back.

They did not even slow him down. The wounds spurted blood but did not leak profusely, thanks to the bindings around his body. His circulation thus maintained, his system flushed with adrenaline and painkilling herbs, Vatu Matalam had continued his holy rampage.

At the far side of the camp, he was finally brought down by a head shot. Along the bloody trail he'd hacked through the encampment lay eleven dead and wounded marines—five completely decapitated, three more dead of partially cleaved necks, two slashed through the body, and one missing a hand. Vatu Matalam had been shot seventeen times, but in his martyr's ecstatic delirium had remained virtually immune to the effects of his injuries until a heavy slug from a .44-caliber Colt revolver had punched a large hole in the center of his forehead.

Allah looked upon warriors who martyred themselves to Islam with special favor. Those who died battling the enemies of Islam dwelled forever in paradise, blessed with riches and the company of dark-eyed houris. For the righteous Muslim, the enemy was anyone who presumed to suppress the will of God as revealed through Muhammad His Prophet, and impose unjust authority on His People the Believers. For the Moros, the enemy had changed over the centuries: first had come the Spanish, with their conquistadores, inquisitors, and macabre Catholicism; next had come the Americans, with their black-iron battleships, flinty-eyed marines, fundamentalist missionaries, and Manifest Destiny; and now the Japanese.

The Matalam clan, warriors all, had always lived by the motto *The enemy of my enemy is my brother.* And one did not leave a brother to die when it was within his power to prevent it. The launch had to escape.

So, even though Salih Matalam had not said a final prayer to Allah, even though he had no time to inhale stimulant herbs or bind his limbs with cloth, and even though he had no close friends or relatives nearby to help him prepare for his martyr's death, he threw off the *Rikusentai* helmet, took his tommy gun in his right hand and his *balisong* knife in his left, and started toward the Japanese.

As he ran, he sang in his native tongue: *"God is great. There is no God but Allah."*

Startled by his lone charge, the Japanese had only begun to disperse and bring their arms to bear as he reached them. Matalam squeezed the trigger of his tommy gun as he drove into their midst, whirling.

"Praise be to Allah, Lord of the universe, the compassionate, the merciful . . ."

The submachine gun roared as he spun, leaving a glittering arc of brass shell casings tumbling through the night air. The encircling Japanese writhed and clawed at the empty darkness.

"Sovereign of the Day of Judgment! You alone we worship, and to you alone we turn for help. . . ."

Salih Matalam felt a bayonet plunge into the left side of his body between his ribs. Still firing, he lunged in that direction, the *balisong* knife flickering in his left hand. He struck, and the ten-inch blade sank to the hilt in the right eye of the soldier on the other end of the rifle.

"Guide us to the straight path, the path of those whom you have favored . . ."

A second bayonet transfixed his right shoulder at the collarbone. He fired the tommy gun along the axis of the stab. The enemy soldier convulsed, screaming. Something impacted his lower back, then his right thigh, knocking him forward.

The tommy gun was empty. He hurled it at a contorted Japanese face directly in front of him and spun sideways in a *balisong* fighting movement, keeping his feet. The butterfly knife in his left hand chattered and flashed.

"Not of those who have incurred your wrath . . ."

Bodies fell back—shrieking, clawing at slashed faces, even as more drove in behind a forest of fixed bayonets. Salih Matalam finished the Exordium to Allah in a state of ecstasy, whirling and striking and whirling and striking. The bayonets, the bullets piercing him—they were nothing.

Nothing.

"Nor of those who have gone astray."

The *balisong* knife was a silver blur in the darkness.

Chapter Twenty-nine

Superior Petty Officer Zenji Kono paused at the top of the trail leading up to the lava dome, fifty feet short of the entrance to the slot canyon, and ten feet from the hidden body of the slain Lieutenant Harada. As the two dozen *Rikusentai* who'd been running up the trail behind him straggled in, he hawked up phlegm and spat, sucking in air like a bellows. A hundred feet ahead was the work site atop the lava dome to which he'd escorted the contrite Seaman Yoshi for punishment detail only hours earlier. A young soldier sleeping on watch had been his most pressing problem until this chaotic evening. How things could change in the span of just a few minutes.

He was looking back down the trail and out over the bay, trying to figure out where the infiltrators who'd commandeered the twenty-five-millimeter cannon had gone, when he noticed three things simultaneously. The first was a narrow black shape sliding rapidly through the flame-tinted central waters of the bay, heading straight for the submarine pen. The second was an ugly blot of white smoke on the peninsula ridge opposite him, where there had once been a seventy-five-millimeter gun emplacement.

The third was the 150-millimeter howitzer—the middle artillery piece of the three on the ridge—firing point-blank at the three-inch naval gun situated next to it. There was a brief flare from the muzzle of the howitzer, a delayed, echoing *BLAM*—and the naval gun disintegrated in a brilliant eruption of light, smoke, and debris. The percussive roar of the direct hit rolled across the bay seconds later.

Stunned, Kono and his *Rikusentai* could only stare as the fallout from the blast tumbled back down onto the ridge. Uchino's grip on his rifle slipped, and he just managed to catch the weapon before it hit the ground. He turned to Kono with stricken eyes.

"Wh-what—?" he stammered.

"Superior Petty Officer Kono!" a desperate voice yelled from back down the trail. *"Superior Petty Officer Kono, sir!"*

Kono spun and peered into the darkness. It was the young seaman Yoshi, with his battle tunic open and minus his helmet, running up the rock-strewn path as fast as his legs would carry him. Across his shoulders was a Nambu 6.5-millimeter light machine gun equipped with a short bipod; in his left hand he carried a metal ammunition box.

"Superior Petty Officer Kono, sir!" he gasped as he reached the group. "American marines are everywhere! They've killed many of us on the beach and on the slopes above the garrison compound—including Warrant Officer Tanabe, sir!"

No loss there, Kono thought grimly. "Calm down, boy. Obviously American marines cannot be *everywhere,* or there'd be some right *here.* I need information I can use. Where did you last see—"

"Excuse my interruption, Honorable Superior Petty Officer!" Yoshi cried, his face working in agitation. "Warrant Officer Tanabe's last order on the beach was to fire on the *Kaiten!*"

"What?" Kono said. "Fire on what *Kait—*"

He stopped talking abruptly and jerked his head around to stare at the surface of the bay again.

"*That* one, sir!" Yoshi shouted, pointing at the silhouette bearing down on the submarine pen. "Saboteurs have stolen it! They are using it to attack the *Sen-Toku!* We have to stop them!"

Kono turned and began to run out onto the top of the lava dome, near the edge where it dropped off to the bay nearly two hundred feet below. "Let's go!" he yelled at the little knot of *Rikusentai.* "We need a decent firing angle! Yoshi—the Nambu! Hurry!"

What we can expect to accomplish with only a light machine gun, he thought as two dozen pairs of boot heels drummed on the rocks behind him, I don't know. Maybe set off the warhead or hit the propellers. If we can get into position in time.

Maybe.

When the heavy-bore artillery piece on the opposite side of the bay unleashed another shell at the *Kaiten*, Horwitch was ready. Fixing the exact location of the firing flash in his mind's eye, he tweaked the howitzer's elevation and signaled to Foster, Mulgrew, Hooke, and Dap.

They turned their backs and covered their ears, and Horwitch pulled the lanyard. The howitzer fired for the third time that night as the opposing gun's incoming shell splashed down in the bay and sent up another huge fountain of white water—well behind the *Kaiten.*

"The bugger's short because he doesn't want to hit the sub pen!" the major yelled as the howitzer's concussion dissipated. "And now it's *too bloody late!*"

There was an explosion on the eastern shoulder of the nearest volcanic cone, in the exact location of the opposing gun's firing flash.

Mulgrew stared across the bay. "Are you sure you hit him, sir?"

As if by way of reply, the unmistakable popping of overheated artillery shells going off began to echo across the dark water.

"Pretty bloody sure," Horwitch replied.

Hooke was on one knee, steadying his binoculars. "The launch is just entering the pass at the mouth of the bay, Major," he reported. "I couldn't pick it out before. Matalam and DuFourmey must have hugged the far shore."

"Excellent." Horwitch took his Bulldog revolver out of its holster and checked the shells in the cylinder. "All still going according to plan, by God." He squinted down at the speeding *Kaiten,* now only a few hundred yards from the grotto. "Foster, Mulgrew, if the Japanese in those two machine gun nests near the slot canyon aren't on their way to this emplacement by now, they soon will be. I suggest you move in that direction posthaste. I will remain here. If the *Kaiten* does not take out the submarine, I will try to bring the roof of the grotto down on it with cannon fire, since I can't depress low enough to target it directly. Also, a great many *Rikusentai* are going to be heading for this peninsula very soon through that slot canyon. It would be most helpful if you could bottle them up at the exit, gentlemen, as we discussed, until our launch arrives . . . and Lieutenant Randall and Gunner's Mate Garth put in an appearance—we hope."

Foster picked up his Sten gun and looped the sling over his shoulder. "It'll be a fokkin' miracle if those two Yanks manage to swim out o' that pickle," he growled, glancing down at the bay. He turned to Mulgrew. "What d'you think, Mick? Two chopper nests? No worries, mate. Just like Kokoda, eh?"

Mulgrew pulled back the bolt on his own Sten and responded with his sardonic smile. "Just bloody like it, Web," he said, moving toward the jungle. "No worries."

Lieutenant Charlton Randall felt like he was getting the hang of the *Kaiten.* He'd wasted six or seven minutes after initially fleeing the dock—oversteering and yawing wildly off course several times, and once coming periously close to stalling the engine by closing an unidentified valve. But now he had the immense torpedo calmed down and running smoothly, if not as fast as he would have liked, straight toward the grotto mouth. The orange glow of the cavernous entrance filled the circular viewing field of the *Kaiten*'s periscope and the sloping black bow of the *Sen-Toku* was silhouetted dead center.

He needed more speed. The concussions from three near misses by heavy shells had struck the *Kaiten* like blows from Thor's hammer, hurting his ears and rattling his spine. The more time he gave the Japanese gunners to shoot at him, the more chance they had of scoring a bull's-eye. He had to get this over with.

He glanced down from the eyepiece of the periscope and probed the mess of tubing on the port side of the cockpit. That oddly shaped valve just above the diving-plane lever—he hadn't tried that. What the hell.

He twisted it open an eighth of a turn—and was abruptly jolted back in his seat as the *Kaiten* leaped forward, its power plant suddenly humming with a high, bansheelike whine. He had no way of knowing that he'd just doubled the supply of oxygen to the engine—only that he'd found the elusive accelerator. Hurriedly, he put his eye to the periscope once again—and immediately discovered that the spray kicked up by the *Kaiten*'s increased speed was completely obscuring his viewing field. The orange glow of the grotto was nowhere to be seen.

"Jesus Christ!" Joe Garth shouted down through the open hatch of the conning tower. "What'd you just do? Put the pedal to the metal?"

Randall twisted his neck and stared up at his friend in shock. *"What the hell are you still doing here?"* he yelled.

Even in the darkness, Garth's white-toothed grin gleamed against his tan. "Just comin' along for the ride, L.T.," he called.

"I told you to jump!" Randall shouted. "Get off this thing, *now!*"

Garth wiped spray from his face. "We'll go together," he said calmly. "By the way, are you watching where you're going? We're veering off toward the rocks."

"I can't see through the 'scope anymore!" Randall exclaimed, seizing the rudder control lever with both hands. "Which way do I steer?"

"Come to port," Garth said. "Not too hard."

Randall pushed the lever forward. The speeding *Kaiten* careened slightly to starboard.

"That's good," Garth called. He shielded his face with one hand as spray flew over the open hatch and battered his head and shoulders. "Straighten her out now."

Randall pulled back on the lever. "How's that?"

"Beautiful. We're heading straight for the sub."

It suddenly occurred to Randall that he could raise the periscope above the level of the spray and restore his forward view. As he cranked on the little brass fly-wheel near his knee, he twisted his neck and looked up at Joe Garth again.

"Joe," he said, not quite shouting this time, "jump. Once I get the periscope extended, I'll be able to see again. You need to jump now. That's an order."

Garth shook his head. "No deal, L.T. I told you—we'll go together."

Randall put his eye to the periscope and adjusted it until the grotto mouth and the submarine silhouette were centered up once more. "Are you disobeying my direct order, Gunner's Mate?"

"Absolutely," Garth replied, spitting salt water.

He clung to the lip of the hatch with all his strength as the *Kaiten* began to smash through the low chop reflecting off the cliffs of the lava dome. The water boiling past the conning tower began to surge up around his thighs—almost high enough to flood into the open hatch. He snatched a glance over his shoulder at the dugout; it was still trailing along in the *Kaiten*'s wake, bouncing at the end of its long tether like a mad thing.

He looked forward again. The orange-lit mouth of the sub pen seemed to be looming very close now; the sharklike profile of the huge submarine was visible from conning tower superstructure to jutting, upswept bow. For the first time, Garth could make out details of the pen's interior. A solid concrete pier, fifteen feet high, extended back along the walls of the grotto. Men were dashing along the pier's edge, as well as on the foredeck of the submarine. There were personnel on the bridge of the conning tower, and on the three antiaircraft gun decks. As Garth watched, a gang of seamen on the bow began to haul in one of the vessel's heavy spring lines. He couldn't help but smile. The sub was going to try to move. But it was much too late for that. At best, it would only expose itself more directly to the onrushing *Kaiten*.

Down in the control seat, peering through the eyepiece of the periscope, Randall came to the same conclusion. Assuming the *Kaiten*'s warhead detonated on impact, he knew the giant submarine was theirs. And it was time to go.

"Joe!" he yelled. Garth's face appeared in the hatchway. "Stand by to cast off the dugout! I'm locking the rudder, opening up the throttle, and we're getting the hell off this thing!"

"Roger that!" Garth shouted back. He pulled a folding knife from his pocket, opened it with his teeth, and set the blade against the dugout's vibrating tether.

"Hang on!"

Randall checked the *Kaiten*'s course once more and slid out of the control seat. Kneeling in the conning tower, he took a deep breath, gripped the throttle valve, and twisted it all the way open.

The force with which the *Kaiten* accelerated threw him into the side of the conning tower, driving the breath from his lungs. White water began to cascade down into the vessel's interior. Gasping, he clawed his way up through the flood, felt the edge of the hatch, and pulled his head and shoulders into the clear. Instantly, he felt Joe Garth's hand on his back.

"Come on, Charlton!" the Texan yelled above the scream of the *Kaiten*'s engine. *"Only a few hundred yards left! We've gotta go now!"*

"Now, Yoshi," Superior Petty Officer Zenji Kono told his young machine gunner.

Lying at the edge of the cliff atop the lava dome, two hundred feet above the giant *Sen-Toku*, Seaman Second Class Iwao Yoshi squeezed the trigger of his bipod-mounted Nambu. The light machine gun chattered. A thin stream of tracer bullets floated down toward the onrushing *Kaiten*, kicking up spray just ahead of it.

Carefully, as his fellow *Rikusentai* began to fire their rifles, Yoshi walked the tracers back through the water and up onto his target.

Randall felt something slam into his shoulder blades. Like Mel Ott connecting. He slumped over the edge of the conning tower hatch, the wind knocked out of him once more. All around, above the piercing whine of the *Kaiten*'s engine, were sharp, metallic snapping sounds.

He tried to push himself up on his arms, but they seemed to have no strength. He could raise his head, though, and when he did he caught sight of Joe Garth sliding backward on his right side toward the *Kaiten*'s stern, clawing desperately at the slick metal hull plates. There was blood on his face. A hundred yards behind him, the dugout bobbed aimlessly, its tether cut.

"Charlton!" Garth yelled, trying to stay aboard. He locked eyes with Randall—then tumbled off the stern into the churning wake, virtually on top of the torpedo's racing propellers.

Randall hoped he would see Joe's head pop up, but it didn't happen. Then he felt himself sliding, banging his knees and elbows, back down into the interior of the *Kaiten.* His limbs felt as if they were made of rubber. He collapsed on the deck plates of the little control room, coughing wetly.

He was so tired.

That was it, then. That was all of them. Fitzgerald, McNab, Bartlett, Drexel, and now Joe Garth. He'd gotten every one of his squad members killed.

Might as well make it an even half dozen. Why should he be special?

With great effort, he crawled back under the periscope housing and maneuvered himself into the cockpit seat.

It was hard to sit up straight enough to look through the periscope eyepiece, but he managed it. He coughed again, and felt a warm gout of sticky blood run over his chin.

The huge black bow of the *Sen-Toku* was just fully emerging from the mouth of the grotto. It almost filled the periscope's viewing field, and was growing larger by the second. Randall reached for the rudder lever. Since he was on board for the grand tour, he might as well make sure he—and the *Kaiten*—didn't miss anything. His right hand felt numb, so he gripped the steering control with both hands. He kept one eye to the eyepiece, fighting the almost irresistible urge to slump back in his seat and relax.

He was so *tired*.

Water continued to beat its way in through the *Kaiten*'s open hatch. The cockpit control room was now flooded a foot deep. The scream of the Long Lance oxygen engine did not quite drown out the reverberating *SNAP-BANG-SNAP* of machine gun bullets striking the hull and the conning tower.

Randall barely noticed. When the black bow of the *Sen-Toku* filled the periscope's viewing field completely, he sat back, keeping both hands on the vibrating rudder lever, and closed his eyes. Breathing had become so difficult that it was easier not to bother anymore.

For the first time in as long as he could remember, he felt utterly content. The burden of being Charlton Randall III of Long Island, New York, with its bitter litany of familial expectations, obligations, and hypocrisies, was gone. The ball of dread that lived in the pit of his stomach—gone. Now there was only Lieutenant Junior Grade Charlton Randall, United States Navy, UDT—measuring up, at last, to the five hardscrabble, working-class men who'd permitted him to lead them into harm's way, and who had already done their part.

Blood clotted in the back of his throat.

He opened his eyes briefly, and was surprised to find that he could not see. It was as if a black shade had been pulled down over his pupils. But that was all right.

He could picture everything that had ever mattered to him in his mind's eye.

Faintly, through the open hatch, he could hear someone yelling in Japanese.

Death wasn't so bad. People were wrong to make such a fuss about it. It actually felt good, especially when you were *so very tired*. Like going to sleep.

Unlike life, it wasn't a heavy, burdensome thing . . . a *weighty* thing . . .

Not at all.

It was light.

As light as a . . . feather.

Joe Garth had just rolled into the half-swamped dugout and raised his head to look toward the grotto when the *Kaiten* hit, traveling at nearly fifty miles per hour.

It struck the giant submarine at the waterline on the port side, halfway between the bow and the conning tower. Its three-thousand-pound warhead penetrated seven feet into the after section of the forward torpedo room before detonating.

The cataclysmic explosion tore off the entire bow and lifted the four-hundred-foot-long *Sen-Toku* out of the water at a twenty-degree angle. A huge pillar of flame, smoke, and water vapor shot into the night sky, extending far beyond the upper edge of the lava dome nearly two hundred feet above. The great submarine staggered back on its haunches, its stern and afterdeck driving under the flattened surface of the bay—its conning tower and superstructure careening violently to port, catapulting men into the air like rag dolls . . . and then the eight-hundred-pound warheads of four of its own torpedoes detonated.

The thunderous explosions—so close together that they sounded like a single drawn-out blast—cracked the forward hull all the way back to the aircraft hangar, splitting it lengthwise. With a terrible convulsion, the *Sen-Toku* bucked backward and down by the stern once more, its conning tower sagging over at a forty-five-degree angle, and began—very rapidly—to sink.

Then, abruptly, it stopped, bottoming out on the rocks in the shallow water of the grotto entrance. It hung there, twisted and ruined, surrounded by a sea of flaming oil, its broad conning tower canted up into the air like a tilting gravestone, a great gaping hole beneath the superstructure where the forward half of the hull had simply shattered and broken off. In the water around the wreckage, the few men who had miraculously been thrown clear but not killed outright by the explosions were screaming—screaming as they tried to flounder toward shore through an ever-widening slick of fire.

Joe Garth was huddled on his side in the bottom of the dugout, hands covering his head, knees drawn up to his chest. Blood from the scalp wound he had received when the initial burst of machine gun fire hit the *Kaiten* ran down over his face and stained the four inches of salt water slopping in the bottom of the canoe. The flimsy boat was leaking badly. Its wooden hull had cracked in three places when the powerful underwater shock waves generated by the explosions slammed into it.

Slowly, painfully, he raised his head again. Shrapnel had embedded itself in the sides of the dugout—even blown a large chunk off the bow—but by random chance, he had not been hit.

He was thoroughly bewildered by the realization that he was still alive.

For several long minutes, he watched the catastrophic scene at the mouth of the grotto. Once, when he was a boy, a Jesuit missionary in El Paso, determined to cure him of the deplorable flaw of youthful exuberance, had shown him a large, full-color painting of Dante's *Inferno*. The priest had reinforced the impact of the gruesome image with dire warnings about the fate of his immortal soul if he did not mend his ways. The painting, with its voluptuous colors and abundance of salaciously rendered agonies, had not looked more hellish than the real-life inferno in front of him now.

Even as a child, Joe Garth's instinct had been to reject such horrible religious fairy tales for what they were—

transparent, ham-handed attempts to control him
through fear. There was enough pain and terror and sacrifice in this life without imagining more in the next.
Hell wasn't some vague netherworld that existed in the
ominous, calculating predictions of priests; it was here,
right before his own eyes, and once again, he'd had a
crucial hand in its making.

Slowly, as Randall and Garth's inferno continued to
blaze up into the night, he got to his knees, retrieved
the crude paddle that had been wedged beneath the dugout's central thwart, and began to stroke toward the
north shore of the bay, where the lava dome joined the
darkened peninsula.

Chapter Thirty

Steward's Mate Henry DuFourmey, having made it through the entrance to the bay and turned westward, had been piloting the stolen launch through two-foot swells along the seaward coast of the peninsula, inside the barrier reef, when the *Kaiten* and the *Sen-Toku* exploded. Even from his perspective, it had been an awesome sight. A column of flame had erupted into the night sky on the far side of the blacked-out ridge, followed seconds later by an air-shaking crack. A more drawn-out blast had come on the heels of the first, emitting an even brighter flash. Immediately thereafter, an intense red-orange glow had spread up above the peninsula like a dome of visible heat.

DuFourmey was standing at the wheel of the launch, staring stupefied at the glow, when the vessel ran up on a small patch reef. The stout wooden keel grated over the jagged obstacle with a terrifying vibration, the launch listed hard to port . . . and then its whirling single propeller slammed into the coral.

The vibration quadrupled in force as the bronze blades of the screw shattered. DuFourmey was thrown off his feet, howling. His left temple struck the port gunwale of the boat and he collapsed to the deck as if poleaxed.

The propeller shaft bound up as the tangle of ruined bronze jammed against the bottom of the hull. With a violent screech the transmission stripped its aging gears. The engine backfired twice and stalled.

Tendrils of dirty smoke began to rise from the engine compartment as the damaged vessel, now silent but for the hissing of overheated water in the engine block, hung at a fifteen-degree list on the fang of coral, rocking in the medium swell. Henry DuFourmey remained flat on his back beneath the port rail, his head lolling from side to side with the motion of the boat, water washing up against his body as it drained in and out of the scuppers.

As the rattle of small-arms fire echoed down from the darkened ridge, the launch gently rocked itself free of the coral outcropping, was caught by the outgoing tide, and began to drift through a narrow channel in the barrier reef out toward the open sea.

On top of the lava dome, Superior Petty Officer Zenji Kono was striding from man to man, shouting at his *Rikusentai* to snap out of it, as they stared down dumbfounded at the twisted wreckage of the giant submarine. The heat rising from the expanse of burning oil immediately below them was intense enough to sear their faces and keep them back from the very edge of the cliff, as was the noxious stink of petroleum fumes and smoke. The waterborne fire had spread back into the grotto itself as thousands of gallons of diesel oil continued to flow out of the *Sen-Toku*'s fractured tanks.

Without warning, there was another gigantic explosion, and the very rock under the feet of Kono's *Rikusentai* seemed to jolt upward. A torrent of flame and smoke belched out of the grotto, past the ruined submarine, and out over the bay. The sub pen began to shake with a rapid series of individual detonations, each accompanied by outflung sheets of shrapnel and debris.

"The fire is setting off the fuel and ammunition stores inside the sub pen!" Kono yelled. *"Move your asses! Get across to the peninsula!"*

One more, by Christ, Horwitch thought. One more little kiss from Big Bertha here for these Nipponese bastards.

He yanked the howitzer's lanyard and the cannon fired for the fourth time. The HE shell shrieked across the bay and landed in the middle of the garrison compound on the far shore. The resultant blast smashed the bamboo huts clustered around the central quadrangle to splinters and toppled the outpost's leaf-camouflaged radio antenna.

Horwitch took a moment to stroke his mustache in satisfaction. A respectable amount of damage had been done in and around the bay in the last half hour. Bloody marvelous.

A scattering of shots—sharp, individual reports, very rapid and very close together—cracked through the jungle shadows from the direction of the lava dome. Horwitch recognized the sounds instantly as coming from at least two Sten guns set on semi rather than full automatic. Foster and Mulgrew were assaulting one of the two machine gun nests, and not wasting ammunition doing it. The major wondered briefly which one they'd decided to take out first, and why, since the emplacements were well within sight of each other, the second nest wasn't shooting.

He waited for the sharp thudding of hand grenades, the staccato hammering of heavy Nambus—but neither came. Nor were there any more Sten gun reports. That boded well, he decided. No return fire from Japanese weapons meant no enemy soldiers still capable of pulling a trigger. Foster and Mulgrew were both irredeemable, convict-class vulgarians, like all Australians, but Horwitch admitted to himself that they knew their business when it came to jungle fighting.

He stepped out from behind the howitzer and drew his old Bulldog revolver. Hooke and Dap had started down the slope toward the bay, hoping to spot Randall and Garth and wave them in. It was fortunate that the finger of land had turned out to be devoid of enemy troops but for the crews of the three cannon emplacements and the two machine gun nests. The lack of opposing personnel gave the members of Horwitch's little makeshift commando group freedom of movement—at least until the remaining *Rikusentai* on the island proper got organized and started to pour through the slot canyon.

He decided to follow Hooke and Dap down the rocky incline to the edge of the bay, assist them in collecting Randall and Garth, and then lead the group back up to rendezvous with Foster and Mulgrew. By that time, hopefully, DuFourmey and Matalam would have the launch on the peninsula's seaward beach, and they could all make their escape. . . .

Horwitch paused just before descending into the jungle and looked out to sea. Nothing caught his eye on the dark waters between reef and shoreline. The only sound he could hear from that direction was the low rumble of surf on sand. No engine noises. Strange. Hooke had reported seeing the launch in the bay's entrance channel only five minutes earlier.

Horwitch ground his teeth in frustration. Where *was* that lippy Yank golliwog? And Matalam, whom he knew to be an effective and resourceful soldier despite his less-than-preferable ethnicity? The Moro, at least, he'd assumed capable of appropriating the boat and getting it around the peninsula to a suitable embarkation point. Bloody foreigners. He turned and began to push his way into the dense jungle foliage.

He would have sent an Englishman to do the job, but he'd been fresh out.

Kono had been afraid of the entire lava dome's caving in as the ammunition and fuel stores inside the grotto detonated, but the seventy-five-foot-thick roof of rock proved to be sturdy enough to withstand the multiple blasts. He and his *Rikusentai* made it to the peninsula side of the lava dome as fire, smoke, and shrapnel continued to lash out of the cavern mouth. He'd half expected flame to surge out of the slot canyon and consume them as they ran along its top edge, but despite the jarring vibrations underfoot, the holocaust had been confined to the interior of the sub pen.

The veteran petty officer was just beginning to turn his attention to the task of finding out why the central artillery piece on the peninsula ridge had fired on and destroyed the two on either side of it, when Web Foster opened up with the heavy Nambu machine gun he'd captured single-handedly only moments before. The four *Rikusentai* to Kono's right emitted strangled cries as they were hammered to the ground. The other men dove for what little cover there was through a hot flurry of 7.7-millimeter slugs.

Seaman Second Class Kiichi Uchino, hunched low behind a little rise of lava, had never before been fired at in anger. It was an educational experience. A bullet made a nerve-wracking noise when it passed only a foot or two over your head, he discovered. *Whiiizzzzzzz-CRACK!* Vaguely, he remembered being told that the *crack* was the lead slug breaking the sound barrier as it went by, and that hearing that crack was a good thing. It meant that you were going to live a little longer. If you didn't hear the crack, it was because the bullet had killed you.

Just ahead of him and to his right, a soldier rose onto his knees and began to wave his hands over his head. Uchino realized with a start that it was Iwao Yoshi.

"Stop shooting!" Yoshi shouted at the machine gun nest. *"We are Rikusentai, not Americans! There are infiltrators on—"*

"Get down, Yoshi!" Kono yelled, stunned that the naïve young seaman had chosen to expose himself so directly. *"Get—"*

Foster, in the first nest, opened up at the same time as Mulgrew, on the Nambu in the second. The crisscrossing fire literally chopped Seaman Second Class Iwao Yoshi to pieces.

"No!" Uchino screamed, horrified, as the torn corpse of his friend was hurled back before his eyes. *"Iwao!"*

Zenji Kono sprang to his feet, firing his carbine at the nearest emplacement. *"Into the canyon!"* he bellowed, scuttling sideways. *"Climb down into the canyon! Hurry up! Move! Move!"* He pulled a fragmentation grenade from his battle harness, yanked out the safety pin, and banged the fuse end once against his helmet to ignite it. As combustion gases fizzed out of the grenade's vent-hole, he threw it toward the nearest machine gun nest with all his strength and scrambled for the edge of the slot canyon. He knew the grenade would fall short, but the explosion would confuse matters somewhat, buy precious seconds for his men.

The effect was better than he could have hoped. The notoriously unreliable fuse of the Japanese Model 97 hand grenade, designed to detonate after five seconds but going off earlier more often than not, lived up to its reputation. At the highest point of its tumbling arc the grenade exploded prematurely, spraying shrapnel down into Foster's captured machine gun nest.

"Aagghh!" the big man cried out, clapping both hands to his right knee. *"Jesus bloody Christ!"*

He was drowned out by a long, sustained burst from Mulgrew's machine gun, located some thirty yards away. The staccato roaring went on continuously for nearly twenty seconds before the Aussie corporal let up on the trigger.

"You hit, Web?" he called, eyeing the lava dome as the last few unscathed *Rikusentai* scrambled over the edge of the slot canyon and disappeared from view.

"Aarrgghh . . . ," came Foster's rasp of a voice. "Bloody bastards . . ."

"Is that a yes, mate?"

"Yeh, fokkin' hell—yes!"

"Bad?"

"My fokkin' knee, mate," Foster ground out. "Shrapnel chewed the bugger to the bone."

"Hurt?"

"Sod you, Mick. What d'you think?"

"All right, all right," Mulgrew called. "Hold tight. I'm comin' over to you. Got me covered?"

The clacking sound of Foster's Nambu being charged with a fresh ammunition strip echoed sharply through the jungle shadows. "Got you, mate. I don't see any of the little bastards at the moment, so come when you're ready, eh?"

"Right." Grunting, Mulgrew hefted his own 120-pound Nambu—complete with mounting tripod—in his arms and stepped out of the gun pit, his spine nearly cracking. Swearing under his breath, sweat popping out of every pore on his body, he lugged the weapon through the foliage toward Foster's position. With every stride, he expected to hear a volley of Arisaka rifle fire, feel hot slugs tear into his flesh.

But it didn't happen. He toiled along for another thirty seconds, bulling his way through broadleafs and strangler vines. Still no fire from the Japanese. He dropped the heavy machine gun on top of the sandbags lining Foster's Nambu nest, jumped down into the shallow emplacement, and collapsed into a sitting position, breathing hard.

"Fancy meeting you here," Foster grunted. Blood was running out between the fingers of the hand he had clasped over his right knee. He was looking over the sandbags at the open end of the slot canyon.

"Fokkin' . . . thing . . . weighs . . . a *ton*," Mulgrew panted, pulling his Nambu into firing position atop the sandbags. "I hope you've got . . . plenty of ammo, 'cause I don't wanna . . . run back to that . . . other nest, mate."

"Four crates," Foster said, indicating the wooden boxes beside him. "Thirty-round strips, not long belts."

"Ah, shit," Mulgrew returned. "I like belts. Less fiddlin' around."

Foster grinned through his pain. "Beggars can't be bleedin' choosers, mate."

"Sad but true." Mulgrew slid over next to him. "Lemme see that knee, Web."

"Okay, but be fokkin' careful, all right? It hurts like a bitch."

"I will if you stop complainin' like a fokkin' schoolgirl."

"Screw you, Mick, you bloody perisher. . . ."

Mulgrew examined the ugly wound. Foster's kneecap had been split in two by a piece of shrapnel. The metal shard had penetrated through the patella and embedded itself deep in the joint. Mulgrew's sardonic expression became grave; he turned his head and spat to one side. Foster wouldn't be going anywhere fast, and when he did, he'd be hopping.

"It ain't good, Web," Mulgrew growled, opening the first-aid pouch on the belt of a dead Japanese gunner, one of the two men Foster had killed when he'd stormed the nest. Mulgrew had jumped the *Rikusentai* in the other emplacement at exactly the same time, preventing one Nambu nest from firing on the other. Tearing open a packet of sulfa powder, the corporal sprinkled a generous amount into his friend's shattered knee, then gently pressed a gauze pad over the wound and began to bandage it in place. Foster grunted once or twice, but said nothing.

"This is the best I can do for now, Web," Mulgrew muttered. "Can you stand it?"

Foster's tough face was pale, but he managed another grin. "Sure, mate. No worries."

"This aid kit's got a few morphine ampules. . . ."

The big sergeant shook his head. "Not a chance. I'll keep my wits about me, thanks. Besides—those are Jap drugs. Might make me permanently barmy, y' know?"

Mulgrew moved around behind his machine gun. "Too late, Web. You're already barmy," he retorted. He inserted a fresh ammunition strip into the Nambu and racked it into the breech.

Falling silent, the two men gazed out through the palm trunks at the slot canyon some seventy-five yards away. A certain amount of motion was visible in the dark opening, well back in the shadows. As random explosions from the burning grotto and fuel depot continued to boom across the bay, Foster propped his knee into a tolerable position and lined up his Nambu on the narrow crevice.

"I'll help you down to the beach," Mulgrew said suddenly, without turning his head, "when Mad Harry shows up." He lit a cigarette and passed it to Foster. "You lean on me, mate—you can make it."

Foster took the smoke and inhaled, smiling. "Yeh. Sure. Thanks."

Mulgrew looked at him as he lit his own cigarette. "I mean it. You can make it."

There was more movement in the slot canyon. Foster squinted over the barrel of his heavy machine gun. "Mick, old son, I appreciate that. But we both know I ain't goin' anywhere on this fokked-up peg."

Mulgrew turned, gazed through the sights of his own Nambu, and blew a long stream of smoke along the barrel. Then he looked back at Foster. The big sergeant's face was running with sweat, creased by lines of pain. "Well, if it's like that, Web," he said.

"You can go, mate," Foster growled, "even if I can't. That's just the way it is. Luck of the draw, and no worries. Both your pegs are still good."

It was Mulgrew's turn to smile. The coal on the end of his cigarette glowed as he inhaled. "Yeh. Sure. Thanks," he said, flexing his hands on the grips of his weapon.

"Remember," Kono whispered to the *Rikusentai* huddled behind him in the slot canyon, "break left and right in pairs as you come out, and run like hell for cover on either flank. Don't stop for anything, or you'll be chopped to bits. Start laying down a base of fire as soon as you can." He raised a rifle with a launcher and grenade fitted over its muzzle. "When the grenade goes off . . ."

He fired the rifle. The grenade flew out of the crevice in a shallow arc, went into the bushes twenty feet in front of the left-hand machine gun nest, and exploded. On that signal, the *Rikusentai* began to pour out of the slot canyon in pairs, alternately heading left and right as Kono had instructed. The twin Nambus opened up, turning the canyon exit into a chaos of ricocheting bullets and rock chips.

The first four men out were killed, but the next ten made it to cover and began to pepper the one active machine gun nest with rifle fire. Petty Officer Kono came out of the canyon behind the last six soldiers, launching another grenade toward the Nambus at a dead run.

"Both machine guns are in that one nest!" he bellowed at the *Rikusentai* who'd taken cover to the right. He ducked instinctively as the grenade exploded in the trees. *"Work up toward that abandoned emplacement! Flank them, flank them!"*

Chapter Thirty-one

Joe Garth had been lying back against a large rock on the shore of the bay, spent, for three or four minutes, watching the sub and the grotto burn, when there was a rustling of foliage on the slope above his head and Finian Hooke stepped down into view.

"If I was a Jap," Hooke said, "you'd be dead."

"What makes you so sure I'm not?" Garth replied. He gestured at the fiery scene several hundred yards away. "What a mess."

The New Zealander stepped forward, switching his Sten gun to his left hand. "So are you," he said, taking in the grease, oil, and blood smearing Garth's naked torso and face. "Lieutenant Randall?"

Garth shook his head slowly from side to side. "He rode the *Kaiten* all the way in."

Hooke blinked, then looked out at the leaping flames. "My God," he muttered.

"I think he was hit," Garth said hollowly. "He was getting ready to jump with me, and there was a burst of machine gun fire. . . ." His voice trailed off.

Hooke put a careful hand on Garth's upper arm. "Perhaps he was dead before the *Kaiten* struck the sub-marine."

"No," Garth said. "The machine gun burst knocked me into the water. When I made it back to the surface, the *Kaiten* was off course again, too far to the left. I saw it veer back onto the right heading in the last couple hundred yards. It was being steered."

The silence lasted only a few seconds, but seemed much longer. "I'm sorry, Garth," Hooke said finally. "He . . . I'm sorry."

The Texan just nodded.

Hooke raised his binoculars to his eyes and examined the wreckage of the *Sen-Toku*. "A bloody fine demolition job, if you ask me, " he said. "The sub is completely destroyed . . . unsalvageable. Only the conning tower looks to be more or less in one piece." He moved the glasses slowly over the exposed sections of the ruined hulk, then frowned and moved them back. "Wait a minute. . . . Wait a minute. . . ."

Garth took a couple of deep breaths and sat up. "What do you see?"

Hooke's frown deepened, his brows knitting together. "Something's wrong. That conning tower. Something's very bloody wrong. . . ."

"Sure there is," the Texan said, getting painfully to his feet, "if you happen to be a Jap sailor. Your subma-rine's blown in half and sitting on the bottom of the bay." He looked up quickly as Yomat Dap emerged from the foliage and stepped down off the slope to the rocky waterline. *"Selamat pagi,"* he said, trying his frac-tured Malay.

The Dayak beamed and nodded, managing to deci-pher "Good morning." To the east, the coming dawn was just beginning to lighten the sky from velvet black to a luminous midnight blue.

A strange sound—like a combination of moaning and singing—began to come from behind a small stand of trees at the water's edge, some thirty feet away. In-stantly, Hooke, Garth, and Dap flinched back among the rocks, bringing weapons to bear.

"What's that bloody racket?" Horwitch hissed, sliding down out of the trees above them. He crept up beside Hooke, brandishing his revolver.

Around the thicket, wading in knee-deep water, came a man—a Japanese—staggering like a drunkard and moaning continuously in a high, singsong voice. His dark blue uniform hung in rags from his shoulders, and at least one of his arms appeared to be broken, dangling twisted by his side. As he approached, it became obvious that he had been badly burned; the skin of his face was blackened and bubbled, hanging in wet, glistening shreds from sharp cheekbones. Long hair, samurai-style, trailed down his neck in tangled strands. He stepped on a submerged rock, nearly fell, and stumbled forward with his one good arm outstretched, probing the air before him. The singsong moaning continued.

"He's blind," Garth whispered, lowering his automatic. "Burned blind. And delirious."

"It'll be my pleasure to put the bugger out of his misery," Horwitch declared, rising to his full height and leveling his Bulldog.

"Wait!" Hooke said, grabbing Horwitch's arm. "Hold your fire."

"Eh?" the major grunted, surprised. "What the bloody hell for?"

Hooke started forward, picking his way hurriedly through the rocky shallows. "Do you see those four bars on his sleeve?" he hissed over his shoulder. "And that patch insignia? He's a captain. A *submarine* captain!"

"Well, what of it?" Horwitch demanded, following Hooke. "We don't need him—"

"*Quiet!*" the New Zealander shot back, his whisper ferocious. "I don't have time to explain, but you must *not talk for the next few minutes!*"

Horwitch frowned, but kept silent. Hooke strode forward, reached out, and put an arm around the injured man's waist. The Japanese shrank away at the touch, flailing the air with his good hand and redoubling his nonsensical babbling. Gently, Hooke guided him to a flat rock at the water's edge and helped him lie back.

Horwitch, Garth, and Dap drew up close, standing in a silent circle behind Hooke, weapons ready, casting watchful glances at the bay and the nearby jungle.

"Captain," Hooke said in Japanese, crouching beside the delirious officer. *"Captain!"*

He shook the man gently by the collar. The response was a high moan of pain and despair. Garth, looking over Hooke's shoulder, averted his gaze. The officer's eyes were little more than empty, puckered holes in his charred face, cauterized by heat.

"Who . . . who is it?" the man wailed, becoming partly lucid. "Who are you?"

"It is Miwa," Hooke said. "Your commander."

If the burned man had had eyelids, they would have fluttered in confusion. He twisted his head from side to side, grimacing in misery. "Mi . . . Miwa?" he repeated. "Vice Admiral Shigeyoshi Miwa? Commander of the—the Imperial Sixth Fleet?"

"The same," Hooke assured him.

"How . . . what?" the officer stammered. "You . . . cannot be . . ."

"I have just arrived with a large surface force to engage the Americans who have invaded this island," Hooke said. "We are driving them off as we speak, Captain."

The empty eyes stared up. "T-truly?"

"Truly." The New Zealander paused. "Medical aid is coming for you. But while we wait, you must help me assess the damage done so far. Can you do that?"

"F-for my emperor, and Japan . . . and for you, Hon-Honorable Admiral," the officer groaned, "I can do anything."

Hooke threw a quick look over his shoulder at Horwitch, then turned back to the injured man. "Excellent," he said. "I knew I could count on you." He cleared his throat. "Now, then. You are the captain of the submarine that has just been destroyed, are you not?"

The officer nodded. "Yes . . . to my—my eternal shame, Honorable Admiral."

"Nonsense," Hooke replied smoothly. "An unavoidable loss of war. There was no dereliction of duty on your part." He paused. "So. you would be Captain Yarizuma, would you not?"

"Ye—" The officer began to nod, then stopped. "I . . . I . . . what?"

"I am confused, Yarizuma," Hooke went on. "In a conversation I had recently with Lieutenant Commander Ogaki, garrison commander of this island's land forces, he referred to you as commander of the *Sen-Toku I-403* . . . and yet the markings on the conning tower of the submarine lying at the mouth of the grotto read *I-404*. Perhaps you could provide clarification. Ogaki misspoke, apparently?"

"I—I," the injured man protested, "I am not Yarizuma. . . ."

Hooke leaned in very close, his dark eyes gleaming. "Not Yarizuma?"

"N-no . . . no . . ."

Hooke nearly seized the man by the throat, but restrained himself. *"Then who are you?"*

The officer moved his head from side to side in pain and confusion. "I am . . . Otsuka," he moaned. "Captain Tadashige Otsuka . . . commander of the *Sensuikan-Toku I-404* . . . Honorable Admiral. . . ."

Hooke was breathing hard. He thought a moment. "And you were going to conduct an attack on Washington, D.C.—utilizing kamikaze aircraft—when you departed this base . . . were you not?"

"I . . . I . . ."

"Answer me, Captain Otsuka! It is your duty to answer your commanding officer!"

"Yes . . . yes," Otsuka whispered, grimacing yet again. "My . . . duty . . ." He drew a long, ragged breath. "I promised . . . Yarizuma . . . that I would not tell . . . but . . . my duty—"

He ran out of air as the chugging rattle of Nambu fire high up on the slopes began to echo off the bay. Garth and Horwitch glanced at each other as several grenade concussions thumped through the trees.

"It was not I," Otsuka said, choking out the words,

"but Yarizuma. . . . Yarizuma did speak . . . of his intention to . . . carry out such a mission, Honorable Admiral. He told me . . . in confidence."

"Yarizuma? The commander of the *I-403?*" Hooke's fingers tightened on the tattered remnants of the injured man's collar. *"There are two Sen-Toku currently operational?"*

"Why . . . of course, Honorable Admiral," Otsuka groaned, bewildered. He began to wheeze as Hooke's grip on his collar restricted his breathing. "You . . . you know that. And five more . . . soon to come . . . from the Kure Shipyards. . . ."

Horrified realization began to dawn on Hooke. "Yarizuma's *Sen-Toku*, the *I-403*—it was here?"

"Yes . . . yes, sir. Of course." His face contorting in pain, Otsuka began to wag his head from side to side again, moaning softly deep in his throat. "My eyes . . . ," he mumbled, "oh, my eyes . . ."

Hooke shook him. "Where is Yarizuma?" he demanded. "When did he leave?"

"My . . . eyes . . ."

"When did Yarizuma leave?"

Otsuka let out an anguished groan. "He put out to sea . . . with the *I-403* . . . the week after I arrived with the *I-404.*"

"When?" Hooke almost shouted. *"Give me a date!"*

"August nineteenth . . . Honorable Admiral," the wounded captain said weakly. "He left for the . . . United States . . . more than two months ago."

Part Four

Chapter
Thirty-two

When it is early morning in the Philippines, it is late afternoon on the east coast of the United States. On this particular October afternoon, the Atlantic seas off the southern New Jersey resort town of Cape May were gray, rough, and wind-whipped, courtesy of a fast-moving cold front that had dipped down out of Canada the day before.

It was, Sonarman Randolph Clarke decided, weather fit for neither man nor beast. He braced himself against the lip of his console, lifting his tin mug of lukewarm black coffee, as the destroyer USS *Reuben Grant* wallowed through yet another set of immense wave troughs, continuing the monotonous patrol that routinely took her from the mouth of Delaware Bay to the mouth of the Chesapeake and back again. And again.

Clarke wasn't sure that being ensconced in the sonar room deep in the bowels of the ship was all that much better than being up on the bridge. The air was stifling, and the lack of a steady horizon on which to focus multiplied the sickening effects of the destroyer's incessant twisting tenfold. In addition, the vessel was suffering from a mechanical problem known as a "shivering shaft"—a warped or misaligned propeller shaft that set up an irritating vibration throughout the hull and would have put the *Reuben Grant* into port for repairs if her captain, one aptly nicknamed Douglas "Donk" Blaine, hadn't been such a salty hard-ass. Finally, and quite possibly worst of all, Clarke was from South Dakota and was prone to seasickness. If it hadn't been for the bitter-tasting pills the pharmacist's mate had provided for him, he'd have been a puking wreck by now.

He put the coffee down on the console as the *Reuben Grant* settled onto a marginally more comfortable heading, readjusted the headphones over his ears, and fine-tuned the sonar unit. It was sending out broad-ranging pings in a standard search mode, sonically scanning the empty water and seafloor in front of, around, and beneath the ship. Clarke yawned. Monitoring the endless pinging was largely a bore. It had been more than two years since Germany's "Operation Drumbeat," when U-boats had been a constant presence in east-coast waters from Newfoundland to Florida; now, the once-feared Nazi submarines were virtually nonexistent.

The return pinging changed slightly in his headphones, and Clarke leaned forward to adjust the unit's signal gain. Then he consulted a handbook and a small chart, both of which were black with penciled-in coordinates and symbols, on the table beside him.

The sudden clap of a big hand on his right shoulder nearly scared him out of his wits. *Christ. Powell.*

"What chew got there, son?" the beefy lieutenant commander drawled. A forty-six-year-old regular-navy lifer of no particular distinction, Harold "Hal" Powell was the officer in charge of the sonar room. He was also exceedingly tiresome. Powell, Clarke had found, delighted in petty cruelties like padding up behind someone intent on their work and startling the living hell out of them by grabbing their elbow or slapping them on the shoulder—then pretending nothing was amiss.

The sonarman slipped the headphone cup off his right ear. "I really wish you wouldn't do that, sir," he said

lamely. What the fuck could he do? Powell was a lieutenant commander.

"What chew talkin' 'bout, boy?" Powell responded,
grinning as he cracked his gum and loomed over
Clarke's shoulder, too close for comfort. "You pick up
somethin' there?"

"Yes, sir," Clarke said, sighing and turning back to
his sonar set. "A good-sized signal off the bottom. The
source is known." He tapped the handbook. "The wreck
of the British freighter *Templar*, sunk in January of 1942
by *Kapitänleutnant* Reinhard Hardegen in command of
the German attack submarine *U-123*. She's lying on her
port side in one piece, in two hundred and forty feet
of water."

"Damn, son!" Powell chuckled, slapping Clarke's
shoulder again. "You're a reg'lar en-cyclo-pedia of information. We musta been over this hulk two dozen times
since July. And this is the first time you're seein' it?"

Clarke resisted the temptation to shrug off the big
mitt clamped on to his deltoid. "No, sir," he said. "I've
marked it off fourteen times before. And I've *reported*
it to you each time."

"Big, ain't she?" Powell commented, oblivious to the
dig.

The sonarman fiddled with the set's controls. "Aye,
sir. Records show she was nearly three hundred and
seventy-five feet long. And she must have broken apart
a little more since the last time we came by."

"How so?"

Clarke relaxed somewhat as Powell's hand finally
lifted off his shoulder. "Because the sonar return's a bit
bigger than I remember it," he said. "But it's the *Templar,* all right. No mistake. Right where she's always
been."

Powell cracked his gum. "Well, that's a relief, son,"
he drawled, strolling toward the door. "Wouldn't be
amenable to the nerves to find a U-boat lurkin' around
on our side of the pond, now would it?"

Clarke turned down the gain of the sonar set as the
return signal from the wreck of the *Templar* began to

fade astern. "No, sir," he replied patiently. "It sure wouldn't."

As the throbbing of the USS *Reuben Grant*'s screws disappeared from the dark waters surrounding the shattered *Templar,* several large bursts of air bubbles rose along the length of the broken hulk. Though there were no human eyes to perceive it, the wreck seemed to split in two lengthwise, the larger section beginning to float ponderously upward at a shallow angle.

There was a second blast of compressed air. Thick schools of cod and haddock fled away from the suddenly unquiet *Templar*, out over the seafloor. The detached half of the wreck rose steadily through the water column, out of the drowned darkness and into the scant ambient light of the North Atlantic's first ten fathoms, resolving gradually into the looming form of a giant submarine.

The four-hundred-foot steel leviathan ascended to periscope depth, blew tanks once more, and began to maintain neutral buoyancy six fathoms beneath the sea's storm-whipped surface. With neither diesel nor electric engines running, the *Sen-Toku I-403* made absolutely no sound.

Captain Toshiko Yarizuma smiled inwardly as he listened to his hydrophone operator's latest report: "No audible indications, sir. No propeller noises, no pinging. The American destroyer has moved on."

The old U-boat commander's trick had worked. German submariners operating along the U.S. east and Gulf coasts in the spring of 1942 had learned that early American sonar had inadequacies of definition and resolution—it would indicate to a sub-hunting vessel that something was nearby, but provide very little information as to the exact size, shape, and depth of the contact. Although Axis intelligence had noted apparent improvement in American and British sonar throughout 1943 and into 1944, the detection systems remained unable to differentiate between objects of similar size lying close together on the ocean bottom. Shrewd German U-boat commanders had taken advantage of this limitation while hunting along U.S. coastal shipping lanes, nestling their submarines up against known, charted wrecks and lying low whenever they felt threatened by patrolling surface vessels. Searching destroyers would record a predictable sonar return from a documented wreck—and pass on by.

Submarine warfare tacticians from Nazi Germany had shared this information with their Japanese counterparts in mid-1942, tempered by the caveat that there was no way to predict when American sonar might improve to the degree that it could determine the exact shapes and sizes of contacts. Apparently, though, as of October 1944 it had not yet reached such a level of sophistication. From Tierra del Fuego at the tip of South America to the Maryland-Delaware shore, Yarizuma had dodged destroyer after destroyer by stealing north from one charted wreck to the next, maintaining a constant visual and electronic lookout while the *I-403* was running on the surface, and diving for cover alongside those wrecks whenever an enemy vessel was spotted.

"Raise the periscope," Yarizuma ordered.

The *I-403*'s executive officer, Lieutenant Hanku Katsura, stepped forward and threw a small lever on a fluid-control panel. With a quiet hydraulic whir, the shaft extensions of the periscope slid upward. Yarizuma caught the shears at the lower end of the 'scope housing as it rose to eye level and stopped.

Complete silence dominated the control room as the commander of the *Sen-Toku* surveyed the world on the opposite side of the tumultuous interface directly above—examining the ocean's surface in every direction to the limits of the unit's visual range. It took Yarizuma three full minutes to walk the 'scope through a 360-degree rotation. Finally, he stood back, slapped the shears up against the housing, and nodded to Katsura.

"Lower the periscope," he said.

The hydraulics whirred again as Yarizuma turned and let his serene gaze wander over the on-duty personnel in the control room. To a man, they stiffened and fixed their attention on their duties with renewed concentration. A slight smile creased the corners of the *Sen-Toku* commander's mouth. He'd trained them well.

"There are no vessels within sight at this time," Yarizuma said. "Storm conditions exist on the surface, the cloud ceiling is low, and night is falling. It is unlikely that patrol bombers will be flying before the weather breaks.

"On one of the most well-defended and tightly patrolled coastlines in the world, fate has handed us an opportunity."

He looked at the navigation officer, who stood at ease at the control room's small chart table.

"Set a course for Lewes, Delaware, following the forty-fathom curve as far as possible."

To the executive officer: "Make speed five knots submerged. Depth ninety feet."

Katsura saluted. "Yes, sir."

"And Katsura . . ."

The young lieutenant paused just before issuing his own string of orders. "Yes, Honorable Captain?"

"All *tokko* personnel and supporting technicians to their stations. Final check of all *Kaiten* and *Seiran*. Final check of the *Ohka*. We attack at dawn."

The *Sen-Toku* commander looked into some unknown, faraway distance just above Katsura's head.

"The hour of our grand gesture is nearly upon us," he said softly. "Dawn. *Dawn.* The true Rising Sun has come to America."

Chapter
Thirty-three

"By Christ," Horwitch exclaimed, breaking the silence that followed Hooke's summary of Otsuka's halting revelations. "This other sub left two and a half *months* ago? Isn't that more than enough time to have reached the U.S.'s east coast by now?"

"At the speed a *Sen-Toku* can probably maintain," Hooke replied, "yes."

"What . . . what is happening?" the blind Japanese captain stammered, hearing the English exchange. "Wh-who are . . . you? Vice Admiral Miwa! Vice . . . Admiral . . ."

Otsuka's voice trailed off into a long, drawn-out moan, and he placed a shaking hand over his ruined eyes.

The chugging roar of two heavy Nambus reverberated through the trees, interspersed with frequent rifle shots and the *thud* of grenades.

Garth moved up beside the New Zealander and the Englishman. "I'd say it's time to leave," he muttered. He nodded in the direction of the firefight. "Foster and Mulgrew?"

Horwitch nodded. "Holding the Japs at the slot canyon. They've taken the two machine gun nests that control land access to this peninsula. We need to rendezvous with them, then withdraw to the beach. DuFourmey and Matalam will have the bloody launch there by now, I should hope."

"Sooner or later," Hooke said, "the Japanese are going to realize that the land approach through the slot canyon is blocked, and start to put across the bay in boats. We'd better be gone by then, because if they get us caught between two attacking forces, the game will pretty much be up."

"Major," Garth said. "We've got to find some way of notifying our high command of the threat to Washington posed by Yarizuma's *Sen-Toku*. There's no telling where that sub is right now." He glanced across the bay toward the burning remains of the garrison compound. "Maybe if we found a radio . . ."

"The long-range radio tower has just been destroyed," Horwitch informed him. "Besides, I don't think our Japanese friends would be all that receptive to the idea of our borrowing their communications equipment just now."

"For all we know, the *Sen-Toku* has already been depth-charged and sunk," Hooke said. "It's nearly twenty thousand sailing miles from the Philippines to the U.S.'s east coast, whether you head east across the Pacific or west across the Indian Ocean. A lot can happen in two months."

Horwitch, Garth, Hooke, and Dap looked up abruptly as a fresh barrage of Nambu fire hammered through the foliage. Again, the raw sound was punctuated by the concussion of grenades. Otsuka, lying on the rocks at the water's edge, writhed and groaned.

"The launch is our best hope of getting out of here," Horwitch said. "We'll climb to the ridge, spot DuFourmey and Matalam, then advance to join Foster and Mulgrew. Let's go." He took a step up the vine-covered slope, then halted. "Bloody hell—I forgot. Where is Lieutenant Randall?"

Hooke glanced at Garth, then looked away.

"Dead," Garth said. "He was wounded by machine gun fire . . . and piloted the *Kaiten* all the way in."

Horwitch's craggy face contorted slightly. "God in heaven," he exclaimed, automatically staring out, as Hooke had done, at the fiery scene in front of the grotto. He swallowed, then looked back at Garth. "Your lieutenant was . . . was . . ."

The major shut his mouth, choosing silence over anything trite.

Joe Garth gazed at him evenly. "He was my friend."

The insistent cacophony of Nambu fire and grenade detonations was now accompanied by the faint sound of voices shouting in Japanese. Yomat Dap leaped up the steep slope five or six strides, crouched on a twisted root, and peered through the shadows toward the commotion. The flickering orange glow from the burning oil slick on the bay partially illuminated his naked body, lending him a lurking, predatory appearance.

Horwitch, Garth, and Hooke spread out, preparing to climb toward the Dayak. As they did so, Otsuka emitted a loud groan and lurched to his feet. One hand clutching at the air in front of him, he began to stagger forward through the shallows again. After a few steps, his groans segued into the same high-pitched singing that had heralded his initial arrival.

"What's he saying?" Garth asked Hooke.

"He's singing 'The Warrior's Song,'" the New Zealander replied. "'At sea we may sink beneath the waves . . . On land we may lie beneath green grasses . . . But we have nothing to regret . . . So long as we die fighting for our emperor.'"

Garth watched the blinded man stumble away. "Doesn't rhyme," he said.

"It does in Japanese," Hooke told him.

Horwitch stepped down off the slope once more and aimed his revolver at Otsuka's back. The singing continued. The barrel of the Bulldog wavered—then came down. "Ah, hell," Horwitch growled, and began to climb toward Dap for the third time.

Garth did the same, sticking his automatic into his

waistband and pulling himself upward, grasping vines and creepers.

A short burst of fire ripped from Hooke's Sten gun. Captain Otsuka cried out in midsong, spread-eagled his arms, and pitched forward into the water.

Garth and Horwitch both looked back at Finian Hooke as he slung his smoking Sten over one shoulder and mounted the slope. They continued to regard him as he drew abreast.

"It was kinder," he said, passing between them on his way to join Yomat Dap.

Superior Petty Officer Zenji Kono knew his business. As his small force of *Rikusentai* had exited the canyon, split left and right, and engaged the hostile Nambu nest, he had sent Kiichi Uchino back to the top of the lava dome to recover Iwao Yoshi's dropped light machine gun. Uchino had barely survived—the enemy gunners had raked the exposed lava dome at the first sign of movement—but made it back without injury, dragging his dead comrade's weapon with him.

Now he was lying behind a low outcropping of rock just outside the slot canyon, firing the light MG continuously. Kono had already yelled at him once to shorten his bursts or he'd warp the weapon's barrel, but in his instinct to match the ferocious output of the two heavy Nambus, Uchino had been unable to discipline his trigger finger. Kono swore aloud as he banged the fuse of his last grenade against his helmet and threw it toward the enemy position. If the light machine gun jammed, he'd lose his base of fire.

Base of fire was key. To assault an entrenched position, it was necessary to lay down a sustained covering fire under which to advance—basic infantry tactics. Engaging one heavy machine gun, let alone *two*, without having some way of keeping the enemy gunners' heads down was an exercise in suicidal futility. Zenji Kono was as willing to die for his country as the next man, but not before he'd exhausted all other options.

"Uchino!" he yelled once more. "*Shorter bursts! Shorter bursts!*"

The young seaman turned and looked at him, wild-eyed, and then resumed firing—a long, uninterrupted burst. Kono swore again and started to roll across the fifteen feet of open ground between them, but a vicious spray of Nambu slugs sent him scrambling back for cover.

The ridgetop between the slot canyon and the Nambu nest was narrow, barely forty yards wide. It sloped away sharply to either side, the opposing drops becoming precipitous twenty feet down. On each of these thinly treed shoulders, his men were pinned down, in poor cover. Without constant movement, the heavy machine guns would inevitably find them, one or two at a time, and chop them to bits.

He had to do something. Now.

"Both flanks!" he bellowed over the deafening fire. *"Sweep around and in! Sweep around and in!"*

"Fock," Mulgrew snarled, swinging his Nambu to the left. "They're on the move on my side, Web! Flankin' us at the run!"

"My side, too," Foster shouted back. He was shaking with pain, but yanked his own weapon around. "Cut 'em off, cut 'em off!"

The two heavy machine guns roared in tandem, sending glittering twin fountains of brass shell casings tumbling up through the smoke-laden air.

"Now, Uchino!" Kono yelled, lunging forward.

A half-dozen strides to his right, Uchino gasped out a single-phrase prayer, seized the light machine gun, and began to advance at an awkward run, firing from the hip. The sandbags lining the hostile gun pit jumped and shredded as the 6.5-millimeter slugs tore into them. The effect was disruptive, if not decisive. The veteran petty officer and the novice seaman received no return fire as they traversed the open ground and set up the MG behind a rotting tree stump some fifty feet ahead of their original position. To either side and slightly ahead of them, the flanking *Rikusentai* continued their respective sweeps, subjected to terrific fire from the twin Nambus.

"I need a grenade!" Kono shouted into Uchino's ear. The younger man yanked one off his battle harness and handed it over, then hunched behind his weapon. As the chatter of the light machine gun filled the air again, Kono rose onto his knees, banged the grenade against his helmet, and lobbed it as hard as he could. This time the hand bomb arced over the sandbags and fell inside the enemy nest.

But the fuse on this M-97 burned two or three seconds long instead of short. It was enough time for one of the occupants of the nest to scoop up the grenade and lob it *back*—directly at the *Rikusentai* attempting to press their sweeping maneuver on the left flank. The grenade went off as Kono counted seven . . . eight . . .

WHUMPFF!

Kono watched from beneath the rim of his helmet as four attacking *Rikusentai*—his boys—were blown back into the trees like so many mangled puppets. The Nambu fire on that flank resumed, hard on the heels of the explosion, as the remaining troops faltered.

Superior Petty Officer Zenji Kono could take no more of seeing his men decimated. There was a shallow gully running left and right between the stump and the rise to the enemy machine gun nest. With an admonition to Uchino to keep firing—in short, rapid bursts, curse you—he dove forward, rolled, and slid down into the narrow depression. In the next second, he was on his feet like a cat and sprinting toward the right flank, where the attacking sweep had also stalled.

The gully ended in a small thicket of thorn trees. From the other side of it, punctuating the incessant roar of the Nambus, came a scattering of individual shots. Kono raised an arm to protect his face and bulled headlong into the tangle of spiky branches. At least his boys on the right were still firing back.

As he plowed through the final ten feet of the thicket, automatic fire of a different pitch—higher than that of either the heavy Nambu or Uchino's light MG—caught his ear. He knew the sound well, from hard-fought campaigns in Burma and New Guinea.

Sten.

He burst out of the far side of the thicket and crashed headlong into Major Harold Horwitch, who was moving equally fast in the opposite direction. The two men bounced off each other and sprawled to the jungle floor, stunned.

Horwitch was the first to recover, clawing his way to one knee and swinging his bulldog around as one of the flanking *Rikusentai* emerged from the brush and raised his rifle. Both men fired at the same time. The Japanese infantryman's head snapped back on his shoulders as the heavy pistol slug hit him just above the left eyebrow. Horwitch jerked sideways and dropped his revolver as the Arisaka rifle bullet drilled through his right upper arm, clipping the bone. He sagged onto both knees again, and when he raised his head he was looking straight down the barrel of Zenji Kono's Luger—from less than three feet away. The Japanese petty officer was also on his knees, still reeling from their collision.

I'm dead, Horwitch thought.

Kono, evidently, agreed. *"You're dead!"* he stammered in Japanese.

Horwitch had just enough Japanese to catch the meaning of the words.

"You're dead!" Kono gasped again. *"Dead . . ."*

His jaw had slackened and his face was blank with shock. The Luger trembled in his hand and sagged off to one side.

Horwitch launched himself at his adversary, wondering desperately why the man hadn't yet fired.

"You're dead!" the petty officer shouted, eyes goggling. *"You're dead!"*

Horwitch took the words as cry of intent. For Kono they were a statement of fact.

The two veteran soldiers collided once more. Kono fell back under the weight of the heavier Horwitch, writhing and trying to bring the Luger to bear. The Englishman grabbed for the pistol with both hands, adrenaline muting the pain of his damaged arm. Kono slammed the hard heel of his left hand three times into the side of Horwitch's jaw, trying to wrench his gun arm free as he did so. The shock and confusion had vanished from his face, and he was no longer shouting.

He brought his knee up into Horwitch's groin. The major grunted, convulsed, and lost his grip on Kono's forearm. The Japanese twisted violently to one side, thrashed out from beneath the bigger man, and came to his knees again. The Luger swung up with a smooth, sure motion, leveling on Horwitch's forehead.

Yomat Dap threw the spear from a distance of eighteen feet. Its broad, leaf-shaped tip plunged into Superior Petty Officer Zenji Kono's back directly between his shoulder blades and emerged a full three feet beyond his chest. Kono arched back with a scream, dropped the Luger, and seized the six-foot shaft transfixing him with both hands. He tugged once . . . then toppled sideways, fell heavily to the jungle floor, and lay still.

Horwitch stared at Dap as the Dayak drew his parang and turned to rejoin Finian Hooke, who was moving through the brush like a dark ghost, firing intermittent bursts from his Sten gun. With each trigger pull, the muzzle flash from his weapon illuminated the jungle momentarily, here and there revealing human figures frozen in the act of clawing the air as they were struck by bullets. The dank foliage continued to shake with the throaty roar of the two heavy Nambus in the machine gun nest nearby.

Major Harold Horwitch staggered to his feet, looking around for his dropped Bulldog revolver. It was nowhere to be seen. His eyes fell on the polished German Luger lying just beyond the dead Japanese petty officer's outstretched fingertips.

Slowly, he stepped forward, bent down, and retrieved the trophy pistol that two years earlier Zenji Kono had taken from the body of his twin brother, Colonel Michael Horwitch, on the steps of the abandoned American embassy in Rangoon.

With a final look at the corpse curled around the blood-streaked spear, Horwitch gathered his strength and began to trot through the jungle after Hooke and Dap, moving up the slope toward the top of the peninsula ridge.

Chapter
Thirty-four

Joe Garth and Finian Hooke came within a hair's breadth of shooting Horwitch when he lurched out of the brush to join them in a tiny clearing overlooking the island's northern beaches. Thirty yards to the west, where the ridge sloped gently downward to a small bald, Foster and Mulgrew were still putting out a ferocious volume of fire from the captured machine gun nest. They'd succeeded in containing the simultaneous flanking sweeps of Kono's *Rikusentai*, aided on the right by the roving disruptions of Hooke, Garth, Dap, and Horwitch. Now the few remaining Japanese were clustered back on the shoulders of the ridge, trying to reorganize. The young infantrymen were having difficulty doing so. Their one infallible constant, Superior Petty Officer Zenji Kono, was nowhere to be seen.

In the dim light of predawn, on the opposite side of the bay, Horwitch could see a large mass of soldiers moving along the path from the garrison compound to the lava dome, approaching the far end of the slot canyon. Several hundred at least.

He knelt beside Hooke, breathing hard. "Have you noticed that?"

The New Zealander was scanning the northern beaches and reefs with his compact binoculars. "The Japanese reinforcements? Yes."

Garth looked down at the machine gun nest, then over the lava dome at the rapidly advancing enemy column. "They're going to be coming through that canyon like water out of a fire hose in about ten minutes," he said. "Over the top of the lava dome, too, most likely."

Horwitch grunted, gingerly probing the leaking hole in his arm. "Ruddy bothersome," he commented.

"What bothers me more," Hooke said, "is what I don't see."

"Eh?"

"The launch. The escape launch. Matalam and Du-Fourmey are not on the beach. There's some kind of vessel drifting offshore, about two miles outside the reef, but it's still too dark for me to be able to tell what it is. And it's not coming in our direction."

The New Zealander lowered his binoculars and regarded Horwitch and Garth with empty eyes. "Our back door is closed."

The twin Nambus stuttered one at a time into a brief lull, then simultaneously resumed firing.

"You all right, Major?" Garth inquired, noticing for the first time the wound in Horwitch's upper arm.

"Quite," the Englishman said, "considering the damned arm's becoming all but useless." He rose to his feet. "Alternatives, gentlemen. While Foster and Mulgrew are still able to keep what Japs there are out here pinned down."

"Let me bind up for you," Garth said, stepping forward. "I'll use a piece of your shirt sleeve."

"Another boat," Hooke suggested. "We work our way back along the shoreline somehow to the other launch." His resigned expression communicated the utter lack of faith he had in his own suggestion.

"The other launch is burning on the garrison beach," Garth responded, knotting a strip of cloth around Horwitch's bloody arm. "An exploding gasoline drum from the fuel depot fell onto it and set it on fire." He paused. "What about the plane?"

Horwitch looked at him. "What plane?"

"The observation floatplane that was tied to the dock behind the *Kaiten*. Is it still there?"

Hooke turned to face the island's mainland and brought his binoculars up to his eyes. "Still there. Still in one piece." He licked his lips. "Still on the far bloody side of the bay."

Garth nodded at Horwitch. "You're a flier, Major. You took over the controls of our transport the other day when the pilots got killed."

Horwitch grimaced. "True, I fly. And that observation plane can probably carry all six of us if we discard our equipment. But like Mr. Hooke just said—it happens to be clear on the other side of the bloody bay. And I'd need the help of at least one other man to keep it in the air—I can hardly close my right hand. Nerve damage, I expect." For the first time since Garth had known him, the Englishman looked genuinely worn-out.

Garth's smile was thin. "What choice do we have?" he demanded. "It's die here or try for the plane. Personally, I'm not too keen to be taken alive by the Japs on this island. After what we've done this morning, they're not in a good mood. How many prisoners did they behead on Bataan?"

"I suppose you'd have us all swim back to the docks," Horwitch muttered.

Joe Garth shook his head. "Perish the thought, Major. I know where there's a leaky dugout canoe, still floating." The thin smile again. "If we keep low, paddle hard, and get moving before it's full light, we just might have a one-in-ten chance of making it."

Horwitch blew out a long breath as the Nambus below suspended fire for a few seconds, then roared in sync once again. "Right," he declared. "A ruddy ingenious plan. Foolproof, I daresay." His tone was ripe with irony. "Let's go collect Sergeant Foster and Corporal Mulgrew."

*   *   *

Seaman Second Class Kiichi Uchino saw the four figures emerge from the ridgetop trees just behind the machine   gun   nest   and   make   for   the   sandbagged
emplacement at a run. At first he thought they were
Rikusentai launching a rear attack, but a blast of submachine gun fire from the lead figure kicked dirt up into
his face and changed his mind. The volume of fire from
the gun pit redoubled—most of it, it seemed to Uchino,
concentrated in *his* direction.

The attack wasn't working. He rolled back from his
light Nambu, abandoning it, and sprinted for the slot
canyon. They needed reinforcements, heavier weapons.
Kono hadn't reappeared after his charge into the thorn
trees, and Uchino had the sickening feeling that his superior petty officer was dead. If Kono couldn't prevail,
none of them could. They needed help.

He ducked behind one of the large boulders near the
entrance to the canyon. It was hard to believe he'd managed to run nearly thirty yards without being shot. Panting, he stared from the canyon entrance to the enemy
nest and back again, unsure whether or not to chance
the last fifteen feet of open ground.

While he was debating, the first *Rikusentai* reinforcement came out of the canyon entrance at a lumbering
trot. Instantly, the twin Nambus opened up. The man
was thrown back against the wall of the lava dome, the
barrage of heavy slugs shredding him like a lump of
beef. He bounced off the rock face, flopped forward,
and landed facedown six feet from Uchino, his torn
flesh quivering.

He was wearing the miraculously undamaged triple-
tank backpack of a Type 93 nitrogen-charged flamethrower.

"What do you mean you're not coming?" Horwitch
demanded as Mulgrew let up on the trigger of his
Nambu.

"Just what I said, sir," the swarthy Australian replied,
squinting through the cordite smoke. "Web might've

been able to hobble down to the beach with our help, if the bloody launch had shown up—but there ain't no way he can make it down this incline and across the whole bloody bay to that plane. So here's where we'll stay."

"Sergeant Foster can't walk," Horwitch argued, "but you can. There's no point in throwing away your life, man. Foster will agree with me. The troops you've got bottled up in the canyon right now are only a small advance party. The majority of the reinforcements are ten minutes away on the far side of the bay. We've got time to slip down to Garth's dugout and make for the plane while it's still fairly dark."

"He's right, Mick," Foster grunted, his face drawn with pain. "I can keep 'em jammed up inside that canyon for a while yet. If they come over the top of the lava dome, I can sweep it clean. Buy you lots of time."

"Yeah, sure," Mulgrew said, scowling. He lit a cigarette, gazing through the sights of his Nambu. "And then what?"

"Sergeant Foster is a legitimate casualty of war," Horwitch persisted. "Since he's no longer mobile, his best prospect is to surrender before this position is overrun. He's in uniform. There's a reasonable chance that the Japanese will remember they are obligated under the Geneva convention to treat wounded enemy combatants decently."

Joe Garth cut his eyes at him. Horwitch was far too experienced a Pacific theater campaigner to believe that.

Mulgrew snorted smoke. "With all due respect, Major," he growled, "don't make me laugh."

"It's better than the chance he'll be able to survive getting down the slope to the dugout under fire," Horwitch said.

There was a deafening rattle as both Foster and Mulgrew opened up on the entrance to the slot canyon. A small knot of *Rikusentai* had emerged and tried to dash for cover. Two of them fell; the others backpedaled hurriedly into the shelter of the rock crevice. A few rifle shots cracked out of the canyon and zipped overhead.

"He's right again, Mick," Foster said, grimacing and shifting his shattered knee with one hand. "If we all go, there'll be nobody to hold them here. They'll bloody well catch us all. Fock it—I'll take a fifty-fifty chance they won't kill me and maybe a Jap doc will tend to this knee, if that's all that's on the bloody table right now."

Mulgrew looked at him. "So you figure they'll honor your surrender, eh? Fine. I'll surrender with you, mate." He shifted his gaze to Horwitch. "After all, they signed the bloody Geneva convention, didn't they?"

"Hell," Foster said, managing a grin, "they'll probably give us a steak dinner."

Horwitch straightened. "Corporal Mulgrew, I order you to accompany us to the dugout canoe and attempt the crossing to that plane."

Mulgrew looked back through the sights of his Nambu, drew hard on his cigarette, and blew a long stream of smoke out into the night.

"Not bloody likely," he growled.

Seaman Second Class Kiichi Uchino's hands were shaking as he buckled on the triple-tank backpack of the flamethrower. Fully charged with nitrogen and fuel, the unit was heavy—well over fifty pounds. The flame gun was a yard-long section of steel pipe with a cartridge-fired igniter at its nozzle tip. Uchino remembered enough of his limited training in the weapon's function to check that the igniter—a small, rotating metal drum resembling a revolver's cylinder—was fully loaded with blank shells. Depressing the trigger lever would fire one of the cartridges, igniting the stream of liquid fuel as it jetted out of the nozzle.

He could not take his eyes off the bloodied corpse of the man who'd worn the unit only moments before.

The reinforcement party of *Rikusentai* had crowded up as close to the entrance of the slot canyon as they dared, trying to maintain a thin barrage of rifle fire. Periodically, the twin Nambus would roar in unison, turning the canyon mouth into a whirlwind of lava dust and rock chips and temporarily driving the soldiers back from the opening.

Kiichi Uchino thought about his friend Iwao Yoshi and the gruff, kindly veteran petty officer Zenji Kono, and turned away from the body of the soldier who'd been killed carrying the flamethrower out of the slot canyon. He steeled himself. The torch, quite literally, had been passed to him.

May I earn my place at Yasukuni, he thought fleetingly, and lunged out from behind the sheltering boulder toward the right flank.

Garth was in the front of the dugout canoe, his paddle at the ready. Behind him sat Horwitch, who had positioned himself so that he would be able to stroke with his one good arm using a short piece of flat driftwood. Yomat Dap was standing in the knee-deep water beside the canoe, preparing to climb in. Finian Hooke was steadying the craft by the stern.

"What the hell are you waiting for?" Horwitch demanded, half turning.

Hooke didn't answer right away, and when he did, there was an odd quality to his voice, a hollowness that made Joe Garth twist around and look back over his shoulder. It was the verbal equivalent of the expression the New Zealander carried perpetually in his eyes—an unsettling mixture of emptiness and pure hate.

"You know full well the Japanese aren't going to take Foster and Mulgrew alive," he said.

Horwitch turned all the way around. "Probably not. But someone has to fly out of here and inform Allied command of the threat posed by Yarizuma's *Sen-Toku*, and since I'm the only flier, that someone has to be me. And I need help to fly, so I need at least one other man to accompany me. The information is more important than Foster, or Mulgrew—or you or me or any single one of us. Foster would hold us up, hamper our escape. Mulgrew refuses to go. I don't want to leave them, but I've made a decision based on military necessity. Someone has to carry this message out of here. Do you understand me, Mr. Hooke?"

The New Zealander stared at him, the flames from the burning oil slick in front of the submarine pen reflecting in his empty eyes.

"Of course," he said. "I understand."

He leaned into the canoe's stern and gave it a hard shove. The dugout lurched forward and slid out over the black water. Off balance, both Garth and Horwitch teetered and grabbed for the gunwales, barely averting a capsize.

When they steadied the craft and looked back toward shore, Finian Hooke and Yomat Dap were gone.

"Gave old Mad Harry a pass, didn't you?" Mulgrew muttered around his cigarette. He inserted a fresh ammunition strip into his Nambu and racked the breech mechanism. "A fifty-fifty chance that the Nippers will let you surrender, you says."

Foster gazed at the entrance of the slot canyon over the barrel of his machine gun. "What's the difference?" he said. "I ain't going anywhere on this chewed-up peg, like I told you. No point in bein' pissy about it. And he's right: somebody's got to get a message to the brass about that fokkin' Jap sub, those U.S.-painted planes." He paused. "I just wish you'd get the hell outta here, Mick. You can still catch up to 'em."

Mulgrew tensed behind his machine gun as his eye caught movement in the canyon mouth once again. "Maybe later, Web," he said.

Foster gave a short laugh. "You always was a contrary bugger, you know? I don't suppose you're really interested in tryin' to surrender to these little bastards, either, eh?"

"Like I told Mad Harry just now," Mulgrew said, squinting through his gunsight, "not bloody likely."

Without warning, the Japanese began to pour out of the canyon in a flood—right, left, and center—firing as they came.

"Me neither," Foster shouted, just before he and Mulgrew squeezed the triggers of their Nambus and the air filled with smoke and flame and shattering noise once again.

It was a banzai charge. Lieutenant Junior Grade Genbei Miyama, the young officer in charge of the first group of *Rikusentai* reinforcements to traverse the slot canyon, had so ordered. The command had been passed by whispers through the crowded ranks huddled behind him in the narrow crevice: there would be no stopping once the attack had commenced. The hostile machine gun emplacement would be overwhelmed by persistence and sheer weight of numbers, regardless of the human cost.

An older, wiser officer would have left the job to a mortar team.

Genbei Miyama, samurai sword drawn and brandished high, was the first man out of the canyon mouth. *"Banzaaiiiii!"* he screamed. Six running steps later, he was the first man killed when the twin Nambus opened up. The *Rikusentai* behind him continued to spill out of the slot canyon, trampling his body into the hard ground.

They fell like wheat before the scythe, the heavy machine gun fire slicing here and there, cutting off—as before—the attempted flanking runs, and mowing down those who chose to attack straight up the slope. Hurled grenades went off in front of and to either side of the Nambu nest; dropped grenades exploded in the midst of other onrushing *Rikusentai*, adding to the chaos. The two enemy gunners sawed their weapons back and forth, staggering their reloads so that at least one Nambu was always firing.

On the far right flank of the battle, behind a little thicket of thorn trees, Kiichi Uchino was kneeling on the ground, panting. The flamethrower tanks were weighing him down terribly; the flame gun lay on the ground beside him, its short connector hose looping back to the unit's gas valves. He was staring at the body of Superior Petty Officer Zenji Kono, curled around the hideous spear that had impaled it as a needle does a collected insect. Kono was staring right back at him, his eyes clouded in death. Uchino gagged once, leaned forward, and threw up.

When he was finished, he wiped his mouth on his sleeve, picked up the flame gun, got shakily to his feet, and began to trot up the slope toward the enemy machine gun nest. It was still dark, but through the trees he could see the muzzle flashes of the twin Nambus.

He had them by the right rear flank. The jungle would conceal his approach until he was less than twenty feet from the emplacement's low bulwark of sandbags. Well within flamethrower range.

And the enemy gunners would be looking in the opposite direction.

FRRAAAAAAAAT!
"Right side, Web! Right side!"
"I see 'em!"
FRRRAAAAAAAAAAT! FRRAAAAAAAAAAAT!
"Look out! Grenade!"
"It's short, it's short!"
"The hell it is—"
WHUMPFF!
FRRRAAAAAAAAAAAAAAAAAAT!
POWPOWPOWPOW!
FRRAAAAAAAAAAAAAAAAAAAAAAAAAAT!
"Mick?"
FRRAAAAAAAAAAAAAAAAAT!
"Mick?"
FRRAAAAAAAAAAAAAAAAAAAAAAAAAAAAAAAT!

The charging *Rikusentai* were a mere ten feet from the machine gun nest, about to surge over the frontal bulwark, when the searing dragon's tongue of the flamethrower lashed out from the trees on the right rear flank.

The burning gasoline shot in a wide jet over the top of the emplacement and enveloped the front rank of Japanese as they pressed forward, fixed bayonets poised to strike. With horrific screams they fell back, human fireballs, thrashing and tumbling down the incline into their stunned comrades.

Foster ripped off a burst from his Sten as three *Riku-sentai* vaulted over his side of the nest, bayonets driving for him. The volley took them high across their faces, killing them instantly; momentum carried them forward so that they flopped on top of him, burying him under several hundred pounds of warm, stinking flesh. Two more *Rikusentai* raised their rifles to bayonet him as he lay pinned. He felt the first blade go in just under his rib cage—and then a great tidal wave of heat and flame washed the two Japanese soldiers away with an ugly, whooshing roar.

Foster struggled up onto one elbow, pushing aside one of the bodies smothering him. Gasping for breath, he clawed his side arm out of its holster and twisted his head around in time to see Finian Hooke leap from the rear of the machine gun nest to the top of the front bulwark, flamethrower tanks strapped to his back, and flame gun nozzle pointing downslope. The New Zealander squeezed the weapon's trigger lever; there was a sharp *crack* like a pistol shot, and another brilliant torrent of fire inundated the battleground. Over the roaring sound, incredibly, Foster was certain he could hear Hooke laughing.

And then he was gone, leaping off the sandbags into the night, throwing fire like a pagan god. Foster turned his head again and another *Rikusentai* infantryman was there, towering over him. The muzzle of the enemy soldier's rifle was immense, a bottomless pit.

Foster jerked up his pistol and fired. So did the Japanese.

The last thing Sergeant Web Foster saw in his mind's eye before everything went black was the bullet coming out of the Arisaka, pushed by a fiery bubble of expanding gases.

Finian Hooke stalked down the charred, flaming ridge between the Nambu nest and the mouth of the slot canyon, unleashing cascades of liquid fire left and right. All around him, men were burning—crumpled into motionless heaps on the ground or staggering blindly off into the brush. Screams of agony reverberated off the walls of the lava dome.

Hooke was still laughing as he approached the entrance to the canyon, spraying fire. Panic-stricken *Rikusentai* crowded into the crevice ahead of him. To Finian Hooke, every one of them looked exactly like the Japanese paratroop lieutenant who had ordered the gang rape and murder of his wife and daughter.

Seeing that lieutenant burn, time and time again, was cause enough for laughter.

Hooke pursued the *Rikusentai* into the canyon. They were bottlenecked in the narrow passage, tearing at each other in their frantic efforts to put distance between themselves and the awful death lurking at their heels. Hooke paused, savoring the moment—and a rifle bullet slammed into his thigh from above. He bellowed in pain, swung the flame gun straight up, and swept the top edges of the slot canyon with fire. More Japanese had arrived from the mainland, swarming over the top of the lava dome.

Hooke kept the trigger lever depressed, jerked the flame gun down, and hosed the retreating *Rikusentai* with burning gasoline. The screams of the damned echoed throughout the narrow crevice above the flamethrower's saurian hiss. Wildly contorting bodies, wreathed in flame, came floundering back toward Hooke. Surrounding him in a frenzied dance of fire.

It was beautiful.

He was consumed by a black joy. The cathartic ecstasy of revenge utterly fulfilled.

A single rifle bullet, fired from above, hit the left-hand fuel tank of the flamethrower backpack.

In the next blinding second, Finian Hooke knew what it was to stand naked on the surface of the sun.

Chapter
Thirty-five

Joe Garth shot the first two *Rikusentai* who attempted to rush onto the dock after hearing the floatplane's engine cough into life. The Arisaka he'd picked up felt strange in his hands—too slender and light—but it was accurate. He retreated to the end of the dock as Horwitch ruddered the aircraft toward the middle of the bay with his one good hand, shouting at him to jump on.

A dozen more *Rikusentai* emerged from the scorched trees, yelling and firing their weapons. Garth stepped over a body, dropped to one knee, and cracked off three quick shots, deftly working the rifle's manual bolt. Three of the advancing soldiers fell.

Garth dropped the Arisaka, took two running steps, and dove toward the taxiing floatplane. He hit the dark water near the front of the right pontoon, grabbed for a strut, and hauled himself onto the float as it swept along.

"*Go!*" he bellowed at Horwitch, clawing his way up into the tiny cockpit.

"Help me!" the major shouted back. "Depress the throttle—here!"

Garth shoved the lever forward as a flurry of rifle

slugs punctured the plane's unarmored skin. One of the cockpit windows blew out in an explosion of glass. The roar of the engine leaped an octave and the aircraft bucked forward, vibrating.

"Grab the bloody stick!" Horwitch gasped. "Straighten her, straighten her!"

Garth seized the control column with both hands. Spray erupted through the whirling propeller, dashing against the forward windscreen and spurting in through the broken side window, as the floatplane gathered speed.

Two sudden concussions shook the plane. A geyser of white water appeared just forward of the starboard wing, and the aircraft skewed sideways. The control column twisted like a live snake in Joe Garth's hands.

"Mortar shells!" Horwitch panted. "Steady the stick, confound it! Steady the bloody stick!"

"I've got it!" Garth replied, exerting all his strength. The aircraft continued to bog down.

Horwitch punched the throttle lever all the way forward. The floatplane burst out of the spray cloud, its twin pontoons skimming over the very tops of the low swells. The dark cliffs on the peninsula side of the bay began to grow with terrifying swiftness in the cockpit windscreen.

"Back!" Horwitch gasped. *"Pull back on the stick!"*

Together, he and Garth forced the vibrating column backward. The nose of the aircraft lifted, the floats bounced twice more—and then the onrushing cliffs dropped away, replaced by stars wheeling across a velvet black sky. Streaks of green-and-red light shot across the field of view, crisscrossing the clear air in front of the plane.

"Tracers," Joe Garth panted.

"This way," Horwitch called hoarsely, guiding his hands. "We'll—we'll bank left . . . away from those guns on the mainland."

The floatplane dipped its port wing and veered off to the west, moving out over the open ocean. Below, Garth could plainly see the burning oil slick in front of the sub pen. The conning tower of the destroyed *Sen-Toku* was silhouetted in the midst of the flames, a sagging black monolith.

They continued the wide bank to port, tracing an arc that carried the small aircraft back over land. As they bypassed the lava dome by less than a quarter mile, a fractured seam of white-orange light, snaking across the top of the immense rock formation, became apparent in the darkness. Smoke and fumes simmered up from it, eerily lit from below by some unseen conflagration . . . as if the earth had cracked open and allowed the smoldering incandescence of hell to leak upward.

"The slot canyon," Garth called. "Something's burning inside." He squinted through the port window. "There are *Rikusentai* all over the top of the lava dome—hundreds of them. Moving past the machine gun nest, too."

"I don't suppose you can see Mulgrew or Foster," Horwitch said, after a pause.

Garth shook his head. "No."

"Hooke or Dap?"

"No."

Horwitch looked down and bumped the engine throttle forward with the heel of his injured hand. The muscles at the corners of his mouth tightened slightly.

"Bloody hell," he muttered.

"I—I think I'm going to be sick," the young *Rikusentai* seaman said.

His comrade, who at nineteen fancied himself a hard case, shifted his rifle to his opposite elbow and knelt beside the body lying at the edge of the trees behind the silenced machine gun emplacement. "It's war," he declared, trying to put a mature rasp in his choirboy's voice. "You have to get used to it."

He squatted down, reached out, and turned over the head that lay three feet to the side of the corpse to which it had recently been attached. "Ugh!" he exclaimed. "I know him. It's Uchino, from Kono's platoon."

"Don't pick it up, don't pick it up," the first seaman implored.

Ignoring him, the second *Rikusentai* lifted the head by the hair. "Incredible," he said. "I wonder what hit Kiichi—gunfire or shrapnel. Look how cleanly his neck's been cut, like a surgeon did it with a scalpel."

The first *Rikusentai* turned pale, turned away, and vomited into the leaf litter.

The first rays of the rising sun were just escaping over the horizon to the east when the floatplane rose above a low cloud and came within visual range of a small land mass, a dull green blot on the shimmering expanse of predawn Leyte Gulf. The usual collection of isolated thunderheads decorated the vast seascape, rising here and there like vaporous Roman columns.

"Minglaat," Horwitch called, pointing with his good hand. After nearly two hours of flying, he no longer even attempted to raise his damaged right arm. Garth, jammed into the cockpit with him and helping to control the plane, nodded briefly. Fatigue was overtaking them both, Horwitch more so due to loss of blood. Garth glanced at him—his complexion looked pale and waxen in the silvery light of dawn.

"Hang on, Major," the UDT man said. "We're nearly there."

"With . . . any luck," Horwitch replied, "we'll be able . . . to set this Japanese-marked floater down in the . . . supply harbor before the island's ack-ack crews open up on us."

"With any luck," Garth agreed dubiously. It was far more likely that the gunners would think their low-flying aircraft was coming in for a suicide run. But maybe if they touched down well offshore and began to taxi slowly toward the—

The cockpit control panel disintegrated in a series of ear-shattering explosions. The forward windscreen blew out, peppering Garth and Horwitch with shards of glass, as the floatplane jinked violently to port and rolled up on its wingtip. The slipstream screamed into the interior of the fuselage, whipping up a choking maelstrom of metal fragments and smoke.

The floatplane rolled over 180 degrees, nosed down, and went into a spin. The centrifugal force pinned Garth against the side of the cockpit, with Horwitch's full weight on top of him. Something sticky was running into his eyes, blinding him. In desperation, he tried to shove the control column away, to center it. It was futile.

"Major!" he yelled.

There was no response.

The aircraft was falling out of the sky like a wobbling top, generating forces that wrenched Garth this way and that without ever releasing him. His head slammed back into the starboard side panel, the impact nearly knocking him unconscious. Once again, he tried to force the control stick back into a central position. This time, through the warm flood obstructing his vision, he saw Horwitch's legs flex, his feet move against the cockpit rudder pedals.

The violent rotation of the world outside the aircraft seemed to slow. Garth felt Horwitch apply pressure to the stick with his good arm. The bloodstained legs of his trousers flexed again . . . and quite suddenly the floatplane rolled out of its spin and leveled off. Long tongues of flame, vibrating like ragged strips of orange cloth, licked back into the cockpit from beneath the engine cowling.

"Major!" Joe Garth yelled again, pushing the Englishman upright and trying to hold the stick back as the yellow-white beaches of Minglaat came up above the nose of the stricken aircraft.

There was a tremendous jolt, an eruption of spray that smothered everything in an overwhelming whiteness— and then the crushing shock of cold salt water slamming into the cockpit interior.

"Tallyho!" Flight Lieutenant Simon Parrish exulted, banking the RAAF Beaufighter over Minglaat Harbor. "How's that then, Pidgey?"

"Bloody gorgeous, Guv," Warrant Officer Alvin Pidgeon replied over the intercom. "Looks like I owes you that ale, sir, once we gets back from this patrol."

"I told you I'd find us a kill today, didn't I?" Parrish

went on, basking in the afterglow of the successful attack. "That damned Nip flew right into our backyard, the impudent bugger."

"He bloody well did that, sir. Good on ye."

Parrish was comfortable with the casual exchange. In the space of two weeks, after a touchy start, he and the cockney radioman had become fast friends.

"Good on yourself, Pidgey," he radioed back, eyeing the smoking ring of white foam on the water outside Minglaat's southern barrier reef, where the wreckage of the Japanese plane he'd just shot down was sinking.

What was left of the aircraft was now six feet underwater and starting to whirl slowly as it descended. The canopy and entire right side of the cockpit had been sheared off, along with the starboard wing. Holding his breath, Joe Garth seized the collar of Horwitch's battle jacket and yanked, trying to pull the Englishman's limp body free. It was no good. Horwitch's legs were trapped under the crushed forward console.

Lungs bursting, Garth grappled frantically around the major's thighs, trying to find some way of working them free. He could feel his eardrums bending inward, starting to needle with pain, as the wreckage sank deeper and deeper. Bracing his feet on the edge of the pilot's seat, he grabbed Horwitch under the arms and heaved with all his strength.

No good.

With a despairing sob, Garth thrashed his way free of the wreckage and took two hard strokes upward, on the verge of blacking out. One more desperate pull and he was at the surface, gasping in air, blinking up at an early-morning sky so vividly blue it hurt his eyes. Somewhere far off, he thought he could hear the throaty pulse of a marine engine.

He took a deep breath and ducked his head under, looking back down.

Beneath his pedaling legs, like the mangled carcass of a broken-winged gull, the wreckage of the floatplane was continuing its slow spiral downward, starkly pale against the deep blue of the abyss. In the mangled cockpit Garth could see Horwitch, his arms floating out to either side, drifting down with the entrapping debris.

He watched without breathing, numb, until the wreckage was nothing more than a small white pinwheel far below, turning languidly in the azure depths. Then, as the thrumming of the fast-approaching PT boat's engines filled his ears, he lifted his head, looked toward Minglaat, and raised his arm to wave.

Chapter Thirty-six

In the cramped officers' mess of the *I-403*, Ensign Hajimi Ona was writing a final letter to his parents. He had been joined by the other two *Kaiten* pilots, Ensigns Kazu Yonehara and Hitoshi Wada, who were making some last-minute adjustments to their wills. Ona was having trouble concentrating. His pen hand was unsteady and there was a constant dull roaring inside his head, as if two large seashells had been clamped against his ears. A slight case of nerves, he told himself over and over again . . . but it was more than that. It was pure, unrelenting, paralyzing fear.

He was all but consumed by it.

Not so Yonehara and Wada.

"Hitoshi and I have decided to leave all our accumulated back pay to the new *Kaiten* training center at Hikari," Yonehara declared buoyantly. "Once we have been reincarnated at Yasukuni, we will have the pleasure of seeing some of our meager earthly wealth used to continue the fight against the Americans and Europeans." He paused, smiling. "Would you care to join us and do the same?"

Ona shook his head slowly. "No. My family is poor. My parents will need all the money I have saved."

"What about your death bonus?"

"They will need that, too."

Wada leaned across the table and weighed in: "Don't forget that you'll get your posthumous promotion, as well—two full ranks. The compensation money that goes to your family will be based on that increased grade. You can't spare even a little for Hikari?"

Ona raised his eyes and fixed them on Wada's. "They'll need all of it, Hitoshi," he said firmly.

Wada looked at Yonehara and shrugged. Yonehara shrugged back. "Well, suit yourself," Wada remarked, slumping back in his chair. He tapped his pen on his will, whistling airily through his teeth, as Ona bent over his letter again.

Tap tap.

Tap tap tap tap.

Ona looked up and glared at him.

"Hajimi," Wada said, smiling sympathetically, "is there something wrong?"

Is there something wrong. In that instant, a flood of thoughts spontaneously organized themselves in Ona's troubled mind.

He had volunteered for *Kaiten* duty, knowing full well that it would result in his own death, and had made it through the many months of grueling training in Toku-yama Bay with relatively high marks. As one of the *Kaiten* service's most promising pilots, he had been assigned to the greatest undersea weapon his country had ever produced, the *Sen-Toku,* under the command of one of Japan's greatest submariners, Captain Toshiko Yarizuma. Ona was a young tiger of the Rising Sun, one of the elite.

He had made arrangements to have his personal effects shipped to his parents from Yokohama. He had written his last will and testament. He had saved fingernail clippings and a lock of his long hair, and packaged them—along with a recent photograph of himself—for delivery to his parents after his death, so that they could be offered in remembrance at the family shrine before being cremated and buried in the homeland.

He had accepted the *wakizashi*—the traditional short sword of the samurai—from no less a personage than Vice Admiral Shigeyoshi Miwa, new commander of the Imperial Sixth Fleet, at a ceremony in Yokohama, just before the *I-403* had sailed out of Japanese waters. He had drunk the vice admiral's sake, which was known to have been a gift from the emperor himself to his brave *tokko* warriors.

He had prepared his *Kaiten* for its intended purpose, checking and rechecking its various systems, going over attack procedures time and time again.

The previous night, he had toasted the emperor in silence with a glass of water—the symbol of purity.

He had secured the ashes of his friend Ensign Isamu Matsura, killed in training at Otsujima, beneath the seat of his *Kaiten*, so that they could take the final ride together.

Ensign Hajimi Ona looked up at Wada, who was tapping his pen against his cheek and studying him openly with an insolent smile playing on his lips. Slowly, Ona straightened in his chair and leveled what he hoped was an implacable gaze at his fellow *Kaiten* pilot.

"No, Hitoshi," he said quietly. "There is nothing wrong."

Lieutenant Mamoru Takagi was the leader of the three *Seiran* fighter-bomber pilots—a quiet, serious young man of twenty-four. In the damp chill of the *Sen-Toku*'s deck hangar, Flight Technician Kameo Fujita, up to his elbows as usual in Sekio Yagi's *Ohka*, watched over his shoulder as Takagi spoke in low tones to his wingmen, Ensigns Matome Fukaya and Sokichi Honjo. The lieutenant was smiling, relaxed; bonding with his fellow *tokko* pilots, infusing them with some of his own apparently limitless natural composure. This in the final hours of their earthly lives.

Fujita turned back to the *Ohka*, squinting in the poor light. It was not enough that the watertight hangar—

loaded with three *Seiran* in addition to the *Ohka*—was cramped beyond belief, that it was so cold he could see his breath; he had to work half blind, as well. It was just one more unbearable complication he was forced to endure. And could he be answerable to a humane, sympathetic officer like Takagi? No. He had to suffer under the abusive dictates of the marginally more senior lieutenant Yagi.

Fujita had grown to loathe the emotionally unstable Sekio Yagi with every fiber of his being. Not a day had gone by out of the past hundred that the *Ohka* pilot had not berated, screamed at, hit, or otherwise tormented him for nothing more than doing his level best under the most trying of circumstances.

A dull metallic boom echoed through the giant submarine above the steady humming of the electric motors. Somewhere forward or aft, a spare drive shaft or perhaps a torpedo was being moved with a chain hoist. Such activity usually accounted for random noises like that—and usually generated a reprimand from Captain Yarizuma, who did not appreciate loud metallic sound signatures being sent out to the waiting ears of any enemy hydrophone operators who might happen to be in the area.

Takagi and his wingmen shared another laugh, and the sound of their quiet mirth echoed around the dim interior of the hangar. Fujita looked enviously over his shoulder again. One after the other, the three *Seiran* pilots, still laughing, began to descend through the narrow hatch that led back down into the main hull of the submarine. Fujita chewed his lip. How nice it must be to feel that sense of brotherhood with a superior officer.

That was what military service should be—a brotherhood of warriors. Not some kind of enforced confinement with a shrieking petty tyrant like Sekio Yagi. The more he thought about it, the more unjust it seemed.

In short order, brooding on Yagi, Kameo Fujita built up an internal rage so intense that his hands began to shake. After working for a few more minutes, he shut the engine cowling on the *Ohka,* and when he did he slammed it down with a bang that reverberated through the cold, dank hangar like a cymbal clash.

Lieutenant Hanku Katsura knocked lightly on the doorjamb of Yarizuma's quarters and waited.

"Come."

The executive officer pushed aside the privacy curtain and stepped into the cramped living space. "Hourly report, Captain."

Yarizuma, sitting propped up in his bunk, set aside the Shinto prayer book he had been reading. "Proceed, Exec."

"Hydrophone officer reports only one contact in the past forty minutes, sir," Katsura said. "Single engine, low rpm, little cavitation—moving slowly and continuously to the south. Rapidly becoming inaudible."

"Fishing vessel," Yarizuma commented, "chancing the weather. Of no concern to us."

"Yes, sir." Katsura rubbed his tired eyes briefly. "All attack preparations have been completed. *Seiran, Kaiten,* and *Ohka* pilots report that their craft are ready to be deployed at your command."

Yarizuma nodded. "Very well."

"The boat is maintaining a speed of five knots at a depth of ninety feet. We continue to follow the forty-fathom curve."

Yarizuma blinked slowly. "Present position?"

"One hundred and ten nautical miles east-northeast of Lewes, Delaware," Katsura said. "We will need to decrease our running depth soon, Captain, if we intend to leave the forty-fathom curve and enter Delaware Bay. The continental shelf shallows rapidly from this point on."

"Proceed on this course for another hour, Katsura," Yarizuma ordered, "and increase speed to seven knots. We will jog to the west just before midnight, and make our way into the mouth of the bay."

Katsura's facial muscles twitched. "How far inshore do you intend to penetrate, sir? There will certainly be mines, listening stations, sonobuoys. . . ."

A rip of a smile unfolded slowly across Yarizuma's face. "Just far enough to pick quality marine targets for our *Kaiten*," he said, "and to ensure that our *Seiran* and *Ohka* will reach Washington."

As the *I-403* continued to glide through the black Atlantic waters off Cape May, the sun was unleashing its full early-morning radiance over the tiny Philippine island of Minglaat. A small crowd of sailors, Seabees, and other assorted personnel with business at the supply depot had gathered outside the old colonial warehouse that served as the island's command post. Several officers, accompanied by a handful of marines wearing sentry armbands, were in the process of dispersing the assembly.

"That's it, that's it," a tall lieutenant barked, waving his hand. "Show's over! You men get back to your assignments. Those supplies still need to be moved, and the war ain't bein' put on hold while you stand around gawkin'. Break it up! Let's go!"

"Goddamn crazy Nips," one Seabee muttered to another as they began to shuffle off toward the supply depot. "Thank Christ that Aussie Beaufighter was flyin' cover for us. That Jap plane was headed right for the ships in the harbor."

"Or maybe for us on the beach," his companion replied. "Lotta ordnance in that there depot."

"Lotta ordnance," the first Seabee agreed.

In a back room of the command post, Joe Garth was sitting—or rather sagging—in a plain wooden chair, supported on either side by a pair of burly marines. His forehead had been creased by a machine gun bullet during the Beaufighter's initial attack on the floatplane, but he had survived the subsequent crash landing unscathed. He had not, however, escaped injury upon being picked up by the PT boat that had raced to the scene. The sailors who had yanked him from the water had proceeded to beat him black-and-blue. Only the captain's intervention had stopped them from killing him on the spot.

"I . . . told you," Garth muttered, blood clotting on his smashed lips, "I'm a . . . UDT man . . . Gunner's Mate Joseph Garth . . . surviving member of . . . a six-man squad from Team One . . . led by Lieutenant Charlton Randall. . . ."

"Bullshit!" erupted one of the PT boat sailors who had helped drag Garth up to the CP from the harbor docks. "You're one o' them half-Japoon types, tryin' to save your skin! So you speak American—so what? So does Tokyo Rose! That don't change the shape o' your eyes, the color o' your hair—or the fact that you just popped out of a fuckin' airplane with a big fat red meatball on the side!" He waved a .45-caliber pistol in Garth's face.

"Lieutenant," Garth said hoarsely, turning to the ranking officer in the room, "I . . . haven't got . . . time to waste . . . talking to this moron. I have crucial infor—"

The agitated PT boat sailor cut him off by stepping forward and whacking him across the mouth with the barrel of his automatic. "Bullshit! *Bullshit!*" He glanced at the officer. "Don't believe him, Lieutenant Miller! I mean—*look* at him! Kinda slanty eyes, high cheekbones, straight black hair—just like a Jap! No uniform, no dog tags, and some goddamned cock-and-bull story about giant submarines attackin' Washington!" He stared back at Garth. "Washington ain't even on the ocean, you Nip bastard."

"Washington State is," one of the marines commented. The sailor looked at him in confusion.

Garth shook his head wearily. "I can't believe this. . . ." He looked up at Miller again. "Sir, I've got American Indian blood. . . . I'm part Apache . . . from West Texas."

"Bullshit!" the sailor screamed in his face. *"You're a fuckin' Jap suicider! Or a—a—a—a spy! Fess up, you yellow sonofabitch!"*

"Shut up, Sweeney," the lieutenant said finally. "I've heard enough of your noise." He gazed uncertainly at Garth. "I'm only the interim commander of this base,

temporarily filling in until Lieutenant Commander
Fletcher gets back tonight from a staff meeting aboard
the USS *Nashville*." He paused. "Personally, I think
you're a fast-talking Jap infiltrator who happened to get
shot down before he could land and start whatever mis-
chief he had planned. I just don't have any solid proof."

Garth shook his head in exasperation. "Sure . . . sure.
I'm an infiltrator. An infiltrator who . . . flew up to a
heavily defended island . . . in broad daylight . . . in a
clearly marked . . . Japanese plane."

"*Ha!*" Sweeney shouted triumphantly.

"Shut *up*, I said!" the lieutenant barked, wheeling on
the sailor. As Sweeney backed down, chastened, Miller
regarded Garth again. "Look, we've got Nip planes diving on our ships, Nip planes strafing and bombing the
hell out of our land bases, and God knows how many
Nip troops running around trying to kill us on all these
goddamn islands. You've got a story to tell; I've got a
supply depot to run and defend. I'm neither qualified
nor inclined to interrogate a suspected enemy
infiltrator—I've got my own goddamn problems to
worry about.

"Fortunately, however, there's an intelligence officer
on Minglaat at the moment, in transit between Peleliu
and Leyte. Complications such as you, my friend, are
right up his alley, so I've sent for him. He can deal
with you." Miller glanced at his watch. "He should be
here soon."

"He's here now," a voice said from outside the open
door. Garth raised his drooping head, blinking through
the fresh blood that had begun to trickle into his eyes.
The bullet crease in his forehead was leaking again, and
it was difficult to see. There was a sound of boot heels
on tile, and the blurry figure of a tall man entered the
room.

"Is this him?" the voice asked.

"Yes, it is, sir," Lieutenant Miller replied. "All
yours."

Joe Garth blinked upward, trying to clear his vision,
as the tall newcomer moved closer.

"What you gonna do to 'im, sir?" Sweeney blurted, unable to contain himself. "Pull his damn fingernails out, like them Japoons done to some of our boys they caught?"

The tall figure half turned. "Who the devil is this?"

"Seaman Sweeney, sir," Miller answered. "Crewman off the *PT-143*. His boat picked up the prisoner after his plane went down outside the southern reef."

"*Jap* plane," Sweeney corrected. "You need anything, sir? Pair o' pliers or somethin'?"

"Yes, I do," the tall officer said. He turned back toward Joe Garth. "I need a medical corpsman in here immediately, with full kit. I need a bottle of Lieutenant Commander Fletcher's excellent bourbon, which you'll find in the lower right-hand drawer of his office desk, and two glasses. I need hot coffee and a tray of food. And I need it *ASAP,* Seaman Sweeney."

"Wh-what?" Sweeney replied.

The tall figure jerked around. *"Move, damn you!"*

As the seaman fled the room, the newcomer stepped forward and carefully began to dab the blood out of Joe Garth's eyes with a handkerchief. His vision no longer obstructed, Garth blinked hard and focused on the face in front of him.

"Easy, Joe," Major Quentin Barnaby said quietly. "Let's get you taken care of."

Chapter Thirty-seven

United States Army Air Forces captain Hiram Gant swallowed the dregs of his coffee and set the mug in a busing tray on his way out of the officers' wardroom. It was cold in late October on the Chesapeake Bay shore just south of Annapolis, Maryland—particularly at four o'clock in the morning. A biting wind was blowing across the dark runways of Salter Field, the temporary air base the USAAF had set up in the navy's backyard—much to the rival service's chagrin. Gant turned up the collar of his flight jacket as he strode across the tarmac, his parachute bouncing against his legs.

On the taxiing line sat his gleaming new P-51D Mustang fighter, *Savannah Gal*, named after his hometown. Beneath the rim of its bubble cockpit, in two neat rows, were fourteen swastika decals—one for each of the German planes Hiram Gant had shot down while escorting B-17 bombers over occupied Europe during the first eight months of 1944. Kills eleven through fourteen had come during one horrific mission over Berlin in July, when the bombers and their escorts had been jumped by a squadron of Focke-Wulf 190s—high-performance

Nazi fighters piloted by battle-hardened veterans of the Russian front.

Gant's sterling record as a combat flier had earned him a Distinguished Flying Cross, a promotion to captain, and reassignment stateside—where, as a bona fide war hero, his duties consisted of promoting war bonds and flying largely symbolic (and safe) daily loop patrols over Washington, D.C., as part of a rotating "honor guard" of decorated pilots who had been culled from both the European and Pacific theaters.

What his exemplary conduct hadn't earned him was a sociable word from three-quarters of the personnel at Salter Field, or the right to sit in the front seat of a public bus in Arlington, Virginia, less than an hour away. Captain Hiram Gant, a graduate of flight training in Tuskegee, Alabama, and a fighter ace nearly three times over, was black—the only black officer stationed at Salter Field.

He had been plunked down into the middle of an all-white celebrity squadron at the behest of army chief of staff General George C. Marshall, a shrewd, forward-thinking man who had seen in Gant an opportunity to promote the idea of a harmoniously integrated U.S. military—and perhaps increase black voter support for his boss, Franklin Delano Roosevelt. An awkward posting, but like many accomplished black men of his generation, Gant had long ago inured himself to the routine injustices of having to function in any white-dominated institution—including the Army Air Forces. General George C. Marshall was open-minded, progressive, and arguably a genius. Unfortunately for Hiram Gant, many of the lesser ranks within the USAAF were not.

Gant considered it a major victory that he was able to sit down in the officers' wardroom at Salter Field and drink a cup of coffee in the company of his fellow pilots without being hounded out the door—although none of them had ever been inclined to join him at his table. Hiram Gant was dryly amused by this. A sizable number of white bomber pilots had been only too glad to have his company when he was keeping Focke-Wulfs and

Messerschmitts off the backs of their Flying Fortresses at eighteen thousand feet over Germany. But this wasn't combat. What could a man do? You couldn't *make* another person like or accept you. All you could do was hold yourself with dignity and perform your duty to the best of your ability, and maybe—eventually—a few minds would change.

Hiram Gant smacked his gloved hands together as he walked toward his Mustang. But not *this* mind. Approaching him from the direction of the other Mustang on the tarmac was Captain Wilmer Jessup, just back from his own two-hour circuit patrol. A native of Tifton, Georgia, Jessup was a seven-kill ace who'd tallied his enemy planes flying a P-38 Lightning out of Guadalcanal during the Solomon Islands campaign. His considerable skill as a combat flier notwithstanding, he was also an unrepentant bigot who made no bones about his dislike of anyone black, Oriental, Hispanic, American Indian, Jewish, Catholic, communist, or non-English-speaking. Serving with a Tuskegee Airman was anathema to him.

The two Mustang pilots converged on each other, exhaling vapor in the cold air. As usual, Gant raised his right hand in a smart salute—a mere courtesy, since both men were of equivalent rank—and nodded.

"Morning, Captain Jessup," he said.

As usual, Wilmer Jessup brushed past him with a scowl, and without returning the salute.

"Haar-*rummphniggah*," he half coughed.

That was the other thing he usually did. Gant closed his eyes momentarily, shook his head, and strode on toward his plane. Jessup's tactics would have been almost laughably childish if there hadn't been so much hate behind them. But Gant knew better than to make an issue of his ongoing insults. Confronted with a formal complaint, Jessup would simply play dumb, supported by his friends, and he, Hiram Gant, would look like just another paranoid Negro who couldn't cut the mustard when given an opportunity to stand shoulder to shoulder with the big boys.

And Hiram Gant wasn't having that.

"She ready to go, Smitty?" he asked the ground technician who was checking *Savannah Gal*'s landing gear.

Blond-haired Corporal Edward Smith, a former Ford mechanic from Dearborn, Michigan, was one of the few servicemen at Salter Field who seemed to have no particular problem with Hiram Gant's presence. He was invariably polite, good-humored, and efficient.

"Yes, sir," Smith said, touching his forehead. "Even warmed her up for ya—made sure that big ol' Packard's tickin' like a clock." He smiled spontaneously.

"Good, good," Gant said, returning the salute. "Well—here I go again. Another pointless figure eight from here to Dover to Washington and back again, waggling my wings at any adoring citizens who happen to be up at this godforsaken hour of the morning."

Smith grinned. "You're a hee-ro, Captain. You gotta play the part." He chuckled. "Nice work if you can get it, right, sir?"

Gant snorted as he stepped up on the frost-rimed wing of the Mustang. "Don't repeat this, Smitty—especially around Captain Jessup—but I'd almost rather be pickin' cotton down in the Georgia sun." Smith was one of the few people to whom he could say something like that.

The ground tech smiled and shook his head. "My lips are sealed, Captain." He saluted again. "You have a safe flight, now."

"Thank you, Corporal Smith," Gant replied, settling into the Mustang's cockpit. *"You* have a nice warm breakfast while I'm out freezing my earlobes off, inspiring the patriotic populations of Maryland, Delaware, and D.C."

He fired up the engine, and the powerful Packard engine belched exhaust from the manifolds on either side of the forward fuselage. The triple-bladed propeller spun into a translucent disk, shimmering in the harsh glare of the hangar floodlights. Smith stepped back as Gant taxied the Mustang out onto the runway and turned it to the northwest, nose into the wind.

He cleared for takeoff with Salter's small control tower, then pushed the throttle forward. The big engine roared, Gant was pressed back in his seat, and in twenty seconds the Mustang was airborne—climbing into the dark morning sky above the twinkling lights of farmhouses . . . soaring out over the icy black waters of Chesapeake Bay.

On the bay below, random patches of fog were starting to coalesce into thick, continuous banks—the result of a temperature inversion that had begun to affect the Atlantic seaboard from New Jersey south to Virginia in the wake of the passing Canadian cold front.

As the night sky began to glow blue low to the east in anticipation of the coming dawn, Hiram Gant leveled the Mustang at an altitude of two thousand feet and began to follow a heading that would take him across Chesapeake Bay to Maryland and Delaware, and finally out over Delaware Bay, where he would make a wide turn around Dover before heading westward once again to buzz Washington, D.C.

Rattle some political teacups in Georgetown, maybe.

It had been decided.

No more wondering.

He, Ensign Hajimi Ona, would die in a fireball of exploding fuel tanks—giant reservoirs that had been built out onto a concrete dock on the New Jersey shore of Delaware Bay, some twenty miles inland from Cape May.

It had all happened so quickly.

Brazenly surfacing the *Sen-Toku* at three in the morning, after penetrating sixteen miles into Delaware Bay by intermittently motoring and drifting with the incoming tide—thereby leaving no consistent sound trail—Captain Yarizuma had calmly picked out a target for the first *Kaiten*—Ona's—by scanning from the bridge of the *I-403* with high-powered binoculars through the darkness and the fog.

"A mist from the gods to conceal us," he had intoned to those assembled atop the conning tower. "It will thicken by first light—can you not feel it?"

Staring at the distant, spotlighted location of his incipient martyrdom, Hajimi Ona had found himself incapable of feeling anything.

"No blackout in effect," Executive Officer Katsura had muttered, gazing at the illuminated fuel tanks. "Unbelievable overconfidence the Americans are exhibiting, Honorable Captain. They think they are beyond the reach of war."

"Ensign Ona will instruct them in the error of their ways," Yarizuma had replied. "Clear the bridge. We will submerge and launch *Kaiten* One."

It had all happened so *quickly*.

Now, in the claustrophobic interior of his *Kaiten*'s control room, Hajimi Ona rested his forehead against the housing of the giant torpedo's raised periscope and tried to slow his breathing. He was staring at the luminous dial of his wristwatch.

It had been one hour since he had climbed into the *Kaiten* and closed the ventral hatch connecting him to the mother sub.

It had been fifty minutes since Captain Yarizuma, using the disposable telephone line, had ordered him to launch—forty-nine since he had started the *Kaiten*'s oxygen engine.

Forty-eight since the clamps securing the *tokko* torpedo had been remotely released from inside the *I-403*'s hull. Forty-seven minutes and fifty seconds since he had powered the *Kaiten* off the deck of the *Sen-Toku*, the flexible tube through which he had crawled to enter the tiny control room ripping away along with the telephone line.

It had been forty-four minutes since he had killed the engine of the *Kaiten*, sure he was clear of the mother sub, and begun to hover just beneath the surface, watching the lights of his shore target through the periscope. Forty-two minutes since the quiet thrum of the *Sen-Toku*'s electric motors had ceased to vibrate through the dripping hull plates that encased him.

Forty minutes since he had found himself completely and utterly alone, with Yarizuma's instructions to attack the fuel dock at 0530 echoing in his head.

The luminous second hand of his watch swept on. Thirty-nine.

Despite the early hour, General George C. Marshall was already sipping coffee in the downstairs living room of his Washington town house, going over some reports, when a knock came at the front door. With a sigh, the general set his cup down and rose out of his chair. Visitors who showed up at five a.m. at the army chief of staff's personal residence were rarely the bearers of good tidings. Marshall opened the door, and a gust of frigid air whirled a few snowflakes into the room.

It was a runner from Central Communications.

"Sorry to bother you this early, General," the red-nosed sergeant said, saluting. He was bundled up like an Eskimo against the cold. "This message from CAID was just decoded a few minutes ago. It came in via top-priority radio relay from the Philippines. Captain Armstrong wanted it brought right over to you personally."

He handed Marshall a plain manila envelope and saluted again. The general returned the salute and nodded. "Thank you, Sergeant. That'll be all."

"Sir." The noncom turned and trotted bulkily down the town house's walkway toward an olive drab staff car.

Marshall shut the door and crossed the room to his chair again. Sitting down, he tore open the sealed envelope, withdrew a single typed page, and picked up his coffee cup.

"Quentin Barnaby," he muttered aloud, one eyebrow raising. "What have you uncovered this time, my academic friend? . . ." The general's eyes roved down the page, speed-reading.

Thirty seconds later, George C. Marshall set his coffee cup down with a bang on the end table beside his chair, picked up the telephone at his elbow, and hurriedly began to dial.

"Perfect," Captain Toshiko Yarizuma whispered, gazing through the periscope of the *I-403*. "It could not be more perfect."

He drew back and slapped the periscope shears vertical. "Lower 'scope," he ordered. As the housing slid downward, he turned to face his executive officer. "A clear sky is dawning overhead," he said, "but the surface of the bay is thick with fog. We will be concealed when we rise, concealed as we launch our aircraft . . . and yet our pilots will encounter optimal flying conditions once they are airborne." Once again, Katsura saw Yarizuma's eyes become strangely distant. "Fate favors us, Exec."

Katsura nodded, feeling a thrill despite his apprehension. "Yes, sir."

Yarizuma put a hand on the periscope housing and spun slowly, gazing at the seamen and officers stationed around the *Sen-Toku*'s crowded control room.

"Surface the boat," Yarizuma commanded. "Antiaircraft gunners to their stations. Open hangar door and ready catapult. Prepare to launch *Seiran* and *Ohka*."

"*Hai*, Captain!"

Katsura's shouted repetition of Yarizuma's orders was followed immediately by the harsh blasting sound of compressed air being forced into the submarine's ballast tanks.

The *Sen-Toku* breached ponderously through the freezing surface of Delaware Bay, streaming water from its massive conning tower and hangar. As the great black warship settled onto an even keel, wreathed in cold mist, hatches were flung open both fore and aft, and seamen began to pour out like ants into the pale light of dawn, running along the decks beside the airplane catapult and the two remaining *Kaiten*. Crews took up stations behind the *Sen-Toku*'s twin-barreled machine guns and light cannon, readying the weapons for action. The huge watertight door at the forward end of the hangar cracked open with a loud sucking sound and swung back slowly on its hinges.

Before the great door had even been secured, seamen were clambering into the hangar and releasing the chains binding down the first of the three *Seiran* fighter-bombers. Encouraging each other with enthusiastic shouts, they began to slide the partially disassembled aircraft out toward the near end of the launching cata-pult. As they did so, Toshiko Yarizuma emerged onto the bridge, accompanied by Katsura and several other officers. He gazed down, surveying the intense activity with an expression of placid approval. Katsura, on the other hand, lost no time in commencing a binocular scan of the *Sen-Toku*'s surroundings.

"What exactly are you looking for, Katsura?" Yari-zuma asked. He sounded bemused.

The exec lowered his binoculars momentarily. "Why—American patrol vessels, sir," he replied, taken aback. "American planes."

The *Sen-Toku* commander raised a hand toward the swirling fog. "In this?"

"Sir," Katsura replied again, his voice tight with ten-sion, "we are deep in enemy territory—surrounded by American warships, attack aircraft, shore batteries . . ."

Yarizuma laughed.

"Sir," Katsura pressed on, "the Americans have mine-fields, radar."

"We have missed their minefields," Yarizuma said, "by keeping to the bay's central channel—as I knew we would. Their own vessels have to get in and out. And on radar we look like any other slow, obvious contact. By the time our presence is questioned, our aircraft will be launched and we will be gone—submerged and run-ning back for the open sea."

Katsura raised his binoculars to his eyes once more. "Just the same, Honorable Captain," he muttered, "I will keep a watch for any threatening activity."

Yarizuma laughed again. "Please yourself, Exec," he said, "but they cannot see us, and they cannot stop us." He spread his arms wide and smiled into the fog. "The gods of war have made us invisible."

The first *Seiran,* piloted by Lieutenant Mamoru Ta-kagi, was launched from the *Sen-Toku*'s long foredeck catapult only thirteen minutes after the opening of the watertight hangar door. It had taken less than eight min-utes to attach the plane's wings, stabilizers, and pontoons. Takagi took off with his cockpit canopy open, one arm extended in an exuberant farewell to the crew, the white *hachimaki* scarf around his head fluttering in the slipstream. The navy blue *Seiran* with the American star insignia rose rapidly into the fog and disappeared.

The next two planes, their assembly completed as the first *Seiran* was being positioned on the catapult, were launched only three minutes apart—a record deployment, Yarizuma noted with satisfaction. First Ensign Matome Fukaya and then Ensign Sokichi Honjo followed Lieutenant Takagi into the air, both emulating their leader's inspirational gesture of waving out their open canopies to the *Sen-Toku*'s crew.

"Banzaaaaiiiiii!" Honjo screamed joyously as his aircraft careened down the catapult.

"Banzaaaaaiiiiiiii!" the crew of the *Sen-Toku* chorused, raising their arms in triumph.

On the bridge of the conning tower, Toshiko Yarizuma smiled his serene smile and nodded slowly, relishing the magnificent moment he had created. The cheers of the crew ebbed away as Honjo's *Seiran* disappeared and a fresh bank of mist began to roll across the bow of the *I-403*. Somewhere overhead, out of sight, the three fighter-bombers rendezvoused and began to vector off toward their target, the combined roar of their engines fading gradually away into the distance.

Muted shouts began to echo out of the hangar, prompting Executive Officer Katsura to lower his binoculars and look down from the bridge. A moment later, the sleek nose of the *Ohka* eased into view, supported on both sides by seamen who were trundling the weapon out toward the catapult. They were followed by Lieutenant Sekio Yagi, resplendent in flying suit, sash, full-length samurai sword, and brilliant white-and-red *hachimaki* head scarf.

Unlike Takagi and his two wingmen, Yagi was not calm. Rather, he was apoplectic.

"Hurry up!" he shrieked at Kameo Fujita, who was trying to direct the nose of the trolley-borne *Ohka* onto the end of the catapult. *"You waste precious seconds with your fumbling, idiot! HURRY UP!"*

Chapter
Thirty-eight

Hiram Gant was just commencing the wide bank that would take him around the port city of Dover when, in the distance, he noticed two sleek aircraft, silhouetted against the dull gleam of the rising sun, rise out of the fog covering Delaware Bay. Their airframe contours caught his experienced eye. They were unfamiliar, and should not have been. As a dedicated combat pilot, he had studied the design characteristics of every known combat aircraft, Allied or otherwise. And yet he had never seen any quite like these.

He nudged the Mustang onto a converging course that would take him several hundred feet above and behind the planes, now flying in a westerly direction at an altitude of about twelve hundred feet. They seemed unaware of his presence. As Gant drew nearer, he was able to make out the familiar dark blue paint jobs and star insignia that identified American naval aircraft.

They were sharp-looking planes, with elegant lines that reminded him of the seaplane racers of the 1930s. But these had long cockpit canopies that suggested a crew of at least two, and of course no pontoons. Gant wondered what the navy was up to—if this was some new design being flight-tested in Delaware/Chesapeake airspace for the benefit of any political eyes that might be watching.

After all, the planes were heading directly for Washington.

He was about to hail the odd-looking pair on the radio when a burst of static crackled in his headphones: "Ace Flight Four, Ace Flight Four—this is Salter Field, do you read?"

Hiram Gant put a hand to his throat mike. "Salter Field, this is Ace Flight Four."

"Roger, Ace Flight Four. Captain Gant, I need to pass this along to you. A General Stage Three Alert has just been issued for all patrolling aircraft in our sector, effective immediately. Some specifics here: a plausible airborne threat to the Washington, D.C., area has just been confirmed, do you copy?"

Gant guided the Mustang onto a following course several hundred feet above and behind the two unfamiliar planes, cutting his speed to avoid overshooting them. He didn't have to cut it much; they were traveling at nearly 350 miles per hour. "Roger that, Salter. Loud and clear."

"Copy. More specifics: possible attack on the capital by suicide aircraft imminent. Be on the alert for one to three high-speed pontoon seaplanes—"

Hiram Gant jerked his eyes down onto the brace of planes ahead of him.

"—of Japanese design—"

These had *no* pontoons.

"—possibly delivered to the U.S. coast by enemy submarine and launched from same."

But they *had* risen out of the center of fog-shrouded Delaware Bay.

What the hell.

Hiram Gant was about to respond to Salter Field when the port side of his cockpit canopy dissolved into a crazed pattern of fractured Plexiglas, sparks exploded

near his left knee, and the Mustang vibrated as if a giant
beast had seized it and begun to shake it by the tail.

Having finally caught up to the American fighter that
was shadowing his two comrades, Sokichi Honjo—flying
somewhat slower than Takagi or Fukaya due to the fact
that the release mechanism of his undercarriage had
malfunctioned, preventing him from dropping his pontoons after takeoff—had quietly gained a few hundred
extra feet of altitude and attacked the lone Mustang
from the port side, diving out of the glare of the rising
sun. His comrades, seeing him trailing with his pontoons
still attached, had reduced their speed by ten percent,
providing him the necessary margin to overtake.

The Mustang wobbled and rolled out as Honjo dove
past, firing until the last second. He could see bullet
strikes pepper the shiny aluminum fuselage from cockpit
to tail, but there was little smoke and no flame. As he
pulled out of the dive and powered on after Takagi and
Fukaya, now approaching the western shore of Chesapeake Bay, he tried again to jettison his *Seiran*'s cumbersome pontoons, yanking on the release toggle with all
his strength.

It was not as if he would ever again need the ability
to land . . . any more than his two-seater fighter-bomber
needed a second crewman on this, its final flight.

Abruptly, the release toggle slackened in his grip. The
Seiran leaped ahead as its twin pontoons fell away and
tumbled into the thinning fog below. Ensign Sokichi
Honjo felt a hot flush rise to his cheeks as, between the
mists, the southern outskirts of Annapolis slipped away
behind the trailing edge of his starboard wing.

"Tenno heika banzai," he whispered, leveling his aircraft in hot pursuit of Takagi and Fukaya.

Hiram Gant tried to blink the gluey blood out of his
left eye as he pulled the Mustang out of its barrel-rolling
dive. The P-51 responded sluggishly, as if one or more
of its control surfaces had been damaged. Aileron, Gant

thought automatically. He looked to starboard in time to see the plane that had attacked him jettison its long pontoons and climb after the two aircraft he had been following.

He didn't bother with the radio; it was a smoking ruin, as were half the gauges on his cockpit console. Nor did he bother with his torn, burned left thigh. The muscle was quivering, but he could still work the foot pedals.

What he did do was take a second to wipe the blood from his left eye before driving the Mustang forward at full throttle.

A fighter pilot without two good eyes—and thus depth perception—wasn't going to be able to hit much.

"I don't get it, Sarge," one of the privates manning the forty-millimeter antiaircraft gun complained. "We've been ordered to shoot down planes with American markings? How the hell are we gonna do that?"

The artillery sergeant in charge of the emplacement—one of several hundred AA positions scattered around Washington and Arlington, and up and down the Potomac River—shook his head, examining the overcast sky. "I dunno, Kirby. Try to spot U.S.-marked seaplanes that don't look friendly, I guess. How the fuck should I know?"

"What a dumb-ass order," Kirby griped. He glanced up at the low clouds. "Can't see a goddamn thing up there. And even if we could, it ain't like there's ever a shortage of U.S.-marked planes flyin' over Washington. What're we supposed to do—blast all our own crates until we hit the right ones?"

The sergeant glared at him. "You can start by getting your eye on the sky, Private. An order's an order."

"Jeez." Kirby tipped his head back. "Hell—I can hear aircraft up there right now. But I can't see a damn thing."

"Maybe we should blast 'em," a second private suggested.

"Without identifyin' 'em first?" Kirby retorted. "You dumb hick."

"There! There!" the sergeant shouted, pointing. "In that hole in the fog! Three flyin' together."

"What are the chances?" Kirby remarked sarcastically. "Three American planes flyin' over Washington, D.C. Gee whiz, never saw that before."

"You want we should blast 'em, Sarge?" the second private offered.

The sergeant shrugged. "Nah. They weren't seaplanes— no floats. We don't want to shoot down the wrong aircraft. And anyway, that damn fog's still so thick we can't track them anymore."

From high above, there came a long, muted rattle of machine gun fire.

The sergeant and Kirby looked at each other.

"Holy shit," Kirby said.

When the fuel tank of Ensign Matome Fukaya's *Seiran* blew up, it detonated the fourteen hundred pounds of high explosive packed into the plane's fuselage. The debris-filled fireball immediately engulfed Ensign Sokichi Honjo's aircraft, which had been following close behind. Another tremendous explosion followed on the heels of the first as Honjo's HE load went up, as well. The sky became a chaos of flame. The bullet-pocked Mustang of Captain Hiram Gant, wing guns trailing smoke, corkscrewed through the ragged fringes of the aerial conflagration.

The first concussion had rocked the *Seiran* of *tokko* leader Lieutenant Mamoru Takagi; the second had blown it over onto its port wingtip. Takagi cursed aloud—something he never did—as he struggled to muscle the aircraft back under control.

Then he saw it—ahead in the distance, through a break in the low cloud. The white dome of the U.S. Capitol building, and, beyond it, the sharp, angular spear of the Washington Monument. Time and time again he had studied and memorized the layout of the American capital—and now here it was, its magnificent architecture gleaming in the rising sun.

The Rising Sun . . .

Mamoru Takagi could not help but smile. Captain Yarizuma had been right. Success must certainly have been preordained by the gods of war.

Even the clouds were parting for him, showing him the way.

He'll nose down, Hiram Gant thought, willing his damaged fighter to somehow power around and line up on the single remaining hostile aircraft. *I'm not high enough, but he'll nose down into a dive . . . head straight for the Capitol building.*

That was exactly what Mamoru Takagi did.

When the *Seiran* plunged earthward, presenting its belly to the trailing Mustang, Hiram Gant was already firing.

Chapter
Thirty-nine

Mamoru Takagi's *Seiran* dove straight through Hiram Gant's line of fire. The slugs from the Mustang's six machine guns chewed into the Japanese plane's underside from propeller to tail, tearing off chunks as it flashed past. Gant threw his fighter into a hard right bank and stared down.

I didn't stop it, he thought wildly, watching the seaplane arc downward through the dissipating clouds toward the brilliant white dome of the Capitol building, leaving a thin stream of dirty smoke in its wake.

A second later the *Seiran* came apart with a blast that jarred Hiram Gant's spine even through the armor of his aircraft. The intensity of the explosion was such that not a fragment larger than a dinner plate was left to fall to earth.

Even the pain of his burned leg and bleeding temple could not quell the exultation that seized Gant as he watched the suicide plane disintegrate.

He forced the Mustang level, juggling the damaged controls, and took stock: low on fuel, shot up, burned and bleeding . . . and three kills. Damned important kills.

Not too bad for a noncombatant loop patrol.

He was still congratulating himself when something rocketed past the port wing of his P-51, trailing a thick column of white smoke, and nearly knocked him out of the sky.

Lieutenant Sekio Yagi let out an ecstatic yell as the *Ohka* missed colliding with the American fighter by less than three feet and continued to roar upward at a steep angle into the shifting overcast above Washington. Nothing could stop him now. His greatest fear had always been that he would run out of fuel before reaching the U.S. capital, but it had proven groundless. The range-extending modifications he had beaten out of Fujita had carried the day. Beneath him lay the buildings and monuments of the city that was the nerve center of Imperial Japan's greatest enemy—helpless, exposed, waiting for him to choose his target.

The noise of the *Ohka*'s rocket engine was brain numbing, but even so, Yagi was conscious of a series of detonations in the sky around him. Antiaircraft fire. He was unconcerned. Fate had not brought him this close to glory only to allow him to be knocked out of the sky by some ignorant Yankee pot-shooter. He looked down at the urban landscape below.

He had thought long and hard about this day, poring over aerial photographs and models of the Washington, D.C, area. And he had long since made up his mind about the specifics of his final attack.

If he came in over the Lincoln Memorial, lined up with the Washington Monument above the reflecting pool, and dove sharply to the left just before reaching the spirelike obelisk, he would hit the White House.

If he came in over the Capitol building (a tempting target itself), lined up with the Washington Monument above the Mall, and dove sharply to the right, he would again hit the White House.

Perhaps even kill Roosevelt himself.

Truly a grand gesture.

But there was one last thing—one final detail.

He swiveled his head, searching the sky.

Surely, after so much had gone right, fate would not deny him this one crowning touch—

There.

A small cloudburst, half rain and half frozen sleet, was lingering over the outskirts of Arlington.

Lieutenant Sekio Yagi was almost overcome by elation and relief.

He would have his crowning touch, after all.

Hiram Gant watched helplessly as the strange missile with the split tail and stubby wings blasted skyward in a long, curving arc, spewing a thick trail of white vapor, and headed into a small cumulous cloud over the Potomac River to the south. It was painted the same U.S. Navy blue as the three suicide seaplanes, and sported the same star insignia. But, even more so than the aircraft he had just shot down, it resembled nothing in the American or Allied air arsenal.

It had to be traveling in excess of six hundred miles per hour. Gant watched the amazing aircraft plunge into the center of the thunderhead and disappear.

He could not hope to catch it. But if its mission was the same as that of its more conventional brethren, it would come back. Back to the heart of Washington. To Capitol Hill, the Mall, and the White House.

His mind racing, Captain Hiram Gant banked his shuddering Mustang over Georgetown and headed back toward the Washington Monument, fighting to gain altitude.

Sleet and rain hammered the fuselage and windscreen of the *Ohka*, completely obscuring Sekio Yagi's vision. It was what he had prayed for—to find himself, in the next-to-final moment, in the eye of the storm. It would provide the pièce de résistance.

When the *Ohka* shot out of the far side of the thunderhead into a patch of brilliant blue sky, it no longer bore the drab, uniform coloration of a U.S. Navy aircraft. The pounding rain had battered away the water-soluble navy blue paint that Yagi had secretly insisted upon many months earlier, revealing the baked-on coating underneath.

The *Ohka* was now a dazzling white, striped with the radiating, fiery red spokes of the Rising Sun emblem. The wings and the dual tail stabilizers bore the same patriotic design, rendered in complementary fashion by an expert hand. Yagi himself had hired the artist, paying for the *Ohka*'s elaborate adornment out of his own pocket.

He was now literally riding a thunderbolt out of the Rising Sun. There would be no mistaking the source of the blow that was about to fall on the American capital.

Yagi looped up through the clear air, rocket engine roaring, as he gained altitude for his final, unstoppable plunge into the White House.

"Sir!" the orderly implored. "You must evacuate now! *Sir!*"

Roosevelt set his teacup down on the arm of his wheelchair and inserted a Camel into his favorite black-ivory cigarette holder. He continued to look up through the tall French windows of the Blue Room, his careworn face impassive, set.

"No," he said calmly, lighting the cigarette. "The president of the United States will not be run out of the People's House like a frightened schoolboy."

He blew a stream of smoke and eyed the pale dot moving rapidly across the sky beyond the tip of the Washington Monument.

"Fetch me another cup of tea, will you, Gregory?"

Hiram Gant fired his machine guns as the *Ohka* was still ascending. For a second or two, watching it emerge from the far side of the squall cloud into the bright sunlight, he hadn't even been sure it was the same aircraft. Somehow, it had changed colors like a chameleon— trading U.S. Navy blue for the blazing red and white of Imperial Japan.

The Mustang's guns fired dry after only three seconds.

The *Ohka* was just reaching the zenith of its upward loop. Hiram Gant saw only one chance to prevent the coming catastrophe.

When the piloted missile dove toward its target—Capitol building, White House—he could ram it.

Kicking the rudder, he banked the vibrating Mustang onto an interception course.

Sekio Yagi squinted downward, locating his landmarks. There. The Washington Monument. To either side, the Capitol building and the Lincoln Memorial. And behind it, just beyond the circular walkway of a small park known as the Ellipse, the White House.

No last-minute turns would be necessary. He would line up the Washington Monument like a giant gunsight and go straight in.

Yagi smiled and nosed the *Ohka* down.

The altimeter Kameo Fujita had jury-rigged to fire a small electrical charge the first time its needle descended rather than ascended did so.

The electrical charge traveled along an extra wire connecting the altimeter to a six-ounce vial of fulminate of mercury buried in the 2,646 pounds of high-explosive trinitroaminol that comprised the *Ohka*'s warhead.

When the *Ohka* exploded, Lieutenant Sekio Yagi was no longer thinking of the actual suicide dive into the White House; in his frenzied mind, he had already accomplished that.

He was dreaming of Yasukuni.

Hiram Gant had realized five seconds after starting his interception dive that he wasn't going to be able to catch the plunging suicide rocket. He had underestimated the speed of his adversary. Despair had turned to panic—and then to wonder as the red-and-white missile simply blew apart seven hundred yards in front of him . . . for no apparent reason.

A tremendous concussion slammed into the Mustang, causing him to lose control. He recovered and rolled the aircraft to port, trying to avoid being hit by the accompanying wave of fire and debris. A black-orange inferno engulfed the Mustang's shattered bubble canopy—

And then he was in the clear, completing a full 360-degree rotation, the seething fireball that marked the destruction of the strange Japanese warplane lingering in the air behind him.

Gant looked around, checking the surrounding sky with the rubber-necked thoroughness characteristic of all combat pilots who lived long enough to become experienced. It was clear above one thousand feet. No other aircraft were visible. Even the low cloud cover that had hidden the initial approach of the attacking planes had almost completely dissipated.

The Mustang stuttered several times, the engine irregularity shaking the overstressed airframe. The needle of the fuel gauge was bouncing on zero, and the cockpit controls were growing more mushy with each passing second.

Enough excitement for one day.

Captain Hiram Gant pressed a palm to his bloodied left thigh, gritting his teeth, and carefully brought *Savannah Gal* around onto a heading for Salter Field.

In the Blue Room of the White House, President Roosevelt turned away from the French windows, lit a fresh cigarette, and held his empty cup and saucer up to his orderly.

"Thank you for the tea, Gregory," he said.

Chapter Forty

In the dark, clammy interior of the *Kaiten*, Ensign Hajimi Ona reached down between his legs and touched the small wooden box containing the ashes of his friend Isamu Matsura. He had found that he was able to temper his awful fear with the reassuring thought that he would soon be reunited with Isamu at Yasukuni.

He squinted through the periscope. The *Kaiten* was moving fast now, running just beneath the surface. Spray flew up over the periscope head, compromising his ability to maintain visual contact with his target, but he had determined the bearing that would take him into the fuel-tank dock and was able to maintain his attack course using the *Kaiten*'s compass. The high-pitched whine of the oxygen engine behind him stung his ears like a human scream.

The fuel tanks were an indistinct blob of bright light against the dim backdrop of the dawn sky. *Saboteurs*, Ona thought suddenly. *The Americans are more worried about saboteurs now than they are aerial or naval attacks. The lights are for security.*

Advantage to him.

There were two black can buoys bracketing the final approach to the dock, approximately two hundred yards apart and half a mile from shore. The *Kaiten*'s course would take it straight between them. Channel markers, Ona decided. But in the event that an antitorpedo net happened to be stretched between the two cans, he would bring the *Kaiten* fully to the surface in the final seconds of the run.

He twisted the oxygen supply valve fully open and squeezed the rudder and diving-plane levers with sweat-slick hands. The Long Lance engine was howling at full capacity now, and the *Kaiten* was vibrating like a struck gong. The intense metallic shimmying shook Hajimi Ona's spine from tailbone to skull, blurring his vision and fragmenting his concentration.

He kept his brow jammed against the eyepiece of the periscope, and caught glimpses of the onrushing fuel tanks. His mouth and throat were sandpaper dry; his stomach had filled with ice. He felt as if he were going insane, for he did not have the courage to do this and he knew it. He had always known it.

And yet, for some reason, his hands stayed steady on the controls and his eye remained fast on the target. He did not claw the oxygen valve shut or veer off his attack heading. It was as if he were locked into a predetermined course of action in spite of himself.

And then the realization dawned on Hajimi Ona that his terror was manageable. That he could still think. That he could force himself to function despite being caught in the grip of an all-pervading dread. He had heard veteran combat soldiers refer to this capacity, this phenomenon, though he had never before experienced it himself. It was the only difference, they said, between a brave man and a coward: a coward is afraid and does nothing; a brave man is afraid and does what must be done anyway.

Tears of relief prickled Hajimi Ona's eyes. He was one of the latter.

He allowed the *Kaiten* to broach through the surface as the black cans slid out of sight at the extreme left and right of the periscope's visual field. Spray flew up from the nose of the craft in a white wall, blotting out the glimmering light from the fuel-tank dock. Ona dropped his eyes to the console compass and gripped the steering levers even more tightly.

Steady on zero-four-zero degrees . . . all the way in.

I am with you, Hajimi, he heard Isamu Matsura whisper.

There was a tremendous impact.

The *Kaiten* surged upward, driving Hajimi Ona down in his seat and herniating two disks in his lower back.

The high-speed props struck hard. The hull of the *Kaiten* bucked violently in time to the percussive din.

Ensign Hajimi Ona's head snapped forward on his shoulders. His forehead slammed into the steel of the periscope housing. Blood erupted from the split skin over the hairline fracture of the skull that occurred instantaneously between his brows.

Ona slumped sideways in his seat, his hands dropping away from the steering levers.

As its pilot fell unconscious, the *Kaiten* continued to plow up onto the broad, invisible mudbank that lay between the two black can buoys—a bank that even at high tide was covered by a mere eighteen inches of water.

When at last the giant torpedo shuddered to a halt in a spray of icy brown muck, it had gouged a trench out of the bank one hundred yards long, and pushed up a fifteen-foot-high mountain of soft mud with its stressed—but undetonated—warhead nose.

It lay hard aground with a slight list to port, its engine silent now. Black and mud-streaked and motionless and impotent. Completely exposed.

Steaming in the frosty air of the October dawn.

The destroyer USS *Reuben Grant* had come out of nowhere, charging through the dissipating fog and ramming the *I-403* as it fled at high speed on the surface out of Delaware Bay. The shivering shaft that had forced the American patrol vessel to turn around and run for Lewes on one screw had also concealed her true identity from the *Sen-Toku*'s hydrophone operator; he had been listening only for twin-screw contacts—the signature sound of sub-killing destroyers and corvettes. The *Reuben Grant*'s master, the pugnacious Captain Douglas Blaine, only just informed of the emergency alert before seeing the Japanese sub suddenly appear on a converging course with his own ship, had recognized a one-in-a-million opportunity and taken it. The force of the collision had crushed the destroyer's bow to the extent that she was unable to pursue the attack further; rather, she was fighting for her own life, with pumps and emergency crews working at full capacity, trying to stay afloat until she could limp inshore and beach—all the while radioing frantically for reinforcements.

They were coming. Dozens of ships and aircraft bearing thousands of pounds of depth charges. Depth charges that would soon rain down upon the crippled *Sen-Toku* like pennies flung from a giant's hand.

The *I-403* had gone to the bottom at a depth of 270 feet, her forward compartments and aircraft hangar flooded, her batteries cracked and gradually filling the remainder of the hull with poisonous chlorine gas as a result of their inundation with salt water. She lay at a forty-five-degree angle on her starboard side in the cold muck of the Atlantic bottom, broken and breaking up more with each passing second, her vital fluids and gases leaking upward through the empty black water in multiple streams. Pinpointing her location for the approaching hunters above.

Ensigns Kazu Yonehara and Hitoshi Wada, ordered to their two *Kaiten* by Captain Yarizuma immediately following the dramatic launch of Yagi's rocket-powered *Ohka*, were still inside their respective *tokko* weapons. Yonehara, in the remaining *Kaiten* on the *Sen-Toku*'s foredeck, was dead—killed instantly when the bow of the *Reuben Grant* had slammed into the giant sub and crushed his manned torpedo's conning tower. On the aft deck, the tremendous impact had wrenched Wada's *Kaiten* sideways in its cradle, jamming both hatches and springing its hull plates. Hitoshi Wada was now up to his neck in frigid seawater, in pitch darkness, frantically trying to kick loose a ventral escape hatch that would not open, his last few inches of breathing space rapidly diminishing.

In the aft torpedo room, Flight Technician Kameo Fujita lay dead beneath the heavy Type 92 conventional torpedo that had shifted off its rack and fallen on him as the sub tumbled downward after being rammed. Until that terrifying moment he had been happy—secure in the private knowledge that not only would Sekio Yagi never return to torment him again, but that the cruel young lieutenant had failed to achieve his precious goal of a glorious *tokko* death . . . thanks to a cleverly booby-trapped *Ohka* altimeter. Revenge, for the scant minutes it lasted, had indeed been sweet.

As Executive Officer Hanku Katsura and those few of the crew who had not been drowned, crushed, or poisoned by the thickening fog of deadly chlorine gas emanating from the *Sen-Toku*'s cracked batteries continued their desperate struggle to clear the dying vessel's blocked escape hatches, Captain Toshiko Yarizuma crawled into his private cabin, bathed in the sanguineous red light of the battle lanterns, and eased the door shut.

He clambered over the ruined jumble of his personal property to his bunk and pulled off the mattress. Jamming it between the sloping deck and the bulkhead, he made a flat cushion on which to kneel, then groped for the picture of his wife and sons that had adorned the wall next to his private Shinto shrine. He found it, set it up against the frame of the bunk.

Sitting back on his haunches, hands on his thighs, he gazed at the portrait, its glass shattered, in the fading crimson glow of his cabin's single battle lantern. All around him, from every direction, the shrieks of tearing metal, the groans of collapsing bulkheads, and the faint shouts of struggling men assaulted his ears . . . invaded and overwhelmed this last, tiny place of refuge.

Toshiko Yarizuma leaned forward, and from beneath his bunk drew his *wakizashi*—the short sword of the samurai. Although he lacked the proper reed mat—a *tatami*—on which to kneel, and wore no formal robes or *hachimaki*, one had to make do under less-than-ideal circumstances.

Keeping his eyes on the portrait of his wife and sons, he opened his coat and shirt, exposing his bare chest and abdomen. He slid the *wakizashi* out of its sheath and wrapped a clean pillowcase around the middle of its razor-sharp blade. Gripping the handle in his left hand and the wrapped blade in his right, he inverted the sword so that its chisel-like tip was touching the left side of his abdomen, its cutting edge horizontal and facing toward the right.

Fresh shrieks of failing metal echoed through the red-tinged cabin interior. The toxic tang of chlorine gas continued to intensify.

Still looking at the portrait of his wife and sons, Toshiko Yarizuma slid the blade of the *wakizashi* deep into the left side of his lower belly. Then, slowly, he drew the blade across to his right pelvic bone, slicing through abdominal muscle and intestine. An immense gout of dark blood spilled over his thighs and onto the mattress.

Turning the blade ninety degrees, he made a slow vertical cut upward, stopping at his lower right rib.

Another ninety-degree turn, followed by a slow cut across the diaphragm to the left side of his rib cage.

Captain Toshiko Yarizuma removed the *wakizashi* from his body and placed it on the mattress beside him as his intestines began to slip out through the massive wound in his abdomen and into his lap. He placed his hands back upon his upper thighs.

He kept his eyes on the portrait of his wife and sons.

After a while, surrounded by the eerie, agonized sounds of his moribund ship, he died.

Throughout the entire act of seppuku, he uttered not a single sound.

He never moved a muscle on his face.

Epilogue

Hiram Gant got out of the army staff car, smoothed down his dress uniform, and began to walk through the chilly afternoon air toward the Salter Field command building, limping on his game left leg. Though it was cold, he had not taken a coat with him before leaving for his midmorning meeting in Washington. Overcoats, he had found, tended to wrinkle uniforms, and for this meeting Hiram Gant had wanted to look sharp.

The meeting had been with President Franklin Delano Roosevelt and General George C. Marshall at the White House.

Gant had felt numb as he was admitted to 1600 Pennsylvania Avenue, even more numb as he'd stood at attention before the big desk in the Oval Office. But despite the unreality of finding himself actually inside the White House, his innate sense of humor had asserted itself. Why should he be nervous? He was only being appraised at close range by two of the shrewdest and most powerful men on the entire planet.

Roosevelt had remained in his wheelchair throughout the meeting, first formally thanking Gant on behalf of the American people for his heroic aerial defense of Washington—and for keeping silent about it, as ordered—then inviting him to relax and take a chair. Gant had seated himself, though he'd hardly been able to relax. Roosevelt had lapsed into amiable chat, gesturing habitually with his black-ivory cigarette holder. Hiram Gant had found him almost irresistibly charming, as even his enemies often did, but thought that the president looked unwell. There was a sickly gray yellow cast to his complexion, and his face was heavily lined. The bags under his eyes were large, puffy, and purple.

All the while, General Marshall had hovered like an elegant sentry at the side of Roosevelt's desk, nodding now and again. Missing nothing. Assessing everything.

The meeting had concluded with several pointed remarks from the cannily genial Roosevelt.

"Now, Major Gant: it has been decided, for reasons of national morale, that the actual events taking place over Washington last week should be left unpublicized—that the entire episode be explained away as an intricate if somewhat overdone aerial exercise designed to test the absolute impregnability of the defenses surrounding our nation's capital." Roosevelt drew on his cigarette, and for once he did not grin, but only smiled. "Do you follow?"

Sensing that the tenor of the discussion had changed, Hiram Gant rose to his feet, tucked his peaked cap under his arm, and came to attention. "Yes, sir."

"That's the story you stick to whenever you are confronted by reporters—or anyone else—demanding to know exactly why you landed in a bullet-riddled Mustang after a routine domestic patrol. We're going to chalk it up to a friendly-fire mishap caused by confusion in a complex training maneuver. Under no circumstances are we ever going to admit that Imperial Japan managed to get four kamikaze aircraft into the skies over Washington. The effect of such an admission on the morale of the country might well be disastrous. Some information is out there, particularly about the giant submarine sunk at the mouth of Delaware Bay, but we'll simply deny it until it goes away." Roosevelt grinned fully this time. "The political art of sustained disinformation, Major Gant. A white lie for the greater good."

Gant gave a slight nod. "Yes, sir."

"Excellent. Good man."

"And sir?"

Roosevelt looked up at him. "Yes?"

"It's *Captain* Gant, sir. Not Major."

The president's face split into another broad grin. With his left hand, he gestured at General Marshall, who moved forward holding a small rank insignia box.

"Not anymore, Major Gant," Roosevelt said. "And after the general pins those oak leaves on your collar, we'll have a short talk about what prestigious and financially advantageous position you might care to occupy for the duration of your career in the United States Army Air Forces." The irresistible grin again. "There are ways to thank a military man—particularly a *discreet* military man—for a job well done other than by simply pinning a medal to his chest."

"Yes, sir," Gant said.

That had been three hours ago. Now reality was the cold afternoon air of mid-November Salter Field, and the impending warmth of a cup of coffee in the officers' wardroom.

Hiram Gant limped up to the main door of the command building and pushed it open, glad to be getting out of winter's bitter clutches. He stomped snow off his feet, then started down the main hallway, blowing on his hands.

The first thing he saw was Captain Wilmer Jessup stalking down the corridor in his direction. The second thing that caught his eye, farther down the hall, was the tall figure of General George C. Marshall, standing outside the CO's office and talking through the open doorway.

How the hell had Marshall gotten here so fast? Maybe via one of those newfangled helicopters. There'd been a few of them showing up around Washington lately.

Gant saw Jessup's eyes shift unmistakably to the shiny new oak leaves on his collar, blink twice, then wander away again. As the two men came within a yard of each other, Gant halted, waiting.

Jessup strode on past, looking at the bricks on the corridor wall.

Hiram Gant cleared his throat. "Captain Jessup."

The white flier stopped, paused, then turned to lock eyes with the Tuskegee Airman.

"In the United States Army Air Forces," Hiram Gant said in a quiet, even voice, "we salute the rank, not the race."

Jessup hesitated. Then his eyes shifted again . . . to the tall figure that had moved up soundlessly behind Gant's left shoulder.

Wilmer Jessup swallowed once and snapped his rigid right hand to his eyebrow. "Yes, sir," he said thickly.

Major Hiram Gant made him hold the salute for an extra second or two before returning it. Released, Jessup dropped his hand, spun on his heel, and continued off down the hall.

Gant whirled and executed another crisp salute, this time in the direction of General George C. Marshall. The severe expression on the army chief of staff's patrician face eased, and the corners of his mouth turned upward slightly.

"Carry on, Major Gant," he said, touching his own brow.

Ensign Hajimi Ona remembered nothing.

Nothing from the moment he had disengaged his *Kaiten* from the deck of the *I-403* to the moment he had woken up in the clean sheets of a hospital bed, his forehead bandaged and leather restraint cuffs secured around his wrists.

Alive. Taken prisoner.

The disgrace was unbearable.

He would rectify the situation at the first opportunity, and hopefully be able to take several Americans with him when he did.

Unbearable.

During his first full day of consciousness, he had lain alone and awake in his cell-like room. Twice, about six hours apart, the single steel door had opened and an American medical corpsman had entered to spoon-feed him broth and adjust his intravenous drip. The corpsman had said nothing, had not smiled. He had merely fed his patient, checked his sanitary condition and the security of the leather cuffs restraining him, and left.

Hajimi Ona bit his lip in frustration. He would bide his time.

What day was it?

Now the door was opening again. A slender American in a neat khaki uniform stepped inside, regarding him with sympathetic, intelligent eyes. Ona stared back at him over his blanket-covered feet.

"How are you feeling, Ensign Ona?" the American asked in perfect Japanese. He looked to be about thirty, and had the gentle demeanor of a student doctor.

Hajimi Ona blinked and continued to stare, his lips clamped shut.

The American smiled, straddled a chair, and sat down. "Healthy enough to want to get your hands on me, it looks like. Understandable, given the circumstances."

Ona's glare softened imperceptibly. What was this Yankee doing? Don't trust anything he says.

"In case you're wondering," the American said, "those burns on your arms and neck were sustained when the navy crew that rescued you was forced to cut open your minisub's conning tower with a blowtorch. Some of the sparks fell on you, I'm afraid. They didn't know where you were, and the hatch was jammed shut." He smiled gently again. "Sorry about that."

Tricks. This was leading up to something.

"I'm also sorry about the restraints, Ensign Ona," the American went on. "But we can't afford to take a chance on you hurting yourself or one of us—at least not until we've had the opportunity to talk to you a little bit. I'm sure you understand."

Ona resisted the temptation to nod out of reflex— the man's Japanese was that good—and continued to maintain his black stare. The American was not in the least intimidated or discouraged. In fact, he appeared not to notice.

"By the way," he said, "my name is Captain Benjamin Shaeffer. I'm your adjustment officer." He chuckled and fished in his breast pocket. "Don't be alarmed at that title. I'm not going to try to make you do anything against your will. I'm just going to chat with you on a regular basis as you heal up and get stronger. Perhaps we'll find we have something in common, eh?"

I have nothing in common with you, interrogator, Ona thought.

"For example, we both speak Japanese. And I love Japan, as I suppose you do. I studied there before the war. Kyushu, the southern island, is my favorite. The seafood is absolutely the best in the world."

Ona scowled, but felt a pang of uncertainty. He was disarming, this Captain Shaeffer, with his mild manner and flawless Japanese. Still, he would not let himself be deceived.

Shaeffer noted the slight change in Ona's expression, then went on: "Just in case you're interested, I know your name because we found one of your testimonial letters in the wooden box containing the ashes of your friend Isamu Matsura. Oh, don't worry—his remains have been treated with the utmost respect. We simply had to investigate everything in your . . . your . . . *Kaiten*, is it?"

"Yes—*Kaiten*," Ona replied before he could stop himself. He was thinking of Isamu.

"Ah." Shaeffer nodded. "Well, no matter. We don't need to pry any further into details like that at the moment." He held up a packet of Lucky Strikes that he had taken from his breast pocket. "Hajimi, listen to me. I know that you look on me as your enemy right now, but perhaps that will change at some point. In any event, I don't like seeing you cuffed to that bed. It's inhumane, somehow. Now, if you were to give me your word that you wouldn't try to harm yourself—or me—I think I could bend the rules and loosen that right wrist so you could at least enjoy a cigarette. Would you like that?"

An obvious bribe to win him over. But what was the harm? He wanted a cigarette right now more than he'd ever wanted anything in the world. And he had no intention of abandoning his sacred duty to join his comrades at Yasukuni. But for now, just one cigarette . . .

Hajimi Ona raised the fingers of his cuffed right hand. Shaeffer smiled, leaned carefully forward, and slipped a Lucky between his knuckles.

"Let me release that cuff," the American said. "One is all I can do for now, I'm afraid, but at least you'll have that much movement. Then I'll give you a light, and we'll smoke. I trust you and you trust me. A gentlemen's agreement, you might say."

He laid his hands on the buckle of the restraining strap and looked Hajimi Ona in the eye.

Ona nodded once. Shaeffer unbuckled the cuff and reached for his lighter.

Hajimi Ona put the cigarette between his lips. The American captain would not fool him, would not manipulate him. Would not change his mind.

But, at least for today, there could be no harm in talking. . . .

Joe Garth was sitting on the second-floor balcony of the mission turned hospital on Minglaat, sipping lemon tea. The gash in his forehead was healing nicely, as were his many bruises, and for the past several nights he'd been able to sleep right through to morning without once waking up.

Captain Art Lucas's mangled Wildcat was still lying just off the edge of the runway, weeds already starting to grow up around its undercarriage. It seemed to Garth a lifetime ago that he had been sitting in this very chair, listening to the lanky fighter pilot describe the desperate naval battle off Samar. Garth shook his head unconsciously and took another sip of tea. It had been all of two weeks.

He looked out over the crowded harbor of Minglaat—at the barges and supply ships and landing craft sitting at anchor or tethered to the hastily expanded docks. The sun was setting, and in its rich light the purple-gray vessels appeared to be floating in a sea of liquid copper. A lone PT boat was approaching the docks at idle speed, its sharp bow cleaving a thin V through the placid water.

Joe Garth watched it, and as he did, a parade of ghostly faces drifted across the idyllic scene before him. Charlton Randall—his squad leader and friend. Fitz and McNab. Bartlett and Drexel. The young British commando—Owen—he'd watched die by inches in the cockpit of the crashed C-47. Major Harold Horwitch, drifting down into a blue abyss in the wreckage of another aircraft, his face and hands upturned as if to catch a last fleeting glimpse of the living world of light and air.

There were others, their fates unknown to him but for whom he held out little hope. Their faces came and went like clouds marching along a distant horizon. Matalam and DuFourmey. The dark, haunted Finian Hooke and his companion, Yomat Dap. Corporal Mick Mulgrew— he of the sardonic commentary and unflinching loyalty. Sergeant Web Foster, the recipient of that loyalty— powerful, fast, and capable. As skilled at tending to the dying young commando in the C-47 as he was at killing the enemy.

A lone Royal Australian Air Force Beaufighter droned across the evening sky, heading in the direction of Leyte. Garth lifted his eyes and watched it shrink into the distance. A night fighter, he thought, noting the radar blister under the plane's nose. Out for a prowl.

Good hunting.

He finished his tea, got out of his chair, and walked down the exterior balcony steps to ground level. The path that led from the hospital down to the docks was sandy and well trodden, and his feet sank to the ankles with every step. He slogged along, his hands in his pockets, breathing in the scent of night-blooming flowers and the ever-present musk of diesel exhaust. Over near the main equipment depot, three sailors were arguing about whose turn it was to drive the forklift.

As he reached the beach, Garth encountered a quartet of denim-clad seamen bearing a stretcher. Lying on it was a fifth man, dressed in rags, his arm crooked over his face. The stretcher party went by at a clumsy trot, heading for the hospital.

A lean PT boat lieutenant was following along behind, not trotting but striding along purposefully. Garth saluted. "Sir."

The lieutenant paused, breathing hard from the effort of walking through the soft sand, and returned the salute. "Evening. *Whew*. Damn sand."

Joe Garth smiled and glanced over his shoulder. "Your man going to be all right, sir?"

The lieutenant nodded. "Not our man . . . but he's gonna be fine."

"Oh?"

The lieutenant tipped his cap back. "Yeah. We found him drifting in a shot-up Jap launch in the middle of nowhere, miles from any island. Half-starved, dehydrated, and nearly wacko from trying to drink salt water. U.S. Navy seaman."

Garth shook his head. "You don't say."

"Yep." The lieutenant scratched his chin. "Funny thing, he's a Negro. Like a steward's mate or something. Musta fallen off his ship, maybe. We don't know—he's too delirious to be able to tell us anything."

Joe Garth looked at him.

"Yeah, uh-huh," the lieutenant went on. "Weird. But maybe when he comes out of it, he'll be able to explain how he ended up drifting around the Philippine Sea in an enemy tub full of holes with its bottom half ripped out. You know?"

The naked warrior stood in the stern of the dugout canoe and tended to its primitive crab claw sail, easily maintaining his balance as the tiny craft coasted along over the dark, running ocean swells. The sky overhead was velvet black and encrusted with stars, showing him the way home. There was no land in sight, but Yomat Dap knew that the islands of the Sulu Archipelago were to his left, and that to his right—much farther away— lay the single long island of Palawan. He could tell by the stars and by the pattern of reflecting wavelets against the hull of his canoe—wavelets that traveled for many miles on top of larger swells, and would have gone unnoticed by anyone unskilled in the ancient art of intuitive navigation.

It would be many days before he would see the coast of his homeland again, but that did not matter. Time was something that a man passed through and that, in turn, passed through him. It was not something that could be caught, and kept, and held unchanged. His blood brother *Fee-nan Huk* had tried to recapture the past, to somehow undo it, and live in another life gone by. It had led him to his death. Yomat Dap had seen it, had known the folly of it, and had nevertheless walked *Huk*'s hopeless journey with him—because, after all, were they not brothers?

The fresh breeze ruffled and lifted the palm fronds that lay in the bottom of the dugout; it threatened to blow them overboard. Dap stepped forward and rearranged the loose leaves with his foot. There.

From beneath them, barely audible over the insistent moan of the wind, came a deep groan.

The big man with the tattooed arms was dreaming again, moving in his sleep. He had lain under the concealing palm fronds for many days now. He would lie under them for many more. Perhaps, in spite of Yomat Dap's best efforts, he would die.

But perhaps not. The big man's friend *Mul-gru* had been dead when Dap had stolen through the scattered patrols of Japanese soldiers and climbed into the ruined machine gun nest. But *Fos-tah* had been alive—barely. A gunshot wound to the head, a stab wound under the ribs, and a badly mangled knee, but alive. It had taken all of Yomat Dap's stalking skills—and all of his strength—to carry the big man off the ridge, through the jungle, and down to the beach without being seen. He had laid *Fos-tah* down in the fisherman's canoe he had found, covered him with palm fronds, and set off immediately, before the sun had fully risen.

Japanese planes had come and gone as he had sailed

the dugout southward, heading for the Sulu Sea. All they had seen was a lone native fisherman in an open canoe, harmlessly going about his unimportant business. The big soldier he had kept covered up, and continued to keep covered up, for if Japanese pilots were to spot a white man in a native dugout, they would surely kill them both.

He had stopped at this island and that along the way, gathering herbs with which to doctor the big man's wounds. Collecting coconuts and helping him to sip the sweet, watery juice.

The big man groaned again, draping one tattooed arm across the canoe's gunwale. Yomat Dap trimmed the crab claw sail and looked down at him. Perhaps he would die soon.

He looked back up at the glittering midnight sky.

But perhaps not.

Author's Afterword

The *Sen-Toku* submarines were real. They were fully capable of traveling around the world and launching aerial attacks against Washington and New York—the purpose for which they were originally designed; only the rapid Japanese surrender in the wake of the atomic destruction of Hiroshima and Nagasaki, and the subsequent end of World War Two, precluded their operational use. In fact, a proposed raid, late in the war, on the Panama Canal by the *Sen-Toku* class I-400 and I-401, and two other smaller aircraft-carrying submarines, was shelved only at the last minute in favor of a simultaneous kamikaze and *Kaiten* attack on the American fleet anchorage at Ulithi Island, scheduled for August 1945.

As fate would have it, hostilities officially ceased as the giant subs were heading toward their target; all submarines in the strike force returned to Japan and were surrendered to American authorities. Two of the extant *Sen-Toku* were sailed to the west coast of the United States by U.S. Navy prize crews, examined thoroughly, and then scuttled in the eastern Pacific in 1946. The third and last fully operational *Sen-Toku*, the *I-402*, was scuttled off Goto Island in the western Pacific, also in 1946.

The *Sen-Toku* were the largest, most heavily armed, most far-ranging undersea vessels of the Second World War. They were decades ahead of their time, were the

probable inspiration for the Soviet Typhoon class submarines (Red October) that followed nearly forty years later,
and to this day remain the only submarines ever built capable of carrying and launching multiple high-performance
attack aircraft. That Imperial Japan ran out of time to use
them operationally as intended is one of the more fortu-
itous developments—from the point of view of the
United States—of the endgame days of World War Two.

Other suicide warriors and weapons mentioned in *The
Sen-Toku Raid* were real, as well. Large numbers of *Fukuryu* divers, or "Crouching Dragons," were fully prepared in 1944 and '45 to man underwater bunkers off
the coast of Japan and sacrifice themselves, if necessary,
to repel the anticipated American invasion of the mainland. *Shinyo* explosive motorboats exacted a constant, if
rather small, toll from American shipping in the Philippines and the southern Japanese island possessions.
Kaiten manned torpedoes were used extensively and
achieved a significant number of hits on U.S. Navy targets (but only one documented sinking). *Ohka* flying
bombs, in various configurations, were responsible for
the outright destruction of at least one American destroyer, the USS *Mannert L. Abele,* and the crippling of
several dozen other vessels, including the battleship USS
Idaho. While most *Ohka* were carried to their target
areas beneath the bellies of Japanese "Betty" bombers,
one variant—the Model 43A—was designed to be
launched from a submarine catapult. The kamikazes, of
course, are well known to all who possess even a basic
appreciation of World War Two history.

It was the British who first came up with the commando concept—hit-and-run assault troops from the
sea—and put it into practice. But commandos did not
swim; they approached their objectives in small boats.
The Americans fully developed the use of demolition
swimmers in the Pacific, but UDT men were not assault
troops; they reconnoitered and cleared beaches of obstacles in advance of major seaborne landings, rarely leaving the water. The impromptu strike force of crash
survivors in *The Sen-Toku Raid* blends these two special-

ties, guerrilla fighter and combat swimmer, in a way that would not, in reality, be fully developed until January of 1962, when the first truly amphibious warriors, the famed U.S. Navy SEALs, were formally commissioned under the administration of President John F. Kennedy.

A few juicy historical tidbits, alluded to in *The Sen-Toku Raid*, for the interested reader:

- After reviewing footage taken at the Leyte beachhead on October 20, 1944, General Douglas MacArthur, not liking the way he looked on film, did in fact stage a more controlled reenactment of his famous return to the Philippines several weeks later, for the benefit of newsreel crews and photographers.
- Legendary Japanese ace Hiroyoshi Nishizawa was right: no enemy pilot ever bested him in combat. He was eventually killed when the transport plane in which he was a passenger was shot down by American fighters.
- The literal translation of the Japanese term *tai-atari* is "body crashing." It is a euphemism for the suicidal ramming—usually air-to-air—of an opponent. Later in the war, B-29 Superfortresses conducting high-altitude raids over Japan were subjected to a concentrated number of these attacks, which—unlike air-to-sea kamikaze attacks—had not previously been common.
- American admiral Chester Nimitz *did* in fact know what his counterpart had planned prior to the Battle of Midway. Yamamoto did not realize that the Americans had broken nearly all Japanese military codes early in the war.
- The death of Admiral Isoroku Yamamoto was not mere chance. American radio monitors had intercepted and decoded a Japanese message detailing Yamamoto's itinerary. It was decided at the highest levels of authority (i.e., the White House) that the chance of eliminating Japan's premier naval strategist outweighed the chance that the Japanese might

realize their military code had been broken. P-38 fighters were dispatched on a special long-range mission to shoot Yamamoto down. They did so, on April 18, 1943.

• According to Japanese belief, Emperor Jimmu Tenno (circa 660 B.C.) was the first *mortal yet still divine ruler of Japan*—great-grandson of the sun goddess, Amaterasu. Emperor Hirohito, who occupied the throne during WWII, was recognized as his direct—and equally divine—descendant.

World War Two was the greatest conflict of the twentieth century and now, nearly sixty years after its conclusion, remains a treasure trove of fascinating and little-known events, personalities, and technical facts. *The Sen-Toku Raid* is a fictional amalgam of a few of these, as well as a speculative examination of the motivations that can drive sane men to the extreme of self-destruction in pursuit of what they consider their penultimate—and inescapable—Duty. For the curious reader, official accounts of the historical facts alluded to in this novel—accounts which provide a degree of detail that cannot be replicated in *The Sen-Toku Raid*'s commercial-fiction format—are readily obtainable, simply for the seeking.

John Mannock is a former commercial oil field diver and boat captain whose work has taken him to the far corners of the world. In the early 1980s, he served in the military in an infantry reconnaissance unit and was deployed on peacekeeping operations in Lebanon and Central America. He has also been a construction welder, journalist, teacher, and professional jazz musician. He and his wife of twenty years, Teresa, live in the Florida Keys when they are not on the road doing research. "Mannock" is a pseudonym. To learn more about John Mannock's writing, please visit his Web site at www.johnmannock.com.